Challenged . . .

"Damn you, Hawk!" She swore at him to mask her disappointment and snatched the bra from the hook of his finger. He laughed, a throaty sound rich with amusement. She struck at him, but he caught her hand before it reached his face and pulled her against him. "Brute!" she hissed.

"And you are a tease," he accused softly and silenced any reply with his mouth. Instantly there was a wild, hungry response to the domination of his kiss. The stiffness fled from her body; every curve welded itself to him.

Passion flamed hot and unchecked in both of them. Hawk let it burn, the heat flowing through his sensitized flesh. Yet there was no haste, no urgency in him. He would take her in his own good time and not be hurried by Carol as she was prone to do if he let her set the pace.

His mind knew no guilt in taking her. In this, there was no confusion. For once, the practices of the Navaho and the white were in accord. Sex and the desire for it were natural things, as inevitable as life and death.

Books by Janet Dailey

Night Way
Ride the Thunder
The Rogue
Touch the Wind

Published by POCKET BOOKS

Night Way

Janet Dailey

PUBLISHED BY POCKET BOOKS NEW YORK

Another *Original* publication of POCKET BOOKS

POCKET BOOKS, a Simon & Schuster division of
GULF & WESTERN CORPORATION
1230 Avenue of the Americas, New York, N.Y. 10020

ISBN: 0-671-83605-6

First Pocket Books printing January, 1981

10 9 8 7 6 5 4 3 2 1

POCKET and colophon are trademarks of Simon & Schuster.

Printed in the U.S.A.

Author's Note

Navaho healing ceremonials, commonly known as "sings," are properly called "Ways," because of the precise manner in which they must be conducted. In these ceremonies, or ways, myth-dramas are acted out.

One of the more popular rites is Night Way. In it, Changing Woman (comparable to Mother Nature), who gave birth to the Navaho race, tried to create light in a world of darkness. On the floor of the hogan, she made a dry-painting: white first for dawn; on it, blue for morning; on the blue, yellow for sunset; and, finally, black for night on the yellow. She prayed but no light came.

She added turquoise and white shell beads. After her prayers, a faint light appeared. The twelve Holy People came to help, bringing more turquoise and shell beads to make a magic circle. Changing Woman held a crystal above it. A bright blaze appeared, but it was so hot and bright, they had to keep raising it and moving it to keep it at a safe distance.

In this way, light was created.

There are some 570 "songs" in Night Way. The verses quoted from selected "songs," beginning each part of this book, are from translations by Washington Matthews, a noted authority on the Navahos.

PART
I

"   With your moccasins of dark cloud, come to us!
With your leggings of dark cloud, come to us!
With your shirt of dark cloud, come to us!
With your headdress of dark cloud, come to us!

. . . Today take out your spell for me."

Chapter I

The land stretched out as far as the imagination, laced with arroyos and crowned with mesas and buttes. Cedar and pinon darkened the slopes while sage and grass tumbled across the floor of the empty plateau. Overhead, the dissolving vapor of a jet trail left a long, white streak in the bright blue sky above the Navaho Indian Reservation. Its boundaries spanned four states—Arizona, New Mexico, Utah, and Colorado—comprising an area larger than the combined size of Connecticut, Massachusetts, and New Hampshire.

On the southern edge of its border in Arizona, a canyon was gouged out of a carmine-red sandstone mass. A giant cottonwood stood tall, its top branches straining to reach the rim. The thickness of its leaves hid the opening of a cave hollowed into the rock face of the wall. It was empty now, long ago abandoned by the ancient ones who had once found it a sanctuary, and had left behind footholds chiseled in the wall. The cave overlooked the entire canyon, which contained only a speck of habitation, a one-room, six-sided log structure with its door facing the sacred east. Near it, the non-walled, crudely constructed "ramada" offered shade from the hot sun. Beyond it was a stick corral, a

weathered buckboard outside it. The horse inside stood
three-legged, its head hanging low, its scrub brush of a
tail swishing at the buzzing flies. A mangy, rib-thin dog
slept in a cool hollow, shaded by the hogan.

A boy, no older than nine, raced from the hogan in a
skipping run. Clad in blue denim pants and a colorful
clay-red shirt whose tail flapped free of the waistband,
he wore soft leather moccasins on his feet. A yellow
headband was tied around his unruly mop of hair, black
and shiny as the crow's wing. His skin was a copperish-
brown, but his eyes were blue like the sky after it had
been washed clean by a spring storm.

The bent figure of a young woman planting hills of
corn straightened at the sound of running feet. She
watched the boy approach, a smile of pride and deep
affection lifting the corners of her mouth. Her eyes
glowed like dark coals, radiating warmth and love.
Straight and sleek black hair was smoothed away from
her face and tied with a white string into a chignon at
the nape of her neck, a style that emphasized her
cheekbones and angling jawline. A silver concho belt
circled the waistline of her blouse of green velveteen.
Many petticoats billowed the long calico skirt, its hem
touching the ankle-high moccasins of fawn-brown with
their gleaming concho buttons. Her slender figure
looked like that of a young maiden, high-breasted and
with hips that hadn't widened.

"Chizh kin góne yah 'íínil." The boy stopped
beside her, barely winded by his run from the hogan to
the cornfield.

"No." She corrected the One-Who-Must-Walk-Two-
Paths with a shake of her head. "You must say it in
English. He thinks you don't speak it well. You must
learn it because it, too, is your language."

A look of calm acceptance stole over the boy's face.
"I carried the wood into the house in one trip." He

repeated his previous statement, choosing his words with care. "Will he come today?"

Her gaze lifted from his upturned face to scan the land to the south. There was no road, only traces here and there on the hard ground to show a vehicle had found its way to this place. The Arizona wind was quick to erase any tracks. Some seventy miles to the east was the Arizona city of Flagstaff. Gallup, New Mexico, was one hundred twenty miles to the west. To the north, there was only Navaho land interlaced with rough trails, questionable roads, and rare highways. But to the south the ranch of her husband was located.

"Perhaps," she hoped along with her son. The planting stick was in her hand, a reminder of the work to be finished. "Now that you have gotten the wood for our fire, you can help me plant the corn." She handed him the pouch of seed kernels.

The corn was not planted in rows, which was the white man's way, but in hills. The planting stick was the tool that poked many kernels nearly a foot into the ground where the Indian corn sent its long roots deep into the subsoil for moisture. "Four kernels for the cutworm, four for the crow, four for the beetle, and four to grow" advised an ancient proverb. Corn was the staple of their diet. Every bit of the plant would be eaten. The young sprouts would be boiled as greens; young, tender stalks would be roasted in ashes; undeveloped ears of corn would be made into soup; the first milk ears were to be used for mush and bread; and mature ears were ground into meal.

Corn was a sacred plant, not simply because of its value as a foodstuff. According to Navaho myth, the forerunners of man were made from two ears of corn, and it was only when four seeds of white, blue, yellow, and all colors were planted that the earth spread out.

White Sage knew this was not the way the white man

believed the earth was formed. On the Reservation, there were many missions operated by members of the white man's religions. The churches of the Franciscan Fathers, Methodist, Baptist, Mormons, and Episcopal, all claimed that their religion was the right one. This confusion among the whites enforced her belief in the centuries-old way of The People.

Besides, these Christians spoke of a far-off land called Palestine and a place named Bethlehem which White Sage could not visualize. The People told stories about the four sacred mountains, and White Sage, herself, had seen the San Francisco peaks outside Flagstaff which was the Mountain of the West. The white man's Holy Book talked only about a male God and leaders who were men. White Sage missed Changing Woman, the principal figure in so many of their stories, and others like Spider Woman and Salt Woman. The white man believed their God was all-good, yet she knew that in all things there was evil, as well as good. The beliefs of the white man did not make sense.

The boy crouched low to the ground to drop the seed kernels in a thick cluster. While she poked them into the hill, he straightened to watch. A thoughtful frown creased his forehead.

"Are we poor?" he asked finally.

"No, we are not poor. Don't we always have plenty of food to eat and warm clothes to wear? Your father provides us with everything we need and more. He is 'rico.'"

Mary White Sage knew this because only a man who was very rich could afford to keep two houses and two families. The white teachers at the Reservation school had always insisted it was wrong for a man to have two wives. Yet Laughing Eyes had told her that white men did it all the time. They had often laughed at the foolishness of the white men's ways, which dictated one thing while another was actually done.

She had understood when Laughing Eyes explained that his first wife would not like it if they all lived in the same house. His first wife's ways were different from Mary's. It had happened to a friend of Mary's who had married a man who already had a wife. Her friend had constantly quarreled with the first wife because the woman was lazy. Finally, to ensure harmony, her friend's husband had built a second hogan a mile away from the first and, thus, separated his two wives.

"Does he have a lot of sheep?" the boy asked. A Navaho's worth was generally measured by the number of sheep he owned.

With the exception of those who lived outside the Reservation, land is not owned by an individual; rather, there is an "inherited use-ownership" which is possessed by the family as a whole. The man who is head of the household has control over it, but he may not give away or remove it from his family. Essentially, he holds it in trust for the real "owners"—his wife and children. Every member of the family inherits the right to graze livestock within a fairly well-defined area, the size of which is determined by the amount of land required to support the stock. The hogan that White Sage lived in was built on land that "belonged" to her mother's family. Less than two miles away was the hogan of her uncle, Crooked Leg.

"He has many, many cattle," she answered, which was more impressive, because cattle needed more land on which to feed. "And he has many, many people working for him—like that man Rawlins who has been here with him."

"We should have sheep," the boy announced firmly. "I am old enough to look after them. Crooked Leg lets me watch his sheep when we go there."

"You cannot watch sheep when you are in school," she reasoned.

The blue of his eyes that had been so sparkling and clear before darkened with resentment and suppressed rebellion. "I don't need to go to school. You can teach me, and he can teach me all that I need to know."

These words seemed strange coming from her son's lips. He had always been so eager and quick to learn, so curious about everything, more inquisitive than the coyote. She paused to study him closely.

"Why don't you want to go to school?"

He was slow in answering. "Because they say I'm not one of The People." Navahos referred to themselves as *dine'é*, "The People." Navaho was derived from the name the Tewa Pueblo Indians gave them, Apaches of Navahu, which means "enemies from the planted fields."

"Who says that?"

"Everybody." He shrugged aside a specific answer. "It's because my hair isn't straight like theirs, and my eyes are blue, not brown."

As Mary White Sage hesitated, a sound alien to any that belonged to the land entered the range of her hearing. She turned to gaze at the dust cloud fast approaching their dwelling. Her large eyes became soft and luminous as she recognized the pickup truck.

"He comes," she told her son.

The bag of seed corn was thrust into her hands. His vaguely sullen expression was replaced by one of boundless joy. He raced with the fleetness of the antelope to be at the hogan before the truck stopped. No more planting would be done while he was here, so White Sage carried the corn and planting stick as she followed her son. Although she didn't run, her steps were no less eager than his, her petticoats swishing with each long, graceful stride.

When the truck stopped, the boy was there, ready to leap into the arms of the tall man who stepped from the cab, and swept him into the air. The ritual of their greeting was always the same. The boy laughed with delight when he was lifted above the man's head, then brought down to be held in the hook of one powerful arm.

"How can a man's son grow in just two days?" The man playfully rubbed the top of the boy's head, rumpling black hair that was determined to escape the yellow headband that tried to straighten the front into bangs.

"I am like the corn. I'm always growing. I knew you would come today."

Held at eye level, it was easy for the boy to see why his mother called his father Laughing Eyes. A thousand tiny lines crinkled the corners of his eyes, making them appear to laugh—eyes that were a lighter shade of blue, as his skin was a shade of brown lighter than the boy's copper hue. Where the sun didn't strike it, it was white.

"I brought you something." The man reached inside the right pocket of his white shirt and pulled out a pack of chewing gum, the boy's favorite treat. J. B. Faulkner gave the pack to the eager fingers reaching for it and set the boy on the ground.

The pack was ripped open and the first stick of gum was unwrapped and he jammed into his mouth. Before it was chewed soft, the second stick was being uncovered. The whole pack of gum inevitably wound up in the boy's mouth to be chewed all at once.

"It would last longer if you chewed one stick at a time," his father pointed out with wry indulgence, but the One-Who-Must-Walk-Two-Paths couldn't reply because his mouth was full of gum.

White Sage watched the greeting between father and son, slowing her pace to give them these few moments alone. Her gaze ran proudly over the man who was her husband, a tall, broad-shouldered figure in his white shirt and brown corded pants. A tan high-crowned Stetson hat covered most of his brown hair.

He looked the same as he had the first time she saw him. It had been the night of the Enemy Way ceremonial when The Girl's Dance, the only part of the ceremony those foreign to The People were permitted to attend and participate in. The whites called it the Squaw Dance, few ever realizing that it was a War Dance. Those girls of marriageable age danced and sought partners from the audience of men. It had been the first that White Sage had taken part in. She had been dressed in her finest, even wearing her mother's heavy squash blossom necklace of silver and turquoise.

At some point in the dance, she had noticed him sitting cross-legged and became aware that he was watching her and none of the other girls. Something had prompted her to ask him to be her next partner, and he had accepted. She didn't remember how many times they had circled the scalp pole until others began to notice. She became worried that perhaps he didn't know that he had to pay her before she could stop dancing with him. Usually the ignorance of the foreigners was regarded with amusement, but White Sage hadn't wanted The People laughing at this man with the smiling eyes. So she had whispered it to him in her best school English.

"But I don't want to stop dancing with you," he had said. When she looked into his eyes, she had seen that he wanted to mate with her. She had felt the faint stirrings of a similar desire, even though she was non-sunlight-struck, a virgin. Finally, he had paid her ten times what anyone else had and returned to the circle of men so she could choose someone else.

But he found out the name of her clan and where her

parents lived. He visited her several times, always
bringing presents for her and her family. J. B. Faulkner
was one of the few whites The People respected. White
Sage learned he owned a big ranch south of the
Reservation and often hired members of The People to
work for him. A month after their first meeting, he
went to her maternal uncle and arranged their marriage
in a ceremony of The People.

On their wedding night, White Sage discovered his
strange habit of sleeping without clothes. The People
always slept in the same clothes they wore during the
daytime, although White Sage recalled the white
teacher explaining that white people wore a different
kind of clothing to bed. But Laughing Eyes didn't wear
any, and he insisted that she should do the same.
Gradually, she had become used to this peculiar trait of
his.

But all that was in the past. Now he was here, smiling
at her. She went eagerly to meet him and be gathered
into his strong arms. His embrace crushed her while he
bent his head to press his cheek hard against hers.

"I've missed you." The gruffness of the voice
whispering in her ear reminded White Sage of the wind
rasping through the cedars. "I think I live only to be
with you." She could feel the hunger in his hands
moving over her and knew the nighttime would not
come soon enough to suit him. With an effort, he lifted
his head and smoothed a hand over her cheek. "I worry
about you when I'm away. Have you been all right?"

"Yes," she assured him and glanced at the young
boy, now devouring the last stick of gum. There was a
lump the size of a wren's egg in his cheek. "This one
helps me all the time."

"I'm glad to hear that." The intensity of feeling left
his voice and his tight embrace relaxed somewhat as he
gazed at their son. "Because I brought him something

besides a pack of gum. You'd better look in the back end of the truck, boy."

With his jaw working vigorously to chew the massive wad of gum, the young boy raced to the lowered tailgate of the truck. His deep blue eyes rounded in surprise. "A saddle!" Hoisting himself onto the bed of the truck, he hurried to the front, where he lifted a handsome, leather-tooled saddle to show his mother. Its weight and bulk were unwieldy, almost more than he could handle, but he didn't ask for help.

The present had to be immediately tried out, which meant catching the horse in the corral and putting the new saddle on it. After the stirrups were adjusted to the right length, The-One-Who-Must-Walk-Two-Paths had to take a short ride. He rode the horse in a large circle in front of the hogan so White Sage and J. B. Faulkner could watch him.

"I wish Chad rode that well," J. B. murmured, then appeared to immediately regret mentioning his other family.

"He has been riding since he was smaller than a yucca stalk." White Sage referred to their son, avoiding his name, since to speak it too often would wear it out. It was common among The People to have several names. Besides his secret name, he had a nickname of the Blue-Eyed-One, and the school had given him the name Jimmy White Sage. "Today he told me we should have sheep for him to watch. He doesn't want to go back to school because they say he isn't one of The People."

"He isn't an Indian." The pronouncement came in a quick, forceful retort, which J. B. tempered with a calmer explanation. "I know children from mixed marriages often consider themselves to be one of The People, but I won't have him deny that he is half-white. And he's going to finish school and go on to college. He is going to have the finest education I can give him. We've talked about this."

She nodded, but she remembered how painful it had been for her at school, where her way of life had been ridiculed and the beliefs of The People scornfully denounced. It had been the same that one time her family had journeyed to Flagstaff, where they had been looked on with contempt. White Sage had been frightened by the things the white men said to her on the street. She had been glad to escape back to the land and all the things that were familiar to her. She was content to make regular visits to the nearby trading post, where she could gossip with other customers. It was run by a Mormon man who had no hair on top of his head; it all grew on his face. His wife was a nice woman with iron-colored hair. White Sage had no desire to venture off the Reservation again. She worried about her son leaving it to get this education, but perhaps Laughing Eyes knew what was best.

"You must talk to him," she said. "He doesn't like being different from the others."

"He is different—and it's only beginning," he announced grimly. When he glanced at her, he smiled, but it was not a genuine smile. White Sage saw its falseness and was troubled. "I will talk to him."

Moving away from her, he signaled to the boy to come to him. The boy reluctantly reined the chestnut horse to the corral, where his father waited. White Sage watched Laughing Eyes take hold of the horse's bridle so their son could jump to the ground. Then she turned to enter the hogan and begin the preparations for their meal.

J. B. led the horse into the corral and tied the reins to a cross-pole. "What's this I hear about you wanting to quit school?" he questioned with seeming nonchalance as the boy stretched on tiptoes to loosen the cinch.

"They say we are poor because we don't have sheep. We are not poor, so we should have sheep to prove that we are not. When you bring them, I will stay home to watch them. I am old enough." Not once did he meet his father's inspecting glance.

"Is that the only reason you don't want to go to school?" He was met with silence. "Do they make fun of you at school because you are different?"

"I am not different. I am the same as they are." The boy tugged at the saddle skirt to pull the saddle from the horse's back. J. B. stepped forward to lift it to the ground.

"That isn't true. You are different."

"No," the boy insisted.

"It's false to pretend you are an Indian. You are neither Indian nor white. You are both. There is nothing wrong with being different." When the boy still wouldn't look at him, J. B. picked him up and set him on the top rail of the corral, so he could see his son's face while he talked. "Be proud of it. You can never be only one or the other. All your life the Indians will expect you to be more Indian than an Indian, and the whites will expect you to be more white than they are."

Blue eyes frowned into his face, skeptical and wary. "How do I be both?"

"Learn everything you can about The People and learn everything you can about the whites. Take what is best and wisest from each of them and make it yours. Do you understand?"

There was a hesitant nod before he asked, "How will I know what to choose?"

"That's something you have to decide." J. B.'s smile was grimly sad. "I can't help you and your mother can't help you. You are alone in this. And it will get harder as you grow older." J. B. was just beginning to realize how hard it would be when the child became a man. His gaze turned skyward to see a solitary hawk soaring on the air currents. "You have to become like that hawk—alone—dependent on no one but yourself, and flying above it all."

Tipping his head back, the boy stared at the hawk, its wings spread in effortless flight. There was not a cloud in the sky, the hawk slicing alone across the great expanse of blue.

"This day I am new," the boy announced in an oddly mature voice. "From now on, I will be called Jim Blue Hawk." He turned to his father. "Do you like it?"

Pride shimmered liquid-soft in the lighter blue eyes. "Yes, I like it," J. B. Faulkner replied.

Chapter II

That summer a life began to grow in his mother's belly. Hawk, as he had come to think of himself, found many things to think about and began looking around himself with new eyes: keen eyes like those of his namesake. When the time came to return to the Reservation school in the fall, he listened to the white teacher, no longer resisting the things that were said which conflicted with what The People believed. Others still mentioned his blue eyes and the waves in his black hair, waves that were more predominant because Hawk had stopped wearing a headband in an effort to straighten the unruly mop. Hawk knew he was different, and because he was different, he was going to be better.

Before spring arrived, he had a sister. Hawk noticed, with interest, that she was different, but not in the same way he was. Her eyes were large and brown like his mother's, but her hair was brown like the trunk of a cedar tree—not the glistening black of the crow. She was given the name Cedar Girl.

Hawk began to call his sister The-One-Who-Cries-at-Everything. She cried when she was hungry, when she was sleepy, when she heard a loud noise, when his mother picked her up, or when she laid her down.

Nothing and no one pleased her except Laughing Eyes. Initially, he suffered the pangs of rejection at the fuss his parents made over his new sister. His needs were of secondary importance to the demands of the baby. He was truly alone like the hawk, pushed out of the nest to fend for himself. But he could. Was he not nearly grown? Hadn't he begun to wear a breech-cloth? Hadn't he been initiated into the tribe? Hawk began to pity his sister because she was dependent on others.

Because his baby sister demanded so much of his mother's time, Hawk had to assume more responsibility. His father still came two or three times a week, bringing presents and food, staying a few hours or for part of the night, but always leaving before dawn. So it fell on Hawk's shoulders to take over the duties that would have belonged to his father if he lived with them all the time.

Thus, when his mother's uncle became ill and it was divined that a Mountain Top Way had to be held to cure him, all relatives were required to contribute to the cost of the ceremony. While others agreed to furnish sheep to feed the hundreds—perhaps as many as a thousand—of guests who would come to witness the nine-night ceremony, Hawk agreed to provide the wood for the fires as his mother's contribution, even though she was at his uncle's hogan every day to help with the preparations.

When school was dismissed early, his first thought was how much wood he would be able to chop before dark. A little snow would not stop him. But it was more than a little snow that fell from the flint-gray clouds that darkened the sky. Two inches were on the ground and more flakes were falling when the school bus let him out more than two miles from his home. Hawk mentally filed away the information that the white teachers had correctly predicted this storm.

The flakes fell heavily and straight down. Before he reached the hogan, the wind caught up with the storm to blow the snow around. Visibility was reduced, but Hawk didn't have to enter the hogan to know there was no fire warming the inside. No smoke curled from the chimney hole. Hawk trudged through the snow toward the door, assured that his mother and little sister had stayed at his uncle's because of the storm.

As he passed the corral, the horse whickered. Hawk stopped still, staring through the screen of white at the sound. Inside the corral stood the chestnut horse, wearing its harness and collar. He searched again, but the buckboard wasn't in the yard.

Turning to look in the direction that led to his uncle's house, he was enveloped in a swirling storm of snow. He could see nothing, no movement except the falling snow. Turning again, Hawk ran to the corral. He didn't bother to unharness the horse and put on the saddle. Hopping on bareback, he gathered the long reins and tied them short.

The chestnut horse did not want to go out in the storm. It took repeated proddings and a slap of the reins to make it leave the corral. Hawk pointed the horse in the direction of his uncle's hogan, a route that the horse knew well.

Into the face of the howling wind, the horse plodded through the snow, which had begun to accumulate into drifts. Almost to his uncle's hogan, Hawk found the buckboard in a dry wash with a broken axle. Taking the chance that he hadn't passed his mother and sister, he rode on to his uncle's hogan. Since she had been closer to it, it was logical to assume she had returned there.

But she hadn't. Hawk stayed long enough to warm the numbness from his bones. His relatives tried to convince him that he didn't have a hope of finding his mother and sister in this storm, but Hawk wouldn't be dissuaded from going out to search for them. In the absence of his father, he was responsible. And Hawk knew he was doing what his father would do in his place.

With a warm Pendleton blanket of his cousin's, Hawk set out again. The storm was worse, the temperatures dropping, and the wind whipping it still lower. Pain lay like a cold bar across his forehead. Snow was drifting over the buckboard. Hawk almost didn't see it.

The snow was deeper and the wind blew it into high drifts. The horse began to labor, plunging through belly-high snows. More than halfway home, the horse staggered to its knees. Hawk finally recognized the futility of going farther. Dismounting, he tied the reins to the harness with numbed fingers and turned the horse loose. Snow and ice were encrusted on its shaggy coat. On its own, the horse would turn its tail to the wind and gradually drift toward its home corral.

Seeking the shelter of a windbreak, Hawk found a tumble of snow-covered boulders and crouched behind it. He wrapped the blanket around him like a tent. It accomplished nothing to rail against the conditions imposed upon him. Indian-like, Hawk practiced the blind acceptance of the circumstances. This was a time to renew his strength from within, to ignore the cold, the wind, and snow raging around him. Surrendering his mind and body, he relaxed into a self-induced torpor where nothing existed but what was within.

Time passed without thoughts. Hawk didn't change his huddling, yoga-like position inside the walls of his blanket-tent. The accumulation of snow on the blanket acted as insulation to keep out the freezing temperature.

An inner sense told him when the storm was over. Straightening, he shook off the weight of the snow on his blanket and drew it around his shoulders, crossing it

in front of him. The world was white and still, newborn
and strange, the familiar landmarks hidden by a
concealing mantle of snow. Gradually, his eyes un-
masked the disguises the landmarks wore. Hawk
started out unerringly in the direction of his home.

If he had survived the storm, then his mother and
little sister could have, too. They might already be at
the hogan, waiting and worrying about him. If they
weren't, he would have to resume his search.

Hawk had traveled no more than a hundred yards
when he saw a patch of bright green against the snow. It
was the same shade of bright green as the velveteen
blouse that was his mother's favorite. In a stumbling
run, he plowed through the snow to reach the spot.
When he stopped, he could see the outline of a human
figure in the snow mound. The extra hump would be
the cradleboard and his sister. There was no movement. Hawk stared for a long, silent moment, then
hesitantly reached down and brushed aside the snow on
the cradle. Tears were frozen on Cedar Girl's cheeks.

He took one step backward, then a second. Quickly,
he turned and ran, putting distance between himself
and the bodies of his mother and sister. The cold tore at
his lungs, forcing him to slow down. Without looking
back, he trudged on toward the hogan.

Across the silence of the white world came the
muffled thud of hoofbeats and the creak of saddle
leather. Hawk lifted his gaze. He stopped at the sight of
the horse and rider approaching at a lunging canter,
puffs of white vapor coming from the nostrils of the
horse. The rider was leading a second horse, the
chestnut, still wearing its harness.

"Hawk!" His father's shout prompted the boy to
wave.

The horse grunted and snorted as it was reined to a
stop, and the rider slipped out of the saddle to rush

forward and grasp the boy's shoulders. Relief briefly overrode the concern in his expression.

"I found the horse. . . . Where is your mother? The baby?" Large, gloved hands dug through the blanket into his shoulders.

"They are gone." It was a flat, unemotional statement.

"Gone? What do you mean—*gone?*" J. B. Faulkner demanded in a desperate kind of anger.

"They are gone—on the path that goes only one way." Hawk returned the piercing gaze with a stoic acceptance of the fact.

"No! Dammit! I won't let them be dead!" His voice was a raging cry. "You are going to take me to them!"

"No!" The boy recoiled in fear, trying to pull free of the powerful hands that held him.

"You are going to take me to them! Do you hear?" The command was reinforced by a brutal shake that snapped the boy's head back.

He didn't give Hawk a chance to refuse as he spun him around and dragged him along by the arm. Following the tracks in the snow, J. B. Faulkner began retracing the boy's route. Frantically, he scanned the snow-covered ground ahead of them. There was an audible breath when he saw the footprints leading to a patch of green where the snow was disturbed to reveal the white-frosted face of the baby girl. He started running, pulling the boy along with him. Hawk lost his balance in the deep snow and fell. He was dragged a few feet on his knees before J. B. released the dead weight to go on alone.

The thick cushion of snow broke his fall. The blanket was forgotten and abandoned as Hawk pushed onto his knees. He was shivering, more from fear than from the cold. The terror built as he saw Laughing Eyes heaving the snow away from the bodies with mighty sweeps of his gloved hands. Terrible sounds were coming from him—sounds of a crazed man.

"No!" Hawk screamed in panic when he saw Laughing Eyes lifting his mother's body from its deathbed of snow.

Ice crystals of blood were frozen to her forehead. Hawk looked quickly away, avoiding the sight of her white-frosted face. His fear increased when his father began rubbing the rigid limbs. In a wretched and tortured voice, Laughing Eyes beseeched her to speak to him, calling her name over and over. When he pressed his mouth to the blue lips and tried to force his life into her empty shell, Hawk's fear for his father was greater than his own.

"No!" He ran to his father's kneeling figure and pulled frantically at his arm. "You must leave them! You must not look upon them! Please! Please!" He was almost sobbing. "Terrible things happen if you look upon the dead! Their ghosts will possess you! Come away from them!"

Some of his warning penetrated because his father turned to look at him. Stark horror held the boy in a paralyzing grip. His father's face was contorted into a mask as frightening as the ones the *kachinas* wore.

"Let go of me!" The snarling voice came from his father's mouth, but it didn't belong to him.

Too stunned by the frightening face before him, Hawk never saw the arcing, backhanded swing until the very last second when it was too late to avoid it. Pain exploded in his right jaw and cheek. The force of the blow sent him reeling backward, but Hawk was unconscious before he crumpled to the snow.

He wasn't aware of the arms that so gently picked him up, or of the gloved fingers that trembled over the vivid red mark covering almost half of his face; nor did he hear the begging to be forgiven. He floated in a black void that nothing penetrated.

When his conscious mind finally surfaced, he was alone in the hogan. A fire was burning, radiating its heat to every corner. Pain throbbed in the right side of his face. Gingerly, he cupped his hand to the swollen flesh running from cheekbone to jaw. It hurt!

As he propped himself up on his elbows, the door opened. Hawk cringed instinctively from the tall, hulking frame. The action was not dictated by a fear of his father, but a fear of the ghosts that had possessed him. As he came closer to the light, Hawk saw that the furious look had gone from his eyes. But so had the laughter. Now his eyes were filled with a tortured sadness, and they avoided looking directly at Hawk.

"Are you hungry?" His father stood in front of the fire and warmed his hands, keeping his back to the boy. "Your cousin fixed some soup."

The gruff voice was abrupt, carrying a hint of self consciousness. But the announcement awakened Hawk's senses to the aroma of food and the gnawing emptiness of his stomach. In a laborious movement, he rolled to his feet and walked to the kettle of soup. The right side of his face felt peculiarly heavy. With a tin mug drawn from the shelf wall of the hogan, he dipped out a cup of soup and carried it to the fire to drink.

His father was uneasy with him. Hawk could tell by the way his eyes kept sliding away without making contact with his. He tried sipping at the hot soup, but when he opened his mouth, the swollen skin on his cheek stretched and sent fiery splinters of pain through him. He winced, unable to conceal it.

"I never meant to hurt you, boy." The husky voice was bitter with regret and remorse.

"You should not have looked on them. Bad things

happen," Hawk repeated. "If the right things are not done, their ghosts will come."

"I don't believe in ghosts. There are no such things," his father insisted with fierce determination. "How can you believe your mother would come back to harm you? You know how much she loved you."

"A ghost is the bad part." As he carefully took another sip of his soup, his downcast eyes watched his father's hands clench into fists, a sign of anger and struggle for control.

"What do you . . . what do The People believe happens to a person when he dies?" His father rephrased the terse question.

"They go to a place in the black north." Hawk didn't like talking about the dead or what happened to them. Speaking about it was inviting ghosts to return. "To reach the place, the dead person must travel four days, and he is guided by a relative who died before. At the bottom of a tall cliff, there is an entrance that leads below the surface to the place. Before the dead can enter this place, those who guard the entrance will test him to be certain he is dead."

His father's eyes were tightly shut and his mouth clenched hard, the point of his chin trembling. When Hawk had finished his explanation, he heard the whispered words of pain his father unconsciously uttered.

"My God, what a terrible place!" His big chest heaved as he took a deep breath and slowly released it. His eyes opened to stare blankly at the fire. "That isn't what the white man believes," he said. "He believes that when a person like your mother dies, she goes to heaven. It's a place in the sky where there is only beauty and happiness—no hunger, no cold, no pain. There, she will know a peace and contentment she could never find on this earth."

Hawk digested this information with a thoughtful frown. A teacher at the school had spoken of such a place, but he had not believed it existed. If his father believed it, perhaps . . .

"If this . . . heaven is so wonderful, why did you not want her to go there? Why did you want her to come back from it?" he questioned.

"Because I was selfish. I didn't want to stay here on earth alone and never again see her warm smile or feel the gentle touch of her hand. I—" The words appeared to choke him. He moved away from the fire and Hawk's watching eyes. "It's late. It will be dark soon." He changed the subject, speaking briskly. "We'll stay here tonight and leave in the morning."

"Leave?" Hawk repeated. "But there are things that must be done. We have to gather the items she wanted buried with her. And there's the four days of mourning and the sacrifices that have to be made on her grave to appease her ghost. We—" He would have continued the list, but his father spun around, interrupting him.

"I told you there are no ghosts!" he declared impatiently. Hawk eyed him warily to see if he was possessed again. With an effort, his father unclenched his fists and rubbed a hand across his forehead. "I'm sorry. I shouldn't have shouted at you. I'm . . . upset because I . . . can't take the bodies of . . . your mother and sister back with me to bury. I have to leave them here—" A brutal look of grief swept over his face before his mouth closed on the unfinished sentence. "Your cousin has already collected the personal things your mother wished to have with her. I have agreed to let them bury her according to *their* belief." The emphasis repeated that it wasn't his belief, and that he wasn't going to let it be Hawk's.

"Are you taking me to your other hogan to live with you?"

Again, his father was uneasy. "I'm taking you with me, but . . . you won't be able to live with me."

"Why?" Hawk didn't understand. "Will not your other wife want me? I am strong. I can do much work, many things to help her."

"Dammit, Hawk! If I explained, you wouldn't understand!" he declared in a burst of impatience, then released a long, weary sigh. "When you're old enough to understand, you'll have discovered the answer for yourself and I won't have to explain. In the meantime, there's a couple I know. I think they will take you in. You know him—Tom Rawlins. He works for me and lives on my ranch."

Some of his father's uncertainty transferred itself to Hawk. The situation didn't please his father; therefore, it didn't please him. He had seen this man, Rawlins, half a dozen times that he could remember. Like The People, he viewed anyone not of his clan with distrust.

"I can live with Crooked Leg. He needs help to watch his sheep." He offered an alternative to his father's suggestion, not wanting to be uprooted from all that was familiar to him.

"No." The denial was quick and decisive. "When your mother was alive, you lived with her people. Now you will live with mine. It's a white world. It's time you began walking its path, learning its values and beliefs. You are going to have to make your own place in it—all by yourself. I would help you if I could, but I'm tied . . . tied by a system you don't understand yet." He sounded tired, beaten. "Once I thought only of myself and what it would take to make me happy. I tried to hold onto too much. I've lost what I cared about the most. Now there are too many others who would be hurt. I didn't think about them before, but I have to now." He glanced at Hawk and saw the bewilderment in his narrowed blue eyes. His mouth twisted in a wry grimace. "You don't know what I'm talking about, do you?"

With a confused shake of his head, Hawk mutely admitted that he didn't—not the last part. Walking the second path of the white world made sense, because he obviously needed to learn more. But the other part about hurting people was something he didn't understand.

"Let me explain it this way," his father murmured. "If you had a flock of sheep and a lamb was separated from them and being attacked by wolves, you would want to save it—protect it. Yet, if you did, you knew the wolves would attack the whole flock and harm them. Would you save the lamb and lose the whole flock? Or would you stay with the flock and hope the lamb might somehow survive?"

"I would stay with the flock," Hawk stated.

"That's what I'm doing. You are my lamb," he explained. "There are some things I can do for you, but I can't stand beside you." Even as he made the statement, he looked away, unconsciously re-enforcing his words by his action. "I'm going to check on my horse, get it bedded down for the night. We'll have to sleep here. I wish we didn't, but—"

"You do not believe in ghosts," Hawk reminded him, since it was the obvious reason for not wanting to sleep in the hogan.

"Not ghosts, no," he agreed. "The only thing haunting me will be my memories."

He walked out the door that traditionally faced east and Hawk was left inside—alone.

With the first streak of dawn, two horses and riders trotted away from the hogan into the immense rumpled blanket of snow. The thin, wavering line of smoke from a dying fire drifted out of the chimney of the abandoned hogan. The pink dawn colored the gray smoke with a lilac flush.

In the bitter cold of morning, the two rode silently away from the canyon. The man had the collar of his heavy parka turned up to keep out the invading chill. His Stetson was pulled low on his head. The boy was bareheaded, his disheveled black hair gleaming in the first rays of sunlight. While the man's shoulders were slumped, the boy sat erect, a natural wild nobility in his bearing.

Traveling ever south, they entered land Hawk had never seen before. Its strangeness heightened his senses. His gaze moved restlessly, always looking, searching, identifying, noting any and all movement within the realm of his vision.

His first sight of a cattle herd came near midmorning. He had seen cattle before, but never in such numbers. And they hadn't been as fat as these redcoated animals with curly white faces. His nose wrinkled at the smell that came from the warm bodies of the cattle. He glanced at his father, but he didn't seem to notice.

Hawk studied the man's profile. Those lines that had once curved upward to make his eyes laugh were now straight, robbing the blue eyes of their happiness and vitality. They looked in his direction rarely, then held the contact only for mere seconds.

Alone. Unconsciously Hawk had been conditioned to accept the fact. Just as his Indian way of life had conditioned him to accept the death of his mother and sister. He wasn't without regret. He missed her. The hogan had seemed strangely silent without the crying of his temperamental sister. Yet it could not be changed; therefore, it must be accepted.

Ride on and forget. The sun is shining on a new day.

Chapter III

When Hawk first saw the cluster of large buildings, he thought they were entering a town. Dirt roads linked each wood building to the next, brown lines crisscrossing the white snow. Yet his searching eyes could find no trading post. There were many corrals, made from smooth boards that were white. Sometimes there was only one or two horses inside them, although one held more. The horses were big, muscled animals like the one his father rode.

Near the corrals, there were three buildings. It was toward one of these that his father was riding. Hawk guessed these buildings were the barns his father had once described to him, where animals were kept, sheltered from the winter storms. Hawk had never been off the Reservation until this day. All of his previous contact with whites had been through the strict teachers at the Reservation school, the Mormons who operated the trading post, and the man, Rawlins, on those few occasions he had come to the hogan with Hawk's father. Hawk didn't include his father in the list of white men he'd met. Yet he had learned much about the world of the whites from all these sources, especially his father. Now he was seeing things that had previously only been described to him, and he was all eyes.

A man was standing on a flat wagon with no sides, pulled by a big machine with three wheels and stopped beside a corral. Hawk identified the big machine as a tractor from a picture he had seen in a schoolbook and felt proud that he knew of such things. With a long fork, the man was throwing dry, yellow grass—hay— into the corral for the horses to eat.

When they rode by him toward the middle building, the man glanced up and waved to his father. He looked at Hawk, then looked again, and stopped his work to stare. Being watched so closely by a stranger made Hawk uneasy. He urged his horse closer to his father's.

The funny-looking, long building called a barn had a tall door at the end, tall enough to permit a horse and rider to enter it without the rider dismounting. His horse shied once at the opening, then nervously followed the horse his father rode inside.

After being outside with the brilliance of the sun reflecting off the snow, it was dark inside. Hawk's eyes quickly sought the darkest corner to make a swift adjustment to the absence of light. His nose was assailed by a dry, irritating dust and the smells of horses and leather and dung. There was a warmth inside the building despite the absence of the sun.

A few yards inside the building, his father stopped his horse. Hawk followed his lead. Saddle leather creaked, a stirrup taking all his father's weight as he dismounted. Hawk hesitated, then kicked his feet out of the stirrup and slipped soundlessly to the hard floor.

Uncertain what to do next, he waited until he saw his father begin unsaddling his horse. Hawk untied the rolled blanket that contained his belongings from behind his saddle and set it on the floor. Laying the stirrup over the saddle seat, Hawk tugged at the cinch strap. He had grown taller in the year and a half since the saddle had been given to him and no longer needed to stand on his toes to reach any part of the saddle.

The strangeness of his surroundings had all of his senses honed to sharpness. His acute hearing picked up the sound of human footsteps approaching before there was an audible crunch of snow outside the opening.

"Someone comes," he warned his father in a very low voice.

The footsteps were close enough for a white man to hear when his father looked up. The smaller-built chestnut horse was on the other side of his father's. The two animals effectively offered concealment to the wary boy, while permitting him to observe the man who entered through the tall door. Of average height and build, the man wore stiff blue Levi's and a heavy jacket lined with sheepskin, buttoned to his throat, and the collar turned up to brush the brim of his hat. Hawk recognized the man, Rawlins, with his muddy-brown eyes and quiet face, a face that always reminded Hawk of a calm stretch of river where the strength and swiftness of the current was hidden from looking eyes.

There was the briefest hesitation in the man's stride as he entered. "You finally made it back. I was beginning to worry about you, J. B."

The man's eyes, unadjusted to the dimness, did not immediately see the second, smaller horse. His father didn't respond as he dragged the saddle off the horse's back and carried it around the animal to set it upright next to an inner wall. When he straightened, Rawlins had stopped only a few feet away and was watching him closely.

"How was . . . everything?" Rawlins hesitated in the phrasing of his question.

A long silence followed in which his father stood

motionless, looking at the man. Then Hawk saw the great shudder that vibrated through his father.

"She's dead, Tom. The little one, too. She'd been to her uncle's and left just before the storm hit." The words spilled from him in a soft, swift rush, like the force of running water that backs up behind a dam, then finally breaks free. "The buckboard broke an axle. She unhitched the horse and must have decided to ride it home. Evidently, she was thrown. There was blood . . . a gash on her forehead. Tom . . . they froze to death—her and the baby. I—" Something choked off the rest, because Hawk saw his father swallow and turn to his horse, lowering his head and spreading his hand across his eyes.

The man, Rawlins, leaned toward his father, then shoved his hands in the pockets of his jacket and looked away. "I . . . I'm sorry."

"Yeah." It was a rasped word that didn't mean anything. His father brought his hand down, roughly wiping something from his cheek, then breathed through his nose. It made a noisy sound, the way it does when the cold makes the water run inside it.

"What about the boy?"

Halting in the act of pulling the saddle pad and blanket off the horse, his father glanced over his shoulder at Rawlins in faint surprise, then looked across his horse's back at Hawk, and quickly bounced away.

"I brought him back with me," he stated gruffly and took the saddle blanket and pad, draping them over the saddle on the floor. He must have seen Rawlins' head jerk, because he added a terse, "I couldn't leave him there."

Taking his horse's reins, his father led it to the opposite side of the wide, long room, thereby exposing the chestnut horse Hawk was unsaddling. The instant

Rawlins' eyes focused on him, Hawk quickly bent his head to the task, staying behind the shield of his horse and keeping to the shadows. His father led his horse to a place on the other wall where there was half a door. Opening it, he unbridled his horse and slapped it on the rump to send it through the opening.

"J. B.—" Rawlins' voice sounded urgent, yet hesitant.

"Dammit, I couldn't leave him there, I tell you. He needs an education, more of a chance at life than he'd get on the Reservation. And . . . I want him near me." The last declaration was tempered to a taut softness.

"But—" Rawlins was frowning, troubled by his father's words.

"I know." His father issued a long sigh and glanced at Hawk when he pulled the saddle from his chestnut and set it against the wall, staying behind the horse. "I can't take him to the house. Katheryn would . . ." He appeared uncomfortable and didn't finish that sentence. "I thought—that is, I hoped—you and Vera would take him in." Rawlins said nothing, but his eyes widened. His father looked grim. "I'm sorry, but there isn't anybody else I can trust."

It was so silent that Hawk heard the whisper of a piece of straw as it floated down to the iron-hard floor. His father broke it by half-turning.

"Hawk, come here," he ordered.

Bending to pick up his bundle of clothes, Hawk ducked under his horse's neck and stepped noiselessly to his father's side. He returned Rawlins' gaze, his dark blue eyes impassively inspecting the man his father wanted him to live with. There was no welcome in the man's look, no warm smile that Hawk usually received from him. Therefore, despite his several brief associations with the man in the past, Hawk would not make the first move to renew the acquaintance.

"He's an intelligent boy, quick to learn. He won't give you any trouble, Tom, I promise," his father said.

"What happened to his face?" After narrowing in on Hawk's right cheek, his gaze had darted in sharp question to his father.

"God forgive me," was the barely audible murmur before he added, "I hit him."

"Why?" The question was filled with shock.

"I don't know." His father tiredly shook his head, as if he didn't want to remember. "There was White Sage, all stiff and cold. You know how Navahos are about the dead, Tom. He started spouting all that superstitious nonsense about ghosts. He was trying to pull me away from her. All I wanted to do was shake him off my arm. I never meant to hit him." There was a great sadness in the look he gave Rawlins. "In his way, he was just trying to protect me. It was a brave thing . . . and I hit him." He paused. "Will you take him?"

In a slow, affirmative nod, Rawlins agreed. "Some will guess who he is. Others will ask. What do you want us to say?"

A muscle was jumping in his father's jaw. "Wouldn't it be natural for a Christian couple to offer a home to an *orphaned* half-breed?"

Rawlins considered the question for a moment, then nodded slowly again. "Yes. Yes, I guess it would."

His father's arm reached hesitantly to place his hand between Hawk's shoulder blades and push him forward, toward Rawlins. "His name is Jim Blue Hawk. He answers to Hawk."

"Hello, Hawk." A faint smile touched the quiet face as he extended a hand toward him. "You remember me, don't you?"

Hawk nodded, the watchful expression never leaving his face. He placed his hand in the man's and felt the man's strength, but it didn't equal that of his father, who was taller and broader. His hand was released after a brief shake.

"You must be hungry and cold after that long ride," Rawlins said. "I'll take you to the house. Vera, my wife, will fix you something to eat. How does that sound?"

Hawk nodded silently and the hand that had just shook his reached out to take hold of his shoulder and guide him forward as Rawlins turned to leave.

"Tom?" His father's hesitant voice halted the man. "Thanks." The word was offered when Rawlins glanced over his shoulder in answer. "I'll . . . uh . . . see to it that you get some money every month . . . for the boy's clothes, expenses, and such."

"Fine."

"What did you tell Katheryn yesterday when she asked where I'd gone?"

"That you were out checking the stock—like you instructed me to do."

"How . . . how did we come through the storm? Did we lose many?" But his father didn't sound very interested, asking the questions only because they were expected.

"A half dozen, no more than that. They drifted quite a bit, but we came out lucky," Rawlins answered.

Something painful and bitter twisted his father's face. "Katheryn will probably be relieved to discover I've decided not to personally leave to check the 'cattle' anymore."

"Yes, she probably will."

Hawk watched his father's unhappy eyes run over the man's face. "You never did really approve, did you, Tom?"

"It isn't for me to judge." Rawlins shook his head.

"I've passed judgment on myself. I'm guilty of not having any guts—not then—"—his gaze skipped to Hawk briefly—"—and not now."

His father grimaced and turned away, signaling an end to the conversation. Hawk's gaze lingered on him before the pressure of the hand on his shoulder prodded him forward. In that second, he sensed that his life was undergoing a more drastic change than he had expected. It wasn't just that he was going to live with white strangers. His mother and little sister were gone. Now he had the feeling that his father was changing, too. He might see him, but the relationship he had known before was gone. He was truly alone.

When he walked out of the building into the bright sunlight, his eyes lifted to the sharp blue sky. Empty. Endless. Its nothingness offered no escape.

With the rolled blanket under his arm, he followed the man Rawlins. The man's boots crunched noisily in the snow; his own footsteps barely made a sound. As they passed other white cowboys, Hawk felt their stares and stoically ignored them. Tucked back in some trees, he saw a big, rambling house, but it was toward a group of smaller buildings that Rawlins walked. Soon, Hawk was aware of the one that was their destination. When Rawlins started up the wooden steps to the door, Hawk held back uneasily.

"What's the matter, Hawk? Come on in. It's all right." The man motioned him forward with a pretense of a smile.

"The door doesn't face the east," he pointed out.

The look in the man's eyes became cool, the smile vanishing. "White men don't believe it's necessary to have the doors of their homes face the east."

Hawk knew this, but it made him uneasy to think of living in such a place. Rawlins waited, the patience of time in his eyes. He didn't attempt to urge Hawk to enter, nor did he scoff at his hesitation. Finally, Hawk moved to climb the steps and follow the man into the house. Inside, the man stomped his feet on a rug, knocking off clumps of snow.

Hawk went no farther than the man did, looking around the small back porch with its coats hanging from wall hooks and a sink for washing. A door opened into a room with white cabinets. Smells of cooking came from within. Rawlins took the rolled bundle from Hawk and set it on the floor.

Seeing his reflection in a looking glass above the sink, Hawk stared. The swelling on his cheek was a purplish-red, the skin puffed near his eyes. He lifted a hand to it. Despite the cool, outside temperature that had chilled the rest of his skin, the distended flesh felt hot to the touch—and very sore.

"Vera?" Rawlins lifted his voice to call the name.

"Daddy! Daddy!" A high-pitched voice cried in excitement as a little girl came running out of the room where the smells were coming from and threw herself into Rawlins' arms. "Mommy is letting me bake cookies!" she announced proudly. "Do you want one? I made them all by myself."

"*Almost* all by herself," a woman's voice corrected.

Hawk was aware of a second person in the doorway, but he was dazzled by the yellow curls on the little girl's head. "How did you trap the sunlight and make it shine in her hair?" he questioned Rawlins with awe. He had heard of whites with yellow hair, but never had seen one with his own eyes.

His question brought silence. Then Rawlins set the little girl on the floor and Hawk's gaze was drawn to her eyes—to be amazed again because they were green. She stared back at him.

"We didn't have to catch the sunlight," Rawlins explained. "Her hair is blonde. A lot of white people have hair that color. There isn't any magic involved, except when a bottle of bleach is used."

"Who are you?" the little girl asked.

But Hawk remained silent, digesting the information Rawlins had given him. "Who is the boy?" It was the woman who asked the question.

"Carol, I'd like you to meet Hawk." Rawlins pushed the little girl forward. "Hawk, this is my daughter, Carol."

"Hawk?" The little girl repeated his name with a curious wrinkling of her nose. "Like the bird? That's a funny name."

"He probably thinks your name is funny," Rawlins suggested.

"What happened to your face?" The little girl demanded, staring at the swollen and bruised side of his cheek and jaw.

Before Hawk could answer, Rawlins was speaking. "He fell and hurt himself. Why don't you take Hawk into the kitchen to sample one of your cookies? Maybe we can persuade your mother to fix him a sandwich. It's been a long time since he's eaten."

"Come on, Hawk." The little girl reached out and grabbed hold of his arm. At first he resisted the tug of her hand, then let himself be led into the next room by the child whose golden head came up to his chest.

"Tom, who does that boy belong to? Why did you bring him here?" As the woman whispered the questions in a demanding tone, Hawk finally glanced around to see who owned the voice. The woman's hair was light-colored, too, but not as yellow as the little girl's. She was wearing a dress the color of the prickly pear flower with half of another dress covering the front of it.

His inspection was halted when the little girl pushed him onto a chair pulled away from the table. She skipped away from him but was back within seconds, carrying a plate with two cookies on it. The noise she made almost made him miss hearing the answer that Rawlins gave.

"J. B. brought him back. He—"

His murmured answer was interrupted by a shocked: "Do you mean that boy is the one his Navaho mistress had?" The words were whispered, but even though the man and woman had remained on the porch, Hawk could hear what they said.

"Yes. She died—in the storm. J. B. asked if we would take care of him. I agreed," the man stated in the same low tones.

"Do you mean he wants us to raise that boy?" Her face was pinched in angry lines. Hawk noticed how thin her lips were. They almost disappeared when she pressed them tightly together—as she was doing now. In Hawk's opinion, all of the woman was too thin. "And you agreed?! How could you? Katheryn is my friend. Do you think—does he think—she isn't going to guess?"

"Katheryn will look the other way and pretend not to know anything—the same way she always has." Rawlins shook his head in a confused gesture. "I've never quite figured out how J. B. can inspire such loyalty from women. It's a pity he can't relate to men in the same way."

"Well, I don't care what you say. J. B. Faulkner has a lot of gall to install his bastard child in this house right under Katheryn's nose."

"Don't you see how much trust J. B. is putting in us, Vera?" Rawlins remained calm despite all the hissing words that had come from his wife. "Once you stop to think about it, it's quite a compliment."

"I just hope he realizes the awkward position he's put us in." The woman sounded less angry now.

The little girl moved to stand beside Hawk, blocking his view of the whispering couple on the porch. Putting a hand on her hip, she demanded, "Aren't you going to eat any of my cookies?" Hawk glanced at the plate on the table in front of him but didn't immediately reach for one of the cookies. "Daddy?" The little girl turned abruptly, her ringlets of gold dancing and bobbing. "He won't eat any of my cookies," she complained in an offended pout.

It was a second or two before the man, Rawlins, answered. "That's probably because he wants to save them for dessert. There's some cold roast beef in the refrigerator, isn't there, Vera?" he asked the woman. "Why don't you fix him a sandwich?"

As the woman entered the room, the little girl asked, "Are you going to eat any of my cookies, Daddy?"

"Sure, I'll have some of your cookies." Taking off his hat, he put it on the wall hook behind him and ran a hand through the sand-colored hair the hat had pressed down. As he unbuttoned and shrugged out of his sheepskin-lined coat, he glanced at Hawk. "Why don't you take your coat off, Hawk? You'll be too warm in the house if you keep it on."

Unlike the white man who takes action, even if it's wrong, it was the way of The People when caught in a situation they had never experienced to do nothing until they discovered how they were supposed to act. Rawlins' suggestion was the first indication to Hawk as to what the correct procedure was. He stood up and began unfastening his coat.

"Yes, and wash your hands," the woman instructed. "In this house, we wash our hands before we eat."

Rawlins motioned him onto the porch, taking Hawk's jacket and hanging it on the hook next to his. When Rawlins walked to the sink, Hawk followed him.

The man turned on the faucets, letting the water run while he wet his hands and lathered them with the bar of soap. Like the white teachers, he used water as if there were a limitless supply. Hawk was silently critical of the water that was being wasted, but he said nothing, and he washed his hands, too. All white men were foolish and wasteful, he decided. It would have taken him two trips to the well to carry as much water as the man, Rawlins, was letting run away. He dried his hands on the cloth that was given to him. Returning to the kitchen in the wake of Rawlins, Hawk sat down again in the chair he had previously occupied.

"Is the coffee hot yet, honey?" Rawlins questioned the woman.

"It's on the stove," she said, nodding with her head.

Hawk watched Rawlins take a white porcelain cup from a cupboard shelf and walk to the stove to pour a cup. Rawlins glanced up as Hawk was breathing in the aroma of the strong coffee, and he smiled.

"Would you like a cup of coffee, Hawk?" he asked. He moved his chin downward in a single, affirmative nod, and Rawlins reached inside the cupboard for another cup like his.

"You aren't going to give him coffee," the woman protested. "It will stunt his growth."

The man, Rawlins, just smiled and ignored her, filling the second cup with coffee and then carrying both to the table. "It will grow hair on your chest, won't it, Hawk?" he winked. But Hawk couldn't imagine why that should be a thing he would want, so he made no comment.

"You really aren't going to let him drink that!" The woman frowned in ill temper. "He's just a boy." She walked to the table, bringing a plate that had meat between two slices of white bread.

"Navaho children are accustomed to drinking coffee and tea, Vera," Rawlins explained. "Besides, after being outside in the cold, it will help warm him up."

His sore and swollen jaw made chewing painful and forced Hawk to eat slowly. The little girl climbed on her father's lap while he ate some of the cookies and told her how good they were. When Hawk finished the sandwich, he ate the two cookies the girl had brought him and sipped at the scalding-hot coffee.

"Why is he so quiet, Daddy?" The little girl twisted around on Rawlins' lap to look up into his face.

"Why do you talk so much?" was his teasing response.

She giggled. "Maybe the cat's got his tongue."

"I doubt it. Unlike you, he probably doesn't talk unless he has something important to say." Rawlins tapped a finger on the button nose of the girl.

"Where's your mommy and daddy?" An unblinking pair of green eyes was fixed on Hawk.

"He's an orphan, Carol." Hawk's gaze darted swiftly to the man holding the girl and answering the question for him. "He doesn't have a mommy and daddy anymore. They went away." The explanation confirmed what Hawk had suspected. His father was still his father, but not in the same way anymore.

"Doesn't he have *anybody*?" The little girl's eyes rounded into limpid green pools.

"I am alone," Hawk answered truthfully. It wasn't said in an attempt to solicit sympathy. It was a statement of fact—nothing more.

"Where do you live?" His answer prompted another question from her.

"He's going to be living with us," her father explained.

"Yes, but first, Tom Rawlins," the woman inserted, "you are going to see that the boy is cleaned up. I wouldn't be surprised if he is infested with lice. Where are the clothes he brought? I'll need to wash them, too—and the ones he's wearing."

"You're right, Vera," the man sighed, as if he were reluctant to agree. "His things are wrapped in that blanket on the porch. He'll need something to wear in the meantime."

"Katheryn left a box of old clothes that Chad has outgrown. She brought them over last week so I could take them to the Women's Club at church. We're sending them to a missionary in South America to distribute to the needy. There should be something in the box of clothes to fit the boy."

Setting the little girl down from his lap, the man rose. "Come on, Hawk. We'll get your head shampooed first; then you can take a bath."

There was a grim resignation in the man's face when he motioned Hawk toward the porch. Hawk found it strange because he understood all about the crawling lice. Once they were so bad in Crooked Leg's hogan that he and his family had to abandon it and build another.

"She soaped my hair again and again and took the blankets outside every day for the sun to kill them." Hawk explained the ritual that had been part of his life—and that of many other hogans, as well. "It was the only way to keep them away. Sometimes they came, anyway."

Rawlins looked disgusted as he turned on the water. "You won't find any lice in this house."

Hawk thought they were very fortunate, indeed, but he wasn't able to say so as his head was pushed under the running water. After his hair was shampooed, he was taken to a small room beyond the kitchen where there was a long white tub standing on four feet that looked like a cougar's claws. It was what his father had once described as a bathtub. Rawlins let water run into it. With instructions to put on the clean clothes folded in a stack on a table hooked to the wall after Hawk had finished his bath, Rawlins left him alone.

Because of the scarcity of water, baths had always been a luxury for Hawk. Perhaps here there was a limitless supply of the precious liquid. Hawk washed very slowly, enjoying this rare opportunity to the fullest. After his bath, he put on the clothes. They were loose on him, but they were clean and smelled good.

When he came out, he helped Rawlins carry boxes from a small storage room and install a narrow bed and a chest of drawers in the vacated space. He was told this was the room where he would sleep.

There was much to observe, much that was new to him, and strange. He was instructed in how to clean his teeth and shown how to use oil to tame the springy thickness of his hair, combing it to one side the way it wanted to go. That night, he was given a different set of clothes to sleep in, called pajamas, confirming what the teachers at school had taught, yet contrary to the habits of his father.

Hawk didn't sleep well. There were too many sounds that weren't natural to him. The minute the sun peeked in his window the next morning, he was up and dressed. Once he left his room, there was very little light to show him the way, but he didn't turn on any of the electric switches.

Making his way onto the porch, Hawk searched through the coats hanging on the wall hooks looking for his own. Behind him, the kitchen was suddenly flooded with light. Startled, Hawk turned sharply to face the door and accidentally knocked over a boot.

"Who's out there?" There was a thread of fear in the imperious demand made by the woman. Before Hawk could answer and identify himself, she was in the doorway glaring at him. "What are you doing sneaking around at this hour?"

"What is it, Vera? Who are you talking to?" The man, Rawlins, walked up behind the woman and saw Hawk on the porch, unconsciously looking guilty. "Where were you going, Hawk?" the man demanded.

"Hunger and thirst will be killing my horse. I must feed it and bring it water before the school bus comes." However, he wasn't at all certain that the school bus would know where to pick him up since he had left his home.

"Don't worry about your horse. Luther will feed and water it when he grains the others," Rawlins told him. "As for school, it's closed for the holidays. Besides, you won't be going to the Reservation school anymore. You'll be transferring to another school that's closer to us. You might as well come in the kitchen. Vera will be starting breakfast."

The woman turned away from the opening and disappeared into the room, yet Hawk hesitated. "Are there not things I should do?" he asked uncertainly.

"Things?" Rawlins frowned. "What do you mean?"

"It was my work to cut wood for the fire, carry water, and help my mother in the cornfield." None of which needed to be done here, since water ran from pipes in the house, heat came from a stove that burned oil, and there was no sign of any garden.

"I see." Rawlins paused to take a deep breath, then smiled. "You'll have chores here, too. I'll be checking the cattle after breakfast. You can come with me."

Chapter IV

The ranch and its way of life was alien to Hawk. There was so little that was familiar to him that he often felt lost and forsaken. Yet his father wanted him to learn of these things, so he accepted the strangeness of it all.

Tom Rawlins gave Hawk his first glimpse of what being a cowboy entailed. The first day he merely observed what was going on around him. The second day he began asking questions.

"Who owns all these cattle?" He gestured to the herd with the Flying F brand on their hips. Their heads were down, feeding on the hay the cowboys had thrown to them from the wagon. Its color was gold against the dirty snow.

Rawlins hesitated an instant. "Mr. Faulkner owns them."

The confirmation that they did belong to his father merely raised another question. "Everyone comes to you to find out what should be done. You give the orders. Why doesn't he if these animals are his?"

"Because he hired me to take care of them. I am what is known as a foreman, which means I'm in charge."

A cowboy called to Rawlins, ending the question

period. But Hawk realized that Rawlins was an important man, much respected by the others.

On the morning of the third day, Rawlins sent Hawk to the house with a message. "Tell Vera I have to be in town early this afternoon and ask her to have lunch ready by eleven-thirty."

When Hawk got to the back porch, he heard voices coming from the room they called the living room. One voice he recognized as belonging to the woman, Vera, although its shrill pitch was muted by a respectful tone. It was the sound of the second voice, soft and pure like the night cry of the owl, that lured Hawk toward the room.

Their talking had evidently covered the sound of the porch door opening and closing, because his presence went unnoticed when he paused in the opening to the room. He stared at the strange woman seated on the long sofa, slim and supple, her hands moving with the flowing grace of a willow in the breeze. Her hair was the color of a newborn fawn, blown away from her face to fall in long waves around her shoulders. Smooth and shiny, her face held the golden hint of the sun, and her lips were as red as the Vermillion Cliffs. She wore a white, bulky sweater that encircled her neck; but, most astonishing of all, she had on a pair of men's trousers. Hawk was so fascinated by this white woman that he barely noticed the tall boy seated next to her.

"J. B. is convinced there is going to be another land boom in Phoenix," the woman was saying. "Can you imagine? The place is an inferno in the summer, although I admit, in the winter it's practically heaven there. Anyway, he's talking about buying up land there—maybe even building a home and spending the winters in Phoenix. He's talking about going there this week to look over the prospects." Her teeth were so white against the red of her lips that Hawk watched the movement of her mouth with increasing interest.

"Is he actually serious?" Vera Rawlins questioned.

"He seems to be. The ranch has always been our home, but you know how bleak and lonely it is in the winter—snowbound sometimes for days, with no outside entertainment. In Phoenix, we could go out for dinner and dancing. Why, it would almost be like it was when J. B. and I were dating." A smile started to spread across her face, then stopped as she finally noticed Hawk in the doorway. Her lips came together, something hardening their curved line.

The sudden change in her expression turned Vera Rawlins in her chair. Her lips thinned and disappeared when she saw Hawk. "How many times have I told you not to go sneaking around?"

As always, the question confused Hawk. She was constantly accusing him of sneaking up on her whenever she failed to hear him approach, which was most of the time. Yet he walked normally, making no attempt to stalk her.

"Is this the *orphaned* half-breed you and Tom have taken in?" The woman stressed the word.

"Yes . . . yes, it is." Vera appeared embarrassed by the admission.

"Come closer so I can see what you look like." The woman motioned for Hawk to approach her.

Even as he obeyed the order, he sensed a change in the air, as if invisible tongues of lightning were dancing all around him. He stopped in front of her, looking down to gaze into her brown eyes, flecked with gold. Across the room, he had thought they held the warm glint of the sun, but up close they held the anger of lightning. Their inspection burned him.

When Hawk breathed in, he caught her scent. "You

smell like a hillside of wildflowers," he murmured in awe.

"What is your name?" she questioned, ignoring his compliment.

"Hawk." When her gaze narrowed with displeasure, he gave her the rest of his name so she wouldn't look at him that way. "Jim Blue Hawk."

"Who gave you that name?" she demanded.

"I took it myself." He would have explained how it had happened, but she didn't give him the chance.

"Do you have another name?"

"Yes." Hawk nodded.

"What is it?"

He hesitated. Perhaps by telling her his secret name, the stiffness would leave her mouth and the sunlight would come back to her eyes if he gave her that power over him. He took the chance.

"The-One-Who-Must-Walk-Two-Paths."

"But you are called Hawk." She didn't seem to understand the knowledge he had given her. "My name is Katheryn Faulkner. My husband owns this ranch. Did you know that?" Hawk shook his head. He hadn't known this woman was his father's first wife. "Do you know what the name Faulkner means?"

Again he shook his head. "No."

"It means 'a trainer of hawks or falcons.' I find that quite a coincidence, don't you?" The tightness in her voice made it sound angry. It was a question that Hawk wasn't expected to answer as she turned to the boy sitting beside her. "This is my son, Chad Faulkner."

He saw the way her face grew soft with pride and warmth when she looked at the other boy. He wished she would look at him that way.

Hawk turned his head to look at his half-brother. He was older than Hawk by four years or so, and several inches taller. His hair was a darker brown than his mother's, but his eyes were the same brown color as hers. Little Carol was sitting on the other side of him, using his knee as a table to rest her coloring book on. Chad Faulkner studied Hawk with a mild curiosity, appearing distantly amused by the situation.

"Hello," he said with feigned disinterest. "What are you doing here?"

The question reminded Hawk of the reason he had been sent to the house. Turning to Vera Rawlins, he related the message he was supposed to deliver.

"He said he had to go into town this afternoon and asked to have lunch at eleven-thirty."

"Who said?" she demanded. And she murmured in an aside to the woman, "I have the hardest time making him refer to people by name." Her attention was returned to Hawk. "Do you mean Mr. Rawlins?"

"Yes. Mr. Rawlins said it." Out of the corner of his eye, Hawk saw his father's wife push back the knitted cuff of her sweater, revealing a slim, gold watch.

"If you have to fix an early lunch, Vera, we should be leaving." She stood up and moved past Hawk, taking care not to touch him.

"Don't go," Carol protested when the knee supporting her coloring book was withdrawn. "I haven't finished coloring this picture for Chad."

"Bring it over to the house this afternoon." Chad stroked a hand over the girl's golden curls with an indulgent affection. "Maybe we'll build a snowman."

"Can we?" The little girl's face lit up with adoration and excitement, as if she had just been promised the most wondrous thing.

"Chad, you spoil her so," Vera Rawlins sighed, but Hawk had never seen her look so happy and contented. Standing apart from them, Hawk watched his father's wife put on a heavy parka with a fur collar, listened to the warmth of her voice when she thanked Vera for the coffee and said good-bye, and heard the front door close. Vera hurried to the kitchen to begin preparing the noon meal, leaving Hawk alone and forgotten in the living room. The fresh, sweet smell of the woman lingered in the room. Hawk felt an ache of loneliness.

Twice in that week, Hawk saw his father. Each time he was asked how he was getting along, and if there was anything he needed. Hawk had seen into his father's empty blue eyes and had known he didn't want to hear the answers to the questions. So he didn't speak of the strangeness and the loneliness he found. Instead, he made the replies he knew his father wanted to hear.

On Monday, he was to start his first day at the white man's school. He was ready to leave early, nervous and unsure of what new changes the school would bring. Would it be like the Reservation? Would the teachers strike your hand with a ruler if you were heard speaking Navaho? A white school would not permit Navaho to be spoken, Hawk decided. He tried not to think about his new classmates.

With his coat on and his hair slicked down, he stood at the kitchen window, waiting with a seeming impassivity while little Carol had her golden hair combed and adorned with ribbons. On this day, the man, Rawlins, would take them to school. After that, they would ride the bus.

"You're going to get overheated with that coat on, Hawk." Rawlins was sitting at the kitchen table drinking coffee and watching his wife combing his daughter's hair. "Why don't you go outside and wait?" he suggested. "Carol will be ready soon."

Hawk accepted the suggestion with alacrity, leaving the house on nearly soundless footsteps. The frosty air nipped at his face and made clouds of his breath. Hawk was gripped by the desire to run from this place and strike out for the north and the hogans of his relatives. His gaze was drawn past the trees to the white house where his father lived. He saw him walking from the house to a car parked in front of it, but his father wasn't wearing the sheepskin-lined parka or blue jeans. He had on a long, dark coat that flapped around his knees and dark pants. A raw sense of forboding shook Hawk. He broke into a run to race through the trees, an unnamed fear tearing at him. His father was standing in front of the car, waiting, when Hawk reached him. Beneath the partially buttoned coat, Hawk could see the suit and tie his father wore.

"Are you going with us to school?" He searched his father's face for an explanation and caught the flicker of guilt that crossed his expression.

"No. I'm going to Phoenix . . . on business. I was on my way over to Tom's to tell you good-bye." He avoided Hawk's eyes as he glanced at the car keys in his hand.

Dread crawled across Hawk's skin. "When will you come back?"

"I don't know. Not for a while." The expressive roundness of the blue eyes staring up at him pulled the man down to crouch in front of Hawk. "Try to understand, Hawk. I have to get away. I can't stay here anymore because it's too easy to believe she's at the hogan waiting for me. There is so much here to remind me of her—too many things that haunt my memory. I need to be in different surroundings for a while. I'll come back. I've gone away before, haven't I?"

But this time was different. His father was the solid rock he could hold onto in this shifting world that seemed to constantly change like the shifting sands of the desert. Hawk didn't understand this need to have his father nearby, so he couldn't express it. His only reply was to stare at his father in a mute plea.

"You're going to have a lot to do—what with school and helping Tom. You won't even notice I'm gone." His father struggled to convince Hawk that his departure was of minor importance. "I want you to pay attention in school and do the homework the teacher gives you. It's important for you to learn everything you can. Tom and Vera will look after you."

Light footsteps approached the car. At the sound of them, Hawk turned his head toward the house. It was the woman called Katheryn who was his father's first wife. Her eyes regarded him with displeasure again, but the look was gone when she glanced at his father.

"I thought you said you were leaving right away, J. B.?" There was a question in her voice.

"I am." He straightened after a last glance at Hawk and walked to the driver's side of the car. Holding the door open, he paused. "Good luck on your first day at school, Hawk." Then his gaze slid to the woman with the fur hood. "Good-bye, Katheryn."

"Don't forget to call me tonight," she instructed with a stiff smile.

His answer was a saluting wave of his hand as he slid behind the wheel. When the motor was started, Hawk moved out of the car's path and watched it drive away. He felt abandoned. His gaze was drawn to the beautiful woman standing on the other side of the driveway. There was a certain forlorn look to her expression that seemed to echo his feelings.

"Hawk!" Tom Rawlins' shouted call summoned him back to the house.

Adjusting to the new school was difficult for Hawk. Because of the low score on a test he had taken, he was placed in a class of students younger than he was. Not only was he older, but he was also much taller, so he always stood out from the others. The students, especially those in his age group, taunted him mercilessly. Instead of making comments about his blue eyes and waving black hair, the remarks they made referred to the copper tan of his skin, or they laughed at his name.

Although Hawk already knew he was different, the experience hammered the point home. He was diligent in his studies. Not because he wanted to excel and prove to the others he was as intelligent as they were—that wasn't the way of The People. He learned because there was value in knowledge.

His life settled into a routine once he started school. When he came to Rawlins' house after school was finished in the afternoon, he was made to change his clothes. From there, he went immediately in search of Rawlins to do his share of work. After the evening meal was over, he would do his homework until it was time for bed.

During the month his father was gone, Katheryn made several visits to the Rawlins' house while he was at school. Hawk knew this because on the days she came, there remained a lingering trace of the wildflower scent in the house when he returned from school. On those occasions, he would sit on the sofa where the fragrance was the strongest and read his assignments. Enveloped by the warm smell of her, he could almost pretend that somebody cared.

It was nearly one month from the day he left that J. B. Faulkner returned to the ranch. Hawk was on his way to the barns to help with the evening chores when he saw the car driving in. Work was forgotten as he raced to meet him, memories of other homecomings running fresh in his mind.

"You're back!" A reckless smile split his face.

"I told you I would come back, didn't I?" his father chided with affectionate huskiness as he reached inside the car to lift out a gaily wrapped package. "I brought something for you."

Hawk fell to his knees and immediately began tearing away the brightly colored paper to get at the box it covered. Inside was a plaid western shirt like the cowboys on the ranch wore. Hawk held it up with pride.

"I thought you'd like it," his father said, viewing Hawk's expression with satisfaction.

"Are you passing out presents, J. B.?" The challenging question came from his father's first wife, who had walked around the hood of the car. Beside her was the tall boy, her son and Hawk's half-brother. Hawk had not seen him since that first meeting. His half-brother called Chad did not attend the same school that Hawk did, but lived at an exclusive boys' academy, so Hawk had heard. Outside of a cursory glance at their first approach, neither of the two paid any attention to him.

"Hello, Katheryn, Chad." His father turned to greet both of them. The smile did not quite reach his eyes, but there was pride in his look when he shook hands with his older son. "I'm glad to see you made it home for the weekend, Chad."

"Yes, sir." The crisp nod seemed to match the severely squared shoulders and the artificially erect posture.

"What did you bring Chad?" Katheryn repeated the question that wasn't answered earlier.

The hesitation was almost imperceptible. "Nothing. Chad already has two of everything."

"Do you mean that you bought that Indian boy something and you don't have a gift for your own son?" Her voice was cold with anger.

His father stiffened, then relaxed with a heavy sigh. "That is precisely what I mean. Shall we continue this discussion some other time? I've had a long drive and I'm tired."

The rigidity left the woman's expression. "Of course you are. Chad, go in the house and pour your father a glass of whiskey." She moved to link her arm with his father's and guide him toward the house. "Don't bother about the luggage, J. B. I'll send someone out to fetch it."

Hawk watched the trio disappear into the house before his gaze fell to the brightly colored shirt in his hands. A wind rustled the paper it had been wrapped in. It was an empty sound.

Shortly after his father's return, there was an unexpected addition to Hawk's nightly routine of chores, homework, and bed. Since Carol was only seven years old, her bedtime was much earlier than his. It was always a drawn-out affair because she would try to wheedle a few extra moments. When that failed, she kissed her mother good night, then her father, and persuaded him to take her to the kitchen for a drink of water. Only after that would she go to bed.

This night, after her drink of water, she stopped beside the kitchen chair where Hawk was studying and kissed him on the cheek. "Good night, Hawk," she declared gaily and skipped away.

At the touch of her lips, he had recoiled instantly,

shocked by what she had done. In the Navaho belief, any contact with members of the opposite sex within the same clan was strictly forbidden, no matter how distant a relative was. He glanced sharply at Rawlins, expecting him to be angry with his daughter. Instead, the man was smiling.

"Is it permitted for her to do that?" Hawk questioned warily.

"Of course." Rawlins laughed at the question and wandered into the front room.

As far as Hawk was concerned, there was only one conclusion to be drawn from the answer. Although he lived in Rawlins' house, he had not been taken in as a member of their clan. He was separate from them.

Through the long winter and into spring, Hawk rarely saw his father. The trip to Phoenix turned out to be the first of many. Before he left and each time he came back, his father would seek out Hawk and, depending on the length of his return visits, would see him several times in between. The discussions were either instructive or related to how Hawk was doing with various school subjects. Never was Hawk asked how he was adjusting to his new life, how he was getting along with the Rawlinses, or if he missed the Reservation life.

Always the time spent with his father was alone. No one else was ever included. Each time his father came back from a trip, he brought Hawk a present. One time it was a shiny new pocketknife, another time a leather belt, and so on. Hawk had no way of knowing whether Chad received a gift, too.

By the time school closed for the summer, he had learned the meaning of words like "bastard," "mistress," and "illegitimate." Listening to the conversations of the cowboys, Hawk heard the contempt they held for most of the Indians.

Gradually, it became apparent to him that his father felt shame . . . shame because Hawk had been born on the wrong side of the blanket and because his mother was an "Indian squaw." That was why his father only saw him alone.

There were times when he remembered wistfully what it had been like when his mother was alive. Seated at the table, he would stare at slices of the soft, white bread. His mouth would wish for the taste of the tortilla-like bread his mother used to make. He would lie in bed at night, listening to the creaking of the wood house, and long to hear the comforting repetitious chants of the "sings." Sometimes he would sing them to himself, but he had to do it softly, or else the woman Rawlins would come to his room and whip him with her stinging tongue.

The advent of summer meant spending most of every daylight hour outside. It was taken for granted that he would work. The cowboys had grown used to having him around all the time and had ceased to regard him as an oddity. Sometimes they even included him in their jokes and laughter. Hawk had such a natural aptitude and an eagerness to learn that they were always giving him tips and pointers.

The first week of June, Chad came home to the ranch for the summer. The first few days after his return, Hawk saw little of him. Late one afternoon he had just finished his assigned task of cleaning out two of the barn stalls when Chad walked in.

"Have you see my father?" Chad followed Hawk to the water hydrant that stood by the horse troughs in the corral. "We're supposed to go riding this afternoon."

"No." Hawk turned on the faucet and bent to drink

from the running water, the excess spilling in to fill the horse tank.

"He'll probably be here shortly," Chad replied with unconcern and rested the toe of his boot on the bottom rail of the corral fence. With his thirst slaked, Hawk shut off the hydrant and glanced at his half-brother. There was nothing in his expression to indicate his presence was unwanted. A natural curiosity to know more about this stranger who was his relative kept Hawk by the corral fence. Chad sent a sidelong glance his way, then let his gaze sweep over the area. "All this is going to be mine someday," he announced, then looked back at him and said nothing. "I know who you are." He began to study Hawk with a quiet kind of curiosity. "I've heard my mother talk about you."

"What does she say?" The fascination he felt for his father's first wife had increased over the months until Hawk became totally entranced by her.

But Chad wasn't interested in answering Hawk's question. "Was your mother really a Navaho?"

"Yes." Hawk could read no contempt in his half-brother's face.

"Have you ever been to any of their ceremonies?" he wondered.

"Yes."

"Jess Hanks, this friend of mine at school, says that they carry rattlesnakes in their mouth."

"The Hopi does this in his snake dance," Hawk explained.

"Don't they get bit?"

"Sometimes." Hawk shrugged to show it was unimportant.

Chad digested that and looked around disinterestedly. "Is it true your mother was a whore and that she would sleep with anyone my father told her to?"

The insult sparked the flames that leaped in Hawk's eyes. "She was his second wife. She slept with no one but him."

Chad laughed at that. "His second wife! A man can only have one wife at a time, and he was married to my mother. If your mother slept with him, then she was a whore."

Anger deprived Hawk of all sense of caution. It ceased to matter that Chad was older, taller, and stronger, or even that he was his half-brother. He hurled himself at him. The ferocity of the attack knocked Chad to the ground. The two scuffled in the dirt, with Hawk kicking and hitting and inflicting some damage, but Chad soon gained the upper hand. Twisting an arm behind Hawk's back, Chad straddled him and pushed his face in the dirt.

"Do you give up?" Chad demanded in a voice that was hoarse from breathlessness. When there was no sound of surrender, he applied more pressure to the twisted arm. "Do you give?" Hawk gritted his teeth and shut out the cry of pain that tried to escape from him.

"What's going on here?" J. B.'s gruff voice loosened Chad's hold. In the next minute, Chad was standing up and Hawk was free. A large pair of hands insisted on helping Hawk to his feet, then brushed the dirt from his cheek. "Are you hurt, boy?" Hawk kept his eyes downcast as he shook his head in denial. "Go to the house, Chad," his father ordered.

"But we're supposed to go riding together," Chad protested.

"I said go to the house!"

"I never started it. He did!" Chad cast an accusing finger at Hawk.

"I don't care who started it! I want you to go to the

house!" J. B. turned his head to enforce the order with a piercing look. With a mutinous set to his mouth, Chad reluctantly obeyed.

"What started the fight, Hawk?" his father demanded when Chad was gone.

Hawk lifted his head to study him with emotionless blue eyes. "Were you married to my mother?"

A certain grimness settled onto his father's features. "Yes, we were married in the way of The People."

"But it isn't the way of the white man."

"No, it isn't."

"Why did you do it?"

"Because I loved your mother; therefore, I respected her ways."

"But in the white man's way, she wasn't your wife."

"In my heart, White Sage was my wife," his father insisted.

"Then why did you not marry her in the white man's way?" Hawk did not relent in his search for an understanding.

"Look around you, Hawk. Your mother would not have been happy here. If I had married her, this would have been her home."

He could see the truth in his father's words. That part was settled in his mind. "I am your son. Why don't I live in your house?"

"It isn't possible," his father declared with a helpless shake of his head.

"At school they call me a half-breed—half-Indian and half-white."

"It would be harder for you if you lived in my house," J. B. explained wearily.

"Because they would call me a bastard," Hawk guessed, speaking the word in a voice that held no feeling.

"Yes. Now do you understand why I don't want you to carry that burden, too?"

"Are you worried how people will think of me, or how they will think of you?" he asked, exhibiting a wisdom beyond his years.

Guilt blanched his father's face. "Try to understand, Hawk. There are more people involved than just you and me. I have to consider Katheryn and Chad, too. I've provided you with a good home. You'll have the best education. There will come a time when you can get involved in my business."

Hawk looked at him with impassive blue eyes. He saw the weak side of his father's character. He was disillusioned but not bitter. Slowly he turned and walked away—alone. There were so many considerations to be weighed.

To celebrate the Fourth of July, the Flying F Ranch held its own rodeo and barbeque. There was a lot of good-natured rivalry and competition among the cowboys as they pitted their skills against each other in calf-roping, bull-dogging, steer-roping, and saddle-bronc riding. Even the children of the cowboys had an event of their own—a goat-milking contest. The last event was a horse race.

When Hawk rode his chestnut horse to the starting line and crowded in with the other riders, there was a slight lull in the talking. Most of the cowboys at one time or another had seen the desert-bred pony stretch into a flat-out run and knew about its speed. Yet they glanced from one to the other, their eyes inevitably straying to a second boy entered in the competition on a sleek, long-legged bay. Chad Faulkner always won. The contest was who would take the second and third places.

At the starting line, Katheryn Faulkner held the pistol, every inch the owner's wife in her split riding skirt of leather and a matching leather vest over a white cotton blouse. Luther Wilcox was the cowboy closest to Hawk. He inched his horse nearer.

"Your horse is good, but you can't beat that bay of Chad's," he said.

"His horse is faster," Hawk agreed. "But I ride better."

The pistol was fired and the horses leaped forward. The race course was a mile-long run, its circuit extending across the grass pasture to a lone cottonwood, then circling back to finish where they started.

Hawk took the lead on his chestnut, then let the bay catch him and pass. Choosing his route with care, he avoided the rough ground that slowed the other horse. Instead of crossing the dry wash where it sloped, he guided his horse to the point where the gully was narrow and the banks were steep, and jumped his horse across it, taking the lead easily.

The bay had nearly caught up with him when they reached the cottonwood, but its circle was wide. Hawk's chestnut curved around it so close that the bark of the trunk scraped his knee. He was bent low over the horse's neck, the wind-whipped mane stinging his face. The fleet-footed bay again made up the lost ground, only to lose it again at the gully.

When they crossed the finish line, the chestnut was ahead by a neck. The pounding of racing hooves and the grunting of straining, equine breathing deafened Hawk to the hesitant and scattered cheers from the crowd.

Flushed and exhilarated by his victory, he reined his horse into a canter and made a sweeping turn back to the finish line for his prize. The resentful look that clouded his half-brother's expression when he rode by didn't bother Hawk. His father was standing in the front of the crowd, wearing a faint smile of pride.

It wasn't his father's approval and recognition of the victory that Hawk wanted as much as it was that of the slim, graceful woman who bestowed the ribbon and prize money to the winner. His blue eyes were shining with excitement as he rode toward her. He wanted her praise more than the prize.

Little Carol was standing beside Katheryn when Hawk stopped his scrawny-looking mount. Long seconds passed before Katheryn Faulkner lifted her head to look at him. Something died inside of him when he saw the icy anger and hatred in her eyes. The smile of victory faded from his face as the chestnut danced and shifted beneath him. Hawk held her gaze with stubborn pride, refusing to be denied the recognition that was rightfully his.

"You cheated," she accused in a low, husky voice that trembled with barely controlled anger. The insulting words stung Hawk. A blinding feeling of hurt briefly darkened his eyes. "You only won because you deviated from the course of the race."

Someone stepped into Hawk's side vision to stand beside the golden-haired girl clutching the woman's hand. "He won fairly, Katheryn." It was his father, speaking low, too, so those looking on couldn't hear. "You can't show favoritism for Chad in front of the others."

The blue ribbon and envelope of prize money were in her hand. Her smile was forced as she turned to the little girl beside her. "Here, Carol. You can give out the ribbon this time."

His father reached down and picked the girl up by the waist so she could reach Hawk to present him with his winnings. As he reached out a hand to take the ribbon and envelope from her, Carol drew them back and sent a frowning look over her shoulder at his father.

"But I wanted to give them to Chad," she protested. "He should have won."

"Yes, he should have," J. B. Faulkner agreed. "But Hawk gets the blue ribbon. You can give the red one to Chad."

With obvious reluctance, Carol gave Hawk the first prize. Carol's defection came as no surprise to Hawk. The rare times that Chad came home from the private school he attended, and deigned to notice the daughter of the ranch foreman, she treated him like a god.

Taking his prize, Hawk relaxed the pressure on the horse's bit and kicked it into a trot toward the barns where the other cowboys and horses were milling. When he joined them to dismount and unsaddle his horse, conversation lagged. A few of them acknowledged his win, tossing out subdued comments.

"Good job."

"Helluva ride, Hawk."

Hawk didn't make a single response, hiding his disappointment behind a mask of stoic indifference.

With the race over, everyone began drifting toward the lawn of the low, rambling main house where the barbeque was to be held. Hawk went, too, although his appetite was left behind. Keeping to the background, he joined the fringes of a group of ranch hands and their families and did nothing that would draw attention to himself. His gaze strayed often to his father's first wife as she laughed and talked with those around her.

Plates became emptied of food, were refilled, and emptied again before bellies became stuffed to the point they could hold no more. Then the adults sat around in groups, talking, drinking, and laughing while the children played rowdily—all except Hawk, who merely sat beneath the shade of a tree and watched them all.

"Hawk?"

He glanced sideways in the direction of the little girl's voice that had called his name. She came running toward him to stop somewhat breathlessly in front of him. Her tightly coiled ringlets of gold were starting to droop, the ends brushing the white ruffles of her pinafore. She was pretty, like a little pink and gold doll, and Hawk smiled.

"Are you really an Indian, Hawk?" Her hands went to her hips as she asked the question, tilting her head to one side.

"Yes, part Indian," he admitted.

His answer widened her eyes, which shimmered with curiosity and a hint of fear. "Do you scalp people?" she murmured in faint alarm.

His eyes laughed with mischief. "Only little girls with yellow hair," Hawk teased and made a playful lunge toward her.

She ran from him, shrieking, "Chad! Chad!" She catapulted herself into the older boy's arms when he appeared. "He was going to scalp me!" she cried. "Don't let him get me, Chad!"

"It's all right, honey," the boy soothed and sent Hawk a glaring look. "I won't let him hurt you."

Hawk watched silently as the tall boy turned and carried the girl away.

Late that night, Hawk slipped out of the house while everyone was sleeping, saddled his horse, and rode north. A full moon lit the way, silvering the land with its bright light. Many times he spurred his horse, feeling the presence of ghosts that traveled in the darkness of night.

Before dawn, he arrived safely at the hogan of his mother's uncle. He spent three days there before his father came to take him back. Hawk wasn't unhappy to leave his mother's relatives. Almost a year away from them had produced significant changes within himself. The absence of modern conveniences like electricity, running water, and indoor toilets didn't bother him as much as the meager amount of food on the table; he also missed the nightly showers and having clean clothes to wear each day.

PART
II

"He stirs, he stirs, he stirs, he stirs.
Among the lands of dawning, he stirs, he stirs;
The pollen of the dawning, he stirs, he stirs;
Now in old age wandering, he stirs, he stirs;
Now on the trail of beauty, he stirs, he stirs;
He stirs, he stirs, he stirs, he stirs.

. . . Happily my head becomes cool."

Chapter V

During his senior year of high school, Hawk was informed by his father that he would be attending an eastern university in the fall. The decision and choice of college was made by his father. A more mature Hawk was not excited by the prospect of being uprooted a second time in his life and thrust into an alien atmosphere. Yet he was aware there was much to be gained from both the experience and the education. When the time came, he went without protest. Only Carol, now a willowy teen-ager, had tears in her eyes when he left.

His father accompanied him to the airport, full of last-minute instructions and advice. Hawk listened as he had always done, then sifted out what was worthwhile and threw the rest away. That was one thing his father had taught him indirectly—to think for himself.

Although Hawk saw his father whenever he visited the ranch, their relationship wasn't close. The way his father had dealt with Hawk's illegitimacy and mixed heritage had created a chasm that his father was unwilling to repair. When they were together, they talked about the ranch, school, or his father's business dealings in Phoenix.

There were always rumors circulating about J. B.

Faulkner's activities. His time seemed to be devoted to acquiring chunks of land in Phoenix, selling some for huge profits, developing others into housing tracts, and constructing commercial buildings on the rest. He dabbled in citrus groves and bought shares in copper mines. It was joked that Faulkner intended to own the state of Arizona before he died.

After starting college, Hawk returned to the ranch each summer to work. Never asking for special favors and accepting his share of the dirty jobs, he earned the respect of his fellow cowboys. Yet there was a barrier between Hawk and the others that he was never able to overcome. He was the bastard son of a multimillionaire. It was a fact the cowboys rarely forgot, and one Hawk could never overcome. There were several he would have liked to call friends, but none that he truthfully could.

Only among the Navahos could he walk as a mere man. Their only distrust came because he was half-white. They didn't care which side of the blanket he'd been born on or how much money his father had. Since that Fourth of July night years ago when Hawk had run away to the Reservation, his father had given his consent to allow Hawk to spend two weeks each summer visiting his mother's relatives.

This summer he had left his pickup at the hogan of a cousin, borrowed a horse, and ridden into the high country where his Uncle Crooked Leg had taken his sheep. Although his main hogan was the one a few miles from where Hawk had lived as a boy, his uncle had several dwellings scattered over the country because of the need to have grazing land and water for his sheep. The air was cooler in the higher elevations away from the desert floor, the summer heat less uncomfortable.

The two weeks always passed so swiftly. During

them, Hawk followed the customs of The People, observing their life-style and taboos. He used water sparingly, washing his hands and face as everyone did, since cleanliness was important. It was bathing that was so rare because of the large amount of water required. Since it was summer, most all of the family slept outside the hogan, but Hawk took care not to step over any sleeping person lest some unknown evil befall him. He avoided lightning-struck trees, never killed a marauding coyote or a rattlesnake. To Hawk, these superstitions were no more ridiculous than the white man's mania about black cats, Friday the thirteenth, and walking under ladders.

Hawk worked, doing his share of whatever task was at hand. He sat in the sweatlodge with the adult males of his uncle's family, singing the chants to the north and purging his body. In the evenings, he gathered with the others around the campfire, exchanging gossip and stories. Crooked Leg was having a government house built for his family, and he discussed this at length with Hawk since he lived in such dwellings. The main hogan would remain standing because the curing chants could be done only in a hogan. There were many questions from his relatives about Hawk's life in the east where he attended college. In all the conversations, Hawk noticed the supercilious attitude his mother's relatives had toward the whites. This arrogance was shared, in varying degrees, by all The People.

It was morning when he left his mother's family. The August sun stayed until the evening hours. Night was drawing its curtain across the sky as Hawk drove the pickup into the ranch yard. He noticed all the activity around the main house and belatedly remembered that Chad was due back. An impromptu party was obviously in progress to welcome home the Faulkner son and heir.

Harboring malice or jealousy was foreign to his nature. Hawk had The People's trait of accepting the status of situations that couldn't be changed. Life went more smoothly that way.

With the truck parked in front of the Rawlins' house, Hawk paused to listen to the beckoning sounds of laughter, music, and English-speaking voices drifting across the yard from the main house. It stirred a need in him different from the one that had taken him to the Reservation. He glanced down at the clothes he'd worn for several days straight at his uncle's, clothes were washed as infrequently as baths were taken, then entered the house to shower and change.

A half-hour later he joined the party in progress. Drifting around the edges of the gathering, Hawk spoke to a few of the ranch hands, unobtrusively worked his way to the bar for a can of cold beer, and stood to one side to drink it and watch the others. He had just located the guest of honor, Chad, over by the buffet table with Katheryn when he observed his father approaching.

"I see you made it back, Hawk." A smile accompanied the gravelly voiced greeting.

"Yes." Hawk nodded and took a swig of beer. "Crooked Leg sent his greetings." Unconsciously, he forced an acknowledgement of where he'd been the last two weeks.

"How is he?" The question was asked with interest.

"Fine." His gaze strayed across the patio to his half-brother. Maturity had given Chad a sophisticated charm to go along with his good looks. At that moment, Chad glanced up, his gaze locking with Hawk's for a fraction of a second before it shifted to the graying man beside him, then narrowed again on Hawk in vague suspicion. Someone distracted Chad and

Hawk let his gaze wander on. "Chad seems to be enjoying his homecoming," he remarked.

"The party is sort of a personal celebration for Chad. I told him tonight that I was putting him in charge of managing my real estate holdings in Phoenix."

The news came as no surprise to Hawk. For years his father had been grooming Chad to step in and take over part of the family business.

"He's been trained for it." Hawk stated the obvious.

"Next year you'll have your degrees in business administration and political science. There's quite a push on now to have minorities working in government. I won't have any trouble arranging for you to be appointed to a high position in the state."

Hawk listened to the plan his father laid out and watched the self-satisfaction settle in his expression. It was easy to read the dual purpose of the plan. His father was buying him the respectability of a high position to overcome his illegitimacy and mixed heritage. At the same time, he was acquiring a beneficial connection in a government office. Hawk had to admit there was a stroke of genius in the plan, but his father invariably gained from his own actions. In this, he gained doubly because he would be assuaging his guilt about Hawk and putting one of his own in a position of influence.

"You have it all well thought out," Hawk remarked and caught the scent of wildflowers. He anticipated Katheryn's appearance before she interrupted his father.

"Yes, I—" he began.

"This is a party, J. B.," she declared in her richly cultured voice. Hawk half-turned to see the woman approach, an arm linked with her son's. "You shouldn't be over here in a huddle."

Amusement twisted at Hawk's mouth. Katheryn allowed him to exist on the fringe of her family, but she jealously guarded any intrusion into the immediate circle. She regarded Hawk as some kind of threat to her son. This suspicion had rubbed off on Chad.

"Hello, Chad. J. B. was just telling me the news. Congratulations." He reached out to shake hands with his half-brother, aware that Chad was testing his remark for envy or resentment.

"Thank you." Then Chad turned to his father and Hawk found himself shut out of the conversation.

Draining the last of the beer from its can, Hawk let his attention return to Katheryn Faulkner. She had an ageless and aloof kind of beauty. Hawk wasn't entirely sure why she commanded so much of his affection. Because of the death of his mother, perhaps he was regarding Katheryn as a substitute. Or possibly the matrilineal society of the Navaho had given him an inbred sense of loyalty to the matriarch of the family. His attraction to her was real; it wasn't something that Hawk tried to figure out, but simply accepted.

He moved to one side to set his empty beer can on a patio table. Petticoats rustled near him and he turned to find Carol nearly at his side. The demure white dress was at odds with the beguiling look in her green eyes. Two weeks of abstinence had made his desires hunger for satisfaction. The sight of Carol whetted his appetite.

Her rose-colored lips curved in a provocative pout. "As late as it is, I don't know why you bothered to show up."

"I just got back." He explained his tardiness without apologizing for it. "You didn't really miss me—not with your beloved Chad here," Hawk teased.

"Chad thinks I'm quite beautiful," she retorted.

For once, Hawk was in full agreement with his

half-brother. Last summer he had noticed the way Carol was blossoming into a woman, the baby fat melting away to reveal round, firm breasts, a slim waist, and curving lips. He had noticed, and he had wanted, but she had been uneasy around him, changeable as the wind. Sometimes she had moved in a way designed to attract his attention; then when he showed it, she would take flight in a kind of panic.

But this summer it had been different almost from the day he had returned from the university. The invitation had been there in her look, her smile, the way she moved, and the absence of innocence in her eyes. It hadn't mattered to Hawk that he hadn't been the first to take her; nor did he care who had lain with her before. The Navaho didn't prize virginity in a woman the way the white man did. He found experience preferable to the time-consuming task of soothing the fears of the uninitiated.

Eventually, Carol had confessed that Hawk had disturbed her the previous summer, arousing in her feelings that she didn't know how to cope with. Hawk blamed it on her mother, Vera Rawlins, who had filled Carol's head with a lot of nonsense about sex being sinful and wicked, and terrible things would happen to her if she didn't wait for a wedding ceremony to sanctify the union.

Even now, Carol's reticence hadn't completely vanished. It was revealed in the excuses she used to seek him out alone, and the discreetly friendly attitude she maintained toward him in front of her parents and others. Hawk had no objections. A Navaho wouldn't flaunt an intimate relationship in front of family members or friends.

"Don't you think I'm beautiful?" she challenged when Hawk failed to reply.

"You know you are," he returned smoothly.

"You could be more forceful about it," she complained with wounded dignity. "Chad didn't have any difficulty."

A trace of amusement slipped across his expression. She was always trying to promote some kind of rivalry between Hawk and Chad. In typical female fashion, she wanted to see the two brothers come to blows over her to prove her feminity. It irritated her when Hawk wouldn't rise to the provocation.

And he didn't accept the challenge this time. "I'm not going to compete with Chad for your attention."

"Who said you could?" she flared, then spun away to seek out Chad.

He watched with a kind of amused indifference while she flirted outrageously with his half-brother and coaxed him into dancing with her. Hawk wasn't surprised when the couple slipped away into the night's shadows. This wasn't the first time Carol had used Chad to even up some imaginary score with him. Hawk knew he would have his turn.

Two days later, he was out on the range. He cantered his horse over the crest of a hill and reined it to a halt near a turning windmill. Dismounting, Hawk checked the motor on the water pump of the well bore. It was functioning smoothly. Turning to walk back to his ground-hitched horse, he paused to scan the raw, wild landscape. The voice of the land and its mysteries pulsed around him, warmed by the heat of a mid-afternoon sun. As far as the eye could see, nothing stirred. Yet its wildness touched him, striking a responsive chord deep inside him.

The pressure that kept his mouth in such taut, controlled lines was eased. Inner pleasure brightened the deep blue of his eyes. Long hours in the summer sun had darkened the skin stretched over lean cheeks, skin that already possessed a natural copperish hue. Even his cheeks were relaxing into a vague smile.

This ancient familiarity with the land was a gift to him from The People. It comforted him and fed him. From it, Hawk knew what white men could never understand. Land owned people, but people never owned land. And this land kept pulling him back, exerting its influence even across the breadth of a continent.

His side vision caught movement. Hawk turned to identify it and saw a horse and rider approaching. He recognized that curved shape instantly and waited for Carol to reach him. Her long, golden hair was no longer forced to curl into ringlets, but allowed to fall free to a point well past the middle of her back, stopping just short of her waist.

At eighteen, she was all woman, versed in the ways to heat a man's blood, as his was heating now. She reined her horse to a stop a few feet in front of him, letting it dance sideways to show off her rounded silhouette. Her breathless smile held the natural sweetness of honey. Hawk craved the wild taste of those lips, but he held that desire in check. The time would come, he knew, as his gaze swept the natural, unrestrained outline of her breasts beneath the thin material of her blouse and knew what it implied.

"I finally found you," she declared.

"Was I lost?" he mocked smoothly.

She wrinkled her nose at him in a provocative protest to his teasing. "Momma wants me to remind you that we're having dinner at the main house tonight. You have to be back in time to shower and change before we go. She didn't want you to forget and be late."

"I hadn't forgotten." He moved to the horse's head, taking hold of the bridle and stroking its velvet nose to quiet it.

"Sometimes, Hawk, you have a tendency to lose track of time when you're out riding alone. I don't know what it is that keeps you out here," Carol murmured.

Turning, Hawk let himself be distracted from the beauty of her by the lasting beauty of the land. "The Navaho believes he is Made-from-Everything, all the things necessary for life. He is made from Water because its wetness is in his sweat, his blood, in the juices that flow from his mouth, the tears that wet his eyes, and the waste that is excreted from his body. He is made from Air. It fills his lungs, and is transmitted through his blood. He is made from the Sun, because like the sun, his body radiates heat. And he is made from the Earth, the dirt that gives him sustenance and to which he will return when he dies. 'Dust to dust, ashes to ashes—'" His gaze swept the rugged terrain. "Look out there, Carol, and you will see the 'Everything' that I was made from. In two weeks, I'll have to leave it again to return east, but it will be the last time I leave. When I come back in the spring, it will be for good."

"But what about your degree?" At her question, Hawk pivoted back to face her. His blood ran warm with desire again. "You aren't going to let it go to waste, are you?"

"Learning is never a waste," he corrected.

"But you know J. B. is going to get you a job. Chad has taken over the management of all the real estate. You—" Hawk reached up to lift her out of the saddle, letting his hands slide up to her ribs as he set her on the ground. An eagerly bright light glittered in her eyes. "Do you think J. B. will turn over the ranch to you?"

"Why should he?" The possibility seemed remote to Hawk, especially in view of the plans his father had for him. That fact didn't bother him. "Your father is managing it very well."

"But Daddy could work for you," Carol reasoned.

He considered her for a thoughtful minute, recognizing the ambition that gleamed in her eyes. "You have always fancied yourself as mistress of the big house, haven't you?" he mused without criticism. "You're always trying to imitate Katheryn. You've even adopted some of her mannerisms."

Tipping her head to one side, she regarded him with an attitude that was both saucy and defensive. "So?" she challenged lightly. "I remember, as a teen-ager, you acted as if she were some kind of goddess. You used to sneak off at night and sit outside the house for hours hidden in the bushes, looking through the glass door of the veranda when she played the piano."

"Were you following me? Or sneaking up there to catch a glimpse of Chad?" he chided, unconcerned that she knew of his obsessive interest in his father's wife.

She pulled back coyly. "Jealous?"

"I've never been jealous of Chad." He had no objections to wild oats being sown by both parties before a marriage. It was only afterward that he expected absolute fidelity. His hands tightened to draw her back to her former position, almost touching him, but she resisted, flattening her hands against his chest, fingers lifting slightly at the contact with the sweat-soaked material of his shirt.

"I have to go back." Her soft red mouth made a moue of regret, and his gaze centered on it. "I only rode out to give you Momma's message."

A smile played with his mouth, faint and knowing. "And that's the only reason you came out here?" The tantalizing fragrance of wildflowers drifted from her skin, the same unique fragrance that Katheryn always wore and Carol had adopted as her own.

"Of course," she insisted.

He let the smile go ahead and curve the line of his mouth as he bent his head toward hers. Instinctively, she offered him her lips, swaying closer to him. Anticipation trembled through her when he brushed them in a teasing fashion. Reaching behind her, Hawk lifted the flap of one saddlebag.

As she seemed to become unconscious that his hand was occupied with a task other than her, he murmured into her mouth, "If the only reason you came out here was to deliver that message, why did you stop to take off your bra?"

Her head jerked away from his, temper flashing green in her eyes when she saw the lacy white brassiere dangling from his fingers. Hawk knew her anger was not caused by his discovery. Rather, it came because he had revealed his knowledge, showing her that he knew how very deliberately she sought to invite him to take her in his arms. Carol liked to pretend their embraces were spontaneous, completely unplanned. Hawk baited her with the fact that she desired him as much as he desired her.

"Why did you have to do that?" Her expression was properly irate.

"You like to be chased, don't you?" He made the circle of his arms smaller. She struggled, but Hawk saw the way her lips parted in an unconscious invitation. "Do you resist because you think it's the proper thing to do, or because it heightens your pleasure?"

"Hawk, stop it! Let me go!" she protested angrily.

Motionless for a second, he relaxed his hold, then let his arms fall from around her and stepped away. "Okay." He saw the look of consternation flash across her expression. Being free wasn't what she wanted at all. His blue eyes glittered with the knowledge as he held out the brassiere to return it to her. "You'll want to put this back on before you ride back. 'Momma' might ask a lot of questions."

"Damn you, Hawk!" She swore at him to mask her disappointment and snatched the bra from the hook of his finger. He laughed, a throaty sound rich with amusement. She struck at him, but he caught her hand before it reached his face and pulled her against him. "Brute!" she hissed.

"And you are a tease," he accused softly and silenced any reply with his mouth. Instantly, there was a wild, hungry response to the domination of his kiss. The stiffness fled from her body; every curve welded itself to him.

Passion flamed hot and unchecked in both of them. Hawk let it burn, the heat flowing through his sensitized flesh. Yet there was no haste, no urgency in him. He would take her in his own good time and not be hurried by Carol, as she was prone to do if he let her set the pace.

His mind knew no guilt in taking her. In this, there was no confusion. For once, the practices of the Navaho and the white were in accord. Sex and the desire for it were natural things, as inevitable as life and death.

Hence, there was no need to deny himself the enjoyment of her body. Her hands were caressing his face and curling into the thickness of his hair while she pressed eager, urgent kisses on his mouth, chin, and jaw. Hawk wedged a space between them with his arm so his adept fingers could unfasten the buttons of her blouse in swift, sure action.

"It's so open here," she whispered in protest even as his hands pushed the blouse from her shoulders. "What if someone sees us?"

It was a question without a satisfactory answer, so Hawk didn't attempt to find one. Sliding the blouse sleeves off her arms, he moved away to spread it on the ground. He removed his hat and hooked it on the horn of his saddle. Then he took off his shirt and laid it lengthwise next to hers to protect their naked flesh from the spiky, sun-scorched grass. When he turned, Carol was standing there half-naked, waiting, wavering uncertainly at his deliberateness.

Hawk held out his hand to her. She hesitated only an instant before she placed her small white hand in the large brownness of his and allowed herself to be drawn to the makeshift bed. Hawk was slow to follow her to the ground, letting his eyes run over her.

"Do you think I have a beautiful body, Hawk?" she asked in a voice that was breathless and needing.

He stretched his long frame alongside the smaller length of hers, raising himself on an elbow. "Yes." His hand glided across the flatness of her trembling stomach to curve itself to the underside of a breast. "I can see your breasts becoming fat and heavy with milk someday and a baby suckling greedily from a nipple."

His thumb moved to the brownish crest and circled it several times to arouse it to a stiff peak. When she moaned in uncontrollable passion, Hawk smiled and moved his hand upward to let his rough fingers slide into her hair. Its length fanned above her head in a headdress of gold.

"Your hair is as bright and shiny as the sunlight." He gave her the compliments he had refused to offer in competition with Chad's at the party. "It feels as soft as cornsilk. Your eyes are the color of the she-stone."

He lowered his head to let his mouth explore the satiny texture of her cheek. As she curved her hands around his middle, an arm brushed the sweat-dampened hair under his arm—the contact brief and tickling.

"What is a she-stone?" she whispered, his compliment arousing a reluctant curiousity to distract her.

"A Navaho believes there are two of everything—male and female." He kissed the side of her neck, evoking another moan from her throat, while his hand began another downward exploration, stopping at the waistband of her jeans. "The Colorado is a male river because of its churning, turbulent waters, and the placid Rio Grande, with its quiet waters, is female. A tall, sturdy plant is male, while the smaller, weaker plant of the same species is female. There are two predominant colors in turquoise stones. The one with the deep blue color is the he-stone, and the one with the greenish cast to it, like your eyes, is the she-stone."

Deftly, his fingers unfastened the snap of her jeans and slid the zipper down. Her hands were there to help him push the denim material off her hips. Leaving her to finish taking off her jeans, Hawk stood up to remove his own faded Levi's. He saw the fevered brightness in her eyes when he shed them.

"God, you look so primitive in that breechcloth," she breathed in excitement. "Why do you wear it?"

"It's more comfortable," he answered with a smooth shrug and loosened the cloth that covered his genitals.

"Seeing you like that makes me feel like a white captive." She tried to laugh at the thought, as if she wasn't serious. "Did the Navaho ever steal white women?" she asked, her voice lifting in curiosity.

Hawk was used to such questions. Each time a woman learned he was a half-breed, she asked similar questions before, during, or after he had bedded her.

His nod was affirmative. "White women, Mexican, Apache—any woman. It didn't matter what the race or tribe was. Because marrying within the clan was forbidden, sometimes the Navaho had to raid in order to capture wives." He sank down beside her in a fluid move that was unhurried, yet one continuous, supple motion.

"What if she resists?"

Hawk read the expression written on her face, the pulsing excitement danger breeds, and his mouth formed a lazy curve. He moved to pin her to the ground with his torso, his weight settling partially onto her.

"You are like the others, aren't you?" he observed. "You are turned on by the idea of a 'noble savage' taking you." His mockery held no condemnation, only a curling amusement. His hands staked her arms to the ground above her head, and she quivered beneath him, her eyes bright and gleaming. "It adds spice, hmm? Acts out a sexual fantasy?"

In her reticence, Carol wouldn't admit such a thing, and Hawk didn't wait for her false denial. Her moist and parted lips told him all he needed to know as he moved to drink from them and spread her legs apart with his knee. Her body arched to accept him, avid, whimpering sounds coming from her throat to be swallowed by his mouth. With his hands, he eased her into a position where he could fit more deeply in the saddle of her hips.

Hawk was absently conscious of the contrast between the whiteness of her satiny skin and the bronze sheen of his strong flesh. It soon escaped his notice under the rhythmic urgency of her hips that invited savage thrusts. Deliberately, Hawk held off her moment of satisfaction, waiting until her nails were digging into the rippling muscles of his back in wild demand. Even as he heard her cry out, he was rocked by the raw explosion of desire that flamed through him. A series of aftershocks shuddered through him, leaving him momentarily spent.

He rested on top of her; then gathering strength, he withdrew to stretch out beside her to let his heart stop its hammering and his lungs end their labored breathing. Carol rolled onto her side to curl against him, her hand gliding over his chest in silent ownership.

"Say you love me, Hawk," she commanded in a husky tremor.

Her lips were still swollen from his kisses. Her flesh was still warm from his body heat. Now the sun's rays continued to make it burn. Satisfaction had been mutual, as it invariably was. Yet her question prompted a glint of amusement to enter his eyes.

"What is love?" Hawk chided. "A Navaho does not believe in 'romantic' love, as the whites know it."

From all that Hawk had observed, the word was so loosely and freely used that it applied to a half a hundred things. Sexual desire was regarded as love. Liking someone was considered love. Caring for the well being of another was love. Several times he had asked someone to define the word. Always it sounded like another emotion hidden under the guise of love.

Whenever he had expressed his skepticism, the response was that something inside would tell a person when they had found the one they loved. Hawk thought it was wiser to look at a prospective mate with your eyes instead of waiting for some mysterious signal.

This romantic love seemed forever elusive— intangible and indefinable. Hawk had concluded that it didn't exist. The way of The People was much more sensible, he had decided after evaluating both.

"How does a Navaho go about choosing a wife, then?" Carol laughed, not certain that he was serious.

"By judging if she has the qualities he is seeking.

Naturally, a wife should be able to cook and keep house. A man would want to enjoy having sex with her. She should be strong and healthy, capable of having his children and working at his side."

These were all qualities he saw in Carol. And there was the advantage that she knew who he was and what he was. They had known each other practically all their lives, which made a very stable foundation for the future. But this was not the time to make her his wife. Next year, after he had graduated from college, he would marry her.

"How chauvinistic!" she declared on a thread of anger. "Cooking, cleaning, and having babies is certainly not my idea of married life. I want more out of it than that."

He read the look in her eyes and knew she was visualizing Katheryn Faulkner, slim and sophisticated, the matron of Phoenix society. It troubled him, but only briefly.

"Chauvinistic? The Navaho is a very matriarchal society. A man owns nothing but his clothes and his saddle. Everything else—land, house, livestock— belong to his wife. He merely works for her," Hawk explained with a lazy smile.

"That sounds better." She snuggled closer to him, but he became aware of the lengthening shadows cast by the sun, and he rolled to his feet, reaching for his breechcloth and pants.

"I thought that might appeal to you." He glanced over his shoulder. She was greedy and spoiled, always scheming to have her way. It didn't worry him. He knew how to handle her. Carol was still lying on the blouse and shirt, stretching out like a smug white cat. "You'd better get dressed," Hawk advised.

"In a minute." She slid him a provocative look.

Chapter VI

"Now. I want my shirt." He snapped the opening of his Levi's shut and reached down to pull the plaid shirt from beneath her hips.

But she deliberately flattened herself more fully onto his shirt, daring him to take it. A wicked light danced in devilish blue eyes as Hawk knelt to engage in a last, playful wrestling match with her.

The instant his knee touched the ground, he felt the vibrations . . . caused by galloping hooves. A second later, he was standing tall, scanning the landscape for the source. The aftermath of passion had drugged his senses, lessening their normal keenness, or he would have been warned of the approaching horses and riders before they were this close.

"Get dressed." This time it was a flat order. "Someone's coming."

"Oh, my God!" Carol whispered in panic and scrambled to her feet, snatching up her jeans and hastily pulling them on.

Even before the four riders came close enough for Hawk to see their faces clearly, he recognized them. The two riders lagging behind were ranch hands, Bill Short and Luther Wilcox. The man sitting so stiffly in his saddle was Chad Faulkner. He was riding beside Tom Rawlins.

"Oh, no! It's Daddy!" Carol sobbed behind him and Hawk turned to find her fumbling with the snap on her jeans.

Making a lightning-quick assessment, Hawk realized there was no hope of fooling Rawlins. His view of the scene might have been limited by distance, but Rawlins would have seen enough to know what had preceded his arrival. Reaching down, he scooped his shirt off the ground and slipped his arms into the sleeves, but he made no attempt to button it or tuck it into his denims. Carol's hands were still all thumbs, unable to fasten the hook of her bra when he turned away to step between her and the quartet of riders, led by her father.

Fifteen feet away, the horses were reined to a sliding halt as the riders piled out of their saddles. Hawk's attention focused on Rawlins, paying scant heed to the riders who flanked the man who was now striding forward. Rawlins was small-built but wire-tough. The man's quietness was deceptive, but Hawk had never underestimated the man's strength or will. Running a ranch this size, as Rawlins did, meant keeping thirty and more rough and rowdy cowhands in line, something the man had been doing for more than half of Hawk's life.

A fair man. If Rawlins had a blind spot, it was his daughter. She could do no wrong in his eyes. Hawk knew this situation was going to rearrange his timetable, moving forward his marriage plans to this summer instead of the next. Hawk respected this man who had taken him in, raised him, and taught him everything he knew about cattle and ranching. No matter how severely tested his temper was, Rawlins had always been a man who listened to reason.

But at the moment, the savagely hard and cold

expression on the man's face didn't appear to belong to someone willing to listen to explanations. Hawk stood his ground, meeting the raging look of the man facing him without flinching. Behind him, he could hear Carol breathing in gasping sobs.

"What the hell is this?" Rawlins thundered. "What have you done to my little girl?"

Prepared for such an outburst, Hawk didn't let the anger touch him. "Tom, I—" He never had a chance to finish the sentence.

"Daddy, I didn't want to," Carol sobbed in shrill hysteria. "He made me, Daddy. He held me down."

Stunned by this false accusation, Hawk jerked his head around to stare at her. Tears were washing down her face, stained red with shame. The white straps of her bra were falling loosely off her shoulders as she huddled behind the blouse she held in front of her. The watery green of her eyes was focused on her father, pleading with him. Hawk felt the sickening shock of betrayal.

"I treated you like a son, you goddamned son-of-a-bitchin' bastard!" Rawlins snarled in hate. "And you repay me by raping my baby!"

Hawk turned back to forcefully deny the charge, but he never had a chance to speak. What felt like a steel rod was rammed into his stomach, driving the air from his lungs and doubling him in half. A fist exploded against his jaw, the force of it straightening him and sending him flying backward to the ground. Pain roared through his head.

A woman's scream echoed through his brain as he shook his head, trying to clear its fuzziness. As he pushed his swaying body to his knees, his blurred vision saw Carol running to Chad. He never made it to his feet as another blow sent him sprawling into the dirt.

Again, Hawk wedged an arm between his body and

the ground to lever himself upright. Before he could carry out the attempt, the toe of a boot was driving into his ribs, lifting the middle of his body, and rolling him over. Sheer instinct took over, rolling his body another revolution away from his attacker and letting the momentum bring him woodenly to his knees.

As Rawlins advanced toward him, Hawk dove for him. A fist clipped his temple, but Hawk got his arms around the man's waist and hung on to drive Rawlins backward. Hawk's superior size and weight should have forced Rawlins to the ground and give Hawk the few seconds he needed to clear his reeling senses so he could defend himself.

But Rawlins didn't go down. Something supported him. In the next second, a different pair of hands was dragging Hawk away from his attacker. His first thought was that someone was trying to stop the fight until he realized no one was holding Rawlins. With his arms pinned in a vise-like grip, he couldn't ward off the swinging fist that slammed into his stomach.

Struggling wildly, Hawk nearly freed an arm, but his captor was joined by a second man. Some distant part of his brain realized the two men holding him for the beating were the cowhands, Bill Short and Luther Wilcox, men he'd ridden with and worked beside. But Rawlins' fists were hammering him to pieces, blotting out the sun and his memory.

Blinded, stunned, and helpless, he felt the strength going out of his legs. He sagged, kept upright only by the two men who held him. A bone popped, enveloping him in a red mist of pure agony. More blows fell, but Hawk had begun to sink into a black oblivion that offered numbness. His weight grew heavier and heavier, pulling at the hands that held him. His head was on a swivel that allowed it to roll with the slamming fists.

The blackness swallowed him and he slumped over like a dead weight.

"He's finished, boss." Luther Wilcox was on Hawk's right. He let go of his arm.

"Pick him up." Rawlins' voice was guttural and winded, vibrating with savagery.

For a pulsebeat, there wasn't a sound. Then Luther hissed an appeal for some rational thinking. "You can't kill him, boss. My God, he's—" His gaze darted to Chad. He checked the words he'd been about to say, not wanting to be the one who called attention to Hawk's blood relationship to Chad.

Moreover, Luther wasn't convinced that Tom Rawlins was within his rights to do more than just work Hawk over. He'd seen Rawlins' daughter out riding with Hawk a couple of times this summer. If Hawk took advantage of the girl, it might have been because he'd been given some encouragement. And he wasn't so sure Hawk was the only one. Besides, there was J. B.'s reaction to consider if Hawk was killed.

The silence lengthened without Luther's appeal for reason being dismissed. Vengeance still burned in the set of Rawlins' features, but the murderous light was fading from his eyes. Luther sent a brief, sidelong glance at the cowboy gripping the waist of the half-crumpled body.

"Let him go, Bill," Luther ordered with a nodding gesture of his head, his voice low and quiet, careful not to let his tone usurp Rawlins' authority.

There was a dull thud as the arm was dropped and the rest of the body hit the ground. It seemed to snap Rawlins out of his poised stance, his hands stiffly flexing out of their fists. He turned to shoot a glance at his daughter. At some point, with Chad's help, she had succeeded in putting on her blouse. His arms were around her, offering both protection and comfort. She had buried her face in the front of his shirt. The handsome face of Chad Faulkner smiled grimly back at Rawlins. Then his hands were moving to her arms to hold her away from him.

Her fingers clutched at the front of his shirt. "Hold me, Chad," she whimpered.

"Wait here," Chad ordered gently. "I'm just going to get your horse."

As Chad moved away from her, Rawlins walked over. Her head was bowed, her face hidden from his sight by a tangled curtain of gold hair. When he laid a hand on her shoulder, she trembled and turned her head away from him. Rawlins murmured something which produced an affirmative nod. It was Rawlins' shoulders that were hunched as he removed his hand, a sensation of helplessness seeming to defeat him.

Halfway to Carol's ground-hitched horse, Chad stopped beside the limp body. He looked down; then he stepped over the still form to gather the reins of Carol's horse and lead it over to the girl.

The bay horse Hawk had been riding lifted its head and whickered a protest at the sight of the five riders trotting away from the wellhead. No one looked back. Its reins were dragging the ground and the horse was too well trained to ignore their significance. The horse turned its head to the man on the ground, its ears pricking, but the man didn't move. Lowering its head, the horse began to graze again, the bit jangling between its teeth as it tore off chunks of nourishing yellow grass.

When Hawk finally regained consciousness, the high desert air was cool and the sky was a black backdrop to a parade of stars. Everything was fuzzy. At first he couldn't figure out where he was or why he was lying on the ground. Then he tried to get up. A pain, so sharp and so intense, stabbed through him and he collapsed with an unearthly cry. When he could think clearly again, Hawk realized that the ribs on his right side were either cracked or broken.

Favoring them, he tried again to rise. This time he succeeded in staggering to his feet, where he swayed drunkenly. The top of his skull hammered, making it difficult to string two thoughts together. His face felt all pulpy and broken. There was something wrong with his nose. His eyelids were all puffed up, the openings merely narrow slits. Every part of him ached, some worse than others, his muscles stiff, cramped, and sore. His mouth felt dry and cracked, throbbing with the pain of a thousand needles. Hawk attempted to moisten his lips and tasted grains of dirt mixed with salty blood and sweat.

He started to lift a hand to his mouth when he heard the rattle of a bridle bit. Turning, Hawk tried to locate the source of the sound. Outlined against a night sky, he recognized the shape of a horse a few feet from where he was standing. He tried to walk to it, but the signals his brain sent to his legs became muddled in the transmission. His steps were uncoordinated, almost drunken.

When he reached for the reins, the horse shied away from the smell of blood he carried. Hawk spoke to the animal, slipping into the Navaho tongue. It snorted nervously, but let him catch the reins and loop them over its neck. Wedging a foot into the stirrup, he used all his strength to haul his body into the saddle. Hawk locked both hands around the saddlehorn in a death grip, leaving the reins slack and giving the horse its head.

The animal needed no urging to turn for its home corral, striking out in a jarring trot. Hawk passed out before they had traveled a hundred yards. Instinct alone kept him in the saddle, his legs clamped to the horse's sides and his hands strangling the saddlehorn.

Hawk surfaced from the pain-induced stupor long enough to realize the horse had stopped. He nudged it with the heel of his boot. The horse shifted, but refused to go forward. Hawk roused himself sufficiently to look around. It was several seconds before his brain could identify the corral. He swayed in the saddle, nearly falling off. Somewhere, not far away, he heard the sound of someone leading a horse, but his haze of pain was too dense to let it mean anything. He concentrated his efforts on dismounting with the minimum amount of pain.

"Hawk!" Someone called his name. It was a voice he should know. Only when the person spoke again did he recognize the concerned and rasping voice as his father's. "I heard there was trouble. I was just going to ride out to look for you."

One foot touched the ground, but he lost his balance when his boot slipped out of the stirrup. Clutching the saddlehorn with one hand, Hawk swung around in a weaving half-circle. The horse's flank was a wall for his back to lean against and stopped him from making a complete circle. With difficulty, he focused his eyes on the stricken face of his father as the man paused in mid-stride.

"Oh, my God, Hawk!" The hoarse words were ripped from his father's throat. Then he raised his voice to shout: "Frank! Pedro! Come over here and give me a hand!"

"No!" Hawk's refusal rang out clear and strong when J. B. took a step toward him.

But a great weariness was threatening to overwhelm him. Pain was a hot fire that burned and pulsed over his face and throughout his body. From the murky depths of his memory, Hawk dredged up the knowledge that this corral shared a long horse trough with the adjoining one. Releasing the saddlehorn, he ordered his weaving, staggering legs to carry him to it.

When he reached it, his hands gripped the metal sides to steady himself. Then he immersed his head into the water all the way to his shoulders. As he surfaced, the shock of the cool water washed his senses clear. His awareness returned. He could think coherently again. Something warm trickled from his nose, and it wasn't the water that was streaming from the rest of his head. Hawk realized that not only were his ribs broken, but also his nose. Out of the slitted corner of an eye, he saw his father approaching and remembered the first words his father had said.

"You were coming to look for me?" It was difficult to make his split and swollen lips shape the words. Hawk knew his speech was slurred. "Did somebody finally do something that wasn't part of your plans? Did you forget to tell Rawlins that you were going to buy me some respectability in a few years?"

Still leaning on the metal sides of the water trough for support, Hawk turned his head to look at his father. Other cowboys had gathered behind J. B. besides the two he had summoned by name. Hawk was beyond caring who heard what he said, gripped by a reckless indifference.

"I never guessed you were so . . . badly beaten up." It was a lame comment, a weak attempt to avoid the rawly worded questions.

"What did you expect?" Hawk spat in disgust. The violence behind his words caused rib bone to scrape against rib bone, resulting in a searing pain stabbing into his side and drawing an involuntary gasp from Hawk.

"We'd better get you to a doctor." His father started toward him again.

"No!" Hawk leaned heavily on the trough until the sickening weakness passed. Hanging his head, he closed his eyes. There was nothing a doctor could do for a broken nose or ribs. No internal damage had been done—no lung had been pierced.

"I'll talk to Tom and get this straightened out," J. B. said.

Gathering himself together, Hawk straightened into an unsteady but upright position and faced his father. "A long time ago, J. B., you counseled me that I would have to make my own way. I don't need you to make plans for me. I'll handle Rawlins alone—the same way I have handled everything else." He rejected the offer of help with careless disdain.

His father hesitated, turning pale. He seemed to make an effort to ignore Hawk's statement. "Under the circumstances, it might be best if you returned to college early."

Hawk's mouth curved into what was supposed to be a smile. "Run away? That's what a Navaho would do, isn't it?" he challenged in a derisive drawl. "When things get too hot and he's outnumbered, he takes flight. I bet you'd like that—you . . . and Tom . . . and Carol. It would make it easy for you, wouldn't it? You'd all like it even better if I never came back. But I'm not going." Hawk let the words hang in the air for a minute, heavy and electric. "What's more, I'm doing things *my* way from now on. And if you don't like it, you can go to hell, J. B."

Hawk walked away with all his muscles protesting. His departure stirred a murmur of voices in the audience of ranch hands. J. B. watched him leave in a numbed silence.

Lights burned in the windows of the Rawlins' house, a house that—for the lack of a better word—had been his home for the last eleven years. Hawk fought off the tiredness that was draining him of feeling and hauled himself up the steps to the back porch with the hand rail. His bruised and battered body wanted rest, but the night wasn't over yet.

As he entered the back porch, he caught sight of a face in the mirror above the wash-sink. It wasn't recognizable as his own. Cut, bruised, and swollen, it belonged to a monster with black hair.

Turning away from the mirror, Hawk shut the door. The movement left him facing the kitchen, where Tom Rawlins sat at the table, glaring at him. His hands were encircling a cup on the table in front of him. Hawk moved into the opening.

"I've come to get my things," he stated in his pain-impaired voice.

"Get them and get out!" Rawlins snarled.

There was a time when Hawk would have held his silence, but all that had changed. "You know me, Tom. And you know I didn't violate your daughter. You may have treated me like a son, but I was the last person you wanted as a son-in-law. What was it that turned your stomach, Tom? The idea of your daughter marrying a half-breed? Or J. B.'s bastard?" he challenged with curling contempt.

A dull red spread across Rawlins' face. He made no comment but averted his murderous stare. Hawk knew he had scored a direct hit. Circling the table, he crossed the room to the hallway leading to his bedroom. Vera Rawlins appeared, stopping abruptly at the sight of Hawk, shock registering first in her expression, then an avenging anger.

Before she could give voice to it, Hawk spoke again, addressing his comment to both of them. "By the way, I wasn't the first man to take your daughter, although I admit it probably wouldn't have stopped me if she had been a virgin."

He shouldered his way past the woman and down the darkened hallway to his small room. Cradling his right arm against his broken ribs, he leaned against the door to summon more strength, then moved to the bed and shook out the woolen blanket folded at the foot. It was the same blanket that had carried his personal belongings when he had first arrived here. Hawk used it again, emptying the dresser drawers and closets of his clothes and dumping them into the center of the blanket. When this was done, he paused to look around the room for any more of his possessions.

A faint sound came from the hallway outside his door, a sound that implied stealth. Hawk remained motionless, listening intently, his back to the door. He heard the furtive turning of the doorknob and his muscles coiled into alertness when it was pushed silently open. There was only one person who would want to see him without anyone else in the house knowing it—and that person was Carol.

"Hawk, I'm sorry." It was her voice that whispered the apology to him. "I don't know why I said what I did. I was so . . . scared. You've got to believe me. Mom and Dad would kill me if they knew I was in here with you."

He pivoted slowly to face her. Her eyes widened as she recoiled at the sight of him, a hand reaching up to cover her mouth while her other arm clutched her stomach. She turned white and looked away, as if afraid she was going to be sick.

"I make a pretty revolting picture, don't I?"

"Please . . . forgive me?" she murmured, unable to look at him again.

"When I forgive you, am I also supposed to forget this ever happened?" He turned away and began tying together the ends of his blanket. "Why don't you run to Chad? He'll forgive you." With his left hand, he picked up the knotted blanket and had to breathe in sharply to control the pain.

"Hawk, please?" Her head was bowed when he turned. She murmured to herself, "None of this would have happend if you were Chad."

The comment twisted his mouth, inflicting pain from his cut lip. He reached out and let a strand of her long hair slide through the fingers of his right hand. "All that glitters . . . isn't sunshine," he mused, then walked out of the room.

It was a long walk across the ranch yard to the bunkhouse. Weariness dragged at his feet. All talking ended the minute he pushed the door open. Hawk was too tired and too hurt to care about the stares directed at him. One eye was nearly swollen shut, but out of the narrow slit of the other, he spied an unmade bunk, the mattress rolled into a cylinder at the head of the bed. With awkward haste, he walked to it and dropped his bundle on the floor beside it.

It took him only a second to spread out the mattress and gingerly lower his frame onto its length. Not bothering to take off his boots or find a blanket to cover himself, Hawk closed his eyes. Instantly, he was asleep. It was a deep, drugged sleep that allowed his body to go to work and begin its mending process, free of pain and unhampered by the conscious mind.

For thirty-six hours straight, he slept—unconscious. When he came to, the blood had been washed from him, his ribs were bound, and there was a steaming cup of broth near him. His gaze rested on the calloused hand holding it and trailed up the arm to the face of Luther Wilcox.

"What is it? Poison?" Hawk's voice was hoarse, his muscles screaming with stiffness when he tried to move. "I suppose you intend to finish the job you started."

"Don't need to." Luther waited until Hawk had

taken the cup, then explained his statement as he walked to a table to resume his game of solitaire. "Carol went to Phoenix to stay for a while with J. B. and Mrs. Faulkner."

The cowboy sat in a chair with his back to Hawk. He didn't speak again, ignoring Hawk.

Three days later, Hawk saddled a horse, packed some supplies, and rode to the canyon. He stayed a month, visiting his mother's relatives. But there was no life for him there, although he found contentment and strength.

After a month, Hawk returned to the ranch. No one asked where he had been or questioned his right to move back into the bunkhouse. In the morning, he rode out with the men to work the cattle. Rawlins never tried to give him an order and never acknowledged the work Hawk did, but his eyes burned with loathing each time they came in contact.

Two months after his beating, Hawk heard the news that Chad and Carol were married. It meant nothing to him. Six months later she gave birth to a baby boy, who was promptly named after his grandfather—John Buchanan Faulkner.

PART
III

". . . With the zigzag lightning flung over your head,
   come to us, soaring!
With the rainbow hanging high over your head,
   come to us, soaring!
With the zigzag lightning flung out high on the ends of
   your wings, come to us, soaring!
With the rainbow hanging high on the ends of
   your wings, come to us, soaring!

. . . He stirs, he stirs, he stirs, he stirs.
Among the lands of evening, he stirs, he stirs;
The pollen of evening, he stirs, he stirs;
Now in old age wandering, he stirs, he stirs;
Now on the trail of beauty, he stirs, he stirs.
He stirs, he stirs, he stirs, he stirs.

. . . I have made your sacrifice,
I have prepared a smoke for you."

Chapter VII

The skies over Phoenix were blanketed with a layer of black clouds that blotted out the sun, throwing the city into premature darkness. At frequent but irregular intervals, bolts of yellow lightning streaked out of the clouds, briefly illuminating the rolling and crashing thunderheads. The brilliant flashes of electric fire were accompanied by explosive claps of thunder that vibrated the air and ground.

The rain fell in wind-whipped sheets, slowing the six o'clock traffic to a crawl. The wipers swished frantically back and forth to sweep the blinding deluge off the Volkswagen's windshield. Behind the wheel, Lanna Marshall flexed her fingers to ease their tense grip. She had heard Phoenix natives talk about the sudden and violent storms that could descend on the land without warning, but she hadn't believed them. Everything was so dry and dusty, baked by the unrelenting heat of the sun, that it seemed unlikely large quantities of rain ever fell on it. Now she knew better.

The traffic around her was traveling slowly but smoothly. Not taking her eyes from the congested lanes of the interstate highway, Lanna leaned sideways to reach down and untie the shoelaces of the white leather oxford on her left foot. The shoe slipped easily off her white, nylon-stockinged heel. While her left foot took possession of the accelerator, she removed her right shoe and wiggled her cramped and tired toes.

"Ah, that's better," she sighed aloud at the instant sensation of relief that flowed through her aching feet.

The traffic ahead slowed to a crawl and Lanna braked to match their reduced speed. It was still five miles to her exit, and two more after than to her apartment. At this rate, it would take her another half-hour to get home.

With a grimace of resignation, she lifted a hand to her hair, sleeked away from her face into a smooth French coil. Searching fingers found the hairpins that secured the restrained style and began plucking them out and slipping them into the handbag on the seat beside her. A combing rake of her fingers sent her shoulder-length hair tumbling free. It was a mink-brown color that gleamed with a rich luster.

A smile lifted the corners of her generously curved mouth. Sometimes Lanna felt like a butterfly emerging from its chrysalis when she shed the disciplined trappings of her nursing profession. Not that the white uniform did all that much to conceal her obvious physical assets. On the contrary, its staid, tailored lines emphasized her curved figure and the nipped-in slimness of her waist.

The combination of summer heat and driving rain made the enclosed air of the car oppressively close. Rolling down a window for circulation would just admit the driving rain. Not for the first time, Lanna wished for air conditioning in her car. In Denver, it had seemed a luxury she couldn't afford, but here . in Arizona, she was learning it was virtually a necessity. She unbuttoned the top two buttons of her white uniform and lifted the sticky nylon material away from the valley between her breasts. The only relief she derived from it was in her mind.

Off the road on her right, Lanna glimpsed the flashing red taillights of a stalled vehicle. Seconds later her headlights illuminated the yellow pickup truck parked on the shoulder of the highway. As she slowed the Volkswagen to pass it, the door on the driver's side opened and a tall, stockily built man stepped out.

In that brief moment when the car lights illuminated him, Lanna glimpsed the bowed shoulders beneath a light tan jacket, white peppered hair below the wide brim of a western hat, and the sagging jowls of a tired face. On the side of the truck was a sign that read FALCON CONSTRUCTION and an emblem showing the black silhouette of the head of the predatory bird. Then she was past the pickup and its driver. Her gaze lifted to the rearview mirror, where she could see the elderly man start out walking, his head bowed against the driving rain

Lanna hesitated only an instant before she flipped on her turning signal and eased the Volkswagen out of the traffic lane onto the paved shoulder of the highway. Leaving the motor running, she leaned across the seat and rolled down the window on the passenger's side.

When the old man swung out to the right to skirt her car, Lanna shouted above the clapping thunder, "Want a ride?"

The man paused in apparent surprise, then bent down to peer in the passenger's window. Rainwater streamed from the rolled point of his hat brim. Beneath thick, iron-gray eyebrows, a pair of pale blue eyes studied her. The accumulation of years had grooved lines in the rugged, sun-tanned face, giving it a certain leather toughness, but Lanna wasn't frightened by what she saw.

"Get in," she invited again with a faint smile.

He hesitated for a split-second, then opened the passenger's door. "Thanks." The gravelly quality in his voice seemed to match his rough exterior.

"It's pretty wet out there. You're already soaked to the skin," she observed as he tucked his big frame into the small car and rolled up the window.

"Yeah, I noticed."

Lanna shifted the car into forward gear and eased it back into the slow-moving traffic. She stole a sideways glance at the big man filling her small car. Crowfooting lines splayed out from the corners of his eyes, relating an impression of deep sadness. There was something about the man that reminded Lanna of an aging Teddy bear masquerading as a silver-tipped grizzly. As if sensing her curious inspection, he turned his head to look at her. Lanna swung her gaze back to the rain-swept interstate lane.

"Didn't your parents ever teach you not to pick up strangers on the road? It's a dangerous thing for a young girl to do—or didn't they ever tell you that?"

This prompted a soft laugh from Lanna. She was being reprimanded by the very man to whom she'd given a ride. "Yes, they warned me all about hitchhikers and strange men," she told him with lilting assurance. "But they also told me the story of the Good Samaritan. I guess that appealed to me more. What happened to your truck?"

"The points got wet, I guess." He sounded disgruntled as he answered her question.

Lanna glanced at the green road sign for the approaching exit. "I can't remember if there is a service station at this exit, but I know there is one at the next." It was the off-ramp that she would take. "I can give you a lift that far. They can probably tow your truck in for you."

There was a rustle of wet clothing. Out of the corner

of her eye, Lanna saw him glance at the watch on his left wrist. "A couple of blocks from the second exit is a construction site. I'm supposed to be there in fifteen minutes. Would you mind dropping me off there?" he asked. "I can ask somebody to go back for the truck."

"Is that the new medical complex that's being built?" Lanna sent him a questioning look.

"Yeah." He nodded.

"Sure, I can drop you there," she agreed. "I have to drive right by it on my way home." Her gaze slid curiously over him. His clothes, his advanced years, and the need to be at a construction site after working hours all told Lanna that he must be the night watchman. "You should have an easy time tonight if this rain keeps up."

"What?" The thick brows furrowed together in a frown.

"Weather like this keeps people inside, instead of pilfering material and equipment from construction sites. It makes your job much easier, I should think," she said, explaining her reasoning.

He turned away, an amused smile touching his mouth for the first time as he realized she thought he was a night watchman. "Yeah, that's right. It will," he agreed.

"When is the building supposed to be finished?"

"The first of October if there are no delays."

"That long?" Lanna sighed. "I have my fingers crossed that I can get a job there when it's completed so I won't have so far to drive to work."

"Do you work in a doctor's office now?" His blue eyes took note of her white uniform.

"Yes. A pediatrician, Dr. Fairchild," she answered. "Depending on the traffic—and the weather—it's about a thirty- to forty-minute drive from my apartment."

"Are you his receptionist?"

"I'm a registered nurse," Lanna corrected.

"There's a hospital not far from here. They always seem to have openings for nurses. Can't you get on the staff there?"

"No, thanks." She shook her dark head in firm negation. "I'm not working in any more hospitals."

"Why?" His curiosity was aroused by her absolute assertion.

"A nurse isn't supposed to get involved with the patients. Unfortunately, I don't possess that necessary emotional objectivity to take care of the sick on a day-to-day basis. I let myself become too close to them. So . . ."—she shrugged—". . . I got out of that emotional wringer. Now I work in a doctor's office, where my contact with the patients is very brief and very limited."

"Do you miss it—working in the hospital?"

"Sometimes," Lanna admitted. "I miss the camaraderie of the large staff—doctors, nurses, technicians, aides—all working together. But now I have a lot less heartache. The hours are better and I always have the weekends off."

"Married?"

She felt his gaze reach to examine her left hand, but she wasn't wearing any jewelry, a holdover from her nurse's training when all was forbidden. Ever since, Lanna never wore jewelry while she was in uniform.

"No, I am not married." There was the faintest suggestion of sadness in her smile. "I have just about decided that the state of holy matrimony is not my destiny."

"Now, I find that hard to believe," he chided dryly. "A lot of men would be attracted to a beautiful woman like you."

"In my twenty-five years, I have received innumerable propositions, but not a single proposal," she confided with a self-mocking smile. "There is something about me that attracts the good-time Charlies of this world."

"I think I detect a note of disillusionment"—the man smiled—"which usually means an affair went bad."

She laughed, surprised at how accurately he had read between the lines, and a little surprised at the personal turn the conversation had taken. What kind of risk was she taking by discussing her love life with a total stranger? Lanna took another look at her passenger. She was simply too comfortable in his presence to feel threatened by him.

"You are very astute," she remarked.

"It comes from years of experience," he told her. "What happened? Did he leave you for another woman?"

"You could say that," Lanna admitted, able to smile about it now. "Of course, the other woman was his wife. For two years, I waited for him to get a divorce before it finally sank into my thick skull that he was never going to get one. Why should he when he had the best of both worlds?"

After their easy exchange of conversation, the dead silence that followed her rhetorical question was heavy. Lanna sliced a curious glance at the man staring out the windshield. He looked sad and very grim.

"Did I say something wrong?" she asked with a puzzled frown.

"What?" he asked blankly, as if he hadn't heard her question, then recalled it. "No, of course you didn't. This is the exit just ahead." He pointed and changed the subject. "Years ago this area around here was nothing but cactus and sage. Look at it now."

Lanna sensed it was a deliberate change of subject, but she didn't object. "Are you originally from Phoenix?"

"No. I was raised in northern Arizona, up around the Four Corners. How about you?"

"Colorado. Denver." She turned the car onto the exit ramp, following a stream of traffic taking the same route.

"How long have you been here, Miss ———?"

She hesitated, but after all she had told him about herself already, her name seemed a minor inclusion. "Lanna Marshall. I've been here less than six months."

"Do you like it here?" he asked.

"It's hot," Lanna replied with an expressive arch of an eyebrow.

"So is hell." The man laughed and the sound had the same rasping texture as his voice, but equally pleasant to hear.

"I guess I miss the mountains, the snow—and trees," she admitted, after giving it some thought. "Of course, Flagstaff isn't far away. I can always drive there if I get too homesick." She waited until the traffic cleared the intersection before she turned the car onto the major cross-street.

"Have you made many friends since you came here?"

"A few." Very few, actually, but Lanna didn't want to sound as if she was feeling sorry for herself. She was naturally outgoing and made friends easily. She simply hadn't been in the city long enough to become well acquainted with many people.

The construction site was just ahead on her right. The shell of the medical building was nearly complete. Lanna slowed the Volkswagen as they approached the construction area.

"You can drop me off at that construction shack."

The man nodded toward a long trailer parked on the site.

A light gleamed from a tiny, square window at one end of the trailer. Below the word OFFICE stenciled on the door was the further identification of Falcon Construction Company. Two yellow pickups, like the one the man had been driving, were parked near the trailer, and so was a dark-colored Cadillac. Lanna stopped her car next to the curb.

"Here you are," she announced unnecessarily and sent the elderly man a warm smile. It had been a welcome change to have someone to talk to. The drive hadn't seemed nearly as long.

His hand was on the door latch, but he didn't immediately open it. He returned her smile, a warm light chasing away the sad shadow in his blue eyes for a moment. "Thanks for the ride. But the next time you see a stranger on the highway, let somone else play the Good Samaritan," he advised her.

"I'll try to remember," she promised. "Don't you have a raincoat or something? You are going to get soaked making your rounds tonight."

He laughed huskily. "If I catch cold, I know just the person to call to nurse me back to health." Then he was opening the door and stepping out quickly into the rain. "Take care of yourself," he said as he slammed the door.

With a wave, he turned and trotted, head down, toward the construction trailer. Lanna waited until the trailer door was opened and a rectangular patch of light streamed out. The man disappeared inside as she drove away from the curb.

For the rest of the week, each time Lanna drove past the construction site on the way to or from work, she thought about the night watchman. Old didn't seem a fair word to describe him, although admittedly, the man was in his sixties. Yet he possessed a healthy vigor with a certain ruggedness that was appealing despite his years. It was odd the way the memory of him lingered so vividly—his gruffness, his gentleness, and the unhappiness that haunted his eyes.

Lanna shrugged it aside, convinced she thought so often about the man simply because she knew so few people in Phoenix. It was natural that a friendly stranger would leave a lasting impression.

It might be more truthful to admit that she missed her father, and the gentle gruffness of the stranger had reminded her of him. Her mother had died when Lanna was eleven. She and her father had grown very close after that. She knew they had begun drifting apart when she had moved away to attend college. It had all been so new and exciting, the first feeling of independence. When her father had met a young widow with children and fell in love with her, Lanna had been delighted for him. She still was.

Only now they were no longer the center of one another's existence. Each led an individual life separate from the other. Lanna didn't want to turn back the clock, yet there were times when she missed the easy companionship, the reliable shoulder to lean on, and the sense of being needed by someone. Someday she'd have a home and family of her own, and that empty place in her life would be filled. Of course, after that last disastrous affair, she wasn't anxious to rush into a new romance. In the meantime, she had her career to occupy her time. Lately, she'd been giving some thought to getting into the administrative side of nursing, maybe taking some night courses at one of the local universities. She hadn't decided definitely.

Setting the basket of freshly washed clothes on the hall floor—the laundry was a regular part of her

Saturday morning routine—she reached into the pocket of her white shorts for the apartment key. She unlocked the door and held it open with a sandled toe to pick up the basket of clothes.

The apartment was small and sparsely furnished. At the moment, it was all she could afford. This was the first time she had lived alone. Always before she had shared an apartment with a fellow nurse. She missed the companionship of a roommate, but it was rather nice to have to pick up after no one except herself. Lanna was considering keeping the small apartment and fixing it up to suit herself, give it a feeling of permanence.

It was a thought that reasserted itself as she stacked clean towels in the bathroom linen closet. She made a face at the gaudy blue fish that swam in the room's wallpaper. They would be the first to go.

She was startled by a knock on her apartment door. She hurried to answer it, lifting damp tendrils of hair away from her forehead and smoothing them into place. Caution made her slip the security chain into position before she opened the door a crack.

"Hello!" There was both surprise and wary alarm in her voice as she recognized the night watchman standing in the hallway outside her door.

"I'm glad you have a chain on your door," he observed with a wry smile.

"What are you doing here? I mean . . . I'm glad to see you, but . . . did you leave something in my car?" She couldn't find the right words to ask why he was there.

Her gaze swept over the tall man. This time he was wearing a white shirt and khaki-colored pants. She noticed his boots were polished, the pointed toes gleaming. There was a turquoise-studded silver buckle at his waist. He was holding something behind his back.

Her hazel eyes widened when he brought his arms around to the front to offer her a bouquet of pink roses.

"I wanted to say 'thanks,'" he said.

"They're beautiful," she responded inadequately as the sweet fragrance of the flowers drifted near her. But there was still confusion when she looked at him. "How on earth did you know where I lived?"

"There was only one Lanna Marshall in the phone directory," he explained.

It was so obvious Lanna laughed, still a little speechless. Then she realized: "I don't know your name."

His hesitation lasted only a split-second. Afterward, Lanna thought she had imagined it. "John Buchanan."

"What can I do for you, John Buchanan?" She was still hesitant about unchaining the door despite the lure of the flowers.

"I thought . . . I'd like you to have lunch with me. Do you like Mexican food?" John Buchanan didn't give her a chance to answer. "There's a little restaurant not far from here. It doesn't look like much on the outside, but the food is great." He noticed her continuing hesitation and smiled. "If it would make you feel safer, you can follow me there in your car."

The remark eased her suspicion and she smiled. "Okay. Give me ten minutes to change into something a little more presentable."

"What about the flowers? Do you want to put them in a vase?" He glanced at the bouquet in his hand.

"Sure." Lanna shut the door, removed the chain, and opened it to take the bouquet. She paused. "Do you want to wait inside?"

"There you are, inviting strange men into your apartment." He shook his head in mock exasperation. "Will you never learn, Lanna Marshall?" She laughed and he joined her with a low chuckle. "I'll stay out here in the hall 'til you're ready." He refused her suggestion and Lanna liked him all the more for his quaint sense of propriety.

"I won't be long," she promised and closed the door.

The restaurant was small and not very crowded, even though it was close to noon. John guided her to a corner booth and sat with his back to the entrance. As he had promised, the food was good. Lanna found herself wondering how much the taste was enhanced by the presence of her companion. He was just as easy to talk to as he had been before. And his dry sense of humor often had her laughing.

The waitress cleared away their dirty plates and refilled their coffee cups. Lanna relaxed against the cushioned backrest. "Tell me about yourself, John," she said. "I think you have my whole life history already."

"What do you what to know?" He smiled, but he appeared to withdraw behind the smile.

"I don't know." She lifted her hands in an expressive gesture. "Anything. Everything. Are you married? Any children?"

"Legitimate or illegitimate?" he countered.

"Quit joking and give me a straight answer," Lanna insisted.

"All right. I'm married. I have two sons and one grandson." It was a completely factual answer, unsatisfactory without elaboration. "He's quite a boy." He removed a photograph from his wallet and showed it to her. "It's hard to believe he's nearly twelve."

Lanna commented on the boy's resemblance to John, the same blue eyes, as she returned the picture. "You can certainly tell he's your grandson. No little girls?"

"I had a daughter once." He returned the photograph of his grandson to his wallet, absently thoughtful.

When he looked up, there was a reminiscent gleam in his eyes and a trace of melancholy. "She died when she was a baby. She would have been twenty-three this summer—about your age. She had brown hair, too—dark like yours—the color of a cedar. I guess maybe you remind me a little bit of her." His mouth quirked in a self-mocking smile. "Please don't tell me that I remind you of your father."

"You don't . . . at least not physically. He's shorter, leaner, doesn't have as much hair." She enumerated the obvious differences.

"And he's probably not nearly as old as I am," John added and tipped his head to one side. "Tell me about your parents. Where do they live?"

"My mother died when I was eleven. My father remarried a few years ago and lives in Colorado Springs."

"Now you have the proverbial stepmother," he guessed.

"No." Lanna shook her head. "Ann is a wonderful woman. She always makes me feel welcome whenever I go to visit. She has made Dad very happy."

"But you don't see very much of them. Why?"

"They have a life of their own. Ann has three children, so that means a lot of school activities, sports, and all the things that go along with raising a family. That puts a lot of demands on Dad's time, and he was never very much of a correspondent. I don't want you to get the wrong impression about him," Lanna inserted. "My father loves me now as much as he always did. It's just that he has other responsibilities now."

"I understand." John said it with such conviction that Lanna believed he really did. "A man has an obligation to more than just one member of his family."

"Tell me about your wife," she urged and tried to

visualize the woman who had been fortunate enough to marry this understanding man.

"Katheryn and I share the same house. Beyond that, there isn't much to tell." He shrugged and Lanna wondered if that was the reason for the unhappiness that always lurked at the edge of his expressions. "She has her interests, her ladies' clubs, things she likes to do—and I have mine."

"I see," Lanna murmured, almost sorry she had asked.

"No, I doubt that you do." John's smile was faint and slightly melancholy. "It isn't much of a marriage by most people's standards, but Katheryn and I are both getting out of it what we want. She has been a loyal wife to me, and a good mother. She has my respect. And I don't fault her for the way things turned out."

Lanna was painfully aware that John had not said his wife had his love. She sipped at her coffee. "Your wife sounds like a remarkable woman. I wish I could meet her someday." It was an offhand comment that immediately slanted John's mouth in a lopsided grin.

"I don't think that would be a good idea," he said. "Katheryn would take one look at you and get the wrong idea. In the past, I admit that I've probably given her reason to be suspicious of other women. I've never claimed to be a saint. Some say I'm a sinner. Who knows? They might be right." He appeared to be only distantly concerned about the opinions of others, his tone amused in a self-condemning way.

Lanna let the conversation drift to another topic, sensing that he didn't want to discuss his personal life in any detail. They finished their coffee, lingered a little while longer, and then John followed her back to her apartment. She asked him in, but he refused.

"Thanks for lunch and the flowers," Lanna said. "I enjoyed them both."

"It was my pleasure, and I mean that," he stated. "I'd like to come see you again, Lanna."

"I'd like to see you again, John." And she meant it. In this sea of strangers, Lanna felt she had found a true friend.

"I don't have many people I can talk to, but I can with you. I'll give you a call," he promised.

As he was leaving, the door to the apartment across the hall opened. Lanna smiled at her neighbor, a middle-aged woman who worked nights. Lanna rarely saw her or her husband, except on the weekends.

"Hello, Mrs. Morgan."

"I'm so glad you're back, Lanna," the woman sighed in an agitated way. "You wouldn't have any cinnamon, would you? I thought I had plenty, only it was nutmeg. Now I have this apple pie all ready for the oven and I have to run to the store for cinnamon. I just came from there this morning. Art's brother and wife are coming over for dinner tonight and I promised Don I'd bake him an apple pie. He says mine are the best he's ever tasted. Weekends," she sighed again, pausing in her nonstop monologue. "To think we wait all week for weekends to come! I think the rat race begins on Saturday morning, don't you?"

"I never thought about it." Lanna shook her head, laughing to herself. The woman was a dear, but she could be very wearing on the nerves over a prolonged period. Lanna turned to the open door of her apartment. "I believe I have some cinnamon. Why don't you come in while I check?"

"You will be an absolute lifesaver if you do." The stout brunette glanced down the hallway at the disappearing broad shoulders of John Buchanan, curiosity flickering in her eyes. "I still have so much to do before Don and Maryann come. Lord, I haven't even cleaned the front room yet. Who was that man?" She followed Lanna into the compact kitchen. "A relative?"

"No, a friend." Lanna checked her spice rack and removed the can of cinnamon. "Here you are. You can bring it back tomorrow."

"What a relief. I just couldn't really spare the time to go back to the store. I wanted Art to go, but I couldn't pry him away from the television set. Baseball!" She grimaced at the cause. "He was a friend? He's a little old for you, isn't he?"

"Not that kind of friend, Mrs. Morgan," she explained patiently. "He's just a regular friend."

"What does he do? Where did you meet him? A girl can't be too careful these days."

"He's a night watchman at a construction site not far from here. His truck broke down the other night and I gave him a lift. John is a very nice man, and it's all perfectly innocent."

"You gave him a ride and you didn't even know him?! You could have been mugged or . . . or worse!" The woman was openly shocked.

"That's almost the first thing John said," she laughed. "But nothing happened. I was perfectly safe with John."

"Safe? Why? Because he's so much older than you are? He's a man, isn't he?" Mrs. Morgan argued. "You are a nurse. You should know that a man's potency has nothing to do with his age."

"We are friends, Mrs. Morgan—that's all," Lanna insisted.

"A girl who looks like you and a man old enough to be your grandfather—humph!" The woman sniffed her skepticism. "If he's interested in you, it isn't as a friend."

"You are wrong." But she knew that once the

woman got an idea in her head, it would take a stick of dynamite to dislodge it. Rather than argue, she steered the conversation back to its original subject. "Apple pie was always one of my favorites. How much cinnamon do you use?"

Sylvia Morgan was instantly diverted into relating her recipe to Lanna while she was escorted to the hallway. When she was finally alone, Lanna shook her head sadly. It was a pity her neighbor didn't understand. She remembered John's parting comment that he could talk to her. She knew how he felt. There was a special affinity they shared that had no basis in sexual attraction. It was rare, and Lanna wasn't going to allow Mrs. Morgan's opinion to damage it.

Chapter VIII

The bond of friendship grew stronger with each visit John made to see Lanna. Twice during the week, he would come to see her and they would have dinner together before he had to report to work at the construction site. Sometimes he would take Lanna out to eat at some out of the way, inexpensive restaurant, but more often she cooked a meal for the two of them since he wouldn't permit her to pay for her restaurant dinners.

There was a large population of retired people, like John, in Phoenix who were forced to supplement their limited pensions with jobs, like being a night watchman. She didn't want to become a drain on his financial resources and have their friendship jeopardized because of money. Sometimes John would come over on a Saturday and they would spend the afternoon together. On those occasions, they would go sightseeing or to a movie, or just sit in her apartment, watch television, and talk. The subject of his family was not discussed. Lanna suspected it was because his marriage was less than happy.

During those summer months, Lanna dated— infrequently. Working in a doctor's office didn't give her many opportunities to meet single men. John's friendship meant she wasn't driven by loneliness to seek male companionship and go from one disastrous affair to another.

The last Saturday in August, John suggested that they tour the Heard Museum. Specializing in anthropology and primitive art, its focus was on the American Indian tribes, especially those of the Southwest.

As they left an exhibit to enter the Kachina Gallery, Lanna murmured, "I've never understood why museums are so quiet. Everyone talks in whispers." She was guilty of speaking in the same hushed tones as the other visitors.

"Maybe," John suggested in all seriousness, "they are reluctant to stir awake spirits they don't understand." His response drew Lanna's sharp and questioning glance. He was staring at the exhibits within the gallery, a distant look to his expression. As if sensing her gaze, he said, "This is one of the finest collections of Hopi and Zuni *kachinas* in the world today."

Lanna turned to view the display. There were dolls, chiseled out of wood and adorned with feathers, snail shells, cactus spikes, bits of bones, and turquoise. They were in all shapes and sizes, alike only in their grotesqueness—bulging eyes, rounded heads with long beaks, tufted heads with toothed snouts, fiercely mysterious and nighmarish.

"Are they idols representing the Indian gods?" Lanna whispered.

"They are dolls, not idols," he corrected and smiled, because this version of a doll didn't match the kind Lanna had played with as a child. "I guess you could say the *kachinas* are reproductions of gods. More accurately, they symbolize the forces of nature as supernatural beings. The one with the winged arms and feathered mask is the eagle doll. Over there is the owl *kachina.* The one with the headdress of cloud signs and spotted corn is the Butterfly Maiden." He pointed each of them out in turn.

Each figure was extraordinarily detailed. "They are fascinating," Lanna admitted, "but in a frightening kind of way. What are they used for? They surely aren't toys."

"In a sense, they are. The *kachinas* are given to children. The idea isn't so much for the dolls to be used as playthings, but to acquaint the child with the various *kachinas,*" he explained. "The word *kachina* is a little confusing since it refers to the dolls, which have no power. The dancers in the ceremonials wear costumes corresponding to the dolls and are also called *kachinas,* as are the spirit forces."

"You said these belong to the Zuni and Hopi cultures?"

"These particular ones do, yes." John nodded. "The Pueblos and the Navahos also have *kachinas.* In the case of the Navaho, the costumes and headdresses are not as elaborate, although they are just as fearsome. Their masks are made of painted buckskin, sometimes adorned with eagle feathers, or a circlet of spruce boughs around their neck. The choice of the various masks depends on the ceremony and which *kachinas* must participate."

"Such as?" It all sounded very alien to Lanna. She was simultaneously repelled and attracted by the subject.

"A Navaho boy is between the ages of seven and thirteen when he is initiated into the tribe, a very impressionable age." A muscle flexed in his jaw as it was momentarily clenched in grimness before John continued. "It takes place during the *Yeibichai,* or Night Way. The boys wear only a breechcloth and their heads are covered with a blanket. They are taken to a fire that's been built, and ordered not to look at the 'gods.'"

Lanna pictured the scene in her mind: the darkness of night, the leaping flames of a fire, and a half-dozen young boys with blankets over their heads, apprehensive, not knowing what to expect, their copper bodies gleaming in the firelight.

"Two assistants of the *shaman,* or medicine man, first wash their hair in yucca suds, then enter the ceremonial hogan to undress and put on their *kirtles,* which resemble kilts, and various ornaments. All exposed skin—arms, legs, chest—is rubbed with white clay. One wears a black mask to represent Grandfather-of-the-Monsters, and the second has on a white mask for Female Divinity. Once they are in costume and their identities are concealed from the children, they go to the fire.

"In turn, each boy is led out to have his shoulders marked with sacred cornmeal by Female Divinity. The black-masked figure has a stick of reeds bound together as a whip. Uttering falsetto cries, he strikes the boy on the shoulders, then on other parts of his body. The crowd of adults can ask the *kachina* to administer light or hard strokes, and he grants the opposite of their request, always making that peculiar cry at unexpected intervals to surprise and scare the boy."

Lanna shuddered, feeling the terror that would build up in a young mind unable to see his attacker, only hear his eerie cries and feel the sting of his whip.

"When this is done, the *kachinas* remove their masks and reveal their identity to the boy. Often they are his cousin or uncle—someone he knows personally. The boy is given pollen from the bag of the medicine man and directed to sprinkle it on the masks, then on the men who wore them. The man who portrayed Grandfather-of-the-Monsters places the black mask over the boy's head and makes the high-pitched cry that had frightened the boy so often. Only after that is the boy allowed to look and is ordered to remember the Holy People."

John paused, seeming to come back from some faraway place when his gaze focused on Lanna. "Psychologically, it's an interesting ritual. By revealing their identity, the *kachinas* show the boy that they aren't really 'gods' at all, just human beings. The masked figure isn't something he has to fear. Letting the boy wear the mask attempts to show, in a symbolic way, that the forces of God or the supernatural reside in man—both good and evil."

His explanation made Lanna understand the ceremony that had seemed so inhuman at first. Lanna was impressed with his knowledge of the subject.

"Have you attended one of these initiation ceremonies?" she asked.

"No." He shook his head, a blandness stealing over his expression. "It's forbidden for whites to attend that particular part of *Yeibichai*."

"How did you find out so much about it, then?" Lanna asked curiously.

"Don't forget, I was raised around the reservations. My neighbors were Navahos, Pueblos, even a few White Mountain Apaches."

"I don't understand how you can tell one Indian from another." The instant the words were out, Lanna saw John stiffen at the prejudice they carried. "I didn't mean it like that," she hurriedly added in embarrassment. "You have to understand that my knowledge of Indians is limited to Hollywood Westerns and the like."

"Members of one tribe can easily be distinguished from those of another, through characteristic features and builds, such as the difference between a German and an Italian. On one hand, you have the arrogant, lean Navaho, and on the other, you have the chunky, broad-faced Pueblo," John stated. "Of course, inter-marriages muddy up the differences sometimes—even between descendants of German and Italian marriages."

"Arrogant. Somehow I would never had attributed that adjective to the Navaho," she mused as they began to wander to another exhibit. "I've always heard they were shepherds. When I think of a Navaho, my first thoughts are of sheep and blankets. I guess I always imagined they were a gentle people. But arrogant?"

"They were—and are—shepherds," John agreed. "But their warriors raided far and wide. The Navaho was the master of the land west to the Colorado. When the Spaniards claimed this territory, the Navahos used to boast that they let the Spanish live here to be 'their' shepherds—which, in a sense, was true, because it was from the flocks of the Spanish that the Navaho stole their sheep. Not even the Apache, probably the most feared of the Southwestern tribes by the whites, ever challenged the Navaho's supremacy." He paused to glance at her. "Have you ever heard of The Long Walk?"

"No," Lanna admitted.

"When the Americans began to settle this area, it was decided that all Indians would be confined to a reservation. The cavalry managed to force the Apache to surrender, but they couldn't militarily conquer the Navaho. So they went out and killed all their sheep, burned their cornfields, and virtually starved them into submission when winter came. They were herded together to make 'the long walk' to Bosque Redondo, southeast of Santa Fe, the Navaho version of the Cherokee's Trail of Tears. Four years later, they were given the wild, barren portion of their former home range—the Four Corners—to live on. Unlike many other tribes that have disappeared into extinction, the Navaho has multiplied—its population increasing."

"You admire the Navaho, don't you?" she realized.

"They are a unique people."

"The plight of the Indian," Lanna murmured.

John followed her train of thought. "We are the only people in the world who attempted to exterminate the natives who inhabited the land when we came. I guess I feel the same confusion every other American does. I keep asking myself: Why did it happen? Was it fear because we couldn't understand their way of life, and because we didn't understand it, we tried to destroy it? Where was our tolerance? Yet, the two systems were incompatible. They couldn't remain unchanged and exist side by side. The Indian had no conception of land ownership, and the white lived by boundaries. Raiding and stealing was admirable behavior to the Indian and looked down on by the white. Conflict was inevitable. The world views were so dissimilar," he concluded. "After that, the laws of nature took over, laws that dictate the strong must survive."

"Yet I think we've learned that Indians had a greater respect for the land. Look at our environment and our struggle to restore it," she offered.

"Yes, and there is a movement to return to the land, go back to the primitive way of life, but I can't agree with that. Mankind doesn't progress by going backward," John insisted. "Even the Navaho believes the Road of Life is one-way. You can't advance horizontally—only vertically."

Their wandering route had brought them full circle to the exit of the museum. John pushed the door open for her and they walked silently out of the building. As they started across the parking lot to the stall where they'd parked the company truck, a groping hand caught at Lanna's arm.

She turned and found herself staring into the red-rimmed eyes that focused on her through an alcohol haze. A red feather was tucked into iron-gray, luster-less hair, shaggy and unkempt. Drawn around his hunched and weaving shoulders was a tattered and dirty pink blanket.

"Cedar beads." In a slurring voice, he held out a necklace, offering it to John. "You buy for lady? One dollar."

Lanna recoiled from the foul and liquor-laden breath that blew from his mouth. The Indian stank of sweat, booze, and vomit. His attempt to stand straight and tall only added to the ludicrous spectacle he made. Her gaze slid sideways, catching the look of pity in John's face.

"No, thank you," he refused.

"Cheap. Fifty cents," the Indian insisted, thrusting the necklace closer for their inspection. "Genuine Indian necklace."

"No," John repeated.

The Indian swayed and made a concentrated effort to focus on John. "I know you?" he questioned.

"I know you, Bobby Crow Dog." The admission was made with a sad smile.

There was an almost visible light of recognition. "Laughing Eyes," the Indian declared, "husband to White Sage." Then he lapsed into a language that was an incomprehensible collection of guttural sounds.

John responded in the same unintelligible tongue. The exchange of conversation lasted a couple of minutes before John held up his hand to silence the Indian. "You are using hard words. It has been too long since I have heard them."

"You should go home," the Indian said.

"You should go home," John countered and reached out to clasp the Indian's hand in both of his.

"Where is home?" There were tears in the Indian's bloodshot eyes, a lost look that was poignant.

"Take care of yourself," John advised as he withdrew his hands. Lanna caught a glimpse of folded green paper left in the Indian's palm and realized John had given him money. In the next second, his hand was gripping her elbow and guiding her away from the Indian. "It always happens," he murmured in a weary voice. "Every time someone starts talking about the noble savage, an Indian like Bobby shows up—drunk, dirty, and selling cheap trinkets."

"I know what you mean," Lanna sighed. "It destroys the image, doesn't it? It must be worse if you know them personally."

"Yes. Bobby Crow Dog is a special case, but he epitomizes many of the problems the Navaho face—problems all Indians face. Thirty years ago, Bobby Crow Dog was in Hollywood making movies. The film people claimed he had the face of the ideal Indian. That was the era when the Indians were always attacking wagon trains. Bobby was never out of work, always had money in his pockets, and a lot of white friends. Unfortunately, he made the mistake of growing old. One day, there wasn't anyone who wanted him in a picture. Bobby had abandoned the Navaho way to embrace the white man's version of success."

"When that success was gone, he had nothing to fall back on?" Lanna guessed.

"Exactly. It's a common problem. Once traditional beliefs and restrictions are given up, they have to be replaced by something else. If all an Indian does is take on the white man's freedoms without assuming any of our values or morals, there is nothing to support him, nothing to give him direction." A furrow ran deeply across his suntanned forehead. "He has to achieve a balance between the Indian way and the white man's.

Somehow, he has to." The last ended on a fervid note that drew Lanna's wondering glance. But she could read nothing in his expression except a hint of strain.

The sun burned brightly, baking the pavement and making it hot beneath their feet. The yellow cab of the truck rose above the other cars in the lot. The intensity of John's feeling on this subject pulled Lanna's thoughts back to the Indian, a contemporary of John's. Laughing Eyes, he had called him, yet Lanna saw so much unhappiness in his eyes.

As they neared the pickup, she lifted her gaze to John again. "White Sage. Is that what the Indians called your wife?"

Beads of perspiration had gathered on his forehead and upper lip. He seemed quite pale despite his dark tan. Her look began to narrow in professional scrutiny, concern surfacing as alarm bells rang in her mind.

"Yes." He bit out an affirmative answer to her question. Its abruptness seemed to be a studied attempt to hide a wavering strength, but Lanna saw his hand trembling as it reached to open the passenger's door for her.

"John, are you all right?" she demanded.

He more or less pushed her into the passenger's seat. "I'll be fine," he insisted, then closed the door.

She watched anxiously as he walked around the front of the truck to the driver's side. He was sweating profusely by then. Reaching into his pocket, he took out a small, square box. Lanna saw him slip a pill into his mouth before opening the door and sliding behind the wheel.

"Your heart?" she guessed.

"It'll be all right." John leaned back, resting his head on the seat's neck rest and closing his eyes.

Instinctively, she reached for his wrist and located his

pulse. "Sit quietly for a little bit," Lanna instructed and watched the second hand of her watch.

"I loved her. I loved her so." His voice cried with an inner anguish.

"Of course you did," she agreed in a soothing tone. One part of her registered surprise at his statement. She had been under the impression that he didn't love his wife. Obviously he had once, since the statement had been in the past tense. Whatever memories he was recalling were upsetting him, and Lanna had no intention of pursuing the topic.

"Have you ever been in love, Lanna?" Haunted blue eyes regarded her through tired, gray-brown lashes.

"Don't talk, John." The pill had already begun to work its chemical magic.

"I've never known such a boundless joy," he murmured. "It was like a light being turned on that chased away every lonely shadow. But when you lose it, the suffering goes on forever." There was a long silence. Lanna was conscious of the strength flowing back through him. "I've always been a selfish man, Lanna."

"I find that hard to believe." Her concern had lessened sufficiently to allow her to mock him affectionately.

"It's true." He smiled at her, and his color returned. "I have always done what was easy, taken the smooth road. I always expected someone else to solve my problems, then wondered why I didn't have any control over the results."

"If you have finished running yourself down, why don't you move over and I'll drive?" Lanna refused to listen to his self-deprecating statements.

"You haven't heard anything I've said, have you?" John accused.

"Not a word." She stepped out of the truck and

walked around to his side. "Move over. I'm driving."
When he hesitated, that stubborn male glint entering
his eyes, Lanna warned, "I can be just as stubborn as
you are, John Buchanan."

"All right," he conceded reluctantly. "You can
drive . . . this time. But I'm okay now. Those pills
always do the trick."

But it left Lanna feeling uneasy. The aura of robust
health was only an illusion. John was vulnerable. When
they arrived at her apartment building, she let the
motor run.

"Why don't you let me drive you home? I can catch a
cab back here," she offered.

"I'm not an invalid. As a nurse, you ought to know
that, Lanna."

Releasing a long sigh, she admitted, "You're right."

"Do you know you might be the only person who
cares—who really cares that I have a problem with my
heart?" He gave her a considering look, a warmth
softening the age-carved lines of his face. "And you
care for no other reason than the fact that we are
friends. I don't think you realize how remarkable that
is."

"Regardless of what you think, I'm sure your family
cares—your wife and your sons," Lanna insisted.

"Are you?" He lifted an eyebrow. "I wish I was."
Before Lanna could comment on that defeated remark,
John added, "I'll see you Tuesday, unless you already
have something planned."

"No. Tuesday is fine," she agreed. Then she climbed
out of the pickup so John could slide into the driver's
seat.

On Tuesday, Lanna fixed dinner for them at her
apartment. John's mood was light, joking and laughing

with her over dinner, as if to make up for his somber and poignant confidences of the previous Saturday.

As Lanna rose to clear the table, he offered, "Do you want some help with the dishes?"

"No, I can manage." She stacked the plates on top of each other and gathered up the silverware. "You just sit there and finish reading your newspaper." She glanced at his empty coffee cup. "Would you like some more coffee? Or how about some sassafras tea?"

He turned down a corner of the newspaper to look at her. "Sassafras?" he repeated with a skeptically raised eyebrow.

"Yes, sassafras. It's marvelous stuff," she insisted, smiling at his reaction. "It builds up the body."

"And you're a professional nurse," he said, mocking her gently.

"We all have our little home remedies," she laughed.

"I'll pass on the sassafras." John smiled and opened his paper again.

She carried the dishes to the small kitchen, which was separated from the living room by a breakfast-counter bar. Then she went back to the table to put the leftovers away. As she passed John's chair, a column headline caught her eyes. Bending to read the story over his shoulder, she tucked a strand of darkly brown hair behind her ear.

"See something interesting?" John questioned with a sideways glance at her.

"This article on Faulkner and the controversy with the hospital about a conflict of interests. I heard Dr. Fairchild talking about it today on the telephone," she explained while she skimmed the first paragraph of the article. "Faulkner's on the hospital board and his construction company just happened to submit the low bid for the construction of a new wing." A name leaped out of the newspaper print. "John! J. B. Faulkner owns Falcon Construction, the company you work for."

"Yes, he does." He nodded. "Personally, I don't see what all the fuss is about. Why wasn't this possibility of a conflict of interests raised when the invitations to bid were sent out to the contractors? I think it's a case of a sore loser. The submissions were made by sealed bids, which were opened in the presence of all the hospital board members."

"You have a point," Lanna conceded. "But you also have to admit that it looks suspicious."

"Only to suspicious minds." His reply was sharp and quick.

She shrugged her shoulders, understanding the loyalty he felt toward his employer. "From all I've heard and read, Faulkner has fingers in just about every pie in town. He can afford to let somebody else have a slice now and then." She held to her point of view without sounding argumentative.

John turned in his chair to send her a curious, twinkling look. "Have you got something against being rich?"

"No. I like to see the little guy get a break now and then, though." She smiled. "This J. B. Faulkner sounds like a pretty ruthless character."

"Oh?" He continued to study her with that same look, amused and indulgent. "How did you manage to learn so much about the man when you haven't even been here a year?"

"He's practically a legend in Phoenix." There was a wryness to her smile. "I don't care how large a city is; the minute you come into any town you hear all about the richest men. There are plenty of stories about Faulkner and how he bought acres of land around here for next to nothing, then sold it for a hundred or two hundred times what he paid for it. He cheated the original landowners out of a lot of money."

John tipped his head back and laughed heartily. "He never cheated a soul. He paid the asking price. It just so happened that he turned around and sold it later for a handsome profit. The man had the foresight to see that this city was going to grow. He gambled that he was right, and the gamble paid off. I don't call that a crime."

"He didn't have to cheat to win, did he? I guess I never looked at it that way," she realized. "I think some people are born lucky. J. B. Faulkner must be one of them."

"I don't know about that," John disagreed. "He might be lucky in some ways. I . . . I've heard he's a lonely man. Money can buy power, influence, and favors, but it can't buy friends. It can't even assure him of the love and respect of his family."

"I know you're right. But when I'm driving down the highway sweltering in my little car and some air-conditioned Cadillac zips past me, I have a hard time feeling sorry for the people inside," she laughed. "I'm too busy feeling sorry for me. What it amounts to is old-fashioned jealousy."

"Now that is the most honest statement I've ever heard anybody make!" John folded the paper shut in a decisive action. "You have just won yourself a dish wiper." As he followed Lanna into the kitchen, he noticed the book of wallpaper samples lying on the counter. "What's this? Planning a little decorating?"

"Yes. I want some new vinyl paper for the bathroom, so I decided to give myself a birthday present." She set the salad bowl down and flipped the book open to the sample she had marked. "What do you think of this one?"

"It looks nice." But he barely glanced at it. "When is your birthday? You never mentioned it to me."

"A week from Friday, but I'm pretending to forget about it. I'll be twenty-six, and I think it's time I stopped counting."

"When you reach my age, that's the time to stop counting," John insisted dryly.

"Yes, well, I've just about decided that I'm not going to have a husband to look after me when I'm your age, so I'd better start putting money away to take care of myself."

"That's not a bad idea," he teased. "An old maid should have some money in her sock."

"Thanks a lot!" She flashed him a look of mock anger, brandishing a tablespoon.

"What are you going to do to celebrate your birthday?"

"I'm open to suggestions. Will you come over for dinner?" Lanna invited.

"I have a better idea. I'll take you out for a steak dinner."

"You have yourself a date," she said, accepting with a decisive nod.

Chapter IX

"White linen, candlelight, champagne. I didn't expect all this, John." The flickering flame brought a burnished glow to light Lanna's mane of brown hair and glittered on the gold combs that sleeked it away from the sides of her face. She reached for the glass the waiter had just filled with the sparkling wine and lifted it in a salute to her table companion. "Thank you."

"This is a special evening," he reminded her in his warm, gravelly voice. "We have a birthday to celebrate."

Lanna sipped at her champagne, laughing softly at the bubbles that tickled her nose. "It would be awful if I sneezed, wouldn't it?"

"In very bad taste." He clicked his tongue in reproval.

"I'm sure the maître d' would frown in his haughty way," Lanna murmured, eyeing the short man showing a couple to their table.

"He wouldn't dare. I'd have him fired for spoiling your evening," John threatened.

Returning the wineglass to the table, Lanna fingered its fragile stem. The pale, effervescent liquid in the glass was only a shade lighter than the amber dress she

139

wore, the whipped cream material softly outlining her figure.

"I feel like this champagne," she remarked, "sparkling with a heady glow. This is a better birthday celebration than having a crowd of people. How do you know where all these wonderful, little out-of-the-way restaurants are? This place has everything—atmosphere, a sense of quiet elegance, and privacy."

"Why do you think I chose it? This is where I bring all my girl friends," John chuckled and leaned forward in an air of confiding. "I am the envy of every man in this room." His eyes danced with a wicked mischief. "Everyone is wondering whether you are my granddaughter or my mistress. Can't you just hear those women asking what a dirty old man is doing with such a young and attractive woman?"

"I'll bet they are wishing they were in the company of such a distinguished-looking man," Lanna retorted. The tarnished silver of his hair glistened in the candlelight, vitally thick and wavy. In a dark suit and tie, he looked at ease in the formal attire, maturely masculine and relaxed. "You look very handsome in that suit. Do you know this is the first time I've seen you wear something other than your everyday work clothes?"

"I haven't been a night watchman all my life. And quit looking at your watch," he ordered gruffly.

"I was thinking we should order." Lanna defended. "I don't know how long it will take to get served, and I don't want you to be late for work."

"Didn't I tell you?" John straightened in his chair. "I have the night off, so there isn't any rush."

"No, you didn't tell me." The initial rush of pleasure had barely passed when a flicker of guilt crossed her expression.

His keen gaze noticed it. "Is something wrong?"

"I was just thinking."

"About what?" John persisted.

Lanna smiled at him and warned, "You aren't going to like it."

"Then it's my fault for asking. What is it?"

"When a man has a Friday night free, he should spend it with his wife and family." She met his gaze with a little toss of her head. John had never discussed with Lanna the details of his marital problems, but she knew the relationship with his wife was strained from the odd comments he'd made.

"As it happens, my wife is out of town," John stated. "She took my grandson and daughter-in-law north for a visit. And my son had other plans for this evening. So if I had stayed home, I would have been alone. Having dinner with you isn't interfering with any family duty at all."

"I'm glad." A curiosity that had been plaguing her refused to be denied its satisfaction any longer. Most people his age talked nonstop about their children and grandchildren, but John rarely mentioned his. "Don't you get along with your sons? You never talk about them. I don't even know their names," she realized. "Do they live here in Phoenix?"

"My eldest son does." He paused a second. "It's very hard to describe your own children. My youngest is sharply intelligent with enormous potential, yet he doesn't seem to have any ambition. We don't get along very well. Now, my oldest son . . . I guess he reminds me of myself in a lot of ways." He looked up, a gleam in his eye. "I don't know whether I've told you this or not, but I've never had a woman friend before. Or maybe I should have said a friend who was a woman," he corrected with a laugh.

"The reverse is true for me," Lanna admitted, aware that he had again deftly changed the subject, but since he was reluctant to discuss his family, she didn't pursue

it. "I have never enjoyed a genuinely platonic relationship with a man before. It's a first for both of us."

"The time I have spent with you has made me the
happiest I've been in years. For some reason, people
don't get around to saying things like that to the people
who are important to them, but I want you to know
how I feel." Tears pricked her eyes at his touchingly
serious confession only to have him suddenly wink and
raise his glass. "Enough sentimentality. For the rest of
the night, we are going to eat, drink, and be merry.
Happy birthday, Lanna."

They did all three. Lanna's wineglass was never fully
emptied of champagne because John constantly kept
refilling it despite her laughing protests. A thick, juicy
steak dwarfed her plate, accompanied by tender aspar-
agus spears and a baked potato drowning in butter and
globs of sour cream. To top off the gluttonous repast,
there was a miniature birthday cake complete with a
burning candle. Most satisfying of all was the lively
conversation between the two, the lulls never lasting
longer than a bite of food.

Sated, and just a little tipsy, Lanna was reluctant to
move when John stopped the borrowed station wagon
in front of her apartment. With an effort, she turned
her head to look at him, a dreamy contentment in her
smile.

"Will you come in for coffee?" she asked.

He hesitated, then nodded. "Of course."

But Lanna heard the thread of weariness in his voice.
"Tired?"

"I'm getting too old for this drinking and carousing
around," he joked and stepped out of the car.

Her legs were unsteady when he helped her out of
the car. The coolness of the desert night air made her
head swim with the aftereffects of all that champagne.

She swayed against the support of his hand under her elbow.

"Whew! I'm a little light-headed," she admitted with a self-conscious laugh. "I'll need more than one cup of coffee. Are you good at sobering up your friends, John?"

"I have a great hangover cure. Should I leave the recipe in case you need it in the morning?" His twinkling glance mocked her mellow state as he guided her to the building entrance.

"I've never had a hangover in my life, but I've never gotten drunk on champagne before, either." In front of her apartment, she stopped to dig to the bottom of her evening purse for the door key.

"You'd better let me do that," John suggested when she found the key, but had difficulty getting it to go into the lock.

"Gladly." She surrendered the key and stood back while he unlocked the door.

Directly across the hall from her apartment, a door opened and Mrs. Morgan walked out. There was a sickly pallor to her face. Lanna's concern was instantaneous.

"Is something wrong, Mrs. Morgan?"

"Influenza. It's going around again. It came on me this morning. I can't work at the plant like this, but it doesn't stop me from doing my laundry. Late at night is the only time you can find an empty washing machine in the building."

"How true," Lanna murmured in agreement.

But Sylvia Morgan had already been distracted by the sight of John dressed in his dark suit. Her scrutiny was so pointed that Lanna felt obligated to make an introduction.

"I don't believe the two of you have officially met,

have you?" she began. "John, this is my neighbor, Mrs. Sylvia Morgan. My friend, John Buchanan."

"I'm pleased to meet you, Mrs. Morgan." John acknowledged the introduction with a polite nod of his head as he returned the door key to Lanna.

"Don't I know you?" Mrs. Morgan frowned and tipped her head to one side.

"I'm sure we have never met," John replied on a faint thread of amusement.

"You look so familiar to me. I just know I've seen you before, but I can't remember where. Things like that bother me," the woman sighed. "You look like someone I should know."

"I have that kind of face." He smiled his unconcern. "People are always telling me I remind them of their uncle or cousin or some character actor on television."

"Maybe that's it." Mrs. Morgan seized the possibility. "Maybe you remind me of an actor. I never thought about that."

"Did you say you had your clothes in the washing machine?" Lanna prompted.

"Yes. Yes, I did." The woman hesitated, as if reluctant to leave. "I'd better be getting them into the dryer or else I'll be up all night. Probably will be, anyway," she grumbled.

Lanna made no move to enter her apartment as she watched her neighbor walk down the hallway toward the building's laundry. Sylvia Morgan paused at the corner to look back, then disappeared down the connecting corridor.

"She was waiting to see if I was going to invite you in," Lanna explained as she entered the apartment ahead of John. "She's convinced you are my sugar daddy."

John laughed, but the sound lacked it's usual heartiness. "I'm not surprised. It's a conclusion more than one person would reach if they saw us together." He moved across the room to sit heavily on a chrome chair at her breakfast table. "Don't take too long making that coffee. My old bones need a pick-me-up."

"It won't take long for the water to boil," Lanna promised, disappearing into the kitchen alcove.

Her high-heeled shoes seemed to add to her wobbly sensation, so Lanna kicked them off, the coolness of the tiled floor pleasant on the bottom of her stockinged feet. She filled a tea kettle with water and put it on the stove to boil, almost turning on the wrong burner. She turned toward the cupboard a little too quickly and had to grab the edge of the counter as a wave of dizziness swamped her.

"Did I tell you I ordered the wallpaper for the bathroom?" she called to John while she opened the cupboard to take down two cups. "It should be here next week. Do you want to give me a hand papering the bathroom next Saturday?" Something hit the floor with a heavy thump. "John?" Lanna turned to look across the breakfast counter. The chair where John had been sitting was empty. Then she saw his body slumped on the floor. She sobered up in an instant. "Oh, my God!" she whispered.

Years of professional training kept her from panicking. She hurried to the fallen man and turned him onto his back, struggling with his heavy frame. Loosening his tie, she unbuttoned the collar of his shirt and adjusted his head, clearing the breathing passages. Her fingers found the vein in his neck and felt the thin throbbing of his pulse. Absently, she noticed the opened box of pills and the white tablets scattered on the floor near him.

She left him long enough to go back to the wall telephone in the kitchen and dial the emergency number. Her voice was clear and concise as she gave her name and address, and requested that an ambulance be sent immediately, advising them it was a heart attack. The phone call didn't take more than a total of thirty seconds.

Assured that help and equipment were on their way, her mind divided into different compartments. One, guided by professional instincts, concentrated on her patient, while her hearing strained to catch the wail of the sirens. A third part was berating herself for not seeing the signs that should have forewarned her. John had probably taken care to conceal them from her so he wouldn't spoil her birthday celebration.

It seemed ages before she heard the wavering scream of the ambulance outside the apartment building. Rationally, Lanna knew it had only been a matter of minutes, but it seemed much longer. Doors were slamming; footsteps hurried along the hall to her door; anxious voices issued questioning exchanges; then there was the sharp knock.

Lanna paused long enough to call, "It isn't locked. Hurry!"

The door was pushed open and white-coated attendants rushed in, carrying their boxes of equipment and pushing Lanna out of the way. She stood back gratefully while they took over with swift efficiency.

One of the men began shooting questions at her. "Are you related to him?"

"No. We're just friends." She leaned shakily against the table, aware that the trembling came from shock.

"Name?"

"John Buchanan."

"Age?"

For a moment, she drew a blank, then resolutely shook her head to get a grip on herself. "Sixty-three."

"Do you know if he has a history of a heart condition? Is he on any medication?"

"Yes, he is. His pills are there on the floor. The prescription information should be on the box."

The attendant grabbed it up and a few of the tablets. "It's blank. Do you know if he took one of these?"

"No. I was in the other room," Lanna explained. "I heard him fall."

The second medic spoke up. "He's stable enough to transport."

"Please, may I ride with him?" she asked.

"Sure." The permission was granted as the two men lifted the body onto a collapsed stretcher.

Lanna hurried into the kitchen for her shoes, pausing to turn off the burner and remembering at the last second to grab her purse. The men were wheeling the stretcher past a wide-eyed Mrs. Morgan in the hallway outside Lanna's open door.

"What happened? Did he have a heart attack?" Her neighbor hurled the demanding questions at Lanna, who ignored both the questions and the woman in her haste to follow the ambulance attendants. "I knew something like this would happen. A man of his age just can't take very much excitement."

Lanna shut her mind to the implication of that statement and climbed into the back of the ambulance. The doors were slammed shut and the vehicle took off amidst the mournful wail of the siren and the rotating flash of light.

The arrival at the emergency ambulance entrance of the hospital started a procedure that was all too familiar to Lanna. Yet, in its familiarity, there was a strange unreality. The nurses and interns waiting at the door to wheel the stretcher-bound victim down the corridor, the clipped, hushed orders issued in calm authority, and the sterile, antiseptic smell of the hospital became pieces of a nightmare. Lanna was kept from taking part in it by an admissions nurse.

"We'll need some information, Miss." The white-uniformed figure with a white cap perched on gray-brown hair blocked her path; a hand laid gently but firmly on her arm.

Lanna stared after the stretcher, reluctantly tearing her gaze away when it disappeared through a set of swinging doors. Dazed, she tried to remember what the nurse had just said.

"Yes, of course," she remembered and followed the woman into a small office cubicle, where she was seated in a straightbacked chair. Threading her fingers together in her lap, Lanna repeated the sketchy information she had already given the ambulance attendants.

"Do you know where Mr. Buchanan lives? His address?" The businesslike tone held no sympathy, its briskness designed to obtain the needed statistics without arousing an emotional reaction.

"He lives here in Phoenix." As she mentally clawed through her memory, Lanna raked her fingers through her hair, dislodging a comb. "I don't know the address."

"What about a home phone number?" the nurse questioned.

"I don't know it." Lanna shook her head.

"Does he have any immediate family? Someone we might contact?" The voice remained unruffled, helping Lanna to hold onto her composure.

"He has a wife. Her name is Katheryn," she remembered and felt the brief, speculative glance the nurse gave her, but the glimmer of curiosity was quickly masked. "He mentioned she had gone out of town . . . north somewhere on a visit. John said their daughter-in-law and grandson had accompanied his wife."

"His son? Perhaps you know where he might be reached?" the nurse suggested.

"No. John said he had an engagement this evening.

I'm not much help, am I?" Lanna sighed as the teeth of the hair comb bit into her palm. Then her head jerked up. "Wait. John works for Falcon Construction. He's a night watchman on one of their sites—the new medical building. They'll have his records on file."

"There, you see, you did know something, after all," the nurse declared with an encouraging smile.

In the hospital corridor there was a sudden flurry of activity. Low voices carried a disturbed note that Lanna was quick to feel. A nurse came bustling into the cubicle to hand the packet containing John's personal possessions to the admissions nurse. A bright flame of agitation burned in the eyes of the nurse facing the desk.

"All hell's broke loose out there." Her voice was sharp with criticism, savagely low. "The next time, you tell those ambulance attendants not to write down half a name. That's John Buchanan *Faulkner* we've got in there!"

The name slapped at Lanna. "There must be some mistake," she protested.

The nursed turned, as if noticing her for the first time. Lanna had encountered looks like that before— the icy steel gaze of a head nurse that would tolerate no nonsense.

The admitting nurse identified her. "This is Miss Marshall. She was with . . . the victim when he suffered his attack."

"He's John Buchanan," Lanna reasserted. "I've known him for months. He's a night watchman, for heaven's sake. I don't know where you got the idea—"

"From his wallet, Miss Marshall, when I checked it for any medical advisories it might contain. After I saw his identification, I recognized him as being J. B. Faulkner." Her gaze swept over Lanna's face and the pale amber dress that so classically draped her curving figure. "I'm sure you had reasons of your own for wishing to conceal his identity."

Lanna's cheeks flamed red at the insinuation, but she answered back, "You are quite wrong, Nurse. I knew him as John Buchanan; therefore, that was the name I gave you."

"It's immaterial now who was misled." The nurse turned away from Lanna to address her subordinate. "There are several emergency numbers listed. You had better start trying to reach someone." Pivoting, the nurse swiftly left the cubicle, her rubber-soled shoes making no sound. There was only the soft rustle of her uniform.

Lanna looked at the admissions nurse and repeated her assertion in a controlled voice. "I didn't know."

The woman's mouth curved in a distant smile, but she made no direct response to the statement. "If you'd care to sit in the waiting room, Miss Marshall, I'll advise you when there is something to report on his condition."

"Thank you." Lanna rose, subdued, her presence superfluous, and retreated to the empty lounge area near the emergency entrance, consigned to the nerve-wracking task of waiting for word.

Chapter X

Lanna sat hunched forward in the lumpy chair covered with plastic vinyl. Her hands were clasped around a Styrofoam cup of cold coffee—its contents remained untouched. Someone had brought it to her more than an hour ago. Straightening, she ran a hand over the silky thickness of her brown hair and sighed.

Her gaze sought the nurse on duty at the window, silently questioning. The woman shook her head, indicating there was nothing to report yet. John's condition was unchanged. John—who was J. B. Faulkner. The full impact of that still hadn't sunk in yet. John or J. B. Faulkner, her only concern was for a friend she had brought here, regardless of his name.

She clung to the fact that he was still alive. That, in itself, gave hope. There was no doubt that he was receiving the best of care. There was no lack of staff, equipment, or specialists to monitor his condition, an indication of the influence the name J. B. Faulkner wielded.

The ring of the telephone drew Lanna's attention again to the nurse on duty. She strained to hear the one-sided conversation, poised motionless in her chair.

"Yes, Doctor. We were able to locate Mrs. Faulkner by telephone nearly two hours ago," the nurse was saying. "She was at their ranch in northern Arizona. She's flying in immediately by private plane." There was a long pause. "His son? No. His housekeeper said he had gone out for the evening and she didn't know where he could be reached. We have left a message for him to contact the hospital as soon as he returns." Silence. "Yes, Doctor. I will."

When the nurse replaced the telephone receiver, Lanna set the cold cup of coffee on the table among the tattered magazines and rose quickly to cross the waiting room to the desk. Anxiety shimmered in her searching gaze.

"That was the doctor, wasn't it?" Lanna queried. "How is John? What did the doctor say?"

"I'm sorry, Miss Marshall. His condition is still listed as critical. I can't give you any more information than that," the nurse replied.

"But surely you can be more specific," Lanna insisted. "Is he conscious? Have they—"

"You must understand, Miss Marshall," the nurse interrupted firmly, "until Mr. Faulkner's family is apprised of the situation, we cannot give out any details. Perhaps it would be best if you went home. There isn't anything you can do here."

"No." Lanna rejected the suggestion with a quick shake of her head. "I'll wait."

Turning away, she retraced her path to the green plastic chair. Her head was pounding and her stomach felt quesy. Lanna didn't know how much of the stress was due to her nerves and how much was caused by the alcohol in her system. She rubbed the spot between her forehead with the tips of her fingers, the pressure bringing little relief.

"Please, God. Please," she whispered a wordless prayer, her soft voice catching on a sob.

Swallowing the hard lump in her throat, Lanna struggled to get a hold on her emotions. The waiting and feeling of uselessness were tearing at her poise, but nothing would be gained by allowing them to overwhelm her. She wished for someone to talk to, something to divert her mind from dwelling so exclusively on John's condition. As a nurse, Lanna knew these next few hours were a crisis period. She lifted her gaze, trying to concentrate on something else.

A couple entered her vision to claim her attention. She focused on the marked contrast between the man and the woman. It was more than just an age difference; it was much more subtle than their obvious difference in age.

The years had treated the woman kindly. Her youthfully slim figure was still intact, fashionably clad in an apple-green skirt and matching bishop vest, complemented by a floral silk blouse. The outfit gave the impression of height to the woman's petiteness, an effect aided by the slender heels of her shoes. They made an imperious click when she walked, demanding attention. Her light brown hair, coiffed in a sophisticatedly simple style, had been permitted to acquire an elegant frost. It was the regalness of the woman's carriage, more than anything else, that insisted she be noticed first.

By contrast, the man appeared almost unassuming. Noiseless like a shadow in the night, he walked abreast of the woman. His stride was smooth, each movement flowing naturally into the next. The way he seemed to glide alongside the woman led Lanna to expect his posture would be slouched. Yet his shoulders and back were straight, although there was nothing of the exaggerated military bearing about them, and his head was tipped at an angle that couldn't be described as subservient. His air of pride was understated, attempting to impress his importance on no one, while being sure of it within himself.

The man wasn't competing with the older woman to be the center of attention, which was why she commanded it, even though he was head-and-shoulders taller. His clothes, too, seemed chosen not to draw attention, but the plain brown slacks and pale tan shirt could not hide the superb fitness of his lean, male body. There was a vague, unrelenting quality to his hawklike profile, his features bluntly sculpted from darkly sun-bronzed skin. His hair was jet-black and waved thickly across his forehead in a careless kind of order.

Despite his seeming indolence, Lanna sensed that the man was aware of everything around him. His gaze sought out and noted every detail of his surroundings, instinctively absorbing every sight, sound, and smell. All of these impressions registered in Lanna's conscious mind in an abstract way, but none of them touched her. As quickly as her interest in the couple had been aroused, it was satisfied. Once again a shudder of apprehension quivered through her body as she thought about John lying somewhere in the hospital, amidst an array of tubes and monitoring devices.

Seeking another diversion, Lanna turned and picked up the cup on the table strewn with magazines. She lifted it to her mouth and tasted its bitter coldness. In the odd way the mind has of refocusing its concern on mundane items in the face of life-and-death struggles, she began worrying whether she had turned off the burner under the water she had been heating for coffee and if she had locked her apartment door. The answers to the two questions became of prime importance to her. She had to find a telephone to call Mrs. Morgan and have her neighbor check.

The woman paused at the desk and identified herself. "I am Katheryn Faulkner. I want to see my husband." By her attitude and tone of voice, she indicated that she asked permission for nothing and from no one.

Standing to one side, Hawk remained in the background and watched the nurse's reaction to the crisp authority of Katheryn Faulkner. Flustered for an instant, both by Katheryn's order and her obvious importance, the nurse quickly recovered.

"One moment, please?" the nurse requested, then picked up the telephone. In a low voice, she relayed the information of their arrival to the party on the other end of the line and murmured an affirmative response. As she hung up the phone, she smiled faintly at Katheryn. "Dr. Sanderson will be here directly, Mrs. Faulkner. If you would care to have a seat—"

The nurse never had an opportunity to complete her sentence before Katheryn was turning away from the desk, freezing the nurse into silence with her abruptness. Outwardly there was no display of emotion as she took several steps into the waiting area. For all the concern apparent in her expression, the man she was here to see could have been a stranger instead of her husband.

But Hawk had observed the way Katheryn had gnawed at her knuckles during the flight to Phoenix from the ranch. He marveled that she had any feeling left for the man she had married. There were times when he admired her steadfast devotion to his father, and others when he found her unrequited loyalty to a man who didn't deserve it completely foolish.

Over the years, he hadn't outgrown his attraction to

this woman. Long ago, Hawk had stopped actively seeking any praise or affection, which would never be forthcoming from Katheryn. Her hatred for him was too deeply rooted. He was blatant evidence of her husband's infidelity, a constant reminder that she was married to a man who cared little about her. Because of his indifference toward her, J. B. couldn't be touched by her jealous anger or pitiful desire for his affection.

It was from this combination of circumstances that the strange relationship between Hawk and Katheryn evolved. She was aware of Hawk's feelings for her. There was a certain irony to wanting the attention of her husband and receiving it from his bastard. So she used Hawk, extracting her own kind of vengeance on him because she couldn't reach her husband—as in this instance, when she had enlisted Hawk to pilot the family owned twin-engine aircraft to fly her to J. B.'s side.

The request wasn't prompted by a sense of compassion; rather, his inclusion in this moment of family crisis was designed to coldly exclude him. She wanted Hawk to be at the hospital, near his father but unable to visit him, restricted by hospital rules that would permit only members of the immediate family to see him. J. B. had never publicly or privately acknowledged Hawk as his illegitimate offspring. There was no reason to believe he might do it on his deathbed.

Born in a Navaho hogan with no birth certificate, Hawk could not prove his identity. No, for him it would always be the word of a half-breed and his Navaho relations against that of the whites. Those whites who knew the truth would deny it—Tom Rawlins and his wife, who continued to nurture their animosity toward him because of their daughter—and the few remaining cowhands who had been working at the ranch when J. B. had been carrying on his affair with Hawk's mother, because they were afraid of losing their jobs and being unable to find anyone else to hire them due to their advanced years and the Faulkner influence.

However, Hawk hadn't accompanied Katheryn because of a desire to be near his father. Even though he was aware of her motive, he was there because of Katheryn. She might need him, and he had to be there if she did.

The almost-silent swish of the elevator doors attracted Hawk's attention. A tall, green-coated man with thinning gray hair walked briskly toward them, his gaze lighting instantly on Katheryn. About the doctor there was an air of professional competence. Yet, beneath it, Hawk sensed an undercurrent of a man who had pitted his skills and knowledge against a problem that was beyond his solution.

As the man drew nearer, the keenness of Hawk's gaze dissolved into blandness. By his manner, he faded into the background of importance, assuming the role of one who served the woman he stood beside.

"Mrs. Faulkner?" The doctor's voice was polite and respectful, shadowed with concern. "I'm Dr. Sanderson. I'm glad you have finally arrived."

"How is he?" Katheryn blinked away a brief gathering of tears and kept her head high.

"We are doing everything we can, I assure you, Mrs. Faulkner." The doctor smoothly evaded a direct answer. "Our Cardiac Unit is one of the best in the state."

"I want to see him," she stated in a voice that would not be refused.

The doctor sliced a glance at Hawk, as if expecting him to intervene, but Hawk remained silently aloof. "Mr. Faulkner is unconscious, but naturally you may see him for a few minutes. If you'll come with me, I'll take you to him."

As the doctor stepped to one side to permit Katheryn

to precede him, she sent Hawk a speaking glance. "Wait for me here, Hawk." The order effectively relegated him to the role of attendant, one which he had already accepted, but he inclined his head in mute agreement.

In the next second, she was moving forward to allow the doctor to escort her to the elevator. Hawk became aware of movement in his side vision. It was the woman he had noticed in the waiting area when they had arrived. Seconds ago, she had been at the telephone booth. Now she was hurrying to intercept the departing pair. The strain of deep concern was etched tautly in her whitened face.

"Doctor?" Her voice was low and firmly controlled.

When the doctor hesitated uncertainly, Katheryn openly displayed her impatience and displeasure. It only seemed to increase the physician's unease. His gaze made a questioning and searching sweep of Katheryn's expression, as if seeking some other reaction. His action aroused Hawk's curiosity.

"Nurse?" The doctor motioned to an elderly, white-uniformed woman. "Take Mrs. Faulkner up to Intensive Care. I'll be there directly."

While Katheryn didn't look pleased by the change of escorts, the young woman slowed perceptibly at the doctor's statement. She looked immediately at Katheryn, her lips parting as if there was something she wanted to say. But Katheryn swept past her to accompany the nurse, without giving the young woman a chance to speak. The snub was forgotten almost instantly as the brunette turned to the doctor.

"How is he? Mr. Faulkner?" She added the name as clarification and Hawk's gaze narrowed on her. What was her interest in J. B.?

"We are doing everything we can," the doctor patiently repeated his earlier phrase.

Irritation flashed in hazel eyes. "I am a nurse. I want to know his condition," she demanded.

"His chances are slim, Miss Marshall," was the clipped response. "We've already brought him through two arrests. If there's a third, it would be a miracle for him to survive."

For all her implied assurance that she could take the truth, the brunette went completely white. The shock of disbelief widened her eyes. Her mouth was open but she couldn't get any words to come out.

Hawk stepped forward. "Who is this woman?" The question was directed at the doctor while his gaze studied the woman who exhibited such concern about J. B. Faulkner.

Her hair reminded him of rumpled brown velvet, attractive in its disarray. It framed a face with features that, taken individually, were not particularly striking, yet the combination of round hazel eyes, classic cheekbones, and wide mouth was definitely attractive. A simple dress of palest gold covered a figure that was slim but well rounded. Firm, thrusting breasts lifted the bodice of the dress with each breath she took. On another occasion, Hawk would have felt the stir of sexual desire upon looking at such a woman, but his present interest in her wasn't physical.

"Miss Marshall was with Mr. Faulkner when he had his heart attack," Dr. Sanderson explained in a somewhat hesitant voice.

Hawk's jaw clenched and unclenched in a sudden surge of anger. It was an anger that was directed at his father for the obvious implication behind that explanation and the subsequent humiliation that would again be dealt to Katheryn.

"Where was this?" His snapped question seemed to free the woman from her dazed state.

"In my apartment," she admitted.

Hawk contained his violent urges and ripped his gaze from the woman to the doctor. "Have there been any inquiries from the media yet?" he demanded.

"I know of only a couple," the doctor replied, following his train of thought. "The hospital has only given out very sketchy reports on Mr. Faulkner's condition. No details as yet."

"I will want the names of everyone who would know the circumstances. The hospital is not to give out any information concerning Mr. Faulkner. Any statement to the media will come from a member of the family. You understand, Doctor?" An iron thread of challenge ran through Hawk's calm statement.

"Perfectly." There was a faint expression of relief in the doctor's face, as if some unwanted burden had been lifted. "I will have Nurse Burroughs, at the desk, give you the names."

"Good. In the meantime, is there a less public place where . . . Miss Marshall can wait?" He paused to glance at the brunette before using her name. She appeared indifferent to the awkward situation or too numbed by the evening's events to care about its effects on J. B.'s family.

The physician considered Hawk's request for an instant. "The staff lounge would afford Miss Marshall some privacy," he suggested and gave Hawk directions to it. "There's always a pot of coffee on. You can help yourself."

"Thank you." His hand gripped her elbow. She offered no resistance when he steered her away from the doctor in the direction of the lounge.

"If Mrs. Faulkner asks—" the doctor began.

Releasing the Marshall woman's arm, Hawk retraced the few steps to the doctor's side. "Tell her I stepped out for a moment. When the time is appropriate, Mrs. Faulkner will be informed about Miss Marshall."

"Of course. I'll leave it in your hands," the doctor agreed with a relieved smile.

As Hawk guided the brunette past the nurse's desk, the doctor stopped to instruct the nurse to provide Hawk with the names he required. Before he could speak, the nurse looked up.

Her voice carried down the corridor to Hawk. "Mr. Faulkner's son just called. He'll be here right away."

Hawk registered the news with grim satisfaction. There was work to be done—and done swiftly. Chad's imminent arrival meant there would be two to accomplish it. Certain aspects of it would require the power of the Faulkner name, which Hawk didn't possess and couldn't invoke. That would become Chad's responsibility. A wry, humorless twist slanted his mouth at the thought of working hand in hand with his half-brother. It would be a first.

Before anything could be started, Hawk needed answers to some questions so he would know exactly what they were up against. Disguising the sharpness of his gaze with the thick screen of his dark lashes, he ran a sideways glance over the woman walking with him. His fingers felt the faint tremors that continually quivered through her. The strain that whitened her face was fear. It was apparent, even to his stranger's eye, that her fear was for the man lying somewhere in this hospital, possibly dying. It was a genuine emotion. That, Hawk didn't doubt.

He found the door to the staff lounge and reached in front of her to open it. The action brought him close for fleeting seconds, and Hawk caught an elusive scent of sandalwood and musk. Then he inhaled the unmistakable aroma of alcohol, identifying it a second later as champagne. Anger hardened him against the young, attractive woman who had so obviously been celebrating with his father.

The lounge was deserted when they entered. With no care for her surroundings, the brunette wandered into the empty room. She seemed unaware that Hawk had released her arm to shut the door. His gaze made a sweeping inspection of the room, all the while keeping track of her. He spotted the coffee urn and the Styrofoam cups stacked beside it.

"Coffee?" His inquiry seemed to surprise her, as if she had forgotten anyone was in the room with her.

"No." On second thought, she changed her mind. "Yes, please."

Hawk filled two cups. A container of sugar and powdered cream sat on the table near the coffee urn. "Cream or sugar?"

"No." She shook her head and Hawk presumed it applied to both.

Crossing the room, he handed her one of the cups. She took it, holding it while he sipped at the scalding black liquid in his cup. She looked brittle, tears lurking somewhere near the surface. She seemed lost in her own mental anguish. He absently admired her control. It was evident to him that she had been deeply involved with J. B., which did nothing to ease his irritation.

"How long have you known J. B.?" He shot the question at her, startling her into looking at him, confused by the seething hostility in his voice. Hawk tempered his features into smoothness. "Why don't you sit down, Miss Marshall?"

"No, I can't sit anymore!" There was frustration in the words that burst from her, frustration at being able to do nothing to help.

"How long have you known J. B.?" Hawk repeated his question, not pressing her into sitting down.

"Since June." She pressed a hand to her forehead and sighed. "It seems longer than three months."

That discounted the possibility that she had met him

a year ago when J. B. had suffered his first heart attack. "You're a nurse? How did you meet him?"

"I was on my way home from work one evening. It was storming. His truck had broken down on the highway. I stopped to give him a lift." She tipped her head back, revealing the clean, smooth line of her throat, and released a short, vaguely incredulous laugh. "I didn't even know who he was until tonight. Isn't that incredible?" She lowered her head to gaze at Hawk, her expression mocking her own ignorance. "He said his name was John Buchanan and that he worked as a night watchman. I believed him. I mean, why should I have doubted him?"

"His name is John Buchanan *Faulkner*," Hawk stated.

The more he considered her story, the less surprised he was by the fact his father had kept his identity a secret. It would be like him to seek anonimity, to have an affair with a woman who wasn't attracted by his status. Hadn't J. B. done that when he'd chosen Hawk's mother as his mistress? A Navaho woman who had no conception of who his father was?

"A nurse found his identification. Why did he keep his true identity from me?" She questioned Hawk in confusion. "I understand why he probably did in the beginning, but later on . . . Did he think it would change the way I felt toward him?"

But Hawk wasn't interested in discussing his father's possible motivations. He wanted details more pertinent to the present situation.

"I want to know precisely what happened this evening, Miss Marshall. What brought on his attack?"

Her downcast gaze stopped on the untouched cup of coffee that she now held in both hands. "It was my birthday." The flatness of her voice indicated how much pleasure had been lost. "John took me out to dinner to celebrate—champagne, candlelight, the works." Hawk could imagine the romantic setting, with his father smiling and laughing across the table at this young attractive woman, bolstering his own ego with her youth and beauty. "He never mentioned that he wasn't feeling well. I suppose he didn't want to spoil my evening. And I never noticed." There was self-blame in her expression. "Afterward, when we went to my apartment, I was going to make coffee—"

"After what, Miss Marshall?" His sudden question cut through the pain of her recollection. "I don't particularly care what sexual activity you and J. B. engaged in. I merely want to know whether or not he was dressed when the ambulance arrived and if he was in bed."

"Yes, he was dressed! And no, he wasn't in bed!" she answered hotly. "John and I are friends! I wasn't having an affair with him! It was strictly friendship on both sides! Why is that so impossible for people to believe?!" She turned away from him, choking on an angry sob.

Hawk made no response, studying her silently. Her outraged disavowal sounded genuine. Perhaps he had misjudged the relationship, but it was immaterial what the truth might be. For the time being, it was enough that he had received the answers to the two most important questions. Now his work could begin.

Turning, he walked away. It didn't occur to him to apologize or offer a word of comfort. He wasn't deliberately callous. Simple thoughtfulness had never been shown to him, so it didn't occur to him to express polite, consoling phrases to someone else.

Leaving his half-empty cup of coffee on the table near the urn, he left the lounge and retraced his path to the nurse's desk. The list of names was prepared and waiting for him. Hawk had barely glanced at it when Chad walked in.

The camel vest suit concealed a waistline that had begun to thicken from too many martini lunches, and it allowed Chad to retain a trim look. He walked with a stiff erectness that came from years spent in the private military school. Not a hair of golden brown hair was out of place as it framed his incredibly handsome, suntanned face. Coldness gleamed in his light brown eyes when he noticed Hawk.

"What are you doing here?"

He moved away from the desk. Chad's striking looks had attracted the nurse's attention, and Hawk wanted their conversation to take place out of her range of hearing.

"I flew Katheryn here—at her request." That information wouldn't sit well with Chad. He didn't understand the cruel game his mother played with Hawk and resented, jealously, any inclusion of Hawk within the family circle.

"Where are Carol and Johnny? Are they here?" His gaze made an arc of the waiting room, looking for his wife and son.

"No. Her parents are driving them here in the morning." It occurred to Hawk that when J. B. died, there would be no one standing in the way of the Faulkners and the Rawlinses. With his father's silent consent, Hawk had been free to come and go these last ten years. Now they would see to it that he left. At the moment, it didn't trouble him unduly.

"What about J. B.? Is he going to make it?"

Hawk wondered if vultures asked such questions when they circled a fallen animal. Whatever feeling Chad once had for J. B. had been eroded long ago by bitterness. Hawk understood about vultures and the

vital role they played, even if sometimes they didn't
wait for death to feast on the flesh of the dying.

"He's alive, but it doesn't look good," Hawk admitted. Through half-closed eyes, he regarded Chad
with amusement as his half-brother attempted to show
concern.

"Where is he? I'd better go there. Mother will need
me," Chad said.

"There is a more immediate problem that needs your
attention." Hawk forestalled the move Chad made
toward the desk.

"What?" Chad immediately challenged.

A corner of Hawk's mouth deepened in wry grimness. "It seems that J. B. was at a friend's apartment
when he suffered his heart attack—a woman friend."

The information slowly sank in, a mottled rage
building beneath Chad's tan. "That son-of-a-bitch!" he
muttered through clenched teeth. "He can't even die
without dragging us through his mud."

"This is a list of the people who know the circumstances." Hawk showed him the paper. "So far, the
media haven't gotten hold of the story, but you and I
know they'll have a field day with it once they get their
hands on it."

"What the hell are we going to do?!" Chad raked a
hand through his hair.

Suddenly it was "we." "Call Judge Garvey. He owes
J. B. some favors. Collect on those political debts.
Garvey's house is in the vicinity of this woman's
apartment and within the radius of the same ambulance. I'm sure you can convince Garvey that J. B. was
with him when he had the attack," Hawk concluded.

"How do you know about Garvey?" Chad studied
him through narrowed eyes, surprised and suspicious.

"I listen." He dismissed his knowledge as unimportant at the moment. "You're going to need to grease

some palms to hush the people on this list. The hardest part is going to be changing the log on the ambulance call. How much cash are you carrying?" Hawk knew Chad generally carried a lot. Turning to shield his action from the nurse at the desk, Chad took out his wallet and checked inside. "Good," Hawk pronounced. "I have some poker winnings on me. Between the two of us, we should have enough to take care of this."

"Cheated the boys out of their pay again, did you?" Chad said.

"I don't have to cheat."

Hawk remembered well the one and only time Chad had sat in on a poker game in the bunkhouse. For all his charming, handsome facade, Chad had a face that was as easy to read as a child's book. He'd lost his money within half an hour. Because Hawk had happened to win most of the pots, there had been an ugly scene that had been prevented from erupting into violence only by the intervention of a couple of cowhands who hadn't been playing.

Since that time, whenever Chad showed up, Hawk would deal himself out of the game regardless of whether he was ahead or behind. Hawk was aware Chad believed he was afraid to fight him. But there were a variety of reasons why Hawk avoided a confrontation. One was he didn't know how impartial the cowhands would be. None of them could afford to be his friend and remain working for the Flying F brand. Rawlins saw to that. Perhaps the underlying reason was buried in the knowledge that Chad was Katheryn's son. To hurt him would be to hurt her.

Hawk never bothered to analyze his motives or actions, nor dwelled on the past. He handled a situation the way it seemed appropriate at the time and didn't concern himself with whether he had been right or wrong—just as he was doing now in a situation that called for swift, decisive action. He wouldn't be thanked for it. More than likely, Chad would take the credit. But Hawk would accomplish his purpose—to spare Katheryn public humiliation. Now that Chad had agreed to the plan, it was the time to act.

"You'd better make that phone call to Garvey," Hawk prompted. "As soon as you get the facts straight, we can start to work on this list."

"Right." Chad made a move toward the telephone, then paused. "What about the woman?"

"We'll discuss that as soon as we have this settled."

After a little verbal arm-twisting, Judge Garvey agreed to the story to protect the good name of his friend. Then it became a matter of talking to the people on the list and appealing on behalf of innocent family members who would be hurt while slipping money into their hands. In total, it took less than half an hour, leaving only the ambulance log to be altered. Although the truth had been suppressed, Hawk knew the story would continue to circulate. Scandal always did. But, at least, it wouldn't be publicized.

By previous arrangement, Hawk and Chad met again near the nurse's desk. A grin was playing about his face as Hawk approached. "Frank Broadmore is going to handle the logbook. He just happens to be their attorney, as well. All that's left is the woman," he concluded.

"She's here—" Hawk began but never got any further.

"Here?!" The word rushed from Chad in a stunned underbreath. "In this hospital?"

"Yes. She rode in the ambulance with J. B.," Hawk replied evenly.

"Where is she now?" Chad wasn't interested in how she had gotten here. "My God, she isn't with him, is

she? I won't have Mother subjected to such humiliation!"

"Katheryn isn't even aware of her existence at the
moment. I'm sure she'll have to be told later on, but the
doctor—Dr. Sanderson—has agreed to keep the
knowledge from Katheryn for the time being," Hawk
explained. "The doctor gave me permission to take her
to the staff lounge, in case any reporters showed up and
started asking questions."

"I want her out of here immediately!" Chad
snapped.

"She seems to be determined to stay until there is
some word on J. B.'s condition. And she claims they
were just friends," Hawk added, remembering how
vehement the young woman's denunciation had been.

"Friends?" An eyebrow was raised in arrogant
skepticism. "J. B. has always had only one use for
women." The look in his eye condemned Hawk to the
same category, cold hatred shining because of Carol,
his wife, who had known Hawk, in the Biblical sense,
before their marriage.

"Either way"—Hawk shrugged—"she doesn't strike
me as the kind you can buy. She seems genuinely fond
of J. B."

"He was, and is, a bastard," Chad declared thickly.
"I have never understood why women couldn't see
that, including my mother. But if she truly cares about
him, she can be persuaded to leave."

"Not by me." After his interview with her, the
woman would never listen to any argument from him.
Besides, Chad was the one with the charm.

"I'll talk to her. You just show me where she is,"
Chad ordered.

Hawk obeyed, but not out of any sense of servitude.
He led him down the hospital corridor to the staff
lounge. When he opened the door, the brunette was

standing at the window looking out into the night. With a certain eagerness, she turned at the sound of the door opening. Coldness invaded her hopeful expression when she recognized Hawk.

Behind him, Chad murmured, "For once, J. B. showed some taste." It was an indirect insult aimed at the Navaho blood Hawk's mother possessed. Fire flashed in Hawk's blue eyes for only a second before it was banked.

Lanna had thought it might be a member of the hospital staff, bringing her word of J. B.'s condition. When a pair of reckless blue eyes returned her look, a faint arrogance in the expression, she went cold with anger. She hadn't thought that man with devil-black hair would dare to return after the vile accusations he had made against her. She should have known he was the kind who dared anything.

His brutally frank questions had made her realize that he was saying what half a dozen other people were probably thinking. Knowing the truth didn't make it easier to face strangers. Therefore, Lanna was on her guard when she noticed the second man.

The man was handsome—breathtakingly so. No taller than the first, he was dressed in an expensively tailored suit that gave him a solid, polished look. As he crossed the room toward her, Lanna saw the faint smile that touched his mouth and the gently sad light in his pale brown eyes. Her wariness began to crumble at this first exposure to someone reaching out to comfort her.

"I'm Chad Faulkner, J. B.'s son," the man said. It explained it all to her. The gentleness, the quiet strength—yes, he resembled John in several ways. "I came as soon as I heard. Thank you for staying until the family could arrive, Miss————" He paused expectantly for her to introduce herself.

"Lanna Marshall." When he took her hand and held it warmly in both of his, she wanted to weep in relief that her anguish was being shared. "H-how is he? I haven't heard anything for half an hour or more."

"He's holding his own," his son reassured her and smiled to enforce the encouragement. "You know how strong he is. He's a fighter."

"Yes." Her gaze slid past Chad Faulkner to the man silently observing them. She saw the mockery in his expression; it seemed permanently stamped there. "John and I are friends," she stated to quickly assert her relationship before Chad Faulkner could receive the wrong impression.

"Yes. I heard you were with him when he had the attack. This must have been very hard for you," he said, comforting her.

Lanna was tempted to lean her head on the shoulder of this man, who seemed to understand so much of what she was feeling. "We had gone out to dinner to celebrate my birthday. I asked John to come in for coffee when we got back to my apartment. When I went into the kitchen to fix it, I heard him fall. I—"

"You don't need to talk about it," Chad offered when Lanna hesitated. "It didn't turn out to be much of a birthday with all this happening, did it?"

"No." She began to feel she was treading unfairly on his solicitude and stood up straighter, withdrawing her hand from the clasp of his. She smiled weakly to show him that she was all right. All the while in the background, she was conscious of the man watching them, so aloof, so unreadable.

"Lanna—may I call you that?" Tipping his head to the side, Chad smiled in an engaging fashion that brought an immediate nod of permission. "I have something to ask you, but I don't want you to misunderstand my reason."

"What is it?" She gave him her undivided attention.

"I would prefer that no one knew my father had been with you this evening when he had his attack. However innocent your friendship is with my father, once the newspapers get hold of the story, it won't matter. I don't want to see my family hurt or your reputation damaged by any sly innuendos that would appear in print," he explained. "With my father being who he is, the news that he has suffered another heart attack will naturally be reported. That can't be avoided. But I can shield you and my mother from the gutter mentality of the press. I can do this with your cooperation."

"How can I help?" His thoughtfulness and his concern for her reputation touched Lanna and disarmed her completely.

"I'd like you to go home. Hawk will take you." At her expression of dismay, he added, "And I promise I'll call you if there is the slightest change in my father's condition. Reporters will be coming. If I'm going to keep your name out of the paper, it will be wise if you aren't here; otherwise, your presence will cause a lot of difficult questions. I wouldn't want to put you through that."

"Yes. Yes, I understand," Lanna agreed.

"Thank you, Lanna." His smile warmed her with its gentleness. "And I promise you, your name won't be mentioned at all in connection with my father. I know it's what he would want."

There was no question in her mind that John was a gentleman in the truest sense of the word. So, it seemed, was his son. She found that very reassuring.

"You are very kind, Mr. Faulkner," she murmured.

"Call me Chad," he insisted, then straightened with a certain grimness. "I'm sorry I can't stay any longer, but you must understand that my mother needs me."

"Naturally. I don't mean to keep you," Lanna assured him with a quick shake of her head.

Chad half-turned, reaching out to touch a hand to her shoulder in silent comfort. "Hawk will see to it that you arrive home safely. And I will call you as soon as there is something to report."

"Thank you." But a certain wariness crept into her eyes when she glanced at the taciturn man who was to escort her back to her apartment. The man Chad had referred to as Hawk returned her look with a blandness that made it difficult for Lanna to tell whether he was displeased that his services had been volunteered.

Chad paused at the door to say something to the man. The indifferent blue gaze swung lazily to Chad. Lanna didn't hear what was said. The man called Hawk nodded in brief response, but whatever was said, it didn't alter his expression. There was an alertness about the man that was never relaxed, even when he appeared to be. It made Lanna feel uneasy when Chad left the lounge and she was alone with him.

"I could take a cab," she suggested.

There was mockery in the rash line of his smile. "You wouldn't want to upset Chad's plans, would you?" His voice drawled around concisely spoken words. "He might worry about you. You wouldn't want that."

"No." Lanna wondered why she had the feeling he was ridiculing her.

Chapter XI

The traffic on the city streets had thinned with the lateness of the hour. The beams of streetlights illuminated the car in a rhythmic pattern, with traffic lights turning green as they approached each intersection with a regularity that seemed uncanny.

Lanna inspected the man behind the wheel with a sidelong study. From shadow to streetlight, his thick hair was the black color of a gleaming onyx stone. There was a faint crook in a nose that was otherwise straight as a blade. His cheekbones were sharp and prominent, intensifying the lean hollows of his cheeks and the deep grooves that arced from his nose to the corner of his mouth. It was a thin mouth, but not lacking in humor. His chin and jaw were strong. It was a hard face, an arresting face that excited interest while it aroused caution.

But it was his eyes that Lanna found most unnerving of all. Their deep cobalt-blue color was such a contrast to that black hair and skin the shade of an old penny. They could dance with humor, taunt with a mocking glitter, sharpen with steel hardness, or become mirror-smooth, reflecting nothing. If eyes were supposed to be mirrors of the soul, he had none.

Her head was throbbing. And Lanna still felt a bit woozy from all the champagne she had drank. The silence inside the car became stifling. She had to break it or scream to release the tension.

"Do you work for John—Mr. Faulkner?" she asked.

He let his gaze leave the traffic long enough to single out her profile in the darkness before it returned to the street. "Not exactly."

"Are you a friend of the family, then?" Lanna was positive he had to be one or the other, since he was obviously in Chad's confidence.

"You could say that," he agreed.

Lanna was irritated. She wanted to talk—to have her mind diverted from thoughts of the hospital and John. Why couldn't it have been Chad who brought her home? But she already knew the answer to that. She tried to remember which of John's two sons was married—the younger or the older? She couldn't recall that John had told her. Chad hadn't been wearing a wedding band, though.

She tried again to make conversation, a stubbornness surfacing. "Chad called you Hawk. Is that your first or last name?"

"My last name." Again there was that brief answer that made her attempt all one-sided. He wasn't abrupt, merely indifferent.

"What's your first name?" Lanna persisted.

"Jim, but no one uses it."

"Just plain Hawk?"

"Just plain Hawk," he agreed, but there was nothing plain about the man.

There was a quality about him that eluded Lanna, something that made him different. She searched for it in his face until he turned to intercept her gaze in silent challenge. Aware that she had been staring, she looked away, forcing her attention onto the city streets.

"You can turn at this corner," she told him.

Her apartment building was only four blocks away. She curled the fingers of her right hand into her palm and stared out the window, rubbing her thumb against her mouth. Fear washed through her again as she remembered the ambulance that had taken her along this same street.

"Chad reminds me of his father—so thoughtful and gentle," she murmured absently.

"Yes, he knows the right things to say." It hardly sounded like a compliment; the tone was much too dry. He slowed the car. "Is this the place?"

"Yes."

When the car was stopped parallel to the curb, Lanna reached for the door handle. The motor was switched off, causing her to turn her head in surprise. The driver's door was already being opened as Hawk stepped fluidly onto the pavement. Obviously, he was going to follow his instructions to the letter and see her safely all the way to her apartment.

Hawk walked at her side, not touching her. He held the entrance door open for her and followed her down the hallway to her apartment. As she reached inside her evening bag for the keys, Mrs. Morgan peered through a crack in her door.

"You're back from the hospital," she observed. "How is he? I checked to see that you had shut off the stove, like you asked. It wasn't on, but you did forget to lock your apartment. Is everything all right? How is your friend?"

"Everything is fine." Hawk answered the question before Lanna could come up with a reply.

"Yes . . . it's fine, Mrs. Morgan," Lanna managed to agree. "Thank you."

Her gaze ricocheted away from the dryness of his look as he moved to block her from the view of her neighbor, effectively ending the conversation between them. Taking the keys from her fingers, he unlocked the door and placed a hand on the small of her back to firmly guide her inside.

A light was still burning above the chrome breakfast table. Lanna paused inside the living room, seeing again in her mind's eye the sight of John crumpled on the floor near that chair now pushed aside.

"I should have asked Mrs. Morgan if she heard my phone ringing." Lanna murmured the thought aloud. "Chad might have called before we arrived." She seized on the possibility. "I'd better call the hospital to be sure."

"No." His hand was on her arm, restraining her when she took a step forward. "I'll call. Why don't you fix some coffee?"

"Are . . . are you staying?" A tremor ran through her nerves.

He was already brushing past her to noiselessly cross the room to the wall telephone in the kitchen. Her question had been ignored. She hesitated, then followed him into the alcove, where the coffee was sitting on the counter. Setting the kettle back on the burner, she turned the heat on beneath it. She strained to hear Hawk's conversation, but he spoke too quietly for her to make out the words.

When she tried to spoon the instant coffee into the cups, her hand shook so badly that the brown granules spilled onto the Formica.

"You'd better let me do that." Hawk was beside her, startling her, as he took away the spoon and firmly set her aside. "Why don't you go in the other room and sit down?"

"I can't." She was shaking all over. It seemed safer to stand in one place. "The hospital? Did Chad call?"

"No. There's no news."

"It's the waiting that is so terrible." Lanna turned to lean against the counter, gripping the edges the way she was inwardly gripping her shredding poise. She closed her eyes, holding on.

"Do you have a headache?"

"Yes." She laughed at the question. It seemed a mild description for the severe pounding in her head.

When she opened her eyes, Hawk was no longer standing at the counter near the stove. She heard the flick of a light switch and placed the sound as coming from the bathroom. The door to the medicine cabinet above the sink creaked noisily as it was opened, then closed. He appeared seconds later with a bottle of aspirin in his hand.

"I bought new wallpaper for the bathroom," Lanna remembered. "A birthday present to myself. I was just asking John if he'd help me hang it next Saturday when I heard this heavy thud. That's when he—" A sob rose to choke off the rest of the sentence, but she didn't let it out.

Effortlessly, he pried the fingers of her left hand away from the edge of the counter and turned her palm upward to shake out two tablets. "Take these." He filled the water glass sitting on the counter behind the sink.

He waited until she had shakily emptied the pills into her mouth, then handed her the glass of water to wash them down. His fingers half-covered her trembling hand to steady the glass and guide it to her lips. The warmth of his touch made Lanna aware of how cold she felt. Her gaze lifted to his face and the blue eyes that seemed to regard her with a life of their own, yet they told her nothing. Lanna wished for some of his control.

As he took the glass from her hand, the tea kettle emitted its shrill, hissing whistle. She started at the piercing sound. In one gliding move, Hawk was there to lift the kettle off the burner and end its scream. Lanna watched him pour the boiling water into the two cups, a brown foam swirling on the surface.

With a sideways glance that seemed to measure her, Hawk picked up the two cups and carried them out of the kitchen. She followed him uncertainly. As if sensing the association of the breakfast table with John, he bypassed it in favor of the green tweed sofa in the living area. He set one cup on the end table and kept the other in his hand.

Standing to one side, he waited for her to take a seat. Lanna sat stiffly on the edge of the sofa cushion, her fingers curling into the delicate fabric of the dress skirt flowing over her knees. It didn't make her feel any more at ease to have him standing there watching her, not batting an eye. It was unnerving. Hadn't she been through enough already?

"Take off your shoes and relax," Hawk told her.

"I don't want to." That implied letting down her guard and allowing emotion to take over, something she didn't want to happen.

In the next second, his cup was sitting on a side table and Hawk was crouching near her feet. Lanna wasn't given an opportunity to protest as his hand cupped the back of an ankle and lifted a foot. After slipping off the high-heeled shoe and setting it aside, he ran his hand firmly over her nylon-clad foot and flexed muscles cramped from the artificial arch. The relief brought by that single motion was instant. Then her foot was being placed on the floor, her sensitive sole feeling the contact with the shag carpet.

As he picked up her other foot to repeat the procedure, she let her gaze slide to his face. Leaning forward as she was, his face was so close to hers that she could see the pores of his dusky skin and the fine lines that fanned out from the corners of his eyes. When his head turned to meet her look, the sudden flare of his nostrils reminded her of an animal catching her scent.

Yes. Lanna grasped at the quality that had eluded her. There was something in the man that was primitive, an elemental streak of wild nobility beneath a civilized facade. From it came the recklessness and the ever-present alertness. It had been refined and controlled, but it smoldered there beneath the surface. The knowledge registered in a disjointed way, implanted amidst the worry, fear, and shock of the night's events.

Then Hawk was straightening, an impersonal hand pressing her shoulders against the high sofa back, forcing her into a relaxed position. A shudder ran through her as she let her head roll back on the firm cushion, her neck muscles no longer responsible for supporting its heaviness. Giving into a surge of weakness, she let her eyes close. The breath she took trembled on a sobbing note. She knew if she really relaxed, she would break out into tears. When she opened her eyes, she found Hawk was still standing above her.

"The woman across the hall—your neighbor—would you want her to come over to sit with you, too?"

Lanna's immediate response was to lift her head from the sofa in a tired shake and comb the hair away from her forehead with her fingers. "No. I don't think I could take one of her well-meaning lectures right now." Then, the phrasing of his question penetrated her mind: "sit with you, too"—meaning as well as himself. "You don't have to stay," she said to his back as he turned to retrieve his cup from the table and sit in the armchair near the sofa, smoothly folding his long frame into the cushioned seat. "I can manage."

His eyes glinted with a doubt which wasn't expressed. "But when time goes by and you don't hear from Chad for whatever reason, you will want to call the hospital.

It might be difficult to explain who the young woman is on the telephone if the question is ever asked. I can inquire without arousing anyone's curiosity."

"I see," Lanna murmured. "That's why you're staying." She should have realized he wasn't trying to make it easier for her—only for the family. "I saw you arrive with Mrs. Faulkner."

"Yes." Hawk was relaxed in the chair, his long legs stretched in front of him, but his opaque eyes were on her.

"John said she was away," Lanna recalled, "on a ranch somewhere up north. You brought his wife here?"

"Yes. When the hospital notified her, she asked me to fly her down," he admitted.

That meant he was a pilot. "The ranch—John owns it?" Part of her still hadn't made the adjustment from thinking of John as a night watchman to realizing he was one of the wealthiest men in the state.

"Yes."

"Was it originally his home? He mentioned once that he was raised in the north—around the Four Corners." It was surprising now to discover how few details she actually knew about John.

"Yes. He hasn't lived there for years. They come back for a visit a couple of times during the summer." Hawk showed more interest in his coffee than the conversation.

Lanna was learning things she wanted to know, satisfying a vague curiosity and diverting her thoughts. "Do you manage the ranch for John?"

"Tom Rawlins is in charge."

"That is where you live, isn't it, Hawk?" It was strange how naturally his name came to her.

"I . . . live there." His hesitation was so slight, Lanna wondered if she had imagined it.

"You don't work there?" A tiny crease etched into her forehead.

"Sometimes." Which was hardly a precise answer. He looked up. "Drink your coffee before it gets cold."

His low-pitched voice was softly steady, its tone not at all the kind that would demand obedience. Yet a fine thread of steel ran through it and asserted his will on her. Lanna took the cup from the end table and held it in both her hands while she sipped at its steaming contents. Its wet warmth briefly steadied her nerves.

"Where do you work?" Hawk asked after she had taken another swallow.

After Lanna began talking about herself, she realized Hawk had deliberately steered the conversation away from any discussion of him. By then, she didn't care. It would have required too much effort to bring the subject back. Instead, she drifted into remembrances of the places she'd gone with John, the things they had done, and the quiet evenings they had spent together. There were so many good memories in recalling how their friendship had developed over the months.

Lanna wasn't even aware of the tears that filled her eyes until one trickled down her cheek. She brushed it away, suddenly self-conscious.

"I'm boring you with all this. I'm sorry." She set her empty cup on the end table, absently surprised that she had drunk it all.

One shoulder lifted in an indifferent shrug. "You needed to talk about it."

"John and I were friends, good friends," she asserted.

"I believe that," he replied calmly.

"You didn't before." A sharp glance accompanied her stiff reminder.

"Is that surprising?" He raked her figure with a dry look.

"No, I suppose not." An utter weariness crept into her voice and expression, her shoulders dropping. Her gaze was pulled to the silent telephone on the kitchen wall. "Why hasn't he called?"

In a slow, effortless move, Hawk got to his feet, pausing there when he was certain of Lanna's attention. "Do you want another cup of coffee?"

"No," she refused, irritated that he could think she would be so easily distracted.

"I'm going to have another cup." He started toward the kitchen.

"Can't you call?" Her flaring temper released frustration that had no other outlet.

She received no answer as he continued to the kitchen. With calm deliberation, he set the kettle on the burner and spooned instant coffee into his cup. Certain that Hawk intended to ignore her request, Lanna's hands tightened into desperate fists. But while he waited for the water to heat, he reached for the telephone and dialed a number. Lanna waited anxiously for the results.

"Nothing," was the word he passed on to her, then turned to fix his coffee.

"That's impossible!" she burst out. "All this time could not go by without *some* developments, *some* change!"

"You are the nurse. Perhaps there have been changes." He admitted the possibility. "Only they weren't conclusive."

Lanna was forced to accede to his logic. John's condition probably had fluctuated without the doctors being able to determine which course it would take. Tiredly, she wiped at the tautness of her forehead.

"You need some rest," Hawk observed. "Why don't you go to bed? In the morning—"

"No!" She rejected his suggestion out of hand. She revealed her agitation in the short, jerky movements of her hands. "I can't go to bed without knowing. I wouldn't sleep. You don't understand. You obviously weren't as close to John as I have been."

"His friends and family generally call him J. B.," he remarked subtly, implying that she didn't really know him.

"They didn't know him the way I did," Lanna defended.

"If you know him so well, then you must realize that J. B. takes from a relationship and gives very little in return." Hawk resumed his former position in the chair, regarding her over his steaming cup of hot coffee.

"That's not true," she denied. "John was very generous."

A jet brow arched. "Generous? Yes, in a material sense—but selfish when it comes to giving of himself."

"No." Lanna refused to believe that.

"Look at you. You trusted him, took him at face value. How did he repay you?" he mocked.

"How can you talk about him like this?" she accused. "He's in the hospital fighting for his life, and here you are running him down."

"I'm only speaking the truth, which shouldn't hurt anyone. As for J. B. fighting for his life . . ."—Hawk paused, his mouth twisting wryly—". . . right now, whether unconscious or not, he's paying an expensive medical staff to do that for him."

"Why do you dislike him?"

"It isn't a question of dislike, Miss Marshall. It's merely a matter of recognizing faults. We all have them."

"Do you have to be so intolerant, then?" she accused.

"Me?" A white smile of humor spread rashly across his face. "You would be amazed at what I've tolerated." With the atmosphere lightened by his expression, he glided on to another subject. "Where are you from originally? Not Arizona."

Again she allowed him to shift the conversation to something safer. She glossed briefly over her childhood in Colorado, her mother's death after she had left grade school, and her father's subsequent marriage when she was in college. But not in this man could she confide the affair with a married man that had left her scarred, but recovering. He wasn't John.

But there had been such an emptiness in her life until she had met John. She guessed that she and John had been drawn together by a mutual sense of loneliness. Her blurring eyes made a slow study of her apartment. It had begun to seem like a home after she'd met John. When her gaze came to rest on Hawk, so contained and so unaffected by the torment she was feeling, a surge of irritation brought her to her feet. The momentum carried her several steps from the sofa before she stopped to hug her arms around her waist.

"You make me feel so damned weak!" Lanna hurled the remark as she rubbed her elbows. "So damned guilty for being weak!"

The tears spilled through her blinking lashes to run down her cheeks. Her lips were pressed tightly together to keep from releasing the sobs that were shaking her shoulders. She lowered her head, letting the brown curtain of hair swing forward to hide her face.

A hand touched her arm and she tried to draw away from its pressure. But it took little effort to turn her and fold his arms around her until she was resting against the flat muscles of his chest. His body absorbed

the shudders that vibrated through her. His strength
offered silent comfort as he held her stiff form close to
his. Her tears dampened his shirt where she rested her
head. Even as she wept, Lanna struggled to control
herself.

"I'll bet you are the type who hates weeping fe-
males," she declared in a wavering voice.

"They are usually more Chad's style," Hawk admitted, but she thought she detected a note of amusement
rather than criticism.

"It's just that it's been so long." Lanna wiped at the
tears with a weak, scrubbing motion while she kept her
head downcast. "I keep telling myself that no news is
good news, but—"

The ring of the telephone was shrill. A cry broke
from her throat as she pivoted within the circle of
Hawk's arms, but they tightened to stop her.

"I'll answer it." The pressure of his hands ordered
her to stay where she was.

Lanna didn't have the strength to move as his long,
rolling stride quickly covered the distance to the
telephone. He lifted the receiver in mid-ring, silencing
it abruptly. It had to be Chad calling from the hospital
as he had promised. No one else would phone her at
this hour of the night.

Hawk faced her as he put the receiver to his ear and
spoke into the mouthpiece. Lanna was motionless,
every nerve, muscle, and sense straining toward him.
His monosyllabic responses told her nothing of what
was being told to him. She searched his face, trying to
read a reaction in his expression, but she could read
nothing there. There wasn't even a flicker of change in
the set of his features. Tension coiled through her until
she wanted to scream. She held her breath when he
turned to hang up the phone, then swung back to face
her.

"Where do you keep the whiskey?" he asked.

"Whiskey?" Lanna released the word with the breath she had been holding. What did that have to do with anything? "That was Chad, wasn't it? What did he say? How's John? Has his condition stabilized?"

"If J. B. had dinner here as often as you said, there must be some whiskey. He always liked a shot before dinner," Hawk persisted. "Where is it?"

"In the cupboard to the left of the sink," Lanna answered, because she knew he would tell her nothing until she did. "I want to know about John. Is he going to be all right?"

Hawk opened the cupboard and took down the half-empty bottle of whiskey and a glass, not responding. He walked toward her, carrying the glass and bottle in one hand. They clinked together, making a flat sound. "He's gone," he said bluntly, not cushioning the announcement with soothing words. "He died at one-twenty-two this morning."

Lanna sucked in a breath and covered her mouth with her hand. All the color drained from her face and she felt sick, her head reeling. Her stricken gaze couldn't leave Hawk's emotionless blue eyes as she silently waited for him to tell her it was all some kind of cruel joke. But it wasn't.

A violent trembling began in her shoulders and spread quickly to her legs. Before her knees buckled, Hawk was there to curve a supporting arm around her and guide her to a chair. Lanna sank into its cushions in a huddled mass of numbed disbelief. Balancing on the balls of his feet, Hawk crouched beside the chair to uncap the whiskey bottle and fill the glass.

"It isn't true. He isn't dead," her thin, wavering voice insisted.

"Drink this."

He pressed the cold, smooth rim of the glass to her

lips, forcing them apart. She inhaled the smell of pure whiskey before the tepid liquid was poured into her mouth. The fiery whiskey paralyzed her throat muscles for an instant, then racked them with spasmodic coughs. Lanna tried to push away the hand that kept the glass hovering near her mouth, but she had no strength.

"Drink some more," Hawk ordered and refused to let her disobey.

The whiskey burned away all her numbness to expose the raw pain. She began to cry and buried her face in her hands to catch the tears that streamed from her eyes. Unconsciously, Lanna rocked back and forth. She had no awareness of the man crouched beside the arm of her chair, staring at the partially full glass of whiskey he swirled in his hand. He bolted it down and then refilled the glass.

Lanna cried until the storm of grief was spent and only a few acid-hot tears were falling. Knotting her fingers together, she lifted her head to gaze sightlessly around the room. She trembled at the frightening emptiness she felt inside. The world had never seemed so bleak and lonely.

"Here." The glass of whiskey was being proffered to her lips again, held by the same set of strong, sun-browned fingers.

With a faint tremor, she lifted her hand to touch his and guide the glass the few inches to her mouth. This time Lanna was prepared for the whiskey's fiery taste. She choked slightly as the muscles of her throat constricted, but she didn't cough. The glass was moved away to the periphery of her sight. She leaned back in the chair and stared at the ceiling, feeling the backlash of whiskey befuddling her senses.

"John said he had a surefire hangover remedy," she remembered. "He was going to give me the recipe because I drank so much champagne tonight." Pain flashed through her head. "Oh, God, was it only tonight?" She closed her eyes as a terrible shudder ran through her.

There was the faint sound of movement beside her. Lanna opened her eyes to see Hawk bending over her. The whiskey bottle and glass were gone from his hand. A resigned grimness was in his eyes. He slipped an arm behind her back, his hand cupping the opposite side of her rib cage.

"What are you doing?" Lanna asked in absent confusion.

"Bed is where you belong now." His other arm hooked itself under her knees to scoop her out of the chair and carry her to the bedroom.

Lanna wasn't convinced he was right, but she didn't protest. She let an arm slide around his neck for balance as she was brought against his chest. Her head rested wearily on his shoulder, distantly aware of the flexed muscles in his arms and back. Again she found a vague comfort in his strength. His solidness was something to lean on.

In the bedroom, Hawk set her on her feet before turning on the switch to light the darkened room. Lanna watched him, swaying slightly and needing to be led by the hand. When he came back to her, it was to turn her around and unzip the back of her dress. She made no effort to help him or stop him when he slid it from her shoulders to fall around her ankles. Next, he lifted up her slip and drew it over her head.

Her mind drifted back in time, to forgotten memories of her childhood when she had fallen asleep in the car and been carried to her room by her father. So long ago, she had stood motionless like this while her father undressed her to put her to bed. This familiar pattern was being repeated now, with Hawk in place of her father, and she was soothed by it. Her brassiere was unfastened and removed. Then her pantyhose were rolled down and slipped from her feet.

"Where is your nightgown?" Hawk asked, standing impassively in front of her.

Lanna blankly returned his look. She wore pajamas. Didn't he remember they were under her pillow? His mouth thinned out into a long, straight line. He turned away to pull down the covers of the bed. Then he was back to lift her into his arms and carry her to the sheeted mattress. He laid her down and drew the covers over her before moving away from the bed.

The click of the light switch threw the room into darkness. The door to the past slammed shut in her mind. Lanna was vividly aware of all that had happened that night as she was engulfed by a wave of panic.

"Hawk!" She called for the one unshakable force she knew, sitting up on her elbows to see his silhouette framed in the doorway to the living room.

"Yes?" He paused there.

"Don't go. Don't leave me." The words rushed from her in an urgent whisper.

He came back to stand beside the bed and look down at her pale face. His gaze took in her semi-prone figure and the sheet stretched across the thrusting round points of her breasts.

"Go to sleep," he told her.

"I'm afraid," Lanna admitted. And she defended her apprehensions with: "You don't know what it's like not to have anyone. I don't want to be here alone."

Her words seemed to freeze him into immobility for a split-second. Then the mattress sagged beneath the weight of his knee. "Move over," Hawk ordered.

Lanna slid away from the edge of the bed as Hawk filled the space she vacated with his long, lean frame. His arm slipped under her to draw her to his side. She shuddered in relief to have his solidness supporting her again. Her hand found his shirtfront, reassured by the steady rise and fall of his chest. She let her forehead rest against his cheek.

"I know it sounds crazy," Lanna whispered, "but I feel so empty inside, and it's frightening." Her mouth formed the soft, trembling words against his skin.

His head moved on the pillow and his face turned to her. Her lips felt the firm outline of his mouth, the warmth of his breath flowing into hers. His hand made an experimental circle on her spine, sensitizing her flesh to his touch.

His free hand weaved its fingers into her hair and slowly applied pressure to make the contact with his mouth more exact. For long seconds, the kiss was no more than that, one pair of lips firmly pressed to another. Yet it carried a vital flame that melted Lanna's stiffness. When his mouth moved in a slow exploration of her softening lips, she could respond.

From his hard vitality, she drew strength. His hands began to slowly caress her, awakening her flesh wherever they touched. Senses that had been used only to register the depth of her pain and grief became aroused to the life force beside her. They registered the brutish fragrance that clung to his hard jaw and the taste of his mouth, the salty tang of her tears coating it. Beneath fingers curling into his shirt was the increased tempo of his heartbeat. More slowly Lanna was becoming aware of his leanly muscled length, the sinewed columns of his long legs beneath the rough material of his pants, the hard, unyielding contours of his hips, the smoothly muscled brawn of his chest and shoulders—masculinity in its pure state, virilely powerful and arrogantly raw.

Bit by bit, she began to be filled by the force of his existence. It was easy to lose herself to the feelings he was creating within her. The shadows of fear were chased away by the fires now being kindled. Sensation after sensation spilled through her: the touch of his hand on her hip, her stomach, cupping her breast while his mouth and teeth played with its point.

Then he was leaving her. She was alone in the bed, confused and adrift, aching with a fresh pain. Incomprehensible sounds came from nearby, drowned out by the erratic pounding in her ears. Despairing that it had all been a dream, Lanna felt herself sinking again into that empty black pit of pain.

"No." Her cry was little more than a protesting moan.

But it brought results. The mattress shifted under the weight of another body. A second later, Lanna was feeling the same solidness and her hands reached for it. A hard, male form fitted itself to her shape. The searing passion of a man's kiss lifted her from the depths and sent her soaring to dizzying heights. The act of procreation was, in itself, a promise of life's cycle being renewed. For Lanna, it was a glimpse of horizons never before seen—glorious, golden raptures yet to be attained.

Their beauty carried her away on golden wings. When they set her down gently, she was too exhausted by the flight to know where she had been taken. She wanted to rest—only for a moment—and curled into the arms of sleep, without fear or dread for the dreams it might hold.

It was nearly dawn when Hawk untangled the sleeping female form from his arms and slipped out of bed. In the gray light filtering through the window, he studied the face etched with contentment and framed by a brown cascade of shining hair. He was tempted to reach out and touch the generous curve of her soft lips while his body sought out the delights of her pliant flesh. Desire flickered to feel again the sensation of a wild wind lifting him high. Instead, Hawk drew the covers over her nakedness and gently tucked them around her shoulders. Then he reached for the clothes lying on the floor.

Chapter XII

Lanna made the transition from sleep to wakefulness in slow stages. She was encased in such a warm, gentle glow that she was reluctant to throw aside the sensation, because she sensed there was something unpleasant waiting for her when she opened her eyes.

Bright sunlight had forced its way into the bedroom and was now glaring through her eyelids. She rolled away from it, wanting to go back to sleep and drift into the dream that had left her feeling so good. But the movement awakened a hammering in her head, a savage ache striking at her temples.

"Why did I have to drink so much champagne?" Lanna groaned and tossed aside the covers.

Like a body blow, it hit her. John was dead. She sat on the edge of the bed, gripping the sides as the painful memory of last night came flooding back in disjointed pieces, out of sequence, some of them hazy.

The haziest of all was just before she fell asleep. Turning her throbbing head carefully, Lanna glanced over her shoulder at the empty bed. Had she dreamed it? Had Hawk made love to her last night? She vaguely remembered asking him not to leave her alone. She was most certain he had stayed, but had he actually gone to bed with her?

Why was her memory so sketchy, the happenings in the latter part of the night so obscure? She had consumed more than her share of champagne, but— Lanna remembered the aspirin, and later the whiskey Hawk had forced down her throat.

A chill crawled over her skin and made her shiver. Lanna suddenly realized she was nude. Why hadn't her father put her pajamas on her last night when he'd undressed her for bed? No, that wasn't her father. It was Hawk. Lanna remembered she had mixed them up last night, too. Maybe Hawk had made love to her. Why would she dream such a thing?

Why would she have let him? She wasn't the type to sleep around. Or, maybe, had she been too drugged to resist him? Yet the thought was associated with pleasure, so obviously there hadn't been any force involved. If she could only get rid of this dull throbbing in her head, she would be able to remember everything more clearly.

A knock echoed through her apartment. It took Lanna a second to realize that it wasn't the pounding in her head growing worse. Someone was at the door. Probably Mrs. Morgan, she thought, and she cradled her forehead in the palm of her hand, willing her neighbor to go away. But the pounding grew more insistent.

Sliding a glance at the alarm clock on the bedside table, Lanna saw that it was nearly noon. Mrs. Morgan had probably gotten worried about her and wanted to be certain she was all right. If Lanna didn't answer the door, her neighbor would probably summon the apartment manager to let her in.

Her chenille robe was at the foot of the bed, its

cranberry color a glaring contrast to the silver satin-quilted bedspread. Lanna picked it up as she rose unsteadily to her feet. She had trouble finding the armholes, but she finally slipped the robe on. There was more knocking on the door.

"I'm coming," she called wearily and tied the corded sash as she hurried from the bedroom. The knocking stopped. When she opened the door, it wasn't Mrs. Morgan who was standing outside. Lanna stared at Chad Faulkner in startled recognition. His light brown eyes ran over her, lingering on the gaping front of her robe, then sweeping over the tousled disarray of her gleaming, dark brown hair. "Hello," she managed to say finally. Self-consciously, she tried to push her hair into some kind of order. "I . . . I just woke up."

"I was beginning to worry when you didn't answer the door." He was dressed in a dark suit, its somberness a marked change from the light sophistication of the vested suit he'd been wearing at the hospital. Lanna was moved again by his stunning looks. His half-smile was gently prompting. "May I come in?"

"Yes . . . yes, of course." She stepped away from the door to admit him. Her hands moved to adjust her robe and try to look more presentable. "I . . . I'm sorry about your father." She remembered to express her sympathy for his loss.

"Thank you." His eyes were gentle with concern as they studied her pale features. "How are you feeling this morning?"

"Probably as awful as I look." Lanna tried to laugh, but the effort made her head pound.

"You are an unusually attractive woman, Lanna, even now," Chad said. "But I expect you know that."

Lanna felt a little too vulnerable to handle his compliments. Sexual desire had been absent from her life since she had broken up with her lover. After last night when Hawk had made love to her—if he had made love to her—it was back. Chad Faulkner was just the type who could arouse it. Her gaze strayed to his left hand, bare of any kind of ring.

"Thank you for calling last night," she offered, instead.

"May I fix you some coffee?" She took a backward step toward the kitchen.

"None for me, but fix yourself a cup, by all means. I must apologize for waking you up." Chad smiled. "It didn't occur to me that you might still be sleeping."

"It was rather late last night." As she entered the kitchen alcove, Lanna saw the bottle of whiskey and the empty glass sitting on the counter. Chad had followed her and noticed her gaze pause on the two.

"You had a rough time of it last night, didn't you? I hope that made it easier," he said, referring to the whiskey.

"It helped me forget," she admitted, and made a lot of things that happened fuzzy in her mind, she thought to herself. "I guess Hawk knew that, which was probably why he poured it down my throat." She lifted a brown tangle of hair away from an ear, then let it fall. "I was pretty well out of it when he left. I never did thank him for staying with me," she realized, then remembered his action hadn't been motivated by kindness. "Oh, I know why he stayed," Lanna assured Chad as she added more water to the kettle. "And I understand why you didn't want me calling the hospital, in case someone got the wrong idea."

"That was only a very small part of it. I didn't want you to be alone." He stood close beside her, his expression earnest. His concern was vastly different from Hawk's impersonal manner the night before. "I hope you accept that."

The provocative fragrance of an expensive male

cologne wove its spell on Lanna's senses. The intensity of his look made Lanna believe she was the only woman he cared about, a very heady thought. She couldn't cope with so much charm and good looks all in one package.

"You are very kind to be so concerned about me, Mr. Faulkner." There was a lump in her throat. She set the kettle on the burner, then forgot to turn the gas on beneath it. "At a time like this, I'm sure you have family, business, and half a dozen more important things demanding your attention."

"I classify you as important, Lanna. And I'd like you to call me Chad. You were very close to my father these last few months. I hope that later on, you and I will become better acquainted."

A stab of sweet pleasure shot through her. Maybe she wouldn't be so lonely, after all. "I'd like that," she agreed simply. Chad didn't seem the type to make idle talk. She certainly hoped he meant it, and she was very relieved to know that he was single.

"I stopped today because I wanted to make certain for myself that you were all right and to assure you that no mention of your name was in any of the reports. As far as the media are concerned, my father suffered his attack while he was visiting Judge Garvey, a close friend of the family who lives near here," he explained. "It's unlikely that this story will be questioned, but if word of your involvement is leaked to the press, some reporter might contact you to check it out." He reached inside his jacket and took out a business card. "Don't let anyone interview you. Outside of denying it, I don't want you to talk to any of them, but call me immediately. I'll handle it for you. I wouldn't want you subjected to some of the snide comments those reporters might make."

No one had ever been so concerned about protecting her reputation except John. She'd always thought this brand of gallantry was a thing of the past. When she took the business card from him, he reached out to warmly enclose her fingers in his grip. It was pleasing to see her hand in his. She couldn't look away.

"You don't have to say anything, Lanna. I don't want you to be hurt by all this. I know I'm doing what my father would want."

When his hand tenderly shaped itself to her chin, Lanna unconsciously swayed toward him. His head made a slow, almost hesitant descent. When his mouth touched hers in a passionless kiss, she quivered at the warm contact. A second later the pressure changed to become seeking and exploring, tentative and curious the way a first kiss often is. With obvious reluctance, he straightened slowly and studied her reaction with his amber-flecked brown eyes.

"I'm sorry," he apologized unexpectedly. "I shouldn't have done that. It's easy to see why my father found you so irresistible."

"We were friends, nothing more." Lanna was sorry he regretted the kiss; she had enjoyed it.

"Yes, I remember." Chagrin flitted across his face. "It's just when I touch you . . . well, let's say that it doesn't arouse platonic feelings."

Lanna experienced a thrill at the admission. He disturbed her and it was good to know it wasn't one-sided. With his looks and charm, Chad probably had any number of women chasing him. She sobered when she realized that as J. B.'s son, he was also likely to inherit a great deal of money, which put him out of her class. Yet John hadn't cared whether she was rich or poor, a member of the moneyed or working class. Wasn't Chad made from the same mold? She kept presuming Chad was the older, since John had said he was like him. She wished she had asked John more. It was too presumptuous to ask Chad now.

Withdrawing his hands, Chad took a step away from her. "I wish I could stay and keep you company for a little while longer, but there are so many arrangements to make," he said regretfully.

"When is the funeral? I'd like to attend the services . . . if I may?" She asked his permission because she didn't want her presence arousing questions.

"Naturally, you may." His quick smile nearly took her breath away. "Since my father was so well known, it will naturally be a large funeral. If anyone asks— which I doubt—simply tell them that you are acquainted with one of the family members and that you came to pay your respects. Specifically, you know me."

Chad waited while Lanna jotted down the time and place of the funeral. "I wouldn't have felt right not attending the services for John, but I didn't want to cause you any trouble, either," she told him.

"I know that the last thing you want to do is cause trouble. I don't have any doubt about that." His expression was a mixture of satisfaction and approval before it sobered into concern. "Will you be all right if I leave now?"

"Yes," she promised.

Still Chad hesitated. "May I call you the first of next week after things have settled down?"

He definitely wanted to see her again. The knowledge shined in her eyes. "Please. I'm home most evenings unless I have shopping to do."

"I'll be talking to you, then." He moved toward the hall door.

A smile curved Lanna's mouth when Chad had left. Unexpectedly, she had found a reason to look forward to tomorrow. Her gaze strayed to the kettle and she realized she hadn't turned the gas on to boil the water.

Slowing down the late-model rental car, Hawk turned into the private driveway marked by two adobe pillars. On either side of the asphalted surface, the sun-scorched earth was landscaped into a desert garden that utilized the native prickly pear and saguaro cactus and scrubby palo verde to achieve its effect. The lane curved in front of a rambling, adobe house roofed with red tiles. Hawk parked the car at the head of the stone walk that led to the front door.

His long, fluid strides carried him with unhurried swiftness to the door with the black wreath hanging in its center. He rang the doorbell and waited, his narrowed blue eyes restlessly sweeping the hazy blue sky and the distant range of mountains that formed a gray blot on the horizon. The turning of the doorknob squared him around to face the door. It opened to frame Carol's fashionably wand-slim figure, clad in an expensive black dress. Her mouth formed quickly into a smile of welcome.

"Come in, Hawk." She pulled the door open wide as she stepped aside. Her corn-gold hair was cut in a feathery, short style that subtracted years from her age. As always, there was the intense search of her bright green eyes when they met his gaze. Hawk didn't know what she was looking for—perhaps forgiveness, even after all this time.

He crossed the threshold and walked onto the polished tile of the foyer while she closed the door behind him. "I'm on my way to the airport. I stopped to let you know I'm flying back to the ranch." His presence wasn't wanted here. And Hawk had no intention of lingering.

"You will come back for the funeral on Monday?" Carol tried to insist.

"No."

"But—"

He didn't let her finish the protest, slanting an eyebrow as he spoke. "Funerals are your way of burying the dead, not mine."

"Who is it, Carol," a man's voice demanded an instant before Tom Rawlins appeared in the mosaic-tiled archway leading into a spacious living room. He stopped at the sight of Hawk, his nostrils flaring in anger. The years had pinched his quiet face into bitter lines, hardening him into an old man. "What do you want here, Hawk?"

"I didn't come to pay my respects." Mockery made a slashing line of his mouth, curved and taunting. "I came by only to tell you I'm leaving. A lot of the boys will want to come for the funeral on Monday, leaving only a skeleton crew at the ranch. With me there, that's one more who can come."

"You don't give a damn if they come or not!" Rawlins snapped.

"That's right. I don't," Hawk agreed smoothly. "But they do. So—?" He lifted his shoulders in an indifferent shrug.

"If you're leaving, then go." Rawlins waved toward the door.

"Daddy, please," Carol murmured in irritation, turning to her father.

A stillness settled into Hawk. "Don't give me orders, Tom, or I might just change my mind."

"This isn't the proper time to be arguing, Daddy," Carol instructed, trying to prevent her father from making a scene.

With a last glaring look at Hawk, he turned on his heel and stalked away. Hawk felt the tension ease from his muscles. His gaze slid to Carol with deceptive laziness. Ever since that time she had betrayed him, she had interceded for him many times against her father.

"I'm sorry," she apologized.

"It stopped being important a long time ago, Carol," Hawk replied and watched her wince.

She opened her mouth to protest. "I wish I could change what happened." But she was interrupted by the sound of running feet.

Hawk glanced at the young boy who dashed into view, a wide grin splitting his face. The boy was a miniature replica of J. B.—from the darkness of his brown hair to the laughing curve of his blue eyes. Only the slenderness of his build had he inherited from Carol.

"Hello, Hawk!" The boy greeted him with open enthusiasm. "Grandpa Tom said you are flying back to the ranch. Can I come with you?"

"Johnny!" Carol's voice was low with surprised reproval. "You know J. B.'s funeral is on Monday. What would people say if his only grandson wasn't there?"

"Ah, Mom," the twelve-year-old complained. "I'm not going to have a chance to ride that new horse Dad bought me. After the funeral, I'll have to go back to school."

"Sometimes I don't understand you, Johnny Faulkner." Carol didn't hide her irritation. "You would rather be riding a new horse than show respect for your grandfather by attending his funeral. What would people think if they knew?"

"Yes, Johnny." Hawk smiled dryly, widening his eyes slightly in mockery. "It's very important what people think. You should listen to your mother. She's an authority on that."

Her head jerked to him, pain whitening her face.

Hawk wondered why he had alluded to her sensitivity toward other people's opinions—possibly because she had reminded him of it, or perhaps because he didn't want Johnny to be as narrow-minded and prejudiced as his parents—and grandparents.

"But you aren't going to the funeral, Hawk," Johnny reminded him. "I heard Grandpa Tom tell Grandma."

"The difference is, Johnny, that no one will care if I'm not there." Which was the truth. Besides, although he no longer believed that dead bodies harbored ghosts, he saw no reason to look on a body pumped full of formaldehyde or at the satin-lined box that contained it. It proved nothing other than the fact that the man was dead.

"Why?" The question was asked out of sheer stubbornness.

Hawk laughed softly, catching Carol's uneasy movement out of the corner of his eye. "I'll tell you the same thing J. B. told me when I was about your age. When you're old enough to understand the answer, no one will need to explain."

Half-turning, he reached for the knob just as the doorbell rang. Hawk continued the movement to open the door to the caller. He recognized the squat, balding man as Benjamin Calder, another one of J. B.'s many attorneys. The man looked stiff and ill at ease, a bearer of bad tidings, Hawk thought to himself. The man's gaze jumped over Hawk, saw him, then dismissed him. Hawk doubted if there was anyone in Phoenix, outside of the Faulkner family, who knew he existed.

"I'm expected." The announcement was addressed to Carol. She had moved to stand beside Hawk, a possessive hand on Johnny's shoulder.

"Yes, Mr. Calder," Carol acknowledged. "Won't you come in?"

Hawk moved to the near side of the door, unconsciously slipping into the shadows of a potted fern and melting into the background, while the attorney entered the foyer. He intended to leave once the man was inside, but the staccato click of heels made him pause as he recognized Katheryn's footsteps. He hadn't seen her since he'd left her at the hospital last night.

"It's about time you arrived, Ben." She greeted the attorney in a sharp, impatient voice. She, too, was dressed in black and looked positively regal. There was no grief in her expression—only anger. She didn't see Hawk standing in the shadows near the door. "What's this nonsense about a new will?"

The attorney blanched under the attack. "It isn't nonsense, Mrs. Faulkner." He attempted to placate her temper with a reasoning tone. "J. B. had me draw up a new will a month ago."

"Who is the chief beneficiary?" she demanded. "So help me God, if he disinherited Chad in favor of that damned bastard half-brood of his, I swear I'll—" She stopped abruptly when Hawk took a step out of the shadows.

"Don't stop now, Katheryn." A corner of his mouth twitched. "It was just getting interesting."

"You'll never see a penny of it." Hatred gleamed yellow in her eyes, savage as a puma protecting her young. "I promise you that. The Navaho bitch who whelped you was nothing but a whore, and I'll have a half-dozen men with blue eyes and the same blood type as yours swear to it on the witness stand. It will be the longest and ugliest court battle you have ever seen."

"Now that J. B. is dead, you can finally say all the things you've been holding back all these years, can't you?" Hawk was unmoved by her threats. None of them could hurt him. Ultimately, she would be the one to suffer. The red-faced attorney was shifting his stance uncomfortably.

Hawk's demeanor merely goaded Katheryn. "Rawlins should have killed you when he caught you raping his daughter." She ignored the sharp gasp that came from Carol. Hawk shot a glance at the sound and saw the shocked confusion in Johnny's wide eyes. The boy would have heard the story sooner or later. Hawk felt only a mild sense of pity that it had to be now and under these circumstances. "People are going to know about that," Katheryn lashed out, continuing her threatening tirade. "And they will know how you've continued to intimidate and terrorize Carol. Everyone has seen the way she acts around you—afraid to cross you, afraid of what you might do. You can't blackmail us anymore."

"Excuse me, Mrs. Faulkner, but—" the attorney interrupted hesitantly. "I don't know who this man is . . . but—"

"Allow me to introduce myself." Hawk stepped smoothly forward, an incautious light gleaming in his blue eyes. "The name is Jim Blue Hawk. I think Katheryn has very luridly explained who and what I am."

The attorney shook his hand uncertainly, his gaze continuing to dart to Katheryn. "This man . . . Mr. Hawk . . . isn't the chief beneficiary. There is a provision in the will for you," he hastened to assure Hawk. "You are to be given a clear deed to half of the ranch property and some cash, while the half with ranch headquarters goes to Chad, but—"

'But what, Ben?" Katheryn challenged, her fury slow to die.

"The bulk of his real estate holdings here in Phoenix—after bequests to you, family members, and certain employees—has been left to a . . . Miss Lanna Marshall." His halting announcement shocked them all into silence.

As Hawk tipped his head back, rich, hearty laughter rolled from his throat, and swept through the room. He was laughing at himself, laughing at the others, and laughing at J. B. wherever he was because he had had the last laugh on them all.

Turning away, Hawk walked to the front door and opened it. He was still chuckling to himself as he started down the stone path to the rental car parked in the driveway. Behind it, another car had stopped. Chad was just climbing out, an irritated frown clouding his handsome features at the sight of Hawk.

Chad walked briskly toward him. "What are you doing here?" he demanded.

Hawk's smile was brash and uncaring, a wicked glint dancing in his eyes. "I was just leaving, Brother. Sorry I can't stick around to see your face when you learn you are about to join the ranks of the disinherited." With a wink and a broad smile, Hawk slapped him on the back and moved easily away, crossing in front of the car to the driver's side.

"What are you talking about?" Chad snapped.

But Hawk just smiled and folded his length into the car. A side glance saw Chad hurrying toward the house, and Hawk laughed again.

It was a hot, dry wind that blew across the cemetery, whipping the minister's prayer out of Lanna's hearing range. Bare-headed, she stood on the outside fringe of the mourners gathered around the grave site. She hadn't owned a black dress. Since it was no longer considered improper to wear another color to a funeral, she had worn a coffee-brown jersey, a shade that almost matched her dark, wind-blown hair.

The sky was a dusty haze, broken only by the glare of a burning sun. It scorched the dry earth and added particles of sand to the raw wind that blasted the somber figures. Lanna's skin was hot and sticky, unable to breathe through the clinging fabric, its dark color absorbing the sun's smothering heat.

Past the heads and shoulders of the other mourners, she had a clear view of the polished casket surrounded by bouquets and wreaths of flowers, the cloying sweetness of their fragrance carried away from her by the wind. Turning slightly, she could see the row of family members facing the casket.

With his arms at his sides, Chad stared at the casket in grave silence. The sun had brought out the blond highlights of his brown hair, ruffled by the wind. Lanna saw how the loss of his father and the strain of the last few days had etched a grimness into his face. As if sensing her gaze, Chad looked her way. The muscles along his jaw flexed as it was clenched. Reading the message of profound sympathy in her eyes, his expression softened before he faced the front again.

Beside him, nearly hidden by his height, was his mother, John's widow. Proudly erect, she looked fragile in black, hidden behind a long, black veil. Lanna guessed that Mrs. Faulkner was one of few women who could carry off such a dramatic touch so naturally.

The woman on the other side of Chad wore black, as well. Although she was without a veil, a black pillbox hat was perched on her shimmering gold hair. She was clutching the hand of the slender boy, standing next to her. Dressed in a dark suit and tie, he resembled John so much that Lanna guessed he had to be his grandson. A man was standing next to the boy. Lanna could see the dark shoulder of his suit, but her view of him was blocked by one of the mourners. She surmised it was John's second son, the married one.

Her gaze wandered back to the casket, a tightness gripping her throat for the friend resting there. Unable to hear what the minister was saying, she let her gaze stray back to the family. Something nagged at her. Then Lanna realized that she hadn't seen Hawk. She searched the faces of the mourners without recognizing him among them. Why wasn't he there? It seemed to Lanna that Hawk had been very close to the family.

The crowd began to stir around her. She realized the service had been concluded. People began to drift away, murmuring to each other. Some started to file toward the family to offer their sympathy. Lanna hesitated. She wanted to join the latter group, but she wasn't certain if that was wise. She lingered for several minutes, trying to make up her mind before she finally turned away.

Her little Volkswagen looked out of place amidst the line of black limousines and Cadillacs. Lanna didn't feel that she belonged there, either. As she started toward her car, walking between the graves, she searched through her purse for the keys.

There were footsteps behind her, but Lanna paid no attention to them until a hand caught at her arm to stop her. Startled, she turned around, brushing away the hair the wind whipped across her face. He said nothing as he held her gaze, his own probing deeply. Up close, the strain was more evident, the grimness more pronounced.

Lanna wanted to say something—to offer some words of comfort and understanding—but she was conscious of the slowly dispersing crowd of mourners that drifted by them. It seemed to her that circumstances dictated a less personal comment.

"It was a large turnout," she offered.

"Yes. The mayor came. Even a representative of the governor and the senator," Chad agreed with a vague dryness.

Chad partially turned and curved an arm around Lanna's waist. "Come. I want you to meet the other members of the family."

The line of friends offering their condolences to the widow had thinned to only a few when Chad ushered her forward. As two men lingered to speak to his mother, he guided Lanna to the blonde-haired woman and her son.

"This is my son, John Faulkner, and my wife, Carol." The introduction sent a numbing wave of shock through Lanna. She tried desperately not to let her surprise show when she smiled at them. "This is Lanna Marshall."

"How do you do, Miss Marshall." His wife extended a slender hand to her in greeting and smiled with an aloof friendliness.

Lanna could only nod in response. The woman was beautiful in that delicate, china-doll way blondes often are. The combination of pale golden hair and green eyes was striking. Lanna felt distinctly plain in comparison.

It was much easier to greet the young boy. "You look very much like your grandfather, John," she murmured.

"Yeah, everybody says that." He shrugged, even while he studied her with curiosity.

It was hard for Lanna to look the blonde in the eye without remembering the way Chad had kissed her—or to forget the hand that remained on the curve of her waist. She felt uneasy and guilty because of the attraction for Chad that she had allowed to grow in her before she realized he was married.

"Mother." Chad's request for the widow's attention allowed the black-veiled woman to excuse herself from the last man and join them. "I want you to meet Lanna

Marshall," he explained. "This is my mother, Katheryn Faulkner."

"I wish we could have met under other circumstances, Mrs. Faulkner," Lanna said and held out her hand in greeting. She couldn't see clearly the widow's expression behind the web of black veil, but she sensed an air of stiff reserve in the cool touch of the woman's hand.

"I couldn't agree with you more, Miss Marshall. I understand you were very close to my husband," she returned in a cultured voice.

"Yes, we had become quite good friends," Lanna felt honor-bound to insist, but her explanation was met with a cool reception.

"Yes, of course," the widow replied, then smiled with stiff courtesy. "Would you excuse me? I'd like to have a word with the minister before he leaves."

"Certainly," Lanna murmured, but John's wife was already withdrawing to seek out the black-frocked man. When she glanced at Chad, she was still trying to assimilate the knowledge that he was John's *married* son. The question rose in her mind: Where was his other son? Her gaze strayed to the only other group of people around the grave site, which included Chad's wife and son, and an older couple. In curious confusion, she glanced at Chad. "Where's your brother?"

His head lifted, drawing back, as if the question startled him. "What do you know about him?" he questioned warily.

Lanna frowned at his reaction. "Nothing. . . . John said he had two sons, but I didn't notice anyone else with the family." The dark-coated shoulder she had seen next to Chad's wife had turned out to be the male half of the older couple.

Chad didn't immediately comment, as if deciding on

a response. "It isn't something that's widely known. You see, J. B. had an affair with another woman. I'm sure you can appreciate how sensitive my mother is about that subject."

"Of course," she murmured, taken aback by the discovery that John's other son was illegitimate.

Mrs. Faulkner rejoined them and angled a glance at her son. "Have you told her yet, Chad?"

"No." His low reply gave the impression he regretted that his mother had asked the question.

"Told me what?" Lanna wasn't sure if she should ask as her gaze wavered between mother and son.

"Why, you are an heiress, Miss Marshall." Mrs. Faulkner seemed to chide her for not knowing that. "J. B. left you a fortune."

"*What?*" She gasped the word. "There must be a mistake." Lanna looked expectantly at Chad for his denial.

"It isn't a mistake." His faint smile seemed to be telling her she should rejoice at the news. "You'll be receiving formal notice from the probate court any time now. The family has already been made aware of the contents of J. B.'s last will and testament. The weekend has merely slowed the legal process."

"But—" Dazed, Lanna couldn't remember what she wanted to say.

"Why don't you give me the keys to your car? I'll have Tom drive it over to the house," Chad suggested. "You can ride with us. It will give me a chance to explain what all this means."

Lanna hesitated, then gave him the car keys which he, in turn, handed to an older, thin man standing near them.

PART
IV

", . . He stirs, he stirs, he stirs, he stirs.
Now Talking God, he stirs, he stirs;
Now his white robe of buckskin, he stirs, he stirs;
Now in old age wandering, he stirs, he stirs;
Now on the trail of beauty, he stirs, he stirs.
He stirs, he stirs, he stirs, he stirs.

. . . Far off from me it is taken!
Far off you have done it!
Happily I recover!

. . . With beauty before me, I walk
With beauty behind me, I walk
With beauty below me, I walk
With beauty above me, I walk
With beauty all around me, I walk."

Chapter XIII

It was a series of shocks, major and minor, that battered down her defenses: first John's death; then the discovery that Chad was the married son; that John's absent son was illegitimate; and, finally, that John had left her the bulk of his fortune. Three days after the funeral, Lanna fell prey to her neighbor's influenza bug.

She was sick most of the following two weeks, unable to go to work and rarely leaving her apartment, but that didn't stop the whirl of activity that went on around her. The telephone rang incessantly: reporters wanting an inside story on her relationship with J. B. Faulkner and her inheritance; salesmen with surefire investments; charities seeking donations. It didn't stop until she had an unlisted number installed.

Her illness didn't slow the legal process of administering the terms of John's will, all of which was beyond her comprehension. Chad gave her a list of reputable law firms in the city and suggested she retain one to represent her. As the other interested party, he was present at any meetings. It was usually Chad who translated the legal jargon into language Lanna could understand, and her own attorney agreed with him.

Before three weeks were up, Lanna had crash courses in estate laws, inheritance taxes, accounting, and real estate practices. All the while, she had suffered the body aches and pains of influenza and drank her sassafras tea. At the end of the period, she was no more adjusted to her changed circumstances.

She would look around her apartment and visualize different styles and colors of furniture to redecorate it; then she would realize she could afford to buy a mansion. Why bother to fix up the apartment? She could return to college full-time and obtain her degree in business administration, but she was rich—she didn't have to work anymore. She could take her Volkswagen to a garage and have an air conditioner installed, but she could also buy a Rolls-Royce. It was no wonder she was still confused even after she started feeling better.

And there was the Faulkner family. Initially, Lanna had expected resentment, justifiably so. She had been extremely wary in her first few meetings with the family before she had fallen ill. Chad's wife, Carol, had been courteous in a friendly way. Lanna hadn't been able to fault Katheryn Faulkner's behavior, although she had been more distant. Since then, Chad had been the only one she was in contact with on a regular basis. Recognizing how susceptible she was to his charm, Lanna was more cautious with him than the other members of the family, but he had proved to be very helpful and cooperative, more concerned with making the change a smooth one than anything else.

Lanna ran a hand over the burgundy velour upholstery of the bucket seat and relaxed against its contoured padding, letting her head recline on the headrest. Outside the windows of the moving car, the sky was a clear blue, free of the haze that usually hung over the valley city. She turned her head to glance at the driver.

Studying Chad, she briefly questioned whether she should have accepted his invitation for a month's rest at his family's ranch in northern Arizona. Its distance from Phoenix promised peace and quiet. She would find little of it in the city where she was still the object of every reporter, charity, and fortune hunter in town.

She looked to the front again. It had been a very generous invitation. Lanna wanted to believe that it meant she was being accepted as a family friend. Remembering how close she had been to John, she wished she could achieve that same relationship with his family.

"Why did he do it?" She asked Chad the question that she had asked herself over and over again. "Why did J. B. make me the chief beneficiary in his will? Don't you resent that?" She frowned.

He hesitated, sliding a look at her. "I did when I first heard about it, but not after I had time to think about it. I'm not exactly a pauper." He smiled. "In his lifetime, my father made a point of transferring to me stock certificates and portions of the interest he held in various companies. He also set up a large trust fund for my mother and one for my son, Johnny. He was distributing his wealth instead of allowing it to accumulate until his death."

"You mean that you believe you have already received your share of his estate?" Lanna sought clarification, hoping to ease some of her guilt.

"In a sense, I have," Chad agreed. "You and I are partners in several ventures."

"I have a great deal to learn about business." Lanna closed her eyes as a tiredness washed through her mind.

"You catch on quickly, though," Chad remarked.

Lanna realized there had been no gentleness in his comment and wondered why. She opened her eyes to look at him, but his attention was on the traffic around them.

"After your bout with the flu—you need a month's peace and quiet, away from all this publicity and endless barrage of legalities."

"Peace and quiet. That sounds wonderful," Lanna sighed.

"I'll only be able to stay a few days, but Mother and Carol are there to keep you company when I leave," he offered. "I'll join you on the weekends."

"It will seem strange not to have you around." She hadn't meant to say it aloud.

When his gaze sought hers, she wasn't able to look away. "It's probably a good thing that we're going to be apart for a while, Lanna." The silent message in his look added all that he couldn't say aloud.

Despite the fact he was married, her attraction for him hadn't lessened, and they had been together so frequently these last weeks. The last thing Lanna wanted was another affair with a married man. She suspected that Chad shared her aversion. Yet, this physical attraction that coursed between them was a constant temptation.

"Yes, definitely." Lanna agreed with his statement in a deliberately carefree voice. "I have leaned on your shoulder entirely too often."

Unexpectedly, he reached across the seat to take her hand. "You can use my shoulder any time. I mean that, Lanna." He threaded his fingers through hers.

They had arrived at Sky Harbor Airport. Chad had to let go of her hand to change lanes, and then he made the turn to the private hangars.

A twin-engine aircraft was parked on a cement apron. Painted on the side of the plane was the head of a falcon. Lanna recognized the insignia immediately. It was similiar to the one that had been on the construction truck John had usually driven. Except this one was different. Off to the side of the silhouette, there were two black, curving lines to signify wings.

"Is that the plane?" she asked.

"Yes." Chad had seen it, too, and was looking for a place to park the car.

"The emblem on the side—it's different from the construction company's. Why?"

"It belongs to the ranch. The ranch is called the Flying F, so wings have been added to the falcon head," Chad explained.

A frown gathered on Chad's features, his attention centered on a flightline office. "What is he doing here?" he muttered under his breath.

Lanna followed his gaze to the man leaning against the side of the building, his coral-red shirt standing out boldly. A brown Stetson was pulled low on his forehead, covering jet-black hair, but she knew without question it was Hawk.

A quiver ran through her at the sight of that supple, masculine frame. The vague memory of being held by those arms lost its dreamlike quality. Lanna could feel the exploring and arousing touch of those hands. Her pulse reacted as it had then, racing to some wild, primitive tempo that had lifted her to a new plane. How could she be so strongly attracted to two men so different—Chad and Hawk?

Hawk straightened from the building when Chad stepped out of the parked car. A smile touched his mouth at Chad's obvious irritation in finding him here. It was fleeting, lasting only until he saw Lanna being helped from the car.

His attention narrowed on her, his electric-blue eyes searching for changes. He found minor ones. Hawk surmised the label on the green slacks and thin, floral blouse belonged to an expensive brand. The sleek, mink-brown of her hair was styled no differently from the way it was when he had last seen her, yet it had the finished look of a professional's hand. He knew these things. His awareness of all that was around him was too keen to miss even minute changes.

When she met his eyes, Hawk noted the faint rise of color in her cheeks. She remembered. He'd wondered if she would. She had been drifting in and out of a dream world that knew only sensation. He was glad her memory of it hadn't dimmed.

"Where is Jake Sanchez? I understood he was meeting us."

The cool demand from Chad slid Hawk's gaze to him. "At the ranch. I came in his place."

"Why?"

A reckless smile curved Hawk's mouth. It seemed to drop the temperature by several degrees. "You know I wouldn't have missed this for anything, Chad." Although his reply was softly spoken, it was in the way of a taunt—a cactus thorn burying itself in the tender nose of a bull.

Untouched by Chad's anger, Hawk let his gaze glide back to Lanna, who silently faced him. His senses vividly remembered everything about her. Nothing had dimmed, not the tantalizing fragrance of her perfume or the disturbed shallowness of her breathing. Both observations affected him now, stirring desire in his loins. Hawk had forgotten none of the discoveries he'd made about her. Catching the sandalwood scent of her cologne, he wondered if she had again applied it to the back of her knees, as well as behind her ears. There was a wild longing to carry her off somewhere and find out, but the civilized side of him subdued it.

"How does it feel to be an heiress, Miss Marshall?" Hawk watched the interplay of emotions on her face. There was strength and pride in her features, two qualities that aroused his admiration. She was outgoing and quick to laugh or smile, unafraid to venture away from her home territory. He sensed a depth to her that had never been tapped.

"It's all been too hectic. I haven't had time to think about it yet," she admitted.

Then she turned her head to look at Chad. Hawk observed the exchange of looks and the tightening of Chad's hand on her waist. Hot-tongued jealousy flamed through him. It shocked Hawk with its force. He had possessed women before and had never been upset if another man held them. Yet his system was charged with this violently possessive emotion, irritating his nerves to a raw state.

"Didn't I tell you J. B. would repay you in his own way?" Hawk's voice was sharp, deliberately antagonistic. He watched Lanna stiffen at the question, realizing that he had been right in assuming her friendship with J. B. would be rewarded monetarily. Hawk noted, with grudging admiration, how quickly pride surfaced in her expression to hide the hurt at the discovery.

"What's he talking about?" Chad demanded with a puzzled frown.

"It's just something we discussed." With a shrug of her shoulders, Lanna belied its importance.

Hesitating, Chad seemed inclined to pursue the subject and obtain a more satisfactory answer, then appeared to decide to leave it to another time—when he wasn't there, Hawk guessed.

"The luggage is in the trunk," Chad stated as he pivoted toward the rear of the car and separated the trunk key from the others on the ring. "Let's get it out to the plane so we can be on our way." Hawk had no argument with that. Neither, it seemed, did Lanna.

Hawk led the way to the plane, toting Lanna's two new suitcases adorned with the monogram of their exclusive designer. Walking beside Chad, Lanna carried the smaller case of the set. She could feel both Chad's tension and her own. And Hawk was the cause.

She knew why she was upset, but she didn't understand why Chad was. She had assumed the two men were close, considering the events that had taken place the night John died. The barely disguised antagonism between them had come as a surprise.

Although she doubted Hawk had told Chad he'd slept with her, would he? She hadn't been herself that night. Surely Hawk knew that. The memory of his lovemaking had returned with such vividness that Lanna wondered why it had ever been vague. The rawly passionate sensations of it licked through her veins each time Hawk's gaze wandered to her. It was unsettling, mostly because she didn't know what Hawk intended to do with his knowledge—a knowledge that was so intimate.

Standing to one side, Lanna watched Hawk stow the suitcases in the luggage compartment of the sleek, twin-engine aircraft. When he turned to take the small case from her hand, his keen gaze read the uncertainty in her expression. An amused kind of satisfaction glimmered in his smile.

"Have you ever flown before, Miss Marshall?" Hawk appeared to mock her with the formal mode of address.

"Only on commercial jets," she admitted. "Never in a private plane."

"We'll be flying over some wild and beautiful country. You're welcome to sit in the seat to my right. You'll have a broader view of the landscape from the cockpit than from a passenger's window." On the surface, his invitation appeared merely polite, but Lanna knew it was in answer to her unspoken need to see him alone.

Still she hesitated, glancing at Chad, not wanting to arouse his suspicion if it turned out there was no cause.

"Do you mind?" she queried, requesting Chad's permission. "I've never been in the cockpit of a plane before. It would be quite an experience to see what goes on and have a bird's-eye view of the country, instead of being five miles up." Lanna schooled her expression, as if her only thought concerned the novelty of having a new experience.

Chad took a second to search her face and appeared satisfied with what he saw. "I don't mind." He smiled with the benevolence of a man granting her a treat. "As a matter of fact, I have some reports I need to study. I'll do them on the flight. That way I can be free to show you around when we reach the ranch."

"Wonderful." Lanna returned his smile and felt like a hypocrite.

Entering the plane, she walked all the wa front and maneuvered herself into the co-pilot's seat. As she buckled her seat belt, her gaze wandered over the confusing array of dials and gaugos. Then Hawk was joining her, folding his long frame into the pilot's seat. The brown Stetson was tossed onto a rear passenger's seat, while a hand combed the flatness out of his thick, black hair.

"Are you all buckled in?" His sidelong glance barely touched her, staying just long enough to see her affirmative nod. "Sit back and enjoy the ride. Just remember to keep your hands off the controls. I wouldn't want to bruise that lovely jaw to make you let go of them."

The set of his features warned her it wasn't an idle threat as he reached for a pair of dark glasses atop the control panel. Lanna clasped her hands tightly in her lap while Hawk began a pre-flight check of the instruments.

The blazing sun beat down on the plane, turning its interior into an oven. Lanna was engulfed by the heat.

The only fresh air came from an opened window on Hawk's side, and it was hot. The left engine turned over and caught in a deafening roar, but it generated a breeze that at least moved the stifling air around. The engine on the right took hold and added its loud vibrations to the first. Then Hawk was on the radio, requesting taxi and runway instructions from ground control. None of the answers made sense to Lanna, and Hawk didn't explain.

The co-pilot's seat might have been empty for all the attention he paid to her while he taxied to the designated runway and prepared for takeoff. The side window was closed, shutting the intense heat inside the plane. When clearance for takeoff came from the tower, Hawk half-turned his head to direct his voice at Chad, seated a row behind them. "We're rolling."

Lanna felt the surge of power as the full thrust of the engines sent the plane racing down the runway, gathering speed. When they lifted off and began a steady climb to the east, a cooling blast of air whooshed through the vents. Lanna turned her hot face to the freshness of its cool spray and breathed in deeply.

On the horizon, the ragged peaks of a mountain loomed. "The Superstititons," Hawk identified, drawing Lanna's glance to him.

The mirrored finish of his sunglasses reflected only her image, and she turned to look out the window. Their flight path took them directly over the forbidding range of mountains. It was a labyrinth of barren mesas and jagged summits interspersed with a maze of arroyos and canyons that held its secret of lost gold. The twisted, tortured land of volcanic debris was studded with cactus and carpeted with dry brush.

As the plane banked to the north, the sunlight glimmered on a body of water. A lake sat in the middle of the raw mountain desert, laughing at the parched terrain that surrounded it. A concrete dam acted the role of Tantalus, holding the water out of reach of the arid wasteland while taunting it with the promise of life. The plane seemed to be barely moving, but Lanna watched its shadow race across the jumble of rocky crags and the tangled desolation of the flatlands.

"How's your knowledge of the Old West?" Hawk asked.

Lanna turned away from the window to answer. "Sketchy." She couldn't see his eyes behind the dark glasses, but she knew he was looking at her.

"That's Tonto Basin just ahead. We're coming up on the Mogollon Rim, roughly a two-hundred-mile-long cliff. The area has been immortalized by nearly every writer of Westerns, including Zane Grey," he told her.

Lanna looked where he pointed and saw the escarpment that dramatically marked the edge of a high plateau. Erosion had laid bare layers of rock, allowing it to rise abruptly from the desert floor. The walls' color was shaded from white to gray to cream, depending on the rock exposed. Crowning the rim was a forest of pine and fir, dotted with aspen, a few maple, and oak. The rim was an impressive sight, its line stretching as far as Lanna could see, broken only rarely by a yawning canyon. Civilization had snaked roads in and around it, but nothing had tamed the wildness of the land.

"It's spectacular, isn't it?" Lanna mused as the plane's shadow climbed the walls to skim over the treetops of its mesa. When there was no response from Hawk, she turned to look at him. He faced her, yet she couldn't tell if he was watching her or looking beyond her out the window at the disappearing line of the rim.

"Yes," he agreed with her comment in a tone of disinterest. "You discovered for yourself that Chad is good at comforting grieving women, didn't you?" The dry remark made Lanna dart a glance behind her to

Chad. He was bent over some papers, his briefcase
cradled on his lap. "Don't worry," Hawk said, reading
her mind. "He can't hear us unless you shout."

"Chad has been very helpful," she replied cautiously, very careful not to raise her voice.

"I'll bet he has." A thread of contemptuous laughter
weaved into Hawk's response.

But the conversation had brought the topic around to
one Lanna wanted to clarify. "That night—" she
began.

"If you're concerned that I'm going to talk, don't
be," Hawk interrupted. "Chad's the one who brags
about his conquests. No one is going to hear about that
night from me."

"I wasn't trying to imply that you would spread it
around. It's just that I don't normally—" She attempted to defend her behavior that night but
wasn't permitted to finish.

"Look, we each satisfied a mutual need. Let's leave it
at that." To ensure that the topic was dropped, he
directed her attention to the front again. "We're
crossing the south boundary of the ranch."

Instead of feeling relieved and reassured, Lanna
experienced a twinge of disappointment. She hadn't
expected Hawk to treat the incident with such an
attitude of insignificance.

Forested mountain slopes gave way to a long valley
corridor that steadily widened. The plane began its
descent. It wasn't long before Lanna spied the private
airstrip lined up directly ahead of them. A collection of
ranch buildings was nestled in a grove of trees not far
from the strip. Lanna had a glimpse of the buildings
before the plane swooped in to land.

Hawk taxied the plane to the metal hangar where a
station wagon was parked. Chad's wife, Carol, was

standing beside the car. The willowy blonde waved at the plane stopping at the hangar but waited beside the car. A cowboy dashed out to slide chocks behind the wheels as soon as the engines were turned off.

The buckle of her seat belt stuck, resisting Lanna's efforts to unfasten it. Finished with shutting down the plane, Hawk turned and saw the difficulty she was having. He reached over and deftly released the catch. His hands made only brief contact with her waist, but it was sufficient to cause a fluttering response in her stomach. Lanna tensed self-consciously. Hawk didn't notice her reaction, or else he ignored it.

She departed from the plane ahead of Hawk. Chad was waiting outside to help her alight. The sunglasses were gone when Hawk joined them, the dusty brown hat again on his head. His blue gaze barely paid any notice to Lanna at all as he unlocked the baggage compartment and began unloading their luggage. The cowboy came forward to help with the suitcases, relieving Chad of the need to carry his own.

"Hello." Carol came forward to greet them. "Did you have a good flight?"

"Of course." Chad leaned down to kiss her cheek. "It was Lanna's first flight in a private plane."

"How are you feeling?" Carol's smiling face was turned to her. That air of friendliness seemed to come naturally to the blonde, although sometimes Lanna glimpsed a silent yearning in her green eyes. She had wondered about it, just as she had wondered about the absence of any affectionate display between Carol and Chad. They didn't appear to have an unhappy marriage, yet it seemed to be lacking something.

"Much better, thank you," Lanna insisted. Her gaze strayed to Hawk, who was stacking the suitcases in the rear of the station wagon.

"You must be anxious to reach the house and relax a little," Carol stated and glanced at her husband. "Do you want to drive, Chad?"

"Yes. You can ride in the front with me, Lanna," he stated.

"No, I'll ride in back," she insisted, not wanting to usurp Carol's position. "Carol can sit with you."

"No, I insist," said the blonde, adding her voice to Chad's. "How can I properly supervise Chad's driving if I'm not sitting in the back seat?" she laughed.

Against her better judgment, Lanna allowed herself to be helped into the front passenger's seat while Carol climbed in the back. As Chad was sliding behind the wheel, Hawk crossed in front of the car and walked toward the parked airplane where the cowboy was fastening the tiedowns. He didn't even glance in the direction of the car when Chad reversed it onto the graded road leading toward the ranch buildings.

"You'll like the house, Lanna. It's old, but it was built to last for generations," Carol stated, then kept up a steady flow of conversation during the drive.

When Chad stopped the car in front of a large, sprawling house, Lanna understood what Carol had meant. Built of stucco and rough wooden beams, it was a solid structure in keeping with the rustic surroundings.

Chad walked around the car to open Lanna's door and help her out—then Carol's door. The blonde started to lead the way to the covered entrance, but Lanna hesitated.

"What about our luggage?" she asked Chad.

"One of the hands will carry it in," he said and slipped a hand under her elbow to guide her to the thick oak door.

The thick walls of the house kept the interior cool. The change in temperature was the first thing Lanna noticed when she stepped into the tiled foyer. White walls added to the spacious feeling, and archways led to the two rooms and a hallway that branched off from the foyer. The room was sparsely furnished; a Navaho blanket splashed color on one wall, while a polished walnut table held an urn of dried flowers and seeds. Lanna guessed that this subtle blend of nature and Indian culture set the atmosphere carried throughout the house.

"Katheryn!" Carol called. "Chad has arrived with Lanna." She started into the room off the left archway. The pressure of Chad's hand on her elbow indicated to Lanna that they would follow.

The living room was dominated by a large fireplace of tawny stone. A grand piano stood near a set of veranda doors. The elegance of the room was not lessened by the odd pieces of Indian pottery that decorated the polished wood side tables, along with bronze sculptures of wildlife.

Lanna's attention was diverted when the slimly regal figure rose to greet her. An aloof smile curved Katheryn Faulkner's mouth. Since their first meeting, there had always been that air of reserve about the woman. Lanna had never been entirely certain that John's wife believed she and her husband were just friends, and no more. Lanna was uncomfortable in the woman's presence. She had strong second thoughts about her decision to accept Chad's invitation to visit the ranch to rest and recuperate from her recent illness.

"I hope you both had a good trip. Would you like some coffee or tea?" Katheryn inquired.

"No, I don't care for any, thank you," Lanna refused and continued to stand. She was conscious of her awkward position as John's friend in his widow's home.

"I think I'd like some coffee, Mother," Chad said, accepting the offer.

"I'll get it for you," Carol volunteered.

"Have a seat, Lanna." Chad motioned in the direction of the cinnamon-colored armchairs.

"Would you like me to show you to your room?" Katheryn inserted when Lanna hesitated a fraction of a second. "You would probably like to freshen up after your trip."

"Yes, thank you," Lanna agreed quickly.

"This way." Katheryn walked through another archway and followed a wide corridor.

There seemed to be a maze of interconnecting hallways and rooms branching out from them. Lanna was certain she would become lost on her own. Finally, Katheryn stopped and pushed open a door.

"This is the master bedroom, which has its own private bath and doors to the veranda," Katheryn explained as she led the way inside the room. "I hope it's satisfactory."

"It's beautiful." The room was nearly as large as the living room in Lanna's apartment. Besides the heavy bedroom furniture, there was a matching loveseat and chair, and a secretary's desk. "I hope you don't object to my coming here." Lanna still felt guilty and wanted to make amends. "I'm sure you don't feel like entertaining guests while you're in mourning, so please don't feel obligated to make any special effort on my behalf."

"I have no objections to your visit," Katheryn insisted. "Chad explained you need rest. I'm pleased you felt you could find it here." The statement didn't ease Lanna's sense of discomfort despite its welcome sound. A noise outside the room caused Katheryn to turn toward the hall door. Hawk stood within its frame, holding Lanna's suitcases under his arm. "Bring Miss Marshall's luggage in, Hawk." Katheryn spoke to him as if he were a servant. His mouth quirked even as he complied with the order, moving in his silent way past

Lanna to the center of the room. "I'll send someone to unpack for you, Lanna," Katheryn stated.

"No. There's no need," Lanna refused gently. "I'll do it myself. Thank you." She was becoming too accustomed to other people doing things for her.

"As you wish." Katheryn's vaguely haughty acceptance of the decision made Lanna more uncomfortable.

All of Lanna's uncertainties returned as Katheryn left the room. She wasn't given time to dwell on them as Hawk reminded her of his presence by asking, "Where would you like me to put your suitcases?"

"Anywhere," she said in a rush of irritation. "By the bed."

Hawk set them down near the foot of the bed, then turned to face her. "Don't be fooled by her."

"What?" She frowned at his confusing remark.

"You aren't wanted here any more than I am," he replied.

Lanna started to deny that, but she, too, felt that despite Chad, she wasn't really welcome in this house. And she definitely didn't blame Katheryn for resenting her.

"I told you once that J. B. was a taker," Hawk continued. "He was an amateur compared to Chad. J. B. always felt remorse. Chad doesn't give a damn about anyone. He'll help himself to everything you've got."

"That isn't true," she denied swiftly.

"You've been warned." Hawk shrugged to indicate it wasn't important to him whether she believed him or not. "I just hope you know what you're signing the next time you affix your signature to a document."

"Are you implying that Chad would try to cheat me?" Lanna demanded.

Her anger seemed to amuse him. "I'm not implying anything. I'm saying he'll take everything you've got if you're stupid enough to let him."

He lifted a hand to touch the point of his hat brim, inclining his head briefly in her direction. The courtesy mocked her. She took an indignant breath, but Hawk was already walking out of the room. Finding nothing to vent her anger on, Lanna spun away from the door and curled her fingernails into the palms of her hands. Hawk had planted a seed of doubt in her mind, and she resented him for doing it.

Chapter XIV

"Good morning." Carol was alone at the table when Lanna entered the sunlight-filled morning room. "I thought I was the only one who overslept this morning. You still don't look like you're completely awake."

"I'm not sure if I am," Lanna admitted and poured a glass of fresh-squeezed orange juice from the pitcher on the sideboard. "I was more tired than I realized."

"I'm glad I don't have to eat alone. Chad's in the study working already, and Katheryn is still writing out thank-you's to everyone who sent sympathy cards," Carol explained. "Did you have any trouble finding your way here this morning?"

"I made a couple of wrong turns. I'm glad Katheryn took me on a tour of the house yesterday, or I would have been totally lost." Lanna glanced over the array of pastries and muffins.

"You could have always followed your nose. Roseanne makes an excellent Spanish omelet. Shall I ask her to fix you one?" Carol suggested.

"No. Coffee and a roll are enough for me. I have to watch my weight." Lanna was envious of the wand-slim figure of her blonde breakfast companion, and of the omelet, hash browns, and coffee cake on Carol's plate.

Choosing a blueberry muffin, Lanna balanced it on the saucer of her coffee cup and carried it to the rattan breakfast table. "Did Chad say how long he'd be working?" Lanna asked. Then she explained: "I was hoping he might show me around the ranch today."

"He didn't say." Carol concentrated her attention on her plate of food, suddenly exhibiting a lot of interest in what she was eating. "But I'm sure he'll show you around if you ask."

There was something in Carol's voice that made Lanna suspect jealousy. It didn't do any good to silently tell herself she was being overly sensitive.

"Maybe I shouldn't ask," Lanna decided, then sliced the muffin apart with a gesture that hinted at her irritation. "I've monopolized his time enough."

"Oh, Chad doesn't mind," Carol assured her quickly.

"But you do," Lanna blurted out, then tried to explain why she had said it. "After all, why wouldn't you want to spend as much time as you can with your husband when he's going to be here only a few days? It's natural."

"I admit that I'm not with Chad as often as most wives are with their husbands, but there are reasons. Chad knows I understand," Carol insisted. "Even in the short time you've known him, you must have discovered what a wonderful man he is. He has been a wonderful husband to me, even though—" Carol stopped as her fork fiddled indifferently with a bite-sized portion of the fluffy omelet.

Curiosity made Lanna prompt: "Even though what?"

When Carol looked up, there was sadness in her eyes. "Even though I can't give him any more children," she admitted in a small voice, then made a valiant attempt to smile. "He says it doesn't matter. We have Johnny. He is a healthy, happy boy, but I know Chad wanted more children. He never liked being an only child. But after three miscarriages, the doctor insisted we shouldn't try anymore."

"You could always adopt a child," Lanna suggested and wondered if she had discovered the reason the two of them weren't as close as they could be.

"It wouldn't be the same." Carol rejected the idea with a brief shake of her head, sunlight from the east windows scattering beams of gold through her hair. "Chad has mentioned it, but I don't want to raise someone else's child. It probably sounds crazy to you, doesn't it?"

"No. I think I can understand what you mean." However, Lanna also thought they were depriving each other of the happiness they sought.

"Chad understands, too, which is part of what makes him so wonderful." Pleasure radiated from Carol's face, animating features that had been so serious a moment earlier. "So you see why I don't object if he feels it's his duty to show you around the ranch? That's a pretty tall order, though."

"I don't expect him to show me around the whole ranch," Lanna clarified her suggestion. "I didn't realize how huge it was until Hawk pointed out the boundaries when we flew in. All I had in mind was a tour of the ranch yard and the immediate vicinity. I could snoop around on my own, but I don't feel right doing that. But if Chad's busy, maybe I can ask somebody else."

"Dad would take you, but he said something yesterday about going into town today on business of some sort. Hawk could show you around. He knows every inch of this place like the back of his hand," Carol stated.

"Yes, well . . . "—Lanna breathed in deeply, finding that suggestion not at all pleasing—". . . I'd rather not go anywhere with him."

Her reply sparked Carol's temper. "I never thought you were the kind who would be prejudiced. Obviously, I was wrong!"

"Prejudiced? I'm not prejudiced," Lanna denied. "I just don't happen to like Hawk. He . . . he rubs me the wrong way." Confusion surfaced over the cause of the accusation. "Why should I be prejudiced?"

"A lot of people look down on him because he's half-Navaho. I don't know why I thought you would be different." Carol continued to eye Lanna with wary doubt.

"I didn't know he was half-Indian. I never even suspected it." She leaned back in her chair, running the information over in her mind to see if it bothered her; instead, it started her wondering about other things. "Is that why Chad doesn't like him?"

When she looked up, Carol was staring at her. "You honestly don't know who Hawk is, do you? Didn't J. B. ever mention anything about him?"

"John? No. Why should he?" Lanna was becoming more and more confused.

"Because Hawk is his son."

"Are you serious?" It was Lanna's turn to search the face of the woman seated across the table. She looked away, realizing it was true and wondering why Hawk—or Chad—hadn't told her.

"Yes. Hawk's mother was a Navaho woman. She was J. B.'s mistress for several years. I was just a small child at the time, so I don't know the details, only what I've heard." Carol became thoughtful, her attention turning inward. "Hawk's mother died—in a snowstorm, I think. Anyway, J. B. didn't want to leave Hawk with her relatives to be raised as an Indian, so he brought him back to the ranch. Naturally, he had too much respect for Katheryn to ask her to raise him."

"Didn't she know about him?" Lanna questioned.

"Oh, yes." Carol nodded. "From what I understand, it was common knowledge that J. B. was keeping this Navaho woman. The ranch is like a very small town. Everybody knows everybody else's business. I doubt that J. B. ever actually told Katheryn himself. I'm certain he tried to be discreet. That's the kind of man he was, but she knew. No one ever talked about Hawk in front of her that I can remember. They always pretended he was an orphan. So did she."

"But who looked after him? Did someone take him into their home?" She steered the conversation back to Carol's original track.

"J. B. asked my parents to look after him. J. B. and my father were very close, so naturally he turned to him. Hawk lived with us. We were raised practically as brother and sister."

"What happened between Hawk and Chad?" Lanna frowned. "There seems to be so much bad feeling between them."

"It's natural under the circumstances. Look at how much Chad had. He was recognized as J. B.'s son. He never publicly acknowledged Hawk. Granted, J. B. did compensate my parents for what it cost to raise Hawk. And he paid for his college education. But that isn't much, is it?" Her smile was sadly rueful. "There was the fact that Hawk was not only illegitimate, but a half-breed, as well. Even if J. B. Faulkner was his father, his mother was still a Navaho."

"I can understand that there would be rivalry—resentment—but such total mistrust . . ." From what Carol had told her, there didn't seem to be sufficient cause, and it puzzled Lanna. "It goes beyond blind hatred. I can't help thinking there is a reason."

"There is," Carol sighed and pushed aside her plate of half-eaten food. "It's me."

"You?" Lanna wanted more of an explanation than that.

"Yes. Remember, I told you that Hawk and I were raised together. He was always 'big brother' and I was 'little sister'—at least that's the way I thought. Then, the summer when I was eighteen, I found out that Hawk wanted to marry me. He was in love with me." Carol paused to cup her hands around a cold cup of coffee. "Chad was always my 'knight in shining armor.' There was never anyone else I wanted to marry."

"And you turned Hawk down?"

"Yes. He didn't understand. He blamed Chad. There was a terrible fight. Chad beat him up, which only made things worse." Carol's bow-shaped lips were set in a straight line, grim with regret. "I tried to tell Hawk how sorry I was, but he wouldn't listen. I think he believes that I didn't want to marry him because he was a half-breed—therefore, not good enough."

"So he feels he's been cheated all the way around. Now I'm part of it," Lanna realized. "I suppose I inherited what rightfully should have been his. Did John leave him anything in his will? Did he acknowledge him at all?" She couldn't believe that John had left Hawk out.

"J. B. gave him half of this ranch. As far as I know, J. B. didn't claim him as his illegitimate son. There was a cash bequest, too, but I don't know what the amount was." Carol held her gaze. "Lanna, I have to be honest. I think Hawk had more right to the rest of the inheritance than you did."

"Yes." Lanna was inclined to agree with Carol, but she didn't know what she could do about it. Was it her fault? Was it her problem to correct? Heaven knew she never wanted John to leave her all this money. Why

had he willed it to her instead of his own flesh and
blood? If John didn't want Hawk to receive it, should
she go against his wishes and give it to Hawk?

It was confusing. She simply didn't know what was
right or fair. Too much had happened lately. She was
tired, both mentally and physically. Chad had suggested that she come to the ranch to rest and relax.
This was only her first full day, and already she felt
worse instead of better.

She took a sip of her coffee. "It's cold," she grimaced
and rose from her chair to pour a fresh cup. "Would
you like yours warmed up, Carol?"

"No, thanks," she refused and pushed her chair away
from the table. "I started a letter to Johnny yesterday. I
want to finish it so I can get it in the mail." She started
toward the door, then paused to half-turn. "Lanna, I
didn't mean to hurt your feelings when I said that."

"You didn't," Lanna assured her.

"Good, because I'd like us to be friends." Carol
smiled.

"So would I," Lanna agreed.

"See you later." She lifted a delicately boned hand in
a graceful wave and disappeared through the archway.

After adding hot coffee to the lukewarm liquid in her
cup, Lanna returned to her chair. Halfheartedly, she
buttered the muffin, but by now her appetite was gone.
A set of footsteps approached the morning room.
Lanna recognized Chad's brisk strides and looked up as
he entered.

"Good morning. I just saw Carol. She told me you
were here," he stated and walked to the sideboard to
pour himself a cup of coffee from the silver urn. "I
decided to join you for coffee."

"Have you finished your paperwork?" she asked.

"The bulk of it." He pulled out the chair nearest her
and sat down. His tawny eyes assessed her in a glance.

"Didn't you sleep well last night? You look tired. Beautiful, but tired."

"Flatterer," Lanna mocked him. "Actually, I slept like a log. I can't remember the last time I slept so late." Yes, she could—that morning after John had died, but she didn't mention it. If Chad remembered, he didn't correct her.

"You obviously needed it." He sipped at his coffee, then glanced at the muffin Lanna had barely nibbled. "Is that all you're having for breakfast?"

"I'm not hungry." Not any more, at least, she thought. "I should exercise to work up an appetite."

"You're supposed to rest while you're here," Chad reminded her.

"That will become boring," she insisted with a laugh.

"After a while it will, but I want you to take it easy for the first few days."

"You sound like a doctor," Lanna reproved. "As a matter of fact, I was going to ask you to take me on a tour of the ranch."

"What for?" His wide smile seemed to regard her proposal with amused curiosity.

"Just to get an idea of what's going on." She shrugged. "I thought it would be interesting to see how it operates."

"This ranch practically runs by itself. Rawlins has managed it for years. It's all very routine, very boring. I don't think it would interest you." He set his cup down, an air of finality in his action, as well as in his words.

"I don't know that I was really interested. Closer to curious, probably," Lanna replied. "I thought I'd like to poke around the buildings and explore the country around here. I haven't been horseback riding in a couple of years. It should be fun."

"I suppose we could do that," Chad agreed. "I can have one of the hands saddle us a couple of horses. We can leave right after lunch. How does that sound?"

"It sounds fine." She nodded.

"You aren't very enthusiastic." Tipping his head to one side, he eyed her curiously. "Is something bothering you?" he guessed. "Do you want to tell me about it?"

Hesitating, Lanna gripped the sides of her coffee cup. "I know Hawk is John's son."

"His bastard, you mean," Chad snapped and immediately looked away, seeking to control his sudden flash of anger. "Sorry, but that's what he is—by name and disposition." When he turned to face her, his smile was stiff. "Now that you've discovered the Faulkner family's skeleton in the closet, what difference does it make?"

"It makes a lot of difference," Lanna declared in agitation. "He is . . . was John's son. I inherited what was rightfully his."

"Rightfully? What makes you think it was *rightfully* his?" he challenged. "What would a half-breed do with all that? John knew what he was doing when he left it to you. Hawk is nothing but a saddle tramp. J. B. threw away his money trying to turn that half-breed into a white man. There isn't an ounce of ambition in his body. He works a little, goes back 'to the blanket' for a while, then comes back to work a little more. He's a worthless no-good who doesn't deserve what he's got."

It seemed a sweeping condemnation. "He appears to be intelligent—" Lanna began.

"Intelligent? He's educated. J. B. paid for that— enrolled him in the finest eastern university, and what happens? Hawk quit before he gets his degree and all

that money goes down the drain. Is that intelligent?"
Chad arched an eyebrow.

"I didn't know."

"Don't feel sorry for him, Lanna. You'd just be
wasting your time," he told her. "J. B. would have set
him up in business, but all Hawk wanted to own was the
clothes on his back, a good saddle, and a Navaho
convertible—more commonly known as a pickup."

"I see," Lanna murmured.

"I hope you do," Chad stated. His handsome
features softened, charming her with the magic of his
smile. "Would you still like to go riding this afternoon?
I promise not to give you any more lectures."

"I would enjoy it." She returned his smile. "But I
don't want to be guilty of monopolizing your time, so
why don't we invite Carol to come along—and your
mother?"

"So you want me to share the pleasure of your
company," he joked, but he wasn't really joking.
Her pulse quickened a little with the temptation
to say no.

Only she didn't. "That's right." Lanna forced the
brightness to stay in her voice.

"If that's what you want, I'll ask them," Chad agreed
without enthusiasm. He finished his coffee and stood
up to leave. "I have a couple of phone calls to make. I'll
see you at lunch, if not before." As he passed her chair,
he paused long enough to lay a hand on her shoulder,
then left the room.

Lanna was glad he hadn't argued about inviting the
others because he could have talked her into letting the
ride remain a twosome. That was the problem. He
could talk her into most anything, she realized. Was she
being too trusting? How did she know if what Chad
said was true?

"Damn you, Hawk, for putting these questions in my mind," she murmured aloud.

That evening Lanna was acutely aware of every minute she had spent in the saddle during her afternoon ride with the Faulkner family. It had been an exhilarating experience, filled with laughter and gaiety and the excitement of new sights. But her muscles, unaccustomed to such exercise, ached at the slightest move she made.

Not even the soothing Brahms melody Katheryn was playing on the piano made Lanna forget her soreness. When the last note faded into the silence of the living room, Lanna forced her protesting muscles to make her stand. Her action drew Chad's gaze.

"I think I'm going to take a couple of aspirins, soak in a tub for an hour, and then fall into bed." Her attempt to laugh at her condition was forced.

"Can you make it to your room?" Chad teased. "Maybe I should help you."

"I'll manage," Lanna assured him dryly.

"We shouldn't have ridden so long. I hope you feel better in the morning," Carol offered.

"I will. Good night." It was meant for all of them. There was a responding chorus. Katheryn's fingers were already gliding over the piano keys with the opening chords of another piece as Lanna left the room.

Once in her room, Lanna didn't waste any time filling the tub with steaming-hot water and adding scented oil. Shedding her clothes, she climbed into the tub and stretched out full length to rest her shoulders against the curved porcelain back of the tub. The liquid heat flowing over, under, and around every inch of her body sent relief surging through her cramped and aching muscles. She closed her eyes in utter contentment and let the bath water wash the soreness away.

The water had turned cool before she summoned enough energy to lather her skin with soap and then rinse. When she stepped from the tub, the quick evaporation of water chilled her. Lanna rubbed at the shivers with a heavy bath towel, its roughness stimulating the return of warmth.

Slipping into the full-length robe of silver satin, Lanna entered her large bedroom. The bath had isolated her soreness, confining it to a few places instead of her whole body. She felt refreshed, not nearly as bone-weary as she had earlier. The softness of the bed didn't look quite as inviting, but neither did she feel like getting dressed and rejoining the others in the living room.

They were still there. She could hear the strains of the sonata Katheryn was playing as it drifted into the room through the veranda door that was standing ajar. Lanna crossed the room to close it before a barrage of insects became attracted to the lights. When her hand closed around the brass doorknob, it hesitated. The clean, dry scent of fresh air wafted through the opening. Outside, the quiet beauty of the night beckoned to her.

Lanna wandered onto the veranda, silently closing the door to the master bedroom. The stone floor still retained the warmth from the day's heat. It felt good beneath her bare feet. She walked to the edge of the veranda and rested a hand on the rough timber post supporting the beamed roof as she gazed at the skyful of stars. They gleamed sharp and crystal bright, a million of them appearing so close that she had only to reach up to touch one. There were no city lights or smog to obscure the breathtaking spectacle of nature's display.

A night bird called from the trees crowding the lawn around the house. Its trill blended with the classical piano music drifting into the night from the opened window in the living room. Lanna's gaze wandered to the trees, trying to locate the bird, but not really expecting to succeed.

Beneath the dark shadows cast by spreading tree branches, the darkness was broken by the flare of a match. Its flame made a short, ascending arc before its light was shielded to a dim glow. Then it was out, leaving behind a tiny red point. Lanna tensed as she realized someone was out there. The red dot was the burning tip of a cigarette.

It moved. The dark outline of a man's shape stepped out from the shadows and moved toward her. Lanna knew it was Hawk by the way he seemed to glide so silently across the space, not hurrying, yet covering ground with lithe ease. She swallowed and wondered what had caused the sudden tightness in her throat.

When he stopped near her, the starlight played over the hard angles and planes of his expressionless face. The night added to the dark hue of his blue eyes. Lanna was unnerved by the steadiness of his look.

"What are you doing out here?" Her voice trembled on the accusation.

"Listening to the music." He nonchalantly leaned a shoulder against the rough-cut post and took a drag from the cigarette, cupping it in his hand. "Katheryn was studying to be a concert pianist before she met J. B. She gave it up to marry him. Did you know that?"

"No, I didn't know that," Lanna admitted in a guarded tone, because she knew something else . . . about him—who he was.

There was a long moment of silence, dominated by the piano music. Lanna stared straight ahead, aware that Hawk was studying her profile. She was uneasy, wondering if she should tell him and how she should word it.

"You know, don't you?" Hawk mused.

"No, I honestly didn't know Katheryn had studied piano seriously—with intentions of making it a career," Lanna insisted.

"I'm not talking about that. Someone has told you who I am," he guessed.

"That you are John's son? Yes, I know." There wasn't any point in denying it. Her gaze wandered nervously, looking everywhere except at him. She was on edge, and she didn't quite understand why she had wanted it out in the open.

"Carol told you," Hawk guessed again, just as accurately.

"How did you know?" Lanna turned to him in surprise.

"It was a simple matter of the process of elimination. " He took a drag on the cigarette and blew the smoke sideways into the night. "I knew Chad wouldn't tell you. Neither would Katheryn. Rawlins wasn't around, and none of the ranch hands would blurt it out. So . . . that leaves only Carol."

"I suppose." But Lanna didn't completely follow his logic. "Why couldn't Chad have told me?"

"If he was going to tell you, he'd have done it before now. Maybe he thought you wouldn't find out." His mouth twisted in a wry line. "He should have known nothing is secret or sacred here. It's somehow fitting that his wife is the one who told you, isn't it? Does he now?"

"Yes. I asked him about you," Lanna admitted.

Hawk chuckled. "And I'm sure he voiced his opinion regarding my character."

"You didn't spare your opinion when you made

accusations against Chad," Lanna reminded him stiffly, but he wasn't paying any attention to her. His head was tipped to one side, in a listening attitude.

"Hear that?" His sharp gaze swung back to her, a faint smile alleviating the harsh line of his mouth. "I knew she'd play it." Lanna realized he was referring to the *Viennese Waltz* being played on the piano. The cigarette was dropped and crushed beneath the heel of his boot.

Before she guessed his intention, his hand was cupping itself to the curve of her waist, and her left wrist was taken, his fingers pressing into the center of her palm. In the next second, she was guided into waltz steps. He danced smoothly, without any flourish, as he circled her around the stone floor of the veranda.

Lanna tripped once, on the jutting edge of a stone. His hand moved to the back of her waist to steady her, then remained there to hold her more fully against his length. Her senses were being affected by more than just romantic music and the starshine. Through the satin material of her robe, she was vibrantly conscious of the sinew-hard column of his thighs pressing against hers. The sensitive points of her breasts tingled each time they brushed the dark blue cotton of the shirt that encased the solid breadth of his chest. His fingers were spread across the small of her back, melting in their warmth. His cheeks were smoothly bronze, the heady fragrance of some male aftershave clinging to his skin.

Conversation became mandatory for Lanna. "How did you know Katheryn would play this?"

"Because it's my favorite, and she knows it." Hawk studied her upturned face through half-closed eyes. "Whenever she thinks I might be out here, she plays it for me—to remind me that I'm outside looking in."

Lanna looked for bitterness, but didn't find any.

"Don't you mind?" The pattern of their steps had grown smaller, staying within an invisible square on the veranda floor.

"It doesn't matter to me what her reasons might be for playing it. I just like the song. Are you disappointed?"

"Why would I be?" Lanna frowned.

"I thought you might expect me to be drinking firewater and dancing to the beat of Indian drums instead of waltzing in the starlight with a beautiful woman and getting drunk on the way she feels in my arms."

His softly spoken words raced through her like a flash-fire. Its heat scalded her and sent her pivoting out of his arms as she tried to bring her leaping senses back under control. His compliment had disrupted her thinking, tearing her mental process to shreds and leaving only the physical in tact. Her heart was drumming against her ribs, as wild as the Indian tom-toms he had referred to.

Lanna tried to take a calming breath, but it became stuck in her throat when his hands circled her waist from behind. She caught at them with her fingers when they met in front. She had already revealed too much of the way he disturbed her by running. She decided against struggling while she collected her wits.

"Were you surprised by what I said or the way I feel?" Hawk questioned in that same sensually soft voice.

"You rarely say anything. Then to come out with something like that—yes, I was surprised," she admitted in a husky tremor.

The soft cheeks of her bottom felt the hard outline of his thighs. His body warmth heated flesh that was already feverish. Lanna felt threatened by the confusing sensations he was arousing—threatened, yet exhilarated.

"Are you surprised that I can express myself?" he mocked gently.

"I know you are educated," she replied somewhat defensively.

"Educated. Yes, I have been educated in the primitive English language. The language of The People—the Navaho—is much more exact and imaginative. Look." He withdrew a hand from around her waist to point to the northern sky. "See the Big Dipper and the North Star?"

"Yes." She wasn't concentrating on them too well, because his cheek and jaw were pressed against her hair. His breath was scented with tobacco smoke, warm and fragrantly pungent.

"The Navaho word for 'north' is *náhookǫs*. Literally translated, it is 'one stiff slender object makes a revolution,' referring to the rotation of the Big Dipper around the North Star. It is more than a direction. It's an identification. English is a passive language of nouns and adjectives, vague and imprecise. Navaho is a language of verbs, exact and precise. A Navaho can never say 'I'm holding it.' He must distinguish with verbs whether the object he is holding is long, like a stick; something bundled like hay or clothes; or an animate object, like a woman."

Her heart did a somersault at the sudden intimacy of his tone. Lanna turned in the half-circle of his arm, facing him as she mentally struggled to direct the conversation to other, less disturbing topics.

"Why didn't you go to John's funeral, Hawk?" She abruptly changed the subject.

His dark lashes came down once to cover the blue of his eyes, a lazy amusement revealed in the action, although his expression didn't change. He kept his hand resting lightly on her waist, but he didn't attempt to close the small distance between them.

"I'm not interested in looking at dead bodies, only living ones." He reached up to let his fingers trace Lanna's hairline along her temple. He followed it to her cheekbone, then explored its classic angle, curling his fingers to rub their knuckles across her cheek to her jaw.

"Will you be serious?" Lanna protested and struggled to ignore the caress of his hand. "John was your father."

"Biologically, yes. He assumed financial responsibility for my upbringing, so not even the Navaho can say that he 'stole me,'" he mused. "Perhaps I didn't go because the Navaho aversion for dead things was too deeply embedded in my subconscious. The truth is"—Hawk paused, a crooked smile slanting his mouth—"I'm too much of an Indian to be truly white. And I'm too white to be completely Indian. I like the creature comforts of the white man's world—classical music, fine brandy, soft beds, the stimulation of a cultivated conversationalist, and beautiful women. But I need space, vast stretches of land to roam, and freedom."

"Is that why you quit college before you received your degree?" Lanna felt the vibrations of her throat when she spoke, his hand lightly stroking the sensitive underside of her chin and jaw.

"You know about that, too?" A brow lifted in amused surprise, then straightened to its normal arch. "At the time I quit, I thought it was because I wanted to punish my father after I discovered that he was ashamed to acknowledge me as his son. But now I don't think that was the reason."

"Then why?"

"Boredom."

Her long hair curled around her neck, getting in his way. So he tucked it behind her ear and smoothed it off her shoulders, exposing her neck to his exploring hand. The pulse in her throat fluttered beneath his fingertips. There was such casual mastery in his caressing fingers that Lanna felt helplessly captivated. It wasn't exactly a frightening sensation.

"Why did you come back here?" she asked. "If . . . if you knew the way everyone felt, why—"

"Because this land is my home. Why should I let them drive me away from it?" Hawk countered with logic rather than bitterness. "Besides, if I wasn't around, that family would fall apart. They need me—the proverbial black sheep, someone they can collectively hate. Right now they can blame me for their unhappiness. But if I wasn't around, they would have to find someone else—probably you."

As his hand pushed aside the neckline of her robe, he bent his head to let his mouth explore the place at the base of her throat where her pulse beat so wildly beneath the skin. The provocative investigation choked off any protest Lanna might have considered making. She did splay her hands across his chest in weak resistance. It soon faded, although her hands remained there. The nuzzling bite of his teeth teased her skin, sending quivers through her nerves. When he pushed more of her robe aside to reveal her shoulder bone, Lanna shuddered openly, her defenses undermined and crumbling.

"You taste clean and fresh, like soap." His mouth formed the words against her throat.

"I just bathed." She heard the throb of desire in her voice and felt confused that this was happening to her—without warning.

But there had been warnings, only she had blundered

on ahead instead of running. Her hands slid to his middle as she swayed toward him, a captive of the raw, searing passion he had aroused within her.

Her head was tipped back, lolling to one side, allowing Hawk the freedom he had said he wanted while she enjoyed the liberty he took. When his hands parted the wrapped front of her robe, Lanna reveled in the license she had given him. Her breasts swelled under the cupping caress of his hands while his lips wandered upward to the lobe of her ear, nibbling at it with his teeth.

Turning her head, Lanna went in search of that mouth that was setting every part of her aflame except her moist and trembling lips. A scorching fire ran through her veins when she found them and succumbed to their male domination. Beneath her robe, his hands curved around to her back and gathered her close, crushing her bared breasts against the cotton weave of his shirt.

A knocking echoed onto the veranda. At first, Lanna thought it was her heart tripping over her ribs. Then it was followed by a woman's voice calling her name. Hawk lifted his head, his gaze burning hungrily over her face.

"They are looking for you," he said. "In a couple of minutes, they'll come out here. Do you want me to stay?" "They" would undoubtedly mean Chad, Lanna realized. She went cold at the thought of what Chad would do to Hawk if he found him here. Fresh in her mind was Carol's statement that long ago Chad and Hawk had gotten into a terrible fight. Lanna didn't want to be the cause of any more bad blood between these two brothers, not when she was attracted to each. Hawk watched her thoughts chasing across her expression and a shutter closed on his. "No, I can see you don't want me to be here," he concluded and set her away from him, straightening the front of her robe.

"Hawk—" Lanna wanted to explain.

"Sit over there in that lawn chair." With a nod of his head, he indicated the chaise longue near the house wall while he tightened the knot of her sash. He had switched off all emotion. "When Chad shows up, tell him you dozed off in the chair."

"But you—"

"He'll never see me," he assured her dryly and moved silently away, keeping to the shadows of the house and melting away into the darkness.

The sound of a door opening and closing, and Chad calling her name, prodded Lanna into action. Her bare feet made no sound on the stone floor as she hurried to the lounge chair. She had barely sat down when the veranda door from her bedroom opened.

"Lanna?" Blinded by the brightness of the interior lights, Chad didn't immediately see her sitting in the shadows.

"Yes. I'm over here." She swung her feet to the floor as if she was just rising, and she lifted a hand to smooth her mussed hair. "Did you call me a minute ago? I guess I dozed off." She used the lie Hawk had provided.

"We wondered where you had disappeared to." He was at her side in an instant. "Carol stopped by your room to be sure you were all right before she went to bed. But you weren't there. And you didn't answer when she called. I guess we panicked. What are you doing out here? I thought you were going to 'fall into bed.'" He grinned.

"I came out for some fresh air. It's a beautiful night." A trace of defiance crept into her voice.

Chad glanced into the night, catching the shimmer of

stars beyond the veranda roof. "It is lovely. I hadn't realized it." He took her hand and folded it warmly between both of his. "Would you like to take a walk?"

"No." She refused his invitation with a quick shake of her head and self-consciously pulled her hand free. "I am tired," Lanna insisted. "Besides, I don't have any shoes on. If you don't mind"—she straightened from the chair; it wasn't difficult to feign tiredness— "I'm going to call it a night. And this time, I'm going to bed."

He moved to block her way. "Don't go wandering off like that anymore, Lanna, not without letting someone know."

She didn't like his tone of voice or his possessive attitude. "Chad, I just stepped outside my bedroom door. I'm certainly not going to ask anyone's permission to do that."

"Of course not. It's just that . . . well, I was worried about you," he appeased.

"What could possibly happen to me out here?" Lanna frowned. "You make it sound as if I'm in some kind of danger." She released a short, incredulous laugh and walked around him. "Good night, Chad."

He half-turned to watch her. "Have a good night, Lanna."

As she turned to close the veranda door, her gaze strayed beyond Chad, unconsciously searching the shadows. She let a faint smile touch her lips when her gaze returned to Chad, then closed the door and pulled the drapes to shut out the night. When she glanced at the bed, she touched her mouth with her fingertips, still feeling Hawk's kiss imprinted on it.

Chapter XV

Sighing, Lanna crossed to the bed and untied the sash of her robe. A pair of silk and lace long pajamas was laid across the foot of the double bed, which looked big and empty tonight. Lanna shook her head to rid her mind of the thought that followed.

Behind her, there was a faint click. She turned to see the drapes billowing out from the veranda door. Hadn't it latched when she closed it? She took a step toward the door, pulling the front of her robe shut.

Hawk slipped silently through the opening of the drapes. He had taken off his hat and was holding it at his side. Pausing inside the door, he made a leisurely study of her from head to toe.

"You can tell me to leave." An eyebrow was raised in silent inquiry.

Lanna moved forward. "Hawk, out there . . . I didn't want you to stay because I didn't want anything to happen to you. The way Chad feels about you . . . I didn't want to be the cause of a confrontation between the two of you." She stopped while several feet were still separating them. "Why did you come back?"

"Because I want you. And I believe you want me." He started toward her.

For Lanna, it wasn't that simple. "I don't know if I want it this way. I've had all I want of sneaking around—little hole-in-the-corner affairs." She pivoted away, her fingers tightened on the satin front of her robe. "I don't like sneaking around behind people's backs."

"I don't know." His hat sailed past her onto the bed as his hands closed around the curve of her shoulders. He stepped closer, fitting his length to hers, and pressed himself firmly against her derriere. Bending his head, Hawk pressed his cheek along the side of her hair to murmur, "I like it behind your back."

Contact with the hard male shape of him set her a tremble with all the raw desires he'd aroused before. Still, she whispered, "You don't understand."

Hawk turned her around and threaded his hands through her hair to tip her head back. Lanna grasped his forearms, hanging on because her knees were so weak. She gazed into his bronze face, stamped with wild nobility and the proud arrogance of centuries of supremacy. The blue-black hair was springy and thick, curling over the collar of his shirt. But it was his eyes that enthralled Lanna more than his virile looks, eyes the color of the darkest sapphires, with their keen intelligence and flash of calculated recklessness.

"You think too much, Lanna," Hawk stated. "Just feel."

The pressure of his hands pulled her onto her toes to meet his descending mouth. The hard kiss took away her breath and her will to resist. She clung to him, her lips parting under the probing insistence of his tongue. It didn't matter that he was drawing away her strength, because she remembered from the last time that his hands, his arms, his body would give it all back later on.

Then Hawk was untangling his mouth from her lips and letting her down until the heels of her bare feet touched the floor. His arms shrugged out of the hold of her hands. Dazed, Lanna didn't protest until Hawk started to walk away from her.

"Where are you going?"

He sent her a brief look over his shoulder, but didn't stop. "To lock the door and turn off the lights. We don't want anyone wondering why you're still up and deciding to check on you."

The click of the bolt sliding into place sounded loud in the room. It was followed by a softer click that threw the room into total darkness. With the drapes drawn, no light entered the windows and Lanna couldn't see in the inky blackness. There was a rustle of clothing, but she couldn't tell where it came from. Disoriented by the sudden darkness, she stayed rooted in the place Hawk had left her, not certain which way to move.

There was no more rustle of clothing and her heart hammered loudly in her chest. A thin thread of panic ran through her. "Hawk?" she whispered, then jumped when his hand touched her arm.

"I'm here," he said.

"I couldn't see," she whispered and turned toward his voice, reaching out for him blindly in the dark.

Her hand made contact with the naked wall of hard flesh. A tiny moan of delight trembled from her throat as she swayed toward him. The sure, firm touch of his hands checked the movement, then moved to slip the loose robe off her shoulders and down her arms. Lanna let it fall to the floor, caring only about the shadowy male outline of the man standing in front of her.

An arm circled her waist, smooth and muscled. Then Hawk was lifting her up and cradling her in his arms, her hip pressed against the flat muscles of his bare stomach. Lanna curved a hand around his neck for balance, letting her fingers slide into the thickness of his black hair. In the darkness, she could barely make out the angles of his profile, but his rugged image was vivid in her mind. The rounded curve of her breast rubbed against his sinewy chest as he carried her unerringly to the bed. He laid her atop the covers and followed her down, stretching his length beside hers.

A bare leg was hooked across hers, as if he needed to pin her down. His mouth opened on her lips in a hungry kiss, raking his teeth over their soft, generous curves. The ravaging kiss fanned hot flames around her. Like a moth, Lanna had to get closer to the fire. Her hands slid around to the corded muscles of his back, trying to press him closer without success. Yet she was shattered by the sheer pleasure of having him beside her.

But the pleasure had only begun, as she discovered under the wayward caress of his hand. He cupped her breast, taking it in his palm and exploring its peak with his thumb, circling it until the nipple was hard and erect. While it was still aroused, his mouth trailed down her neck to the hollow of her throat, then finally to the rosy point. A stifled moan of searing delight whispered from her lips as Hawk rolled his tongue around it and nibbled at it gently with his teeth.

Sensation after sensation washed over her. While his mouth intimately investigated the perfection of her breasts, his hand continued its roaming. It wandered over her quivering stomach, paused to examine her navel, and teased her arching hips. These tormenting caresses brought her to an ardent, feverish pitch. Her lips scattered helpless kisses over his shoulder, her nails digging into the rippling muscles of his back in wild frustration.

She moved against him, straining for closer contact, her body recognizing him as the perfect lover. Driven mindless by this hard tension gnawing within her, she was clinging to him. Her face moved over his skin, so scented of the male and so solid. His hand returned to cup her chin and quiet her restless movements so his lips could claim her mouth again. Kissing her senseless, he wedged his knee between her legs and offered the throbbing lower half of her body partial satisfaction, swallowing her moans of wild need.

Lanna thought she was going to die with wanting before he finally shifted his weight onto her, spreading her legs as he pinned her to the covers with his heaviness. Relief cried through her nerves at his thrusting entrance, but it didn't last. She was swept into a tumultuous storm of sexual radiance and charged with a desire wilder than any she'd ever known. The fury of it grew and grew, lifting her higher and higher until she broke through the storm clouds and was bathed in the hot brilliance of the sun.

Male hands that had so expertly guided her hips now relaxed their biting grip on her cheeks and moved to the mattress on either side of her head, relieving her limp body of part of his crushing weight. When Hawk's mouth moved gently over her throbbing lips, Lanna could taste the salty beads of perspiration that had gathered on his upper lip and chin. Her hands could feel the faint tremors going through him, aftershocks of the shuddering climax.

His lips brushed along the curve of her cheek. "It was like this before. Do you remember?" His voice was husky, and rawly disturbed, like his deep, quivering breaths.

"It seemed more like a dream," Lanna admitted with soft regret. "Only it wasn't a dream."

"No. Not even a peyote dream." His lips curved in a quiet smile against her skin.

Using his arms to lever his chest off her, Hawk eased himself from between her legs and shifted to lie beside her. Lanna rolled onto her side to face him and reached

out to trace the contours of his face with her fingertips.
There was a silent claim of possession in the way his
hand moved to rest on her hip bone and maintain the
physical contact between them. She let her hand move
to the taut column of his neck, and sensuous black hair
curled over her fingers in the back.

"Your hair needs to be cut." It was a somewhat
absurd observation, but Lanna couldn't express the
awed wonder she was feeling.

"It keeps the sun off my neck," he replied.

He slid an arm around her shoulder to nestle her to
his side. When Lanna tried to bend her right leg to rest
it on his knees, a sore muscle made a searing protest.

"Mmm." The faint sound of pain escaped as she
involuntarily winced.

"Did I hurt you." There was a frown in his voice.

"No." Lanna managed to maneuver into the position
she wanted, then explained when her head was resting
in the crook of his shoulder: "I went riding today, and
it's been a while."

"Now you are sore." Hawk laughed silently against
her hair. "What you need is a good rubdown."

"Unfortunately, the only masseuse I know is in
Phoenix—a therapist at a local hospital, not at one of
the massage parlors," she added.

"Do you have any lotion in the bathroom?"

"Yes. Why?" Puzzled, she tipped her head back,
trying to see his face in the dark.

Hawk shifted her out of his arms and Lanna felt the
mattress spring back when he swung out of the bed.
"I've rubbed down many a sore horse in my time
without any complaints. I think I can take care of a
long-legged filly like you."

Raising herself up on her elbows, Lanna watched his
shadowy figure move across the dark interior toward
the bathroom. She heard the door open. A second

later, there was the click of the switch and the sudden
illumination that sent a rectangular patch of light
streaming into the bedroom. She had to briefly shield
her eyes from the brilliance, then heard the muted clink
of bottles.

Hawk didn't turn out the light when he left the room,
giving Lanna a glimpse of his nude form before the light
was behind him to send him into shadow. What she saw
made her hold her breath. Long and lean, his body was
all hard, copper-toned flesh, excitingly male. She
hadn't completely recovered when he stopped beside
the bed.

"We'd better pull the covers down or we'll get this oil
all over the spread. That might take some explaining,"
he reminded her.

Lanna sat up to roll the covers down to the foot of
the bed, then shifted to the middle of the mattress and
lay down. The patch of light from the bathroom came
over his shoulder to illuminate her. She felt his eyes
wandering over her and was a little shocked by her
complete lack of shyness.

"Roll over on your stomach," Hawk instructed.

"Why?" she protested, because she wouldn't be able
to look at him if she was on her stomach.

"It's usually the posterior that's sore from riding,"
Hawk mocked. Pink-cheeked, Lanna rolled onto her
stomach, pillowing her face on her hands. Self-
conscious and a little nervous in this position, she still
attempted to relax, but her muscles tensed when the
mattress dipped under Hawk's weight.

He started with her feet, spreading lotion over the
sole and arch, then rubbing it in with slow, firm strokes,
separating her toes. The sensation was altogether too
pleasant for Lanna to remain stiff under his soothing
touch. Her ankle was flexed and massaged as Hawk
worked his way to the calf of her leg. When his

kneading fingers reached the inside of her thighs, where she was the sorest, she flinched from the hands that bestowed a strange combination of pleasure and pain.

"Relax," he chided gently.

"That's easy for you to say," Lanna murmured, but she didn't resist again the hands manipulating her stiff muscles into a state of relaxation. "Don't you have any ambition, Hawk?"

"Are you planning to reform me?" He repeated the procedure on her other leg, starting with her foot and working up to her thigh.

"No." She smiled against her hand, and closed her eyes to savor the delicious tingling of her flesh. "I don't think I'd want you to be any different from the way you are. It's just that Chad mentioned it, and I . . . wondered if it was true."

"Do you mean you're doubting Chad? That's a step in the right direction," Hawk murmured the dry comment. "If by ambition, you mean a desire for power and excessive wealth, the answer is 'no,' I don't have any ambition."

Straddling her legs, he began rubbing the tender flesh of her derriere, massaging its dimpled cheeks. His touch both soothed and stimulated, impersonal yet intimate. Lanna tried to keep her pulse from running away with itself.

"Is something wrong?" Hawk questioned in an amused and knowing tone.

"As if you didn't know." She shifted under his hands, seeking to escape them, but he pressed her flat.

"Lie still. I'll behave."

Lanna obeyed and tried to divert her mind to thoughts other than those connected with this absorption with sensation. "Wouldn't you enjoy the challenge of running an enterprise? You own half the ranch now. What will you do with it?"

"What do you think I should do with it?"

"Why do you keep dodging my questions? You're worse than a politician," Lanna grumbled. "What was your major in college?"

"Business administration." Hawk paused before he added: "With a minor in political science."

"I might have known," she laughed softly. "You're a natural."

"So I've been told." His hands began working their magic on her waist and lower back. "I've had a lot of practice at riding the fence."

"Mmm, that feels good," Lanna murmured as his thumbs glided up her spine to the base of her neck. "I think Chad feels threatened by you. Is it because you are intelligent and educated, probably as capable of running Faulkner Enterprise as he is?"

"Chad has never had to learn to think on his feet. He's a plodder. He has to have a plan before he can act. If something upsets it, he becomes disorganized." Which wasn't a direct answer to her question. "If you have to talk, try a subject other than Chad," he advised and began pummeling her shoulder blades with the sides of his hands. Under the circumstances, Lanna couldn't talk about anything.

When he was finished, Hawk straightened to stand on his knees. "Roll over."

Lanna twisted around to lie on her back, facing him. Shifting his position, he began rubbing his lotion-slick hands on the taut cords just above her knees. Lanna watched the rippling muscles in his shoulders and sinewy arms with growing fascination. The light from the bathroom gleamed on the pale copper hue of his skin and glistened on the blackness of his hair.

Stimulated by a slow-growing desire, she became sensitive to his touch. Instinct prompted her hips to move in silent invitation to his massaging hands. Hawk ignored it. She might have controlled the leaping fire inside if she hadn't seen he was becoming aroused.

"Hawk." She reached for his hand to draw it to her breast and pull him forward.

There wasn't any need to say more. His mouth covered hers with drugging force. It was a spontaneous combustion of passion as Hawk fitted himself to her arching hips. He dragged his mouth away from her lips to bury it in her throat long enough to murmur, "If you wake up stiff and sore in the morning, you have the consolation of knowing the others will assume it's from riding, instead of being ridden. But how the hell am I supposed to explain it if I wind up sore?"

But he didn't expect an answer from Lanna. Which was just as well, because she wasn't capable of giving him one. Passion whipped their bodies to the point of exhaustion. Physically drained and emotionally spent, Lanna fell asleep in his arms. In repose, her face was soft with satisfaction.

As he had done the last time, Hawk slipped silently away when the first streaks of dawn were lacing the night sky. The sun was high before Lanna awakened to discover she was alone in the bed. Her disappointment was tempered by the knowledge that it had to be that way.

Strolling under the shade trees, Lanna was heading for the stables. The birds were singing among the spreading limbs. Their cheerful melodies matched her own spirits, so she dawdled to listen. Her gaze roamed the branches overhead, but only rarely did she catch a flash of color as a bird flitted through the leaves to another perch.

In addition to being dressed in designer jeans, new boots, and a cream-colored silk blouse, she wore a flat-crowned hat, more Argentine in style than Wild West. The throat string dangled loosely below her chin. As she emerged from the trees into the ranch yard proper, Lanna heard voices. She glanced in their direction, hoping that Hawk might be among them. But the trio consisted of Chad, his mother, and Tom Rawlins, all walking in the general direction of the main house.

Abruptly, she angled away from them, taking a more direct line to the stables. She hadn't seen Chad or his mother yet this morning. Even though Carol had noticed nothing amiss when they had shared coffee, Lanna wanted to be by herself a while longer. The three had seemed very engrossed in their conversation; she hoped they wouldn't notice her.

"Lanna?!"

When Chad called to her, she turned and waved. "Good morning!" Then she continued on her way.

"Wait." He wasn't satisfied with only a greeting and came after her in a jogging run. Lanna stopped when she heard the crunch of his boots on the gravel and waited for him to catch up with her. In her good mood, it was easy to smile, even if she didn't welcome his interruption. Chad looked fresh and vigorously handsome when he finally reached her, a puzzled smile splitting his expression. "Where are you going?"

"To the stables. I thought I might go for a ride." With luck she might see Hawk. "I mentioned to Carol that I was considering it," she added to stave off any lecture from him.

"But it's nearly lunchtime," he protested.

"I overslept again this morning. I just had a big breakfast, so I decided to skip lunch." Actually, she had been positively ravenous when she had sat down at the table in the morning room.

"You don't look nearly as tired this morning," Chad observed as his gaze wandered over her in open admiration. "There's more color in your cheeks. All this rest is agreeing with you. I'm glad."

"Something definitely is." She nodded and smiled broadly.

"Is there any reason you have to go riding now? If you wait until after lunch, I'll come with you. By the way, how are the muscles this morning?" His glance slid suggestively downward to the rounded curves of her hips, outlined by the snuggly fitted denims.

"Just a little stiff," Lanna admitted. "I thought if I rode today, they would loosen up. Thanks for the offer to come with me, but I don't expect you to hold my hand all the time. I can manage on my own."

"I don't like the idea of you riding alone. It's easy to get lost in this country," Chad explained with a wry grimace. "This is the busy time of year on the ranch, too. I'd hate to have to pull the boys off the range to organize a search party for you."

"I hadn't thought about that." She nibbled at her lip, recognizing the logic of what he said. "I guess I could wait."

"Come up to the house. You can have some coffee or iced tea while I eat lunch." His hand reached out to take her arm, expecting her acceptance as a matter of course.

"I'd rather just wander around outside." She eluded the suggestion without making it a rejection of him. "It's too nice to be indoors." As she turned her head in an encompassing gesture to indicate the pleasures offered by the sunny day, Lanna noticed the solitary figure walking up the ranch driveway. "Who is that?"

Chad followed her gaze. "Looks like an Indian," he said on a note of contempt. "Probably coming for a handout. The fool should know better than to come here. Rawlins will send him on his way fast enough."

As the figure grew more distinct, Lanna felt a tug of recognition. "I think I know him," she murmured.

"You know him?" Chad repeated in surprise. "Why should you know an Indian?"

She stared at the torn and dirty pink blanket wrapped around the stooped shoulders. It wasn't possible that it could belong to any other Indian. There was even a bedraggled red feather stuck in straight, gray-black hair. The major difference from the last time she'd seen him was that the Indian wasn't weaving in a drunken stagger. He was tiredly marching in a straight line.

"I don't actually know him," Lanna admitted. "But I met him once when I was with your father."

"Where did you meet him?" The sharpness of Chad's demand surprised Lanna.

"Outside a museum. Does it matter?" She frowned at the grimness he was trying to conceal. Katheryn and Tom Rawlins had come up behind Chad. Their attention, too, was focused on the Indian.

"No. Of course not," Chad assured her.

Lanna turned back. The Indian had seen them standing there and proudly squared his shoulders as he approached, striving for an air of dignity. He was dirty; there was a sallowness to his brown skin; but this time he was sober. Plodding wearily, he didn't stop until he reached them. His eyes were black and bright as he searched their faces.

"Hello, Bobby Crow Dog," Lanna greeted him by name and smiled.

He stared at her with a puzzled look. "Do I know you?" His speech no longer followed the idiomatic pattern of an uneducated Indian.

"I don't think you would remember me," she told

him. "But I met you about a month ago. You had a
necklace of cedar beads that you wanted John—John
Faulkner—to buy for me."

"It is possible," he conceded, then pulled himself up
to his full height. "I have come to see J. B. Faulkner."

"He's dead," Chad announced with almost brutal
frankness.

Hope faded from the black eyes, leaving them flat.
Lanna watched his posture slump under the weight of
the news, his height decreasing by several inches. He
looked vaguely lost and bewildered.

"I'm sorry, Bobby Crow Dog," Lanna offered in
sympathy.

"White Sage was there, as he remembered her, to
take his hand and guide Laughing Eyes on the long
journey to the afterworld. I know this," he stated dully.
His words drew a stifled gasp from Katheryn. Lanna
glanced behind her, but Katheryn was already walking
rigidly away from the group. "He said I should go
home." Bobby Crow Dog was talking again and Lanna
turned back. He lifted his tired and wrinkled face to
Chad. "I have come a long way to see my old friend."

"You didn't walk all the way from Phoenix, did
you?" Lanna was amazed that he would have the
strength to make such a trek.

His expression changed as he adopted the look of a
buffoon. "I ride my thumb." Then he was aping the
action described by his words—hopping around with
his hand between his legs. Lanna shuddered at the
spectacle he made of himself. "I look ridiculous, don't
I?" Bobby Crow Dog laughed, revealing a fine row of
teeth that had grown yellow with neglect. "It is funny to
ride your thumb."

"Yes, it's very funny." She smiled weakly and
realized he had probably often made himself the butt of
a joke to gain acceptance or a handout.

His face became sad, a little pleading. "I have a hunger that is killing me. Is there food for an old friend of his? Maybe a warm place to sleep? The ground is hard and cold, and my blanket has holes."

The humble questions were directed at Chad. Lanna turned to him, too, her hazel eyes adding her own plea to Bobby Crow Dog's. There was a reassuring warmth in Chad's expression.

"I remember that my father knew you, Bobby Crow Dog," Chad said. "Rawlins will take you to the bunkhouse. You'll find there's plenty of food and a good bed to sleep in. You are welcome to stay as long as you like."

The broken red feather dipped as the Indian bowed his head in grateful acknowledgment of the invitation. "Thank you. You are a good son. He would be proud of you for remembering an old friend."

"Tom." Chad motioned the ranch manager to come forward. "Take him and see that he gets something to eat."

Rawlins didn't seem too pleased with the order, but he obeyed. He waved to the Indian to come with him. As they walked away, Lanna saw Bobby Crow Dog bend toward the wiry, thin foreman.

"Maybe there is whiskey," he suggested eagerly. "I have cedar beads, a genuine Navaho-made necklace. My cousin strung it. Or I could give you a magic eyescope with a naked lady inside."

Lanna's gaze made a downward sweep, away from the two men walking toward the bunkhouse. "I'm glad you asked him to stay, Chad."

"Yes. Isn't he the one who used to make movies in Hollywood?" His head tipped toward her. "I vaguely remember J. B. mentioning that name."

"Yes, he's the one." Lanna nodded.

"If you'll excuse me, I think I'll go see if Tom and I

can find some clean clothes for him, and arrange for a bath. He could use it. I could smell him from where I was standing." Chad smiled faintly before he moved to follow the foreman and the old Indian.

His thoughtfulness warmed her. It was so typical of Chad. Lanna had started to turn away when she saw Hawk crossing the yard toward her. His gaze briefly followed the departing Chad and lingered for several seconds on the blanket-clad figure walking with Rawlins. It struck Lanna how intensely the two brothers disliked one another—and she was attracted to both of them. It was an uncomfortable situation. What would she do if she was ever forced to choose? And how much trouble would it cause?

Hawk's look was sharply questioning when he reached Lanna. "Was that Bobby Crow Dog?"

"Yes. Do you know him?" She was faintly surprised that he would recognize him when Chad had only vaguely remembered him.

"I met him a few times." A frown narrowed Hawk's gaze as he looked again in the direction of the trio. "Where are they taking him?"

"To get something to eat," Lanna explained. "Chad told him he could stay as long as he liked."

"He did?" An eyebrow was lifted in open skepticism.

"Bobby Crow Dog was a friend of your father's. He came here looking for him. When he found out John was dead, he looked a little lost. It was sad," she murmured.

"He doesn't have anyplace to go. The hogans of his relatives aren't open to him anymore, because he shames them with his stealing to buy liquor," Hawk admitted. His mouth twisted in a slanting line. "I find it a little hard to believe that Chad actually invited him to stay here."

"Chad is very kind and generous," Lanna retorted, defending Chad in his absence. "He's been very helpful to me."

"Only because he could gain from it," Hawk stated, then flashed a quick smile. "I think we'd better find a subject we can agree on. How do you feel this morning?"

"Fine." The sparkle returned to her eyes. "You?"

Hawk studied her look with lazy satisfaction. "Fine."

"Not sore?" she asked with a faintly provocative smile.

"Nope. Where are you going?"

"Originally, I was going riding, but"—Lanna hesitated, glancing toward the house beyond the trees—"I thought I'd go to the house to check on Katheryn. She appeared upset by something Bobby Crow Dog said."

Turning, Hawk stared at the house, his features expressing a quizzical concern. "Maybe you should check," he agreed. "I'll see how Bobby Crow Dog is making out with your kind and generous Chad."

His smiling taunt sent a flash of irritation through Lanna. She glared at his retreating shoulders, her loyalties divided between the two brothers, and conscious that this wouldn't be the last time. Pivoting sharply on her heel, she retraced her steps back to the house.

When she opened the front door, she heard the shrill anger of Katheryn's voice coming from the living room. Its sound didn't match the image Katheryn had always presented publicly to Lanna—that of a refined and composed lady. Her curiosity was aroused. She closed the door quietly, careful not to make a sound.

"I could kill him! I swear I could kill him!" she raged. "It was bad enough at the hospital! Carol, when J. B. reached out with his hand, I thought it was for *me!*

God, I thought finally—*finally*—he was turning to me! Then he whispered her name—*her name!* Now, that filthy Indian shows up here!"

"Katheryn, it's over," Carol soothed.

"No, it isn't over!"

"You are letting yourself get all worked up over something that isn't even important anymore." There was an angry edge to Carol's voice now.

"Isn't important?"

"Ssh!"

Realizing that they suspected their conversation was being overheard, Lanna took a tiptoeing step back to the door, opened it noisily, then closed it. She had heard enough to know that Katheryn was still jealous of John's association with Hawk's mother, a jealousy that had gone beyond the grave.

As Lanna walked toward the living room archway, she hooked her thumb through the throat string and slipped her hat off her head. She was wearing a bright look of interest when she entered the room.

"I thought you were going riding, Lanna." Carol eyed her with equal brightness.

"I decided to wait until after lunch. Chad said he would go with me then." She sank into a chair, stretching out and letting the hat dangle from the armrest. "Is anything wrong?" She glanced from Carol to Katheryn.

The older woman pivoted away. "I have a bit of a headache. Too much sun, I expect." Her voice was as still as her posture. "Foolishly, I didn't wear a hat outside this morning."

Lanna wished she hadn't asked the question and forced the woman into a lie. Rising from the chair she had just taken, she excused herself. "I think I'll see if there's any coffee left."

The conversation she had interrupted wasn't resumed after she left. But her thoughts kept turning back to what she had heard as she sat alone in the morning room. She felt sorry for Katheryn. Her life had been consumed by bitter jealousy that fed on itself. It must have tainted her every waking minute—and still did, evidently. Lanna sighed.

Chapter XVI

Hawk let his gaze stray from the poker game to the corner of the room where a couple of the older hands were sitting with Bobby Crow Dog. The old Indian was regaling them with tales of his Hollywood days—the movies he'd made and the stars he'd known. He'd tried to sell just about everything he owned for a drink of whiskey, but so far he was still sober.

"Did you really make all those movies with John Wayne, like you said you did?" Bill Short was eyeing Bobby Crow Dog skeptically.

"He always asked for me." Bobby nodded. The dirty pink blanket was gone; so was the feather. In place of the ragged shirt and pants, he had on a bright plaid shirt and Levi's. The new clothes emphasized the gauntness of his frame. "I called him Duke and he called me Crowbait."

"Were you really in *She Wore a Yellow Ribbon?* I saw that movie four times and I don't remember you in it." The other cowboy exchanged a glance with Bill Short, half-grinning. "The only Indians I saw in that were dead."

"That was me!" Bobby explained with a toothy

smile. "That's why I was such a good Indian—I was always dead. That's why Duke called me Crowbait, because I was always sprawled in the dust." He laughed and his audience joined him.

"What are you going to do, Hawk?" The Mexican, Sanchez, directed his attention to the poker game. "Dan just raised. It's three bits to you if you're staying in."

Hawk glanced at his cards showing on the table. A pair of fours was all he had, nothing in the hole, and the seventh card had been dealt. Dan already had him beat with a pair of ladies on the table. There was maybe three dollars in the pot. Chances were he could bluff Dan out. He'd done it often enough in the past. But there was a stronger impulse running through him— powerful and impatient. It was wearing down his restraint, making him feel reckless and uncaring about the possible consequences—the same way he'd felt last night.

Throwing in his hand, Hawk rose abruptly from his chair. "I'm out."

There was a desire for haste in him, but he made himself wander slowly across the room to the door. Outside, Hawk paused beneath the overhang to let his eyes adjust to the night's darkness. His gaze was drawn immediately to the lights glittering through the trees from the windows of the main house. A quick heat rushed through his veins. He took a step toward the lights and stopped in cold shock when a voice came out of the darkness near him.

"All that smoke get to you?" Luther Wilcox inquired with too much nonchalance. "I had to come out for some fresh air, too. It was cloggin' my lungs." There was a dull thump as the front legs of his chair came down.

Irritation ran wild through Hawk's nerves. Why hadn't he known Luther was there? The answer didn't put him at ease because Hawk knew he had allowed himself to be distracted by the image of Lanna's face, the steadiness of her hazel eyes, and the quiet beauty of her features.

Hawk turned, with apparent casualness, to face the man in the chair. Age had widened Luther and grizzled his hair. For all the easy talk they exchanged over the years, there was always a brittleness between them. Luther and Bill Short had been the ones who had held Hawk for the beating Rawlins had given him. Hawk had never forgotten it. Both men knew it and were wary around him, despite what might appear on the surface.

"Yeah, I needed some air." He accepted the excuse Luther had provided and walked past the man to lean a shoulder against a windowframe.

The position gave Hawk a view of what was going on inside the bunkhouse as well as with the door, the old cowboy, and the distant house. Luther shifted in his chair with an effort, angling himself toward Hawk. It was age that stiffened the man after a hard day's work.

"You should retire, Luther. You're getting too old for this work." It was a statement of fact, rather than interest in the old man's well-being.

"Retire? Hell! I'm going to cowboy until I'm dead or crippled!" Luther snorted. "And if I get crippled, well, you can just tie me in a saddle. I ain't gonna retire. I'd just as soon be dead."

Impatience gnawed at Hawk, although it didn't show in his expression. A burst of laughter came from inside. "You should be in there, Luther, listening to Bobby Crow Dog. He made all those films in your heyday, didn't he?"

The Indian's presence was another thing that didn't rest easy in Hawk's mind. Chad had a reason for it. Lanna might believe it was merely a gesture of goodwill, but he didn't—not for a minute.

"Never went to movies much. Couldn't afford it." Luther coughed up some phelgm and turned to spit. "After supper tonight, that Indian was trying to sell me this telescope he's got. It ain't a telescope. It's one of them girlie-peep things. You look in it and there's a picture of a naked woman. It was something. Stirred this old man's pulse." He chuckled, then turned his bright gaze on Hawk. "Chad's new friend has a face and figure that can give a man ideas, don't she?"

"I haven't seen much of her." Not as much as he wanted to. "Chad doesn't seem inclined to introduce her around." The mere mention of Lanna turned Hawk's hungry gaze toward the main house.

"She ain't playin' the piano tonight," Luther remarked. "Kathcryn does have a way of playin' it that fills a man's soul."

"She is a very accomplished pianist," Hawk agreed.

"She really must have worked her spell on you last night. Why, it was practically mornin' before you came back."

"Were you checking on me, Luther?" Hawk coolly drawled the challenge, but his eyes were coldly sharp and piercing.

The cowboy hesitated, pursing his lips. "No." He shook his head. "No, I wasn't checkin' on you." His sun-weathered face looked sad. "I know you aren't goin' to listen to any advice from me. But, boy, you are headin' for a pack of trouble. You've already known more than your share. Back off, boy, while you can."

"I don't know what you're talking about." Hawk didn't change his relaxed pose.

"Have it your way." The cowboy shrugged.

"You're tired, Luther. It must be past your bedtime. Why don't you turn in for the night?" Hawk suggested.

"No, I'm goin' to sit out here for a spell. I don't sleep too good anymore. When you get old, the body doesn't seem to need as much sleep as it used to."

Hawk swore silently. Throwing a last glance at the beckoning lights of the main house, he straightened.

"I'm going to turn in," he announced. "Good night, Luther."

"Night."

It was nearly sundown when Hawk rode into the ranch yard the next day. Hot, tired, and dirty, he hadn't slept worth a damn, lying awake in his bunk most of the night and remembering the pleasures he had enjoyed in another bed. It angered him that he couldn't forget. He'd pushed himself hard today in self-punishment. Damn, but he wanted a shower and something clean against his skin—like Lanna. Hawk clenched his jaw savagely.

With a check of the rein, he halted his horse's shuffling walk in front of the barn. He swung out of the stirrups and started to lead the horse inside to unsaddle it. From the near side of the building, he heard a wavering voice monotonously chanting and paused. Curiosity moved him to investigate.

Looping the reins around a corral rail and securing them in a half-hitch, Hawk left the horse and ducked between the boards. When he rounded the corner of the building, he saw Bobby Crow Dog facing the setting sun and swaying as he sang. Hawk stopped to listen, his brows drawing together in a puzzled frown as he tried to catch a word or a phrase that would help him identify the chant. But the guttural sounds were garbled and indistinct.

"What is this song?" Hawk interrupted the singer. "I don't recognize it. Where is it from?"

Bobby Crow Dog regarded this display of ignorance with contempt. "It is from *Flaming Arrows*, 1949."

The information prompted a wry shake of his head. But Hawk's amusement vanished when he saw the fifth of whiskey in the Indian's hand.

"Where did you get the whiskey?" Hawk thought it had been strictly understood that no one was to give him liquor. "Who gave it to you?"

"I trade," he insisted, offended by Hawk's implication that he had accepted charity. "Give big magic for bottle."

The corners of Hawk's mouth were pulled grimly down. The "big magic" was probably that picture of the nude woman the Indian had tried to peddle to all the cowboys last night. Somebody had finally given in.

"Who traded the whiskey for the magic?" Hawk demanded.

The Indian frowned as he tried to remember. "The Two-Faced One."

"That description fits a lot of people on this ranch," Hawk muttered to himself. Louder, he said, "Do you know his American name?"

"She give me good whiskey." He took a swig and made a sound of satisfaction. "Want some?"

She? On second thought, Hawk doubted if that meant anything. Bobby Crow Dog had reverted his speech pattern to the old way. The Navaho language didn't have pronouns that distinguished between the male and female gender. The Navahos tended to use the American ones interchangeably.

Hawk asked, "Was it a man or a woman?"

The liquor Bobby Crow Dog consumed deafened him to the question. He was staring again at the golden ball of the sun and chanting his unintelligible lyrics.

Shaking his head, Hawk turned away. With a certain fatalism, he decided that it didn't matter who had given Bobby Crow Dog the whiskey. One way or another, he probably would have gotten hold of a bottle, anyway. It was the only way the old man could recapture his lost days of glory.

"Did I tell you Johnny received a perfect score on his math test, Katheryn?" Carol glanced up from the petit point design she was stitching, holding the needle in mid-air. "It was in the letter that came today. He was so proud."

"No, you didn't mention that. I'll have to remember to send him a little something as a reward for doing so well," Katheryn declared with the typical generosity of a grandmother.

"Johnny does so well in school, just like his father." Carol directed the remark at Lanna by way of explanation. They were sharing the sofa, Carol busy with her needlework and Lanna leafing through the pages of a magazine.

"Chad had to study hard for his grades," Katheryn inserted. "They weren't given to him simply because he was a Faulkner."

"Of course not," Carol agreed. "But Chad is very intelligent. Everyone knows that."

Lanna made a halfhearted attempt to appear interested in the conversation. But it didn't hold her attention any more than the magazine in her lap did. She cupped a hand over her mouth to hide a tired yawn.

"Am I boring you with all this talk about Johnny?" Carol apologized.

"No, not at all," Lanna insisted. "I'm just tired. I didn't sleep very well last night."

She had tossed and turned all night long, waking up at the slightest sound, thinking it might be Hawk. It had been unsettling to realize how much she had counted on seeing him last night. She had felt very tired and rundown all day, which indicated she didn't have much reserve strength after her recovery from the flu.

"Maybe you should have an early night," Katheryn suggested.

"I think you are right," Lanna sighed. Tossing the magazine aside, she rose from the sofa. "Good night. Tell Chad good night for me. I don't want to disturb him while he's busy."

"We will," Carol promised. "If he doesn't come out of that study fairly soon, I'm going in there and drag him out. He works much too hard."

"Would you like some hot milk? Or perhaps some cocoa?" Katheryn offered.

"No, thank you," Lanna refused, then hesitated when she turned to leave. Looking back at her hostess, she asked, "Do you have any sassafras tea? That's my remedy for everything."

There was the smallest hesitation before Katheryn nodded. "I believe we do. I'll ask Roseanne to bring a cup to your room."

"Thank you. Good night."

She followed the corridor to her bedroom. As she entered, her gaze was automatically drawn to the glass-paned doors leading to the veranda. She paused, then crossed the room to close the drapes. Her hand hesitated on the drape cord as she gazed out into the blackness of night. A few lights glimmered through the trees. Lanna turned the small knob that locked the doors and pulled the heavy drapes shut.

Fifteen minutes later, she had creamed her face, brushed her teeth, and changed into her silk pajamas.

Lanna walked to the bed to turn down the covers. There was a light rap on her door. Then Carol called brightly, "Room service."

Lanna smiled. "Come in." She finished pulling the covers down as the door opened and reached for the rolled pillow to plump it. "You shouldn't be waiting on me. I don't expect that."

"I know you don't." Carol set the china cup and saucer on the table beside Lanna's bed.

"Thanks for bringing it." Lanna took the cup from its saucer and inhaled the enticing aroma rising from the hot liquid.

"It was no trouble." Carol shrugged. "Are you feeling okay? It would be terrible if you had a relapse when you're here to rest."

"I'm just tired," Lanna insisted and sipped the tea. "This is a different brand," she noticed and took another sip. "I like it. Do you know what it is?"

"No. Katheryn fixed it. Roseanne had already gone to bed. That's why I volunteered to bring it."

"It doesn't matter." She took another sip before setting the cup back in its saucer.

"You're tired. I won't keep you up." Carol started toward the door. "Good night."

"Good night." In a naturally graceful half-turn, Lanna sat on the edge of her bed. She switched on the small lamp on the bed stand. "Would you mind turning out the light?"

"Sure." Carol opened the door and paused to reach back inside to switch off the bright overhead light. She smiled and closed the door.

Picking up the cup again, Lanna made a silent wish that the soothing tea would help her sleep. She didn't want to spend another night like the last one. Yawning, Lanna reached for the cup of tea and finished it, then slipped under the covers, reaching over to turn out the lamp.

Within minutes after snuggling onto the pillow, she felt a little nauseous, but it soon passed and she fell asleep. She began to dream almost immediately. Hawk was there, in the bed with her. His eyes were so vividly blue, intensified and electric, every pinpoint of color sharply defined. His hair was even blacker, its sheen throwing off so much light that Lanna had to close her eyes against the glare, even in the dream.

There was an explosion of color behind her eyelids. Her heart was pounding so loudly that Lanna was certain it was outside her body. When she looked, Hawk was holding it in his hand. She begged him to give it back, but he just smiled in that careless way of his and walked away. Then Chad was there, promising to get her a new heart, reassuring her the way he always did. She could hear his voice so clearly, yet his face kept becoming distorted, waves running through it like in those mirrors at a carnival.

Carol came to tell her about the letter from her son, Johnny. Lanna tried to explain about Hawk stealing her heart, but Carol laughed and insisted Hawk would never do that. He was her brother; hadn't she been raised with him like a sister?

The dream became a parade of characters—first Hawk, then Chad, Carol, followed by Katheryn railing in jealousy against John. John came to see her, thousand-dollar bills sticking out of his pockets. He kept forcing the money into her hands, insisting she take it. The old Navaho came swooping into her dream, flapping his dirty pink blanket and cawing like a crow. His gnarled fingers were talons that kept grabbing at her arm, a cedar bead necklace dangling around his neck.

Her breathing was hard. She could hear the air whooshing in and out of her lungs. Her heart was back. She could hear it beating. Had Hawk returned it? Was it the new heart Chad had promised? If there were fingerprints on it, she would know. Fingerprints? How could she find fingerprints on her heart when it was inside her? What if it wasn't her heart, but someone else's?

Lanna tried to run from the dream, but her legs wouldn't work. There was color . . . so much color. Dazzling. It was the Fourth of July. She relaxed to watch the brightly beautiful red, blue, green, and yellow stars cascading in the sky. Whirling and twisting. She was inside a kaleidoscope. Stunning patterns and combinations created especially for her. Amethyst, orange, fuschia, ruby, emerald. She was surrounded by jewels. Enormous, hundred-carat stones. Someone kept heaping them on top of her until her hands were weighted down with rings.

All night long, she hovered between beautiful dreams and nightmares. It was never totally one or the other. When she awakened, it was with a twinge of regret. She didn't want to leave all that beauty behind her. The exhilaration of it had left a fading trail in her veins. She felt rested, yet faintly listless.

When she entered the morning room, Katheryn was seated alone at the table. She smiled pleasantly. "You are up a little earlier this morning. How do you feel today?"

"Better." Lanna smiled back.

"Would you like orange or grapefruit juice this morning? We have both." Katheryn slid her woven-rattan chair away from the table and stood up to walk to the sideboard, laid out with the morning's breakfast array.

"It doesn't matter. I can get it," Lanna offered.

"Sit down," Katheryn insisted. "I was going to pour myself some more coffee, anyway."

Lanna took a drink of her orange juice. "Where's Carol? Is she still sleeping?"

"No. I believe she is busy packing for Chad." Katheryn added a lump of sugar to her coffee.

"Is Chad leaving?"

"Yes. He has to fly back to Phoenix this morning. He doesn't feel he should stay away from the office any longer." There was a musical clink of the spoon against the side of the china cup as Katheryn stirred her coffee. "He's in the study, collecting all the papers he needs, if you want to speak to him before he leaves."

"Yes. Maybe I should," Lanna murmured with a trace of a frown in her expression. "I should ask him about my new heart." The instant she said the words aloud, she realized that had been part of the dream she'd had last night, and she laughed. "That's crazy."

"What is, dear?" Katheryn glanced up curiously.

"Nothing." Lanna shook her head and pushed her chair away from the table. "I just had the wildest dreams last night. Excuse me."

"Certainly."

Leaving the morning room, Lanna hurried along the corridor into the foyer and took the second archway leading to a set of carved mahogany doors. It was the only room, other than the bedrooms, that had doors to ensure privacy. She rapped twice on the polished wood.

"Come in." Chad called.

With a turn of the ornate brass knob, Lanna pushed the door open and walked in. The study was a very masculine room, stamped with John's personality. Lanna noticed it immediately in the heavy Indian influence of a decorative Navaho blanket on a wall and *kachina* dolls on the fireplace mantle. They were balanced with several trophy antlers, as well as solid oak furniture and a leather sofa and chair. It was all countered by a draftsman's table, its pigeonholes filled with rolled-up blueprints. It was definitely John, the outdoorsman, the contractor, and the student of the Navaho culture.

Chad was standing beside the massive, antique oak desk, sorting through the papers on its top, where his briefcase was laid open. A smile spread across his handsome features when she entered.

"Good morning. Katheryn just told me you are leaving this morning." Lanna crossed the room to stand in front of the desk. "You didn't mention anything about it yesterday."

"I had planned to leave later on this afternoon. Then Carol asked if I would stop at my old alma mater to see Johnny. She has some books for him, and Roseanne baked his favorite cookies, so I'm being sent with a 'care' package." He added some papers to the folder in his hand and slipped it into the briefcase among some others. "It's Carol's way of making up for not seeing him this last weekend."

"I hope I wasn't the cause of that." Lanna frowned.

"You weren't. There were several activities going on at the school this weekend. Johnny didn't want to miss out on them. He's on the football team, first string."

Lanna felt reassured by Chad's explanation. "I imagine Carol is very proud of him, then."

"Proud? That's almost an understatement," Chad declared. "She practically lives for that boy. I know it's because she can't have any more children, but it worries me sometimes the way she makes him the center of her existence. She writes to him four or five times a week. Sometimes I think she cares more about our son than she does about—" He stopped, a look of chagrin spreading across his face. "I'm sorry, Lanna."

"For what?" She tipped her head to the side, shiny brown hair swinging across her shoulder.

"It's an old story. Husbands are always complaining about the way their wives neglect them." He snapped his briefcase shut with an air of finality. "I never intended to use that line on you. Carol isn't perfect, but neither am I."

"You are just closer to being perfect than she is," Lanna teased in an effort to ease the sudden tension.

Chad moved around the corner of the desk to stand in front of her and take hold of her shoulders. He studied her with an intent look that seemed to transmit his utter sincerity. Yet Hawk didn't trust him—the unbidden thought crossed her mind.

"Carol is a good wife—and a good mother," Chad stated emphatically. "I want you to understand that so you will know it isn't because I lack something that I—" He stopped again without finishing the sentence. "I almost wish you hadn't come here to tell me good-bye," Chad murmured in a half-groan. "If Mother or Carol were here, it might be easier. Lanna."

His urgent tone made its own explanation as his fingers tightened on her shoulders. She stared into his eyes and the gold dust sprinkled through their light brown color. Its glitter seemed to hypnotize her. Lanna realized what a dangerous charm he possessed— dangerous because he could claim to respect his wife while making a pass at Lanna. His image began to acquire a tarnish in her eyes. But she made no attempt to stop—just to see how far he'd go, and what it would be like.

As his hands pulled her toward him, Lanna tipped her head back. His mouth was warm and firm in its possession of her lips, moving against them with expertise. His arms curved around her and gathered her close. Instead of feeling emotionally threatened, Lanna felt turned off. She missed that feeling of excitement, that heady wonder Hawk so uniquely aroused. She began to withdraw from the kiss, regretting that she had allowed it to happen.

When the study door opened, she was firmly in Chad's embrace, their lips just separating. The unexpected intrusion made them both turn their heads. Lanna's eyes widened in dismay when she saw Hawk poised inside the doorway. His gaze was glacial blue, its iciness freezing her. Chad's arms loosened their hold, yet remained protectively around her.

"The plane will be ready to take off in fifteen minutes. Jake will fly you to Phoenix." Hawk paused on the information, then allowed a chilling smile to touch his mouth. "Sorry I disturbed you."

He retreated into the hallway, pulling the door closed behind him. Lanna hung her head in silent despair, guessing what Hawk had assumed, and wondering how she could ever possibly explain. She didn't even try to move out of Chad's arms.

"Lanna, what can I say?" he murmured. "I never should have allowed the kiss to happen. It was only Hawk, but it could have been—" He cupped a hand under her chin and lifted it. "I'm sorry. I can't help the way I feel about you."

She twisted out of his grasp. "Chad, don't say anymore."

"I know I don't have any right to say the things I'm saying." He caught at her arm to stop her when she would have walked away. "And I don't have the right to feel the way I do. But it doesn't change the situation. I feel as rotten as you do right now, believe me."

"I believe you." Did she believe him? Or was it possible it had been deliberately planned to make sure Hawk would be alienated from her?

"I never wanted to hurt you or embarrass you," Chad offered huskily. "These last few days have been torture being so near to you and not being able to hold you in my arms and kiss you."

"It won't happen again, Chad," Lanna stated.

"I don't blame you for feeling that way, darling." He tried to turn her into his arms, but Lanna resisted.

"No," she said firmly and pulled free of his grip.

He called her name but she ignored the summons as she hurried from the room. She wasn't running away from Chad. She was running after Hawk. But she didn't intend to explain that to Chad.

Outside the house, the sun was so brilliant it hurt her eyes. She had to shield them against the glare until she reached the shade of the trees on the lawn. When she reached the open ranch yard, Lanna paused to scan the premises for a glimpse of Hawk. There was no sign of him.

By one of the buildings, a cowboy was loading something into the back end of a pickup. Lanna crossed the yard to the truck. The man might have seen Hawk when he left the house and noticed where he had gone.

"Do you know where I can find Hawk?" She was slightly winded when she stopped beside the lowered tailgate. The cowboy turned his head. Lanna felt the quiet speculation in his look, but she didn't care what this older man was thinking. "Have you seen him?" she repeated insistently.

"I saw him going into the barn a minute ago," he admitted, gesturing with his hand to indicate the building he meant.

"Thank you." She tossed the phrase to him as she started in the direction of the barn.

She slipped through the narrow gap where the wide sliding door had been pushed ajar. The dim interior smelled of stifled air, horses, and hay dust. At the far end, the other set of double doors was pushed wide open to let in the sunlight. Hawk was leading a haltered horse through the opening into the barn. By the time Lanna had crossed the length of the concrete passageway, he was tying the lead rope through a steel ring on the wall. A Western saddle with its blanket and pad were propped on the floor a few feet away. Hawk didn't even glance at her when she reached him, his expression a mask.

"Hawk, I want to explain what you saw in the study," she began.

"Why?" He ran a currycomb over the horse's back, dislodging the dust. "It has nothing to do with me."

The flat indifference of his voice warned Lanna that he wasn't going to make it easy for her. Somehow she had to make him understand, and she didn't know how to start.

"It wasn't the way it seemed," Lanna protested, wishing he would at least look at her while she was talking.

But Hawk's attention remained on his task. "I'm sure the two of you are just friends." There was no special inflection on the last phrase to make it a jibe, yet it stung just the same.

"That isn't what I was trying to say at all. I mean, yes, we are friends. Chad has been good to me. He's helped me a lot these last couple of weeks." In her agitation, Lanna knew she wasn't saying what she really meant.

"You were just thanking him for all he's done," Hawk said smoothly. Hooking the currycomb on a nail in the wall, he reached down to pick up the saddle blanket.

"I didn't kiss him because I was grateful," she denied as she watched him smooth the blanket over the horse's back. The severity of his sharply male profile was making it difficult for her. "Will you at least look at me when I'm talking?" Lanna demanded in angry frustration.

He turned to face her, a hand resting on the striped blanket. "What are you going to tell me?" The enormous amount of patience in his eyes seemed to emphasize his total indifference to the discussion. "That you struggled but he forced you to kiss him?"

"No!" She reacted as if he was silently taunting her, although there was nothing on the surface to indicate he was. Hawk turned away to pick up the saddle pad. "If you give me a chance, I'll tell you the way it was."

"What's between you and Chad isn't any of my business." He positioned the pad on the blanket. "I stay out of his way, and he stays out of mine."

"I'm going to tell you, just the same," Lanna retorted in a choked voice. "Chad is a very handsome man, sophisticated and charming. I doubt if you can appreciate what I'm going to say, but a woman is flattered when a man like that appears interested in her. It builds up her ego, even if he is married. Besides, I wanted to see if he would kiss me even if he had a wife. You don't slap a man's face for that."

"With sufficient flattery, I suppose you'll hop into bed with him." Lifting the saddle, he swung it onto the horse's back and settled it into place. "Of course, you'll have to tell Carol to move over. She does like the taste of the forbidden, so maybe you and Chad can talk her into a threesome."

"Dammit, Hawk! Will you quit twisting everything I say and making it come out worse! I'm trying to get it through your thick skull that I kissed Chad mostly out of curiosity. I wondered if I would feel the same excitement that I did when you kissed me."

"A kissing contest?" His mouth twisted, but there was little humor in its slant. Hooking the stirrup over the saddlehorn, he reached under the horse's belly for the cinch. "That's a new line. You are very original." He threaded it through the cinch ring and took up the slack.

Lanna waited, but Hawk never asked the question she expected. "Don't you want to know what I found out?"

"Not particularly." With the cinch tightened, he brushed past her to put the bridle on.

"There wasn't any comparison." Her voice was soft, almost humble. "I barely felt half-alive in his arms."

"Too bad." Hawk forced the bit into the horse's mouth. The metal jangled as the horse chewed the bar between its teeth.

"Is that all you can say?" The pain of disbelief flickered across her expression.

"We all have our troubles." He buckled the throat latch, then removed the halter. "But I never get involved in other people's affairs."

Lanna watched him gather the reins to lead the horse away. "Where are you going?"

"I have some fences to check."

"Wait." She reached out to lay a hand on his forearm. "I'll ride with you. Let me saddle a horse."

Hawk stopped and glanced down at the hand on his arm. It looked small and white against the faded yellow of his shirt sleeve. When he slowly lifted his gaze to her face, his blue eyes were opaque, totally emotionless.

"I ride alone," he stated.

Lanna refused to take the hint. "You don't have to ride alone this time. I'll come with you and keep you company."

"It wouldn't be a good idea to be seen in my company," he replied.

"I don't care. Can't you understand that it doesn't matter to me who or what you are? I want to come with you." She threw aside her pride even as she faced him with quiet determination.

"I ride alone because that's the way I want it." Hawk moved his arm, shrugging off her hand.

"Don't you need anybody, Hawk?" Lanna wondered in bewildered pain.

"What for?" He gave her another one of those blank looks.

It roweled her. "Will you stop looking at me like some damned—" She checked her outburst to search for another word.

But Hawk supplied the one she was going to say. "Like some damned Indian! That's what half of me is! Which half did you want to ride with—the Navaho, or the white?" he challenged in a raw fury.

There was no justification for his attack. Lanna lashed out in self-defense, slapping his face hard. Her arm hadn't completed its arc when she was grabbed and hauled roughly against him. Her arms were pinned to her sides in his steel vise, crushing her brutally to the unyielding wall of his chest. He grabbed a handful of hair, insensitive to the pain his yanking hold inflicted on her tender scalp.

Her gasping cry went unnoticed as he brutalized her mouth, raping and plundering with merciless anger. Her lips ground against her teeth, breaking the tender skin and leaving the taste of her own blood on Lanna's tongue.

As violently as it was begun, it was ended. Hawk released her with a backward shove that had Lanna stumbling to regain her balance. Instinct lifted the back of her hand to her injured and throbbing lips.

"Go." His eyes blazed with barely restrained fury. "If you hurry, you'll be able to see Chad before he leaves and cry on his shoulder."

Lanna felt the tears on her cheeks and impatiently

brushed them away. "You aren't free, Hawk. You have condemned yourself to a life of solitary confinement." Her choked voice wavered but remained strong. "You'll never be free until you let somebody love you and learn to love them back. You have to trust and need others to really live."

But her declaration appeared to make no impression on him as he pivoted and swung into the saddle. Lanna watched him ride to the open doors and duck beneath the crossbeam. The dappled buckskin danced eagerly into the sunlight, but Hawk kept the horse at a walk. Lanna shuddered.

Chapter XVII

For a week, Lanna rarely ventured out of the house. She had kept hoping Hawk would seek her out, but she hadn't seen him at all, not even at a distance. A depression settled into her, growing with each passing day.

She continued to have her nightly cup of sassafras tea. Each morning Lanna would wake up feeling revived, but by midday the restorative powers of the tea had worn off, leaving her with even less interest in what went on around her.

She wandered into the living room with no special purpose in mind. Katheryn was arranging a bouquet of bronze and white mums in a crystal vase, adding sprigs of fern. Seated in a chair by the fireplace, Carol was finishing another one of her letters to her son, Johnny.

"Hello, Lanna. We wondered where you were." Katheryn paused in her task long enough to glance up. "Chad called to say he would be arriving on Thursday."

"That's nice," she murmured.

"He asked how you were. I assured him that you were taking it easy." She snipped off the end of a flower stem. "There isn't a great deal to do here. I hope you aren't becoming bored, Lanna."

"No, I'm not bored." It was closer to being indifferent. She watched Katheryn expertly arranging the bouquet and realized how useless she was. She did absolutely nothing. The cook fixed the meals and washed the dishes. The housekeeper made the beds and cleaned the house. Katheryn and Carol added the odd touches, like the flowers, while she sat around letting everyone else wait on her. "I'm certainly not contributing very much. All I do here is make work for everyone else. I should be doing my share to help."

"Nonsense, Lanna. You are here to rest," Katheryn reminded her. "I'm not going to let you lift a hand. Chad would be furious if he heard you suggest such a thing."

Sighing, Lanna turned away. She didn't have the energy to argue. She had offered, so her conscience was eased. She strolled over to the window and gazed outside at the long shadows the trees cast on the ground. There was a rustle of paper as Carol put aside her stationery.

"Would you like to go riding, Lanna?" Carol suggested. "We would be just in time to watch the sunset."

"If you want to." Lanna shrugged. She didn't really care, but she knew Carol was making an effort to entertain her.

"It will take me fifteen minutes to change. How about you?" Carol tossed the challenge with a bright smile.

"Fifteen minutes," Lanna agreed.

It took her less time than that because it didn't matter what she wore. There was no one she wanted to impress. Even if she saw Hawk, it was unlikely he would pay any attention to her. It was only in her dreams that he came to her, Lanna was still absently amazed to discover she dreamed in color. She hadn't been aware of it before, but she had also rarely remembered what she dreamed.

All the way to the barns, Carol chattered incessantly. Sometimes the blonde's bubbling personality made Lanna absolutely weary. Yet she knew Carol's intentions were the best. She was trying to cheer her up and persuade her to take an interest in something. It wasn't Carol's fault that Lanna wasn't receptive to her attempts. She knew the cause. She hadn't seen Hawk for days.

Three days of dust, sweat, and stink had accumulated on Hawk. He'd slept outside the last two nights. Not because he had ridden so far from the headquarters of the ranch that he couldn't have trailered his horse back with one of the other riders. He had stayed out deliberately to be out of sight of the house lights. But he hadn't slept any better on the hard, cold ground with a blanket of stars above him than he had in the bunkhouse.

The conflict within himself hadn't been settled. He wanted Lanna as much as he ever had—if not more—because he had been without her. Yet his anger was still very real. Her honesty kept reaching out to him. She had admitted she wanted Chad to kiss her, had even explained her reasons—which should have given him immense satisfaction. But every time he pictured her in Chad's arms, it seared him raw all over again.

So he was back, wanting her and knowing he wouldn't go to her. The People didn't believe in repressing sexual urges. By the same token, they believed too much sex was a bad sign. They believed in witches, too. Lanna had certainly bewitched him, Hawk thought with a wry grimace.

Reining the horse to a stop at the barn door, he

swung out of the saddle. His joints were stiff as he led the bay horse inside the barn and tied it to the wall ring. Untying his bedroll from behind the cantle, Hawk carried it over to the wall and leaned it against it, then returned to uncinch the saddle. The stirrups slapped against his legs when he hauled the saddle off the horse. The sound of footsteps absently drew his gaze to the opened barn doors. When Tom Rawlins appeared, Hawk ignored him to set the saddle, horn down, on the floor.

"What are you doing here?" Rawlins demanded in a baiting tone.

"Taking care of my horse," Hawk answered with the obvious, rather than understand the actual question the foreman was asking.

"I thought you were helping with the roundup."

"You *hoped* wrong." Hawk changed the verb with emphasis.

"I don't see why you're hanging around here. I told Chad you would be out when he came back. He'll be here tomorrow." His statement contained a threat.

"You should have checked to find out what my plans were." He peeled the sweat-dampened saddle blanket and pad off the horse's wet back and spread them over the saddle. "I'll be going back out in a few days."

"Don't you think you should be checking on your share of the cattle?" Rawlins asked.

Hawk unbuckled the throat strap of the bridle and slipped the headstall off the horse's ears. "It will be an honest count."

"Two ranches can't work the same land because there isn't room for two bosses. I thought you'd be smart enough to know that," the foreman jeered, satisfaction glittering in an embittered face.

"Did you?" Hawk smiled with cold recklessness. "I'm just a dumb half-breed."

"You'd better get back to the roundup."

"I don't take orders from you." He wiped the sweat from the horse's back and withers, its skin shivering in reflex under his gloved hand. "I'll be riding out in a few days. If that isn't good enough for you—or Chad—it's just tough."

"What if it isn't?" Rawlins challenged as his jaw turned white.

The grating rasp of the other barn door sliding on its track half-turned Hawk, not completely, because he wasn't about to turn his back on Rawlins. A fiery pleasure flared through his veins and into his bones when he saw Lanna walk through the opening. In his mind, he reached for her, although he didn't move, except to slide a glance at Rawlins.

"I'll leave in my own good time, Tom. You'd better let it go at that," Hawk advised in a low voice that would not carry down the wide passageway of the barn.

"Hello." Lanna's voice swept through his senses like a windsong, swirling and dipping.

Rawlins was angered by the interruption, but he hid it well. "Are you and Carol going riding, Miss Marshall?" he inquired smoothly.

"Yes, we thought we would," Carol answered for Lanna.

"I'll catch up the horses for you," Rawlins volunteered.

Hawk was aware that Rawlins had left, but he continued to study Lanna. Her round hazel eyes looked wounded and tired. There was no joy of life in her face. Had he broken her fine spirit with his cruelty? Hawk experienced a wild need to hold her in his arms and give back that vital spark he had destroyed.

With a quick step, Carol came between them to take Lanna's arm. "Let's give Dad a hand with the horses." She escorted Lanna toward the doors.

Not once did Lanna look back as she left willingly with Carol. Hawk's gaze followed her every step of the way until she was out of sight. What had he expected? He cursed bitterly because he knew he wasn't going to seek her out and apologize. He hated himself for that.

Lanna's dreams were violent and confused. She was out on the roundup, riding with Hawk. Only instead of driving cattle, they were herding people. All of them were wearing grotesque masks. Yet Lanna easily recognized them. Every time she rode past the one with the yellow mask, the figure would wave a letter under her nose and insist that she write a note to Johnny and sign her name. Lanna knew it was Carol. Chad was carrying a heart of solid gold, which he kept trying to give to her.

The nightmare lasted for a long time. All the while she kept riding in circles around the masked people, never getting anywhere. She kept asking Hawk which way to go, but he kept asking if she wanted to ride with him.

When she woke up, she had to struggle to separate fantasy from reality. The vivid colors of their masks kept flashing in her mind, and the intensity of her confusion lingered until well into the morning.

Not even Chad's arrival in the early afternoon could bring Lanna out of her depressed mood. His smiles weren't able to charm her anymore, and his compliments sounded flat to her ears. Yet he appeared just as sincere and concerned as before. Lanna realized that the difference was she didn't care. It confused her. She thought she would feel better once Hawk had returned, but this dull mood persisted.

"Tom was mentioning to me that he has decided to start the fall cattle drive tomorrow, bringing the herds down from the summer pastures." Chad stirred his martini with the olive. "It should be in full swing by Saturday."

"He's left it late in the year as it is," Katheryn murmured in vague criticism. "It's already the last week of October."

"But it's been very mild," Chad reminded her, then smiled. "That isn't the point I was trying to make. When he told me about starting the drive, I thought it would be a great opportunity to show Lanna the more glamorous side of ranching. She's had more than two weeks of rest, leading a tame existence. She needs a little adventure to spark her enthusiasm. What do you think, Lanna?" He put the idea to her. "Would you like to spend a couple of days on the drive? We could sleep out at night under the stars, providing it doesn't rain, of course."

The suggestion didn't appeal to Lanna in her present mood. Normally, she would have been quick to agree. What was the matter with her? Yet she was about to beg off the trip when Carol spoke to enthusiastically add her approval to the plan.

"It's a marvelous idea, Chad. It would be so much fun, wouldn't it, Lanna?" she insisted. "I haven't been on one since I was in school and Dad took me. It's absolutely fascinating, Lanna. You do want to go, don't you?"

In the face of so much optimism, Lanna couldn't find an adequate reason to refuse, and she definitely needed something to shake her out of this lethargy. "Sure," she agreed with a surrendering shrug.

"Good." Carol rose from her chair and reached for Lanna's hand like a schoolchild. "Let's see what you have for clothes to wear. We'll need something warm in the high meadows. Do you have a sturdy parka? If you don't, I have one that you can borrow. It might be a little tight in the shoulders for you, though."

Chad's suggestion was quickly turned into a project. Lanna was swept along in the tide of planning and packing, whether she liked it or not. She let Carol make most of the decisions, which invariably meant consultations with Katheryn, who seemed to be the final authority on everything. Lanna was thoroughly tired of the subject by the time she went to bed. Oddly, there was serenity in her dreams that night, her sleep-world filled with rainbows and light prisms, sunsets and sunrises.

In the morning she awakened feeling revived and eager to embark on the ranch adventure Chad had proposed. By midday, her interest in it had waned. Lanna was certain Carol had talked it to death, then wondered why she couldn't summon the same amount of enthusiasm. She was bound to see Hawk, so why wasn't she excited? Was she coming down with the flu again? Or had it taken more out of her than she realized?

With lunch over, Lanna followed Katheryn into the living room. Carol and Chad were behind them, laughing and exchanging anecdotes of their separate adventures on previous roundups. It occurred to Lanna that this trip seemed to bring the couple closer together.

"I almost forgot." Chad snapped his fingers. "I have some papers that need your signature, Lanna. They're in my briefcase in the study. I'll get them." Separating himself from the group, he walked swiftly to the double set of doors.

"Go with him," Katheryn suggested. She didn't wait for Lanna's answer as she called to her son, "Don't bother to bring them out. Lanna can sign them in there."

The instant Lanna entered the study, she felt like a puppet on a string being pulled in the direction the puppeteer wanted her to go. Then she chided herself for having such cynical thoughts. Katheryn had pulled the string, not Chad. She quickly lost interest in the entire subject.

Removing a sheaf of papers from his briefcase, Chad flipped to the signature page. "There are only a couple of places where you need to sign."

"What is this?" She didn't feel up to deciphering several pages of legal jargon.

"It's more or less a proxy, giving me the right to vote your shares of stock the way I see fit," he explained. "There's a board meeting coming up with a lot of major decisions to be made. There really isn't time to brief you thoroughly on all the issues so that you can intelligently participate in the meeting."

Lanna hesitated. "I should at least read it."

"You'd only get confused." Smiling, he offered her a pen. "It's just a proxy agreement."

"For something so simple, there are an awful lot of pages to it," Lanna noticed. "Let's go over it later, Chad."

"Lanna, there isn't any need to go over it." His short laugh was tinged with exasperation. "I've already told you what it's about."

"I know you told me. If that is what's in there, you shouldn't object if I read it," she reminded him.

"Of course, I don't mind. It's just so time-consuming."

"I'm sorry I'm so stupid about these things," Lanna retorted. "But I'm not going to sign anything without reading it first. I haven't up to this point, and I'm not going to start now."

"Don't you trust me, Lanna?" Chad looked hurt and surprised.

"Yes, I trust you," she insisted. But she realized she didn't—not completely—when he was trying to pressure her like this. "It's just that I'm tired. And I really don't care about all this right now."

"I should have it signed before I go back to Phoenix. I don't like letting things go until the last minute. Sit down," he suggested. "We'll go over it page by page, paragraph by paragraph."

"No. Not now." She wasn't capable of concentrating on any one subject for a long period of time. "Later. After we come back," Lanna promised.

Chad considered her for a minute, then gave her a wry smile and nodded. "All right. And I didn't mean to sound like I was pushing you."

"I know." Perhaps he hadn't.

Sitting on her horse atop a butte, Lanna had a clear view of high canyon meadows below. The burnt red hides of Hereford cattle made a steadily growing blot on the yellow grass below. The cowboys added to the herd in scattered groups of three and four animals, driven out from hiding by the searching riders. Chad had explained to her that the gathering had been going on for the last couple of weeks in preparation for this final drive.

Hawk stood out from all the other riders—in Lanna's mind, at least. He worked alone, yet she often saw him directing the others. Wearing a blue chambray shirt and a buckskin vest lined with sheepskin, he was riding a fractious, bald-faced chestnut, rangy and unruly. Briefly, Lanna thought that the horse and rider were well suited to one another.

At this altitude, there was a briskness to the sun-warmed air. Lanna felt it and burrowed a hand inside the pocket of her down-lined jacket. A stiff breeze ruffled her mane of brown hair under the flat-brimmed hat. This tumble of jagged rock, yellow aspen, and straw-green grass should have had an appeal to her. She sighed because it didn't, and she wondered why.

Her placid mount twitched an ear. A second later, Lanna heard the clatter of metal-clad hooves on stone and half-turned in the saddle to see Carol approaching on her pinto.

"Hi!" Carol greeted her in a breathless voice and reined her horse to a stop beside Lanna's. "Chad said he saw you ride up here. You have a great view!" She patted her horse's neck as she surveyed the land spreading out before them.

"Yes, it's really something," Lanna supposed.

"How do you like it so far? It's fascinating, isn't it?" Carol enthused.

"Yes, it is." Lanna felt like a wet blanket compared to the blonde's ebullience. She was being a drag, yet she felt helpless to change. "I think I'll go back to camp and get some coffee. It's chilly up here." Aware of the protesting expression forming on Carol's face, Lanna reined her mount in the opposite direction. She didn't enjoy faking enthusiasm when she didn't feel any.

Giving the sorrel its head, she let the horse pick its way over the wind-smoothened rock to the animal trail leading down from the butte. Its weaving path quickly led her out of sight of the butte, behind boulders and into a stand of blue spruce edged with shivering gold aspens. The stiff breeze carried the distant bawl of the cattle and the occasional shouts of the outriders. The sounds disturbed the more peaceful thud of her horse's hooves as it ambled slowly through the whispering trees.

As she rounded a bend in the sloping trail, the trees thinned into a grass and rock-strewn glade. Another rider was approaching the clearing from the opposite direction. Lanna saw a flash of blue and white stripes edging a brown vest. Then the horse and rider were out of the trees and directly across from her. The bald-faced chestnut tossed its head in a blowing snort and sidestepped impatiently under a checking hold. Hawk held her gaze for a long moment, then eased the pressure on the bit to let the horse go forward at a quick-stepping walk.

"Where are you going?"

Lanna couldn't read anything in the mild inquiry or in his seemingly pleasant expression. "Back to camp for a cup of coffee."

"I'll ride with you," he said and reined his head-strong mount alongside hers.

"I thought you rode alone." She couldn't resist making the stiff reminder.

"I just want to make sure you get there safely." Hawk shrugged.

The impulse to question his sudden interest in her safety died as Lanna realized this might be his way of showing he regretted their last argument. He was a man with a lot of pride. Apologies wouldn't come easy to him.

His resistive mount stayed a half-stride in the lead as they crossed the clearing. It worried at the bit and tossed its head, flashing a marled eye at its rider, as if hoping to catch Hawk off guard.

"Why didn't you ever leave the ranch, Hawk?" Lanna ended the brief silence between them.

"Why should I have left?"

"Why did you stay? Why did you want to stay?" She rephrased the question.

"I've asked myself the same thing."

"And?" she prompted.

"I was dealt a hand. I have to play it out. Maybe when all the cards are on the table, I'll find out whether

I've won or lost." His side glance said it was the only answer he was prepared to give for now.

A bird took flight from a bush in front of them. Hawk's mount reared and plunged, finding a perfect excuse to misbehave. It took him a moment to bring the chestnut under control and back alongside Lanna's sedate horse. Hers had barely flicked an ear at the bird.

Wry humor underlined Hawk's expression. "No one else wanted to ride him."

"I can't imagine why," Lanna murmured dryly. The amused feeling didn't last long before her thoughts were pulled down. "Why doesn't Rawlins like you? He practically raised you."

"He did raise me."

"Then why? Was it because you wanted to marry Carol?" she asked.

"Let's say that he didn't want me for a son-in-law." Hawk smiled thinly.

"Do you still resent her for marrying Chad?"

"She's welcome to him. They are two of a kind. They belong together."

She saw the hardness in his eyes and wondered what he was remembering. "When Chad gave you that beating—"

"Chad?" Hawk interrupted. "He never gave me any beating."

"But Carol said—" Lanna began.

"Carol lied. The only beating I ever got was at the hands of her father, while Bill Short and Luther Wilcox held me. Chad was there, all right, but he just watched. That's when I got this broken nose, as a souvenir." He touched the bump on the bridge of his nose with a gloved finger.

"Tom Rawlins beat you?" Lanna was confused by the conflicting stories. "Why?"

For long seconds, the only sounds were the creak of saddle leather, the jangle of bits and spurs, and the uneven tempo of two horses walking on the hard ground.

Hawk watched the bobbing head of his horse. "He claimed I raped his daughter."

Lanna couldn't respond immediately. She vividly remembered his violent assault on her, aware of the anger that could be aroused within him. Knowing that, she still asked, "Did you?"

Tipping his head back, he laughed silently at the sky. "Do you know you are the first person to ask me? Tom didn't. None of the men. Not even J. B. asked." Lanna felt his bitterness and understood its justification. "If you asked whether I had sex with her, the answer is yes—too many times to count. But that was a long time ago."

"And she married Chad," Lanna murmured.

"She always wanted to become a fine lady like Katheryn. From what I've heard, Carol is the sunshine of Phoenix society, so she got her wish."

Hawk didn't appear to harbor any malice toward her. Lanna couldn't even say that any of what he had told her had made him cynical. There was a certain bitterness, yes, but he had accepted the events in his life as the natural way of things. They hadn't twisted him as they so easily could have done. That said something for his inner strength.

The mention of Katheryn made Lanna ask, "Was your mother's name White Sage?"

"Yes." His sliding glance seemed to ask how she knew.

"John loved her very much. I thought it was Katheryn's Navaho name. The day Bobby Crow Dog came, Katheryn went into a jealous rage. I overheard her tell Carol that John whispered your mother's name before he died." The weight of depression began to settle on her again. Those initial moments when Hawk's presence had uplifted her spirits were slipping away.

"Why are you so preoccupied with the past?"

"Because I'm trying to understand what's going on and why," she sighed. "It's like being lost in a large house with many rooms; only there aren't any lights. Each little piece of information lights a candle so I can find my way."

"You can't change anything. You can't even try without it changing you," he warned.

"We all change, Hawk. It's part of living." Her voice became flat and expressionless.

Reaching out, Hawk took hold of the reins of her horse near the chin strap and forced it to halt. Then he pivoted his mount into a half-circle, overriding its objections, so he was facing her, positioned so close that their legs were rubbing. Lanna was subjected to the narrowed and thorough study of his keen gaze.

"What's wrong, Lanna?" he questioned in faint puzzlement. "Something is. I can feel it. You don't act the same. If I hurt you—"

"It isn't that. It seems to be everything." The vague lift of her shoulders indicated she didn't know the exact cause. "So much has happened—John's death, the unexpected inheritance, and all the confusion after that, being sick, then coming here. I think it's just all finally caught up with me." How could she explain that she didn't seem to care about anything anymore? It was something that bewildered her, too.

Leaning, Hawk encircled the curve of her neck with a leather-gloved hand and pulled her toward him. The hard pressure of his mouth held a hunger that fed on her strength, draining the little she had. Yet, the kiss thrilled her.

Hawk's chestnut didn't like the close contact with her horse and lashed out with a hindfoot, breaking them apart. Hawk punished it with the jab of a spur and reined it even with her horse again. The impatience smoldering in his blue eyes had nothing to do with the vagaries of his mount.

"I'll be missed if I don't get back to the herd soon," he stated.

"I know. You'd better go back," Lanna advised and despised her own apathy. She turned her head away, gathering the reins more firmly in her hand. "I'm not very good company, anyway. I'm sorry."

Ignoring Hawk's frown, she dug her heels into her mount and started for camp. A despondency weighed even heavier on her when she heard the tattoo of the chestnut's hooves cantering in the opposite direction.

Chad was already in camp when she arrived. Coming forward, he helped her dismount and handed the reins of her horse to one of the ranch hands. When she mentioned she wanted a cup of coffee, he got it for her and one for himself.

"What's wrong with me, Chad?" she sighed and glanced at the man sitting next to her on the felled log.

"Don't you feel well?" He was quick to show concern.

"I'm not sick. I just don't have any energy or the desire to do anything but sit. I'm beginning to feel like a vegetable."

"I'm sure you are exaggerating." he smiled.

"I'm not, Chad," she insisted with a weary shake of her head.

"You've been through a lot lately, both physically and emotionally. Your body is probably demanding a rest. What better way than shutting down some of the systems?" he reasoned. "You'll be feeling better soon. You'll see."

"I suppose you're right." It did sound logical, but she continued to worry, anyway.

The rest of the afternoon, Chad stayed by her side, making certain that she took it easy. His undemanding solicitude was reassuring. When he suggested she might prefer to return to the ranch instead of spending the night sleeping out, she refused. She had already created enough problems for him without interrupting more of his plans.

That evening, Lanna didn't have any chance to speak to Hawk, not with both Chad and Carol sitting beside her. Although she felt his eyes on her often during the evening, he didn't approach her. It was early when Carol suggested they turn in for the night, advising Lanna that they would be rising with the sun in the morning. Chad brought their bedrolls from the truck.

"I'll fix your bed for you," Carol volunteered.

"You really don't need to wait on me like this," Lanna protested.

"It's no trouble." Carol shrugged.

"Here." Chad offered a tin cup to her.

"I don't want any more coffee, thanks," Lanna refused.

"It isn't coffee. Mother put some sassafras tea in a canteen and sent it along for you," he explained.

Lanna took the cup, confused by the effort Katheryn had made on her behalf. It didn't seem like her. "That was very thoughtful of her."

"We have all grown to care a great deal about you, Lanna." Chad smiled with affection. "Drink up."

This compassion and concern the Faulkner family expressed for her made Lanna feel as though they really cared. Yet she was bewildered by it, too, when she considered the way they had treated Hawk. It seemed out of character.

Chapter XVIII

Hawk sat in the shadows outside the circle of the firelight. A horse stamped restlessly in the rope corral holding the remuda. His gaze made an absent sweep of the area, then returned to the camp and its snoring occupants. Automatically, he sought out Lanna's sleeping figure.

Hawk wasn't certain what he had expected during their encounter earlier in the day. He had known Lanna wouldn't throw herself into his arms but he hadn't believed she would be so ambivalent. And he didn't accept her explanation. This change in her personality kept nagging at him, depriving him of sleep.

The fire was flickering and dying. Its glow was cast by the red ember remains of dead wood. Soon the night's chill would be invading the camp. Wearing moccasins, instead of boots, in camp, Hawk walked soundlessly to the firewood stacked near the edge of the circle and picked up two of the larger chunks. Sidestepping sleeping bodies, he moved to the fading fire and added the fresh logs to the hot coals.

The hungry flames leaped over the dry bark, enlarging its circle of light in a sudden burst of fire. Hawk watched the fire cast its illumination on Lanna's sleeping form. His gaze sharpened when he saw the involuntary twitching of her body beneath the quilted blanket. He moved to her side to awaken her from the nightmare.

"Lanna, wake up," he whispered very softly so he wouldn't disturb Carol, on the other side of her. When his hand touched her shoulder, she jerked in a convulsive reflex. He quickly covered her mouth with his hand, anticipating her outcry of alarm and stifling it. "You were having a nightmare," he explained when her widened eyes focused on him and removed his hand.

"Your eyes," she murmured in a peculiarly absent voice, "they are so blue."

Something was wrong. The feeling was so intense, it left him shaken. He studied her with a new sharpness, noticing the dilation of her pupils and the flush of her skin. The pieces to the puzzle began to fall into place: the vividness of color, the disinterest, the twitching. Hawk recognized the symptoms and cursed silently for not suspecting something like this before.

"Listen to me, Lanna," he whispered urgently. "It's very important." She gave him a wide-eyed look of unnatural concentration. "When you drank that coffee before you went to sleep, did it taste funny to you?"

"No coffee." She tried to shake her head, but her coordination was poor. "Katheryn sent tea."

Hawk rocked back on his heels, glancing beyond Carol's slumbering shape to Chad. His jaw flexed in hard anger. Lanna whispered something to draw his attention back to her. It was part of a hallucination and unimportant at the moment.

"Close your eyes, Lanna. Go back to sleep. Everything is all right. Do you understand?" He watched her relax and close her eyes. The rest of his questions would have to wait until the effects of the drug had worn off. He couldn't risk upsetting Lanna in her present state. First, he had to confirm his suspicions; then he had to make plans.

Leaving her side, he slipped cautiously past Carol and Chad. Logic dictated that the tea had been previously prepared, since Chad wouldn't risk fixing it when so many people were around. It narrowed Hawk's search considerably. He found the canteen of tea in Chad's saddlebags. A taste confirmed it was peyote, a very weak blend.

He had the proof in his hands, but who would believe him? In her present drugged condition, Lanna could be too easily influenced against him. It would take forty-eight hours, at the very least, for the effects of the peyote to wear off. Which meant if he wanted her to rationally consider his evidence, he had to get her away from here. Recapping it, Hawk returned the canteen to the pouch and put everything back the way he'd found it.

With a quick glance around the campfire, Hawk made sure no one had awakened before he retraced his steps to the outer circle of the camp. This was one time when it was an advantage to be isolated from the others. Using the saddle blankets and pads to muffle the clunk of metal and leather, Hawk carried his gear to the rope corral. Then he returned to raid the camp mess of a sackful of supplies.

The horses snorted and milled nervously when he appeared, then settled down when they recognized the quiet sound of his voice. He was able to walk right up to the gentle-natured sorrel Lanna had been riding, catching it with ease. Outside the corral, he tied it to a tree and put his saddle on it. He went back to drop a loop around the big dappled buckskin and lead it out.

There was no saddle for it. Hawk couldn't risk trying to take Lanna's. When the time came, he would have to ride it bareback.

Gliding silently back to the campfire, he went directly to Lanna. He didn't awaken her as he gently picked her up in his arms and carried her back to the horses. The sorrel stood quietly as he set Lanna in the saddle and swung on behind her. It didn't object to its double burden. The buckskin resisted the initial pull on the rope around its neck, then yielded to follow the sorrel and its two riders.

Staying at a walk, Hawk kept the sorrel to the carpet of grass. Its thickness would muffle the sound of the horses until they were well away from the camp. As soon as there was distance between them, Hawk urged the horse into a trot to cover more ground.

Chad would follow them as soon as he discovered Lanna was gone. If the rest of what Hawk suspected was accurate, Chad wouldn't let her be taken from him without a fight. Hopefully, he wouldn't leave until morning. He might guess that Hawk was taking her onto the Reservation. Rawlins would know where his mother's hogan was located, but Hawk was counting on the fact that he wouldn't know about the cave in the bluffs above it. It would take at least two days, maybe more, for the effects of the peyote to wear off. He had to keep Lanna hidden out that long.

Every hour, Hawk stopped to rest the horse. It was nearly two o'clock when he switched the gear to the buckskin and started out again, leading the sorrel. At four o'clock, he crossed the interstate, only a short distance down from the southernmost boundary of the Navaho Reservation.

Although she mumbled incoherently several times, Lanna never roused from her trance-like sleep. Each time Hawk looked at the woman in his arms, swaddled in the quilt from her bedroll, he was stirred by a great feeling of protectiveness. Its powerful force drove out the weariness in his own body and pushed aside the need to rest and sleep.

When the sun peered over the eastern horizon, Hawk stopped the buckskin to study the terrain ahead. It was less than three miles to the abandoned hogan of his mother. The buckskin shifted beneath him and blew loudly in the dawn stillness. Careful not to disturb her, Hawk eased Lanna into a more secure position in his arms. The early light of a new morning touched her face, highlighting the wing of her brow and the proud bones of her cheeks. His gaze lingered on the alluring curve of her lips, soft and generously wide. He smoothed the brown satin hair away from her forehead with humble gentleness.

"It's going to get rough from here on," he murmured aloud. "I've left tracks a blind man could follow. We're going to have to take to the rocks now. It's nothing you have to fear." Hawk knew how sensations could be intensified in her drugged state. "It's just going to be a little bumpy. You're safe. Remember that. Nothing is going to hurt you."

She made a faint sound, as if she'd heard him. It was likely she had, since peyote intensified the user's perception of sight and sound. His voice had probably inserted itself into one of her dreams. Violence trembled through him, directed toward those who had done this to her. But it wasn't the time for such an emotion, and Hawk suppressed it with iron control.

Ahead was a dry wash. Hawk pointed the buckskin at it and tugged on the sorrel's lead rope. The horses would leave no distinct tracks in the loose sand. There wouldn't be any way to distinguish them from the impressions left by a flock of sheep that had passed this way a few days ago.

A hundred yards down the gully, a bank had been caved in by a gravel slide. Hawk spurred the buckskin up the loose rock. It plunged and bucked its way up the slope, sending a cascade of new gravel down to cover its trail. At the top of the slide was a jumble of boulders and a clay sand that the desert sun had baked as hard as concrete. Hawk followed it to the stone mesa that formed the walls of the canyon where the abandoned hogan stood.

His roundabout route added two miles to their journey. Their destination was ahead, below the canyon rim. He halted the buckskin and wrapped the lead rope around the saddlehorn in a half-hitch. Dismounting with Lanna in his arms, Hawk laid her on the ground well clear of the ground-tied buckskin, then went to investigate the last leg of their trip on foot. It had been a long time since he'd traveled the narrow trail winding down the cliff to the cave gouged in the canyon's rock face. The erosion of wind, rain, and time might have wiped out part of it or all of it.

Crouching at the rim, Hawk studied first the canyon floor. It looked deserted in the early morning hour, but its inhabitants were many. A coyote was feasting on a rodent it had unearthed, and a long-eared hare was busy washing its face, pausing often to test the air for the scent of danger.

Almost directly below Hawk was a spring, the only source of water for several miles. During drought years, even this spring had been known to go dry. But where it trickled out of the rocky desert soil, a stand of cottonwood trees grew. One giant towered high, hugging the rock wall and reaching for the canyon rim. It was this tree, with its thick and spreading limbs, that concealed the cave entrance from the view of anyone on the canyon floor, unless they specifically knew of its existence and exact location.

The old trail stopped at the narrow ledge outside the mouth of the cave. From there, the canyon wall sheered straight to its floor. Handholds had been chiseled into the rock face by the long-ago dwellers of the cave. They came within a few feet of reaching all the way to the bottom of the canyon. Hawk hoped they were still intact, since they would provide his quickest access to water. Otherwise, he would have to lower himself by rope and hope it was long enough to reach the bottom, or else ride all the way around to the mouth of the canyon, which meant leaving tracks for the searchers to find.

The rounding roof of the hogan was barely visible from his position, but he could see the remains of the stick corral and its fallen *ramada*. Satisfied that he could observe most of what went on in the canyon, Hawk began to move cautiously down the ledge of rock that formed the narrow trail to the cave.

There were places where erosion had cut into the trail, yet it was still possible for a sure-footed horse to traverse it. A fallen boulder blocked a third of the entrance, but it only added to the natural concealment of the cave opening. Entering the cool darkness, Hawk struck a match and held it high. The interior had been crudely hollowed out to form a large cavity, large enough to accommodate the horses, just as Hawk had remembered. He hadn't trusted his memory because he didn't know how much of it had been exaggerated by a child's perception of size.

Emerging from the cave, Hawk climbed the trail to the top where he'd left Lanna and the horses. He gathered Lanna in his arms and carried her down the narrow trail to the cave. After making her as comfortable as he could, he went back to lead the horses down, first the buckskin, then the sorrel. He checked to be sure Lanna showed no signs of waking up before he left the cave again.

A glance at the position of the sun in the morning sky warned Hawk that he was running out of time. When Chad discovered that he was gone, as well as Lanna, he would set out in pursuit of them. Hawk guessed that the search party would be split up into two groups—at Rawlins' directions, since Chad would never think of it. One group would track them on horseback. But the other group, the one Chad would lead, would travel by pickup to the canyon. Depending on how quickly they got organized, the first group could be here within an hour—certainly not more than two.

It was the second group that concerned Hawk now, and the wiliness of Tom Rawlins. He retraced the last mile of their route. Where a metal horseshoe had left a white gash on the stone, he rubbed dirt into it. He sprinkled sand over any vague imprint of a hoof on the ground. He knew better than to sweep them away with brush, since the marks left by the branches would leave their own trail. Painstakingly, he repositioned stones that had been overturned, revealing their ground-darkened underbelly instead of the sun-bleached whiteness of the others around them. All the while he took care not to let his moccasined feet leave any tracks. He found the place where the flock of sheep had grazed and cut a shirtload of grass to feed the horses.

Satisfied that the only thing that could follow their trail now was a bloodhound, Hawk returned to the cave, tossed a third of the grass to the horses, and shook the rest out of his shirt near the rear wall before putting his shirt back on. Gathering twigs and broken pieces of branches the wind had blown onto the ledge from the towering cottonwood, Hawk built a tiny fire in the rear of the cave and put coffee on to boil. He flexed his tired muscles and knew he would have to be content with snatched minutes of sleep for the next forty-eight hours. He rubbed his eyes, feeling their grating rawness, and rocked back on his heels to patiently wait for events to unfold in their own time.

What would happen if Chad found them? Hawk wasn't sure how desperate his brother was. He would have to play it as it happened and prepare for the worst.

Lanna's eyes opened slowly in the shadowy darkness. She had difficulty figuring out where she was. A horse stamped restlessly somewhere nearby. She felt the vibration of it beneath her. A light flickered and she focused on it. A man's figure was hunched beside a small fire, his hands cupped around a tin mug. She began to understand the hardness of her bed and the darkness. They were camping out with the cowboys on the fall drive.

She turned her head to see if Carol was awake and was blinded by a patchwork of light flooding in through an opening in the darkness. It startled her, causing her to become instantly wide awake. Two horses were standing behind a rope strung in a diagonal line and tied around opposing rocks. In the shadowy dimness, she recognized the sorrel horse she had ridden the day before. The second animal was light-colored and a hand taller.

It slowly began to dawn on her that she was in some kind of a cave. Lanna scooted uneasily into a sitting position, her alarmed gaze racing to the man near the fire. Her movement had drawn his attention. With a trace of relief, she recognized Hawk, but his presence didn't solve her confusion.

Straightening, he walked over to her and offered her

the cup in his hand. "Coffee? We only have one cup, and it has to serve as both pot and drinking mug." He didn't refer to the strangeness of her surroundings.

"Where am I?" Lanna absently accepted the cup he handed her. "How did I get here?"

"I brought you here," Hawk admitted with casual ease.

"Yes, but . . ." —Lanna looked around her again—". . . where is 'here'? And how did you manage to get me here without me knowing it?"

"You were drugged."

"Drugged? That's nonsense!" She laughed in disbelief, then sobered when she realized he was serious. "What did you do? Give me something while I was asleep?" Her question held more bewilderment than accusation.

"Have you ever heard of peyote? You would probably be more familiar with it as the drug mescaline, which is obtained from the button-top of the peyote cactus." He crouched down to be nearly level with her, balancing on the balls of his feet.

"Mescaline, yes." Lanna had heard of that. "It's a psychedelic drug, in most instances non-habit-forming and rarely leaving any lasting side-effects, depending on the user." She recited what she remembered about it. "Are you saying that I took it?"

"It's usually brewed into a tea," Hawk stated.

"A tea." Lanna began to realize what he was implying, although she didn't understand how he knew about it. "Sassafras tea? I've been drinking a cup before I go to bed at night. Carol usually brings it to me."

"Last night it was Chad."

"Yes." She nodded as a cold chill shivered down her spine. "He said Katheryn had sent some in a canteen for me. It explains the dreams I've been having, doesn't it? Why didn't I suspect something before?" Lanna wondered as the truth became starkly clear. "But how did you guess?"

"I tried to awaken you from what I thought was a bad dream last night. I've seen the peyote dream-trance before. The Native American Church uses it as a sacrament in certain religious ceremonies under very controlled conditions. When I found the canteen of tea in Chad's saddlebags, it confirmed my suspicions."

"But why? What did they hope to gain?"

"The dream state or the time of heightened awareness lasts about twelve hours. Usually the effects of the drug wear off completely after twenty-four. But when it's used regularly—and you've been taking it every night—those last twelve hours you lose interest in what's happening around you—you don't feel like doing anything."

"That's exactly what happened." She brushed a hand across her face, suddenly realizing why she had been acting so strange. "I couldn't understand why I was feeling so apathetic about everything. That's why! But what does that accomplish?"

"Since you started having these dreams, have you signed any documents without reading them first?" Hawk questioned as he watched her closely.

"No, I—" Then she remembered. "Chad had some papers that he wanted me to sign. He said they were proxies so he could vote my shares."

"Did you sign the papers?" His mouth thinned grimly.

"No. I didn't feel like reading them, and, even though he explained to me what they contained, I wouldn't sign." Lanna was amazed that she hadn't signed them. "I couldn't understand why he was pushing me so hard." She stared at him, reading in his face his mistrust of Chad. "He was trying to cheat me in some way. That's why he was drugging me."

"I can almost guarantee it. Drink the coffee before it gets cold," Hawk ordered.

She obediently took a sip, but her mind was still racing. "What do you suppose was in that document? Was I signing everything over to him?"

"It was probably much more subtle than that," Hawk replied dryly. "More than likely, it was a legal document that gave him control of your inheritance, similar to a power of attorney, giving him the right to act in your behalf and depriving you of any say-so."

"But Chad is already well off—rich in his own right. Why did he do it?" Lanna protested the lack of reason.

"It's commonly known as greed." Hawk smiled. "Why should he settle for half when there was a way he could get all of it?" He scooped up a handful of loose dirt from the cave floor and let it trickle through his fingers. "There might be another reason, too. All his life, Chad has been second. He was second to J. B. in Katheryn's affections. Even Carol came to his marriage bed secondhand. In business, he was second in command to J. B. Maybe he even believed he was second to me. Chad hated sharing. When he learned he was sharing the inheritance with you, it was probably more than he could take."

"And I thought he was being so good and kind to me." She shook her head at her gullibility. "I kept thinking how much like John he was—so considerate and thoughtful."

"J. B. was really considerate and thoughtful," Hawk mocked. "He should have known that when he left you all that money, he was making you a target for every swindler in the country. That's probably why Chad brought you to the ranch—to eliminate all the competition for control of your money."

"But why drug me? I already trusted him." Lanna combed her fingers through her hair as if to smooth out her feelings of confusion. "It never even occurred to me that I shouldn't—not even after all the negative things you said about him. I thought you were just prejudiced."

"Maybe he was worried that the Faulkner charm wouldn't work on you. He might have discovered that you weren't susceptible." He crooked a finger under her chin and lifted it. "Were you?"

The searching fire of his gaze examined her expression. A tremor started in her heart and spread throughout her veins.

"I am definitely susceptible to the Faulkner charm, but not Chad's," Lanna informed him.

The corners of his mouth deepened in a pleased smile as his thumb held her chin still for his kiss. There was restraint in his passion, arousing, yet controlled. Lanna yearned for him madly, and she realized the lingering influence of the peyote was heightening the sensation. Hawk reluctantly ended the kiss to rub his thumb over the outline of her trembling lips.

"Under the circumstances"—his voice had a husky catch to it—"Chad must have decided he needed an alternative to his charm. At a guess, I'd say the solution came to him when Bobby Crow Dog showed up at the ranch."

"Why?" Lanna was disappointed when Hawk took his hand away.

"If you aren't going to drink that coffee, I am." He lifted the cup from her hand and straightened to stand above her. "It was out of character for Chad to let Bobby Crow Dog stay at the ranch. But the old man would know where to get the peyote and not arouse anyone's curiosity. Chad certainly couldn't, not without starting rumors about his possible drug habits."

"So he had Bobby Crow Dog obtain it for him," Lanna sighed.

"Chad probably paid him with whiskey. I asked Bobby where he got it and he told me he had sold some big magic. I thought he was talking about one of the trinkets he was peddling—not peyote," Hawk admitted. "He even told me that he sold it to the Two-Faced One, but the name applied to too many people who I was acquainted with, including Chad."

"And Katheryn and Carol," Lanna added to the list. The names sparked her anger, but it was self-directed. "I can't believe I was so damned gullible! I wasn't fooled just by Chad, but by them, too!"

"You aren't the only one who was fooled. So was I. In my arrogance I thought they wanted to get rid of me because I was an unwanted reminder of the past. But they wanted me out of the way so I wouldn't uncover the game they were playing with you," Hawk explained. "I must have had a premonition when I said they would turn on you if I wasn't around. Any real or imagined threat from me against them died with J. B."

"I'm glad you didn't go," Lanna declared. On her own, she would never have discovered what was happening to her until it was too late.

"We aren't through this yet," Hawk cautioned.

Which brought Lanna full circle back to the first question. "Where are we?"

"I'll show you. Come look." Hawk held out his hand to pull her to her feet.

Folding back the quilt that covered her feet, she took his hand and stood up, a little awkwardly. He led her to the mouth of the cave. The sunlight spilling through the brown leaves of the tree outside created an intricate pattern on the interior walls of the cave. Lanna stopped short of the outer ledge and looked straight down to the canyon floor. Quickly averting her gaze from the dizzying sight, she noticed the narrow trail leading up to the rim.

"See the roof of that building near the entrance to the canyon?" Hawk pointed and Lanna nodded, just barely making out the convex roof. "That's where I lived as a child with my mother. We are on the Navaho Reservation." When his arm came down, it was to curve around her waist.

"Why did we come here?" She turned to look up to him, liking the strength and self-possession she saw.

"Because I needed somewhere to keep you for a couple of days until the effects of the peyote wore off. Maybe by late tomorrow, you'll be back to normal." His eyes moved over her, keen and assessing. "Right now, your senses are still under its influence, which is half the reason I'm not going to bed with you. I don't want an exaggerated response from you to taint the experience with phoniness."

Lanna wouldn't argue with that, although she longed to. "What's the other half?" she asked instead.

"Because we're going to have company soon, and I want to know the moment they arrive." His gaze left her face to make a slow, thorough sweep of the canyon, the rim, and its entrance.

"You haven't explained why you picked this place. There must have been half a dozen other places we could have gone."

"Rawlins and several of the older hands know every inch of the ranch as well as I do. If we had tried to make it to a town to hole up, we would have been seen. The Faulkner money and power can persuade a lot of people to talk about what they've seen. But this place"
—with a nod of his head, he included all of the surrounding countryside—"is homeground only to me. Rawlins knows the location of the hogan, but I'm

staking everything on the ace he doesn't know about this cave."

"It's Rawlins you expect to come here."

"Chad will be here first. Rawlins will tell him how to get to it, but he'll track us with a couple of riders, hand-picked to keep their mouths shut."

"He's following our trail. It will lead him right here, won't it?" she questioned in faint alarm.

"He'll lose it about a mile away, if not before," Hawk assured her and turned to study her for a silent minute. He ran a leather-gloved finger down the curve of her cheek in a subdued caress. "I might be getting you into a worse mess, Lanna. Before, all you stood to lose was money. It's hard to say how desperate Chad might be feeling right now or what lengths he might feel compelled to go to in order to cover up what he tried to do or carry it through."

Lanna recognized the potential danger of the situation. "I'm not afraid." Which was strangely the truth. And the knowledge lent a calmness to her voice.

"As long as we aren't out there, moving around, we won't be spotted. We can stay hidden away in here until they get tired of looking for us."

"What about food and water?"

"I took the liberty of raiding the camp supplies before we left," Hawk confessed with a rash grin. "As for water, there's a spring directly below us."

"And the pump to get it up here?" Lanna asked in jest.

"You can't see them, but there are handholds chiseled into the face of the rock leading down to the canyon floor. All I have to do is climb down and fill the canteens."

A glance at the perpendicular rock wall alarmed Lanna. "What if you fall and break your neck?"

Soft laughter came from his throat, mocking her concern, as his arm tightened to curve her closer to his length. "Now why would I do a foolish thing like that?" He brushed a kiss on her cheek. "I'll be careful," Hawk promised.

Lowering her head, she rested her forehead against his shoulder bone. "We can't stay here forever, Hawk. After a few days, then what?"

"Then . . . we'll choose the time to confront Chad." He was almost offhanded with the statement.

Lanna closed her eyes, liking the way Hawk kept saying "we." "You once told me that you didn't get involved in other people's affairs. You aren't exactly a disinterested observer now."

"This time there's a difference—" His explanation was never finished as he stiffened, his fingers biting into her shoulder. Lanna could feel his whole body coming to a state of full alertness and lifted her head to see what was wrong. She heard the rumble of a vehicle an instant before Hawk warned, "They're coming." He pushed her toward the inside of the cave. "Kick the fire out and keep the horses quiet."

The tiny fire had nearly burned itself out. All Lanna had to do was smother the coals with the loose dirt from the cave floor. She moved to the horses, stroking the nose of the buckskin while the sorrel nuzzled her shoulder. Tension was coiling in her stomach as she glanced toward the opening. Hawk was lying flat on his stomach at the cave entrance. She wished she was with him so she could watch what was going on, too, but she had to guess what was happening by the distant sounds she heard.

The vehicle stopped; its motor switched off. There was the tinny clap of metal against metal as doors were slammed. That was followed by a tense silence. Lanna strained and caught the faint sound of voices, or so she imagined. She couldn't be sure. The buckskin turned its head toward the opening, pricking its ears. Remembering her job, she caught at its nose.

Time creeped. After what seemed like hours had passed, her mind began to question the need to remain with the horses. This time Lanna didn't listen to it, recognizing her waning attention and determination as side-effects of the peyote. Finally, Hawk inched backward into the cave before he rolled quietly to his feet and came to her.

"What's happening?" Lanna whispered and searched his impassive features. "Are they leaving?"

"No." A slight negative shake accompanied his low voice. "I think Chad intends to wait to see if Rawlins trails us here."

"How long will that be?"

"This afternoon, probably late. Tracking is slow business," he explained. "Rawlins will keep to the trail even after he guesses where we're heading."

"You said he'd lose it a mile from here," she reminded him.

"When he does, he'll send one of the riders on ahead to meet up with Chad. But Rawlins will stay behind to worry the area—ride a few circles around the point where he lost our tracks—trying to pick up a trace. He won't give up easily." But Hawk didn't sound concerned as he moved to the rear of the cave and picked up an armful of yellowed grass to feed the horses. "You might as well relax for a while," he advised. "It's going to be a long day."

It was made even longer by the pressure of confinement and the need to keep all sound and movement at a minimum. As Hawk had predicted, it was the middle of the afternoon when a lone rider approached the hogan.

More than an hour later, two more riders came. A short while after that, Lanna heard the slam of doors and the truck starting up.

"Are they leaving?" Lanna whispered from her post by the horses.

"No." Hawk was crouched in the shadow of the boulder at the cave entrance. "Chad is leaving, but Rawlins and his men must be planning to camp here for the night. They've picketed their horses and are building a fire."

Lanna stifled a sigh and glanced at the sack of supplies. "We might as well eat, too. I'll make coffee and fix the meal," she volunteered.

Before she could open the sack of supplies, Hawk was standing beside her. "No coffee and no fire," he told her. "We'll have a cold sandwich, the same as we had for lunch. There is still enough bread and meat left."

"But why?" she protested.

"Right now they only *suspect* we are in the vicinity." Hawk stressed the verb. "But if they smell food cooking or woodsmoke, they will *know* we're around here."

"You're right, of course," Lanna conceded reluctantly.

Both the bread and the cold beef had begun to dry out, and there was only water from the canteens to wash it down. It was tepid and flat. A cup of hot coffee would have gone a long way in keeping out the night's chill that invaded the cave when the sun went down. Lanna wrapped the quilt around her and huddled in its warmth near the feet of the horses. A fire at night would carry the added risk of exposing a light that might be seen by the men camped in the canyon. Lanna knew it was out of the question to suggest it, so she shivered in silence.

Leaving his vigil, Hawk moved noiselessly into the heart of the cave and stooped to pick up his bedroll. He untied it and separated the groundsheet from the quilt. Shaking it out, he spread it on the ground lengthwise from the saddle.

Glancing at Lanna, he said, "There's no point in both of us losing sleep. You might as well get some rest." He wrapped the quilt around his shoulders like a cloak and moved back to the entrance.

Lanna looked at the tarp with the saddle for a pillow and ignored its invitation. Instead, she got up and walked to where Hawk was sitting with his legs stretched out and his back resting against the hard cave wall.

"Let me watch for a while and you get some sleep," she suggested.

In the dim light cast by the moon, she saw the tired smile curve his mouth as he shook his head in refusal. "Go lie down," he ordered softly.

"If you aren't, neither am I." Lanna sank to her knees beside him. "I'll stay here with you."

He hesitated, then lifted an arm to open the front of the blanket. Lanna accepted the invitation to join him inside the fold of his blanket and rested her head against the curve of his shoulder. She spread her quilt over both of them.

"We'll be warmer this way," she said.

"Mmm." She felt the vibration of Hawk's agreeing sound and the stir of his breath on her hair. "As long as it doesn't get too warm," he murmured.

She smiled in the darkness, enjoying the comfortable weight of his arm across her stomach and the invigorating warmth of his body heat combining with hers.

Chapter XIX

There was a whir of wings and Hawk's eyes snapped open. Angrily, he realized his half-conscious catnap had become a sound sleep. For how long? He shot a glance at the sun, newly risen in the sky. Two hours, maybe, not much more than that. Lanna was heavy in his arms, breathing deeply in sleep.

His body was stiff and numb from being in the cramped position, but Hawk held off moving. Something had alarmed those birds, so he remained motionless and listened. It was several seconds before he separated the rustling sound of a breeze stirring the brown leaves in the tree from the swish of something or someone walking through tall grass. Then he heard the distinctive sound of a horseshoe striking stone. It came from almost directly below, and there was more than one.

He covered Lanna's mouth with his hand to awaken her and smother any involuntary sound she might make. She stiffened, then relaxed under the silencing pressure of his hand. The snorting of a horse was followed by the sound of pebbles rolling under a boot. Hawk glanced at their own horses, but they didn't appear interested in the sounds.

There was a splash of water, which told Hawk they were at the spring. "Ah, that's the sweetest water I've ever tasted." Hawk recognized Bill Short's voice.

"Fill the canteens before the horses muddy it up," Rawlins ordered.

"How do you suppose he managed to vanish without a trace?" Short questioned on a confused note. "I figured he would show up before now."

"Which shows how cunning he is. That's what he wants us to think so we'll waste time waiting around here while he lights out for other parts. That's why he led us up to within a mile of this place."

"Then where is he?"

"Most of these Navahos have themselves a summer hogan up in the hills. I'd guess that's where Hawk has taken the girl," Rawlins said. "He's probably up there now, laughing. He won't be laughing when we find him."

"Do you know where to look?" Short sounded skeptical.

"I remember J. B. mentioning a couple of places in the hills where there was water. We'll find it, if we don't cut his trail before then," Rawlins was confident. "Let's mount up."

There was the squeaking groan of saddle leather and horses splashing through water before the ground vibrated with the thunder of cantering hooves. Hawk waited until the sound had receded, then shifted Lanna out of his arms to rise stiffly and watch the departing riders.

"Have they gone for good?" Lanna asked hopefully when he turned back to her.

"I don't know. Why don't you water the horses and give them the rest of the grass?" he suggested and swung the blanket off his shoulders.

"Where are you going?"

"Maybe I'm just naturally suspicious"—Hawk shrugged—"but I want to make sure they are really leaving and that conversation we overheard wasn't part of a setup. I won't be long," he promised, then started up the narrow trail to the canyon rim.

Within half an hour, Hawk returned. "They're gone," he stated, answering the silent question in her look. "They rode into the hills west of us. This is one time when Rawlins outsmarted himself. We should be safe for a couple of days." Lanna heard the tiredness in his voice as he almost sighed the last words. The lines deepened around his eyes in a faint smile. "How about some coffee and some hot food?"

While she cut slices of bacon from the slab he'd brought, Hawk started the small fire. They shared a cup of coffee while the bacon sizzled in the small skillet. Lanna used the last of the water to stir up the dehydrated eggs, then fried them in the bacon grease. It was the most delicious meal she'd eaten in ages.

"There are a couple of swallows of coffee left." Hawk passed her the tin mug.

"We don't have any more water," she told him before taking a drink and savoring the rich coffee flavor. It revitalized her, but her muscles were still stiff from the cramped sleep she had had.

"I'll get some." He moved to string the canteens over his shoulder. "The horses need some more grass, anyway."

"Wait." Lanna quickly drained the last of the coffee, not wasting a drop. "I'll come with you."

"What? And break your neck?" Hawk joked.

Lanna thought of the makeshift ladder he'd described, with footholds carved into the stone, and she shrugged. "I did a little climbing when I lived in

Colorado. Nothing particularly challenging or danger-ous, but if you can make it, so can I." Then added the final, and most telling argument: "I'm tired of being cooped up inside this cave, anyway. I'm getting claus-trophobic." Which was a slight exaggeration, but she didn't want to be left behind.

Hawk hesitated a second, then agreed. "Okay, you can come. I'll go down first."

"So you can catch me when I fall," Lanna joked.

"That's right." Hawk smiled and reached down to toss her his quilt. "Throw that down to me so I can bundle the grass in it and have something to carry it in coming back up."

She followed him onto the ledge outside the mouth of the cave and watched as he swung over the edge, searching with his feet for the first foothold. He disappeared slowly from her view. Lanna held her breath until she saw him on the ground. She threw him the folded blanket.

"It's your turn," Hawk called, cupping his hands to his mouth and issuing the challenge. "You can change your mind if you want."

"Not a chance." Lanna mimicked his movements, lying belly down over the edge and swinging her feet over.

She wasn't as confident as she had implied, but once she had started, there seemed to be only one way to go—and that was down. She preferred using the footholds to reach at her destination rather than falling. Her knees were shaking when she got to the bottom and Hawk's hands closed around her waist to lift her the last couple of feet. Lanna could have accused him of exaggeration. The erosion of time had turned many of the footholds and handholds into finger and toe holds, but she was too glad to be safely on the ground to worry about them now.

"Is your heart still beating?" Hawk smiled with his eyes.

"A hundred times a minute," Lanna admitted.

"You can fill the canteens from the spring while I cut some grass for the horses." Unslinging the canteens from his shoulder, he handed them to her.

"Aren't you worried about leaving tracks for them to find if they come back?" she asked.

"They've ridden and walked all over this canyon. They'll never be able to tell our tracks from theirs," he assured her.

Removing his hunting knife from its sheath, he carried it and the blanket over to the tall, yellowed grass beneath the trees. Lanna walked the few feet to the spring with the empty canteens. At the point where it seeped from underground, the water flowed gaily over a washboard of pebbles and emerged into a small pool about the same width and depth of a washtub. Over many years, the water had eaten a narrow channel into the solid rock at the opposite end of the pool, where it escaped in a silver ribbon. Lanna lost sight of the tiny stream as it entered a tunnel of lush grass.

She held the canteens under the pool's surface and listened to them gurgle as the water rushed in. The water was almost icy-cold. She scooped a swallow up in her hand and sipped its sweet wetness, then splashed some on her face. Her skin tingled, revived by the chill of the water.

When the canteens were full, Lanna set them by the canyon wall and wandered over to where Hawk was working. The hogan was plainly visible beyond the stand of cottonwoods. Her curiosity was aroused when she noticed a much smaller building half-hidden among the trees.

"Hawk, what is that?" She pointed to the small

building that was almost a miniature of the hogan. "An outhouse?"

He looked and turned back to continue cutting swaths of grass, but not before Lanna saw the grin that split his face. "No, that's a sweathouse."

"What's a sweathouse?" It didn't upset Lanna that her question amused him.

"Just what the word implies—a house where you sweat." Hawk paused in his labor. "I suppose you could call it the Navaho version of a sauna."

"That sounds heavenly," she murmured wistfully. "I don't suppose it's been used in a long time."

"As a matter of fact, it has. I use it whenever I'm here for any length of time." He began slicing at the grass with the knife blade, then tossing the clumps on the nearby blanket.

Lanna gazed at the building. "I don't suppose that maybe . . ." She turned back to Hawk and found him watching her with a dancing glint in his blue eyes.

"A sweathouse is an exclusively male institution," he stated.

"No women allowed?" she questioned with faint challenge.

Hawk looked to the west. Lanna knew his thoughts were on Rawlins and where he might be. Just for a minute, she had allowed herself to forget about their pursuers. She reluctantly shelved the idea of using the sweathouse, realizing it might be too risky.

"You cut some grass for a while." He stabbed the point of the knife blade into the ground. "I'll start a fire and get the stones hot."

"If you don't think we should—" Lanna began in a reasonable tone.

"We'll never have a better time," Hawk interrupted. "Tomorrow they might swing back here to see if they were right all along."

"You talked me into it." A pair of dimples dented Lanna's cheeks when she smiled.

"I thought I could," he murmured dryly.

Hawk was gone for what seemed a long time. When he returned, Lanna had added enough grass to the mound he had accumulated to fill the blanket. Hawk was carrying a hollowed-out gourd, shaped like a pitcher. He set it aside to tie the four corners of the blanket.

"I'll take this to the cave." Slipping the knot of two corners over his head, Hawk slid one arm free so the bundle was positioned on his back. "Why don't you fill that pitcher with water while I'm gone?"

"Okay."

But Lanna watched him make the climb, worried that he might not make it safely with that awkward bundle on his back. When he hooked a knee over the ledge and swung onto it, she released a sigh of relief and walked to the spring.

Hawk hadn't come down by the time she had filled the pitcher with water, so she walked to the sweathouse. A dusty blanket acted as a door to the dirt-covered building. Lanna lifted it aside and immediately felt the rush of heat. She stepped inside, letting the blanket fall into place behind her. The smallness of the building made it quick to heat, with the earthen walls holding it in. Smooth stones were piled in the center. Lanna dipped her fingers in the pitcher of water and sprinkled drops on the stones. The droplets sizzled and were quickly gone.

Leaving the gourd inside, Lanna went back out. She looked toward the cave, but there was no sign of Hawk. The temptation to use the sweathouse-sauna was simply too great. Without waiting for him, Lanna undressed, neatly folded her blouse and jeans with her underclothes, and laid them near the door.

Before the brisk autumn air could chill her skin, she hurried into the lodge. This time she was liberal in the amount of water she splashed on the hot stones, sending a rush of steam into the air. Sitting down, she stretched out her legs on the hard ground and leaned back on her hands. Within minutes, she felt the moist heat surging through her body, soothing tired muscles and easing the tension of the last twenty-four hours. Tilting her head back, Lanna closed her eyes to enjoy the sensation.

A cool draft of air fanned her skin. She opened her eyes to see Hawk towering above her, dressed in a breechcloth that hid so little. His flesh was a smooth, pale copper, from the long length of his legs to the flat muscles of his torso. There was a darkness to his blue eyes as they swept over her. Lanna felt the thudding of her heart grow louder. The breechcloth revealed the way the corded muscles of his thighs attached themselves to his hipbone and exposed the hard curved line of his buttocks. There was a tightness in her throat, an exhilarating tension racing through her nerve ends.

"The stones were hot," she murmured. "I didn't think you'd mind if I came in before you were back."

"I don't." Hawk reached to splash more water on the stones, and steam billowed in a thin white fog.

Fascinated by the sheen that his perspiration was bringing to his skin, Lanna missed the movement of his hand that untied the cloth covering his loins. But when he unwrapped it and tossed it carelessly to the floor, it suddenly hurt to breathe as she was suffocated by a heat that came both from without and within.

With an animal grace, Hawk lowered himself to the floor beside her, his gaze locked with hers. Their primitive surroundings, their nudity, and the volcanic heat rising from the core all pressed Lanna backward. Hawk followed her. He tangled a handful of hair in his fingers, holding her head still while he studied her flushed face. Lanna's breath left her in a sigh as his mouth began a slow descent to her lips.

She lifted her hands to his sweat-slick skin, letting them glide over the rippling muscles of his back and ribs. Their mouths explored each other in devouring sensuality, tongues investigating and mating. Yet there was a slowness, a languor, a stoking of the flames to make them burn hot and long.

His hand moved over her glistening body, her flesh burning under his touch. His caressing fingers seemed to enjoy discovering again every sensitive inch of her body, tracing the tantalizing hollow of her throat and circling her breasts. The earthy smell of him filled her senses, blocking out everything but the long-denied aching within her.

Dragging his mouth from her lips, he didn't let it leave her skin as it moved over her cheek to the pulse beating wildly in her throat. His lips parted, letting her feel the wetness of his mouth against her skin.

"I've waited so long for this." There was a ragged edge to his voice, a roughness to his breathing. It echoed much of what Lanna was feeling.

When his lips brushed the curve of a breast, she slid her fingers into his hair. Sweat had separated the jet-blackness of his hair into wet tendrils, making it cling like damp silk to her hands.

Unable to bear the way his mouth was teasing her breast, Lanna arched toward him, forcing his head down. His mouth opened to surround the hard center and the dusty rose circle around it, devouring its ripeness. A moan of wild longing quivered from her throat as the intimate stimulation of his mouth tightened the pit of her stomach, making it throb with a fiery need. His hand glided down to massage away the burning ache. Her hips moved under his soothing manipulation that eased the hurt but aroused her to a pitch of fevered desire. Her raking hands and quivering body pleaded with him to fulfill the promise of satisfaction with which his hands and mouth were torturing her.

His male lips came back to her mouth, piercing its dark recesses with his hard tongue. His body shifted to cover hers, the welding film of perspiration uniting their flesh. The hot humidity of the air stifled her lungs. Under the crushing weight of his body, Lanna couldn't breathe, pinned between the rock-hard floor and the equally unyielding solidness of him.

She struggled free of his mouth to murmur in choked regret: "Hawk . . . you're too heavy for me. I can't breathe!"

In one fluid, continuous motion, he rolled onto his back, pulling her with him so that she was in the dominant position. Partially lifting her from his torso with his hands, he slid his disturbing gaze over the white globes of her naked breasts.

"I thought you would prefer the proper missionary position," Hawk murmured in faint mockery.

Then his hands were on her—arousing, building, and caressing. The heat became a golden inferno as their bodies moved together in a wild rhythm. Lanna was enveloped in the flaming warmth that went beyond passion. At some point, they surpassed the mere physical union of the flesh to experience the dazzling fusion of the spirit.

The enchantment was slow to leave as Lanna laid within the circle of Hawk's powerful arms. She didn't speak, finding words an inadequate means of expressing her feelings. Closing her eyes, she savored the violent ecstasy that lingered in her nerve ends. Hawk stirred beneath her, his hand gliding over her perspiring skin. She murmured an incoherent protest.

"This steam will sap the rest of our strength," he warned huskily and forced her to sit up.

When he rolled to his feet, Lanna remained sitting with her legs curled to the side. Her hazel eyes were luminous and soft as she gazed up at him, openly acknowledging that she belonged to him. The possessive glitter of his gaze confirmed his ownership. He reached down to help her up, then changed his mind when she was almost standing and swung her off her feet and into his arms. She linked her hands around his neck, pressing her mouth to his throat and scattering loving kisses over his warm, wet skin. The salty taste of him was headier than any after-dinner liqueur; she was drunk with the sensation of him.

He carried her to the door, pushing aside the blanket with a shoulder. After being in the dim interior of the sweathouse, the sunshine was brilliant against her eyes. She shut them and hugged nearer to the warmth of his body as her bare skin felt the chill of cooler air. Hawk didn't set her down, but continued walking with her in his arms.

"Where are we going?" Lanna asked, not really caring as she let her thumb trace the jutting line of his collarbone.

"The Swedes believe in a dip in a fjord after a sauna, don't they?" he replied.

It was a second before the implication of his words registered. It lifted her head from his shoulder and opened her eyes wide. Turning her head, she saw he was carrying her to the spring. Her gaze jerked back to his face and to the faintly devilish glint in his eyes.

"Hawk, you wouldn't? You aren't?" But she already knew that he would, and he was. "No! Put me down!" Lanna struggled in laughing panic. "Please, Hawk, don't!"

"I'll put you down in a minute," he chuckled.

"No! Don't drop me into that!" she protested, neither frightened nor angry, just anxious to avoid that part of the ritual.

"Okay." He stopped beside the spring. "I won't drop you into it," he promised.

Relief sighed through her and she relaxed in his arms, believing him. Suddenly, the arm that had been supporting the back of her legs was removed. Her feet swung down, straight into the cold spring water. Lanna shrieked from the shock of the cold water on her hot and sweaty legs.

"Is it cold?" Hawk laughed and splashed water on her thighs.

"You promised!" she accused, trying to keep her balance on the slippery bottom long enough to step out.

"I promised not to drop you," he reminded her, then began splashing more water on her, aiming it higher.

Lanna retaliated, using the heel of her hand to send up a spray of water to drench his chest. He stepped into the pool and the water fight began in earnest: a playful, shrieking, laughing fest that succeeded in washing the perspiration from their skin. Drenched from head to foot, Lanna scooped a handful of water directly into Hawk's face, laughing at him when he recoiled. She started to repeat it before his counterattack was launched against her, but she let the water trickle through her fingers when he put a hand to his eye. The game was instantly forgotten.

"Are you all right?" She moved quickly to him.

The minute she was within reach, Hawk captured her wrist and pulled her into his arms. His hard mouth came down on her own and her heart raced. In a state of limpness, she leaned against his masculine form, arching her curves to his shape. Her lips parted under the insistence of his mouth, responding to the need for deeper contact. His bold masculinity touched her feminine core, making her pliant to his every want, and he wanted her.

His hands lifted her into the air, raising her above him until his mouth could reach her breasts. To keep her there, he circled an arm around her waist and another around her thighs below the curve of her bottom. Lanna curled her fingers into the sinewy cords of his shoulders, seeking balance in this mind-spinning embrace. With her hips arched against his stomach and her legs dangling against his, Hawk walked out of the pool.

When he reached the giant cottonwood, he let her slide down to his level and braced her against the trunk of the tree. His encircling arms cushioned her from the scrape of striated bark so his possession would give only pleasure.

It seemed a long time before she was finally aware her feet were on solid ground. Her arms were still wrapped tightly around him, reveling in his indomitable male strength. His mouth was moving in a rough caress against her hair.

"You are mine, Lanna." His voice was thick and forceful. "No other man will ever touch you again." He lifted his head, framing her face in his hands while his searing gaze challenged her to deny his claim.

But Lanna could not. Her agreement shimmered in her eyes. "Yes," she whispered gladly.

Hawk took a deep breath and released it slowly. The fierceness seemed to go out of him as he relaxed. His look ran gently over her. "You're cold," he observed.

Lanna glanced down and noticed goosebumps that the cool air had raised on her skin. Upon seeing them, she shivered, only then feeling the chill.

He stepped away from her, taking her hand. "We'd better get dressed before you catch cold."

"What about you?" she countered.

"I'm thicker-skinned than you are, in many ways," he said and led her back to the sweathouse.

His clothes were folded in a pile next to hers, but he disappeared inside the earthen hut while Lanna quickly began to dress. She was fastening the snap on her jeans when he stepped out wearing his primitive loincloth. He dressed as quickly as she had, but his motions appeared less hurried.

"Do you think you can make the climb back to the cave?" he asked.

"It should be easier going up," Lanna replied.

It was, although Hawk stayed on the ground until she was safely on the ledge. Then he climbed up, bringing the canteens. The darkness of the cave added to the cool temperature.

"Shall I fix some coffee?" Lanna suggested.

"I could use some." He tossed her a canteen.

When the coffee had boiled in the mug, Lanna added a spoonful of springwater from the canteen to settle the grounds. They sat close to the small fire, sharing the cup, in an atmosphere of quiet intimacy.

Hawk flexed his shoulders in a weary gesture and handed her the cup. "You finish the rest," he said. "I'm going to take a nap. I haven't had my quota of sleep in the last forty-eight hours—for one reason or another." Rising to his feet with catlike ease, he moved to the tarp spread out from the saddle and stretched out on top of it. Before he covered his face with his hat, he sent her a glance. "We shouldn't have any visitors, but you'd better keep an eye open just the same."

He fell asleep almost instantly. Any moving around Lanna did, she was careful to be quiet. She found a comb in his saddlebags and sat in the sunlight-drenched entrance to unsnarl her hair. When the shadows moved in, she noticed the way Hawk was sleeping with his

arms clutched across his chest, as if staving off a chill.
She shook his quilt free of any wisps of grass and
covered him with it. He stirred but didn't awaken.

Before the sun went down, she fixed their evening
meal, guessing that Hawk wouldn't want a fire going
after nightfall. Light could be seen for miles in this
clear desert country. She didn't awaken him until the
food was ready. One touch of her hand and he was fully
alert.

When they had eaten, Lanna fixed one last cup of
coffee. The sky was purpling with the coming night as
she smothered the small fire. Hawk was standing at the
cave entrance, looking out into the dusk. She brought
him the coffee.

"Where do you suppose they are?" she asked,
guessing where his thoughts were.

"I don't know." He turned to her with a faint shrug.

She offered him the coffee, her skin tingling sensi-
tively to the brush of his fingers when he took it. "Are
you going to stay up and keep watch tonight, too?"

"No. I don't see any need to." He blew at the hot
liquid before taking a sip. "They aren't likely to come
back in the middle of the night."

In the purple-orange light, Lanna could barely make
out the roof of the hogan. The sweathouse wasn't
visible at all. "What was it like growing up here?" she
asked, curious about anything connected with him.

"Innocent. Cruelly so, as it turned out," Hawk
replied, but without bitterness. "Yet, it's from here—
from my childhood as a Navaho—that I've derived a
sense of stability. Someday I want to show you this
land—the Four Corners."

"I'd like to see it," Lanna admitted, because he
wanted to show it to her since it was special to him.

"Its mesas and buttes stretch between sage-covered
plains, rock-ribbed and empty." He looked out, seeing

in his mind's eye what wasn't visible in the twilight. "Blue spruce canyons, tawny sands, dull red rocks. How can I explain how dramatic the colors are, shifting and intensifying in sun and shade? This land is vibrant and dynamic, filled with the force that created it."

Lanna could hear the intensity in Hawk's low voice and realized this profound indentification with the land was something she would probably never be able to share with him. It was perhaps wise to understand that now.

"An Indian is inseparable from the earth," Hawk said, not speaking directly to her, but merely voicing his thoughts aloud. "Every tribe that's been separated from its ancient homeland has withered and died—the Chippewas, the Mohicans, the Chickasaws. Yet the Navaho, the Pueblo, and the Apache live where they have for centuries, within the sacred four peaks, and they survive." He stopped, sending her a sideways glance, as if just remembering she was there. "Sorry."

"There's no need," she insisted.

"You might as well know this about me. I could never leave this place if I didn't know I could always come back. Neither can I stay, because I know there's more out there. There will always be two parts to me. I've learned how to make them walk together and compromise their needs for the sake of the whole."

"Two parts, like your name—Jim and Hawk—one American and the other Indian," Lanna mused.

"Jim Blue Hawk is my full name," he corrected.

"Jim Blue—" she began before the significance penetrated. "J. B., the same initials, and Hawk for Faulkner."

"Purely coincidental. I took the name when I was a boy. J. B. probably saw the analogy and was amused by it, maybe even subconsciously proud. I don't know." He shrugged to indicate it held no importance to him.

"But you have so many of his traits. Chad inherited his weakness, perhaps his shallowness." Lanna was willing to concede that J. B. had possessed human failings. "You have his strength, his intelligence. Taking charge comes naturally to you. I watched you during the cattle drive. And this—bringing me here when you found out what Chad was trying to do. Why haven't you ever made use of your talents? You dodged the question the last time I asked you."

"There are times when I have to come and go as I please. Bosses have the nasty habit of expecting people to keep regular hours."

"But if you were your own boss, you could arrange your schedule to suit yourself," she pointed out.

He smiled lazily and handed her the cup. "I told you once before that you think too much," he mocked and moved away from the entrance. "I'm going to water the horses and see that they're settled in for the night. We're going to have to do something about getting them some exercise tomorrow, or they may wind up with cabin fever."

Lanna stayed at the mouth of the cave, listening to the faint sounds going on behind her. Her mood was a little pensive as she watched the stars come out and the moon rise in the sky. She drained the coffee to the dregs, swirled it, and dumped all but a few grounds on the cave floor. When she turned, she saw Hawk was lying down.

He folded back a corner of his quilt. "Bring your blanket," he invited.

She noticed he was fully clothed beneath it, so she didn't remove her own. Placing the coffee cup with the sack of supplies, she gathered up her own blanket and walked over to lie down beside him. He offered his shoulder for a pillow and she curved into the hollow of his arm.

"Tired?" she asked.

"I don't have a headache, if that's what you're asking." There was a smile in his low voice.

Lanna felt the warmth in her cheeks. "That isn't what I was asking, exactly." But her flesh was fully aware of the male outline of his body stretched out beside hers.

Sighing, he turned onto his side, partially facing her. His hand glided over the curve of her waist and hip in an absent caress. "You could steal a man's potency," he accused lazily.

"Could I?" She tipped her head back on his arm, eyeing him with a faintly provocative look.

"The Navahos believe that too much sex is harmful," he said while his hand continued its wayward wanderings.

"Why?" Curiosity gleamed in her eyes.

"Because it can—Navaho translation—'affect the spine where it joins the brain.' An anatomy professor would tell you that's a reference to the median nerve. Have you ever studied yoga?"

"No." Lanna unfastened a button on his shirt and slid her hand inside to make direct contact with the warmth of his skin.

"In order to achieve the transcendental Illumination, a yogin must redirect the course of sexual power up the median nerve to the brain. A great many of the esoteric ceremonies of the Navaho deal with parables and myth dramas. From the physical life force comes spiritual power," Hawk explained. "In Buddhism, it is believed the spirit exits the body, after death, near the crown of the head, where the median nerve exits—which is why many Buddhists shave their heads, except for that spot. When they die, a few hairs are plucked to ensure the safe exit of the spirit." He wound his fingers around a thick lock of hair on top of her head. "It's also the reason why many Indians scalped their enemies, to ensure that their ghosts escaped and didn't return to haunt them."

"Fascinating," she murmured. Her mind meant it, although her senses were concentrating on other things.

"I should hate to see your beautiful hair dangling from someone's belt." His hand pressed her hips flat against the ground sheet.

"Not even yours?" Lanna whispered as his fingers began to make short work of the buttons on her blouse.

"Not even mine." Hawk formed the words against her mouth and chose a more satisfying means of communication than with words. Lanna acknowledged the excellence of his choice with a smothered murmur of pleasure.

Chapter XX

Watching the interplay of sunlight on a distant butte, Lanna remembered how Hawk had described his land last night. She saw its vibrance for herself as the clay butte leaped with red fire, then shadowed to brick. Far away, a low cloud fell on the horizon—a hill darkened with juniper and pinon.

She lifted her face to the strong wind, feeling the tiny particles of sand it carried. It whipped her hair away from her shoulders, streaming it like a brown silk banner, and plastered the material of her cream yellow blouse against the thrusting outline of her breasts, billowing the material at her waist. The air was scented with the pungent smell of sage and dry with dust. Yet it lived—it all lived.

"What the hell do you think you're doing, wandering off like that?" The anger of concern in Hawk's demand made Lanna turn from the waist.

"I was just looking around." The wind lashed a swath of hair across her face. She pushed it away and turned back to face the stiff breeze. "I wanted to see the hogan where you lived as a boy," she explained.

"But there wasn't much to see," he said, supplying the conclusion for her.

"Not in there," Lanna agreed without looking at him, her gaze still wandering over the land. "But out here—" She left the sentence unfinished. She couldn't put it into words better than Hawk had, so she didn't try. He moved to stand beside her, his gaze lingering on her profile for a minute before turning to scan the countryside.

When her silent communion with the land was over, she turned to study him. She recognized his innate dignity, his fierce pride, and his strong-willed independence. It was the right moment, somehow, to speak from her heart, when her thinking wasn't influenced by passion or desire.

"Hawk, I love you." It was a simple statement, without embellishment.

It held him motionless for an instant before he turned to her, implacable. "I don't know this word 'love.' I haven't had any experience with it, Lanna." His hands moved to take her shoulders and hold her still while his blue eyes probed her features. His reply brought a quiver of disappointment, but Lanna told herself she understood. "I do know that when another man touches you I'm filled with a murderous rage. When I hold you in my arms, I'm lifted higher than any creature has ever flown. And unless I'm with you, I'm not content. If there is more to love than this, you'll have to teach me."

Her tiny gasp became caught in her throat as Lanna realized what he was saying. She swayed toward him, a radiant disbelief dampening her eyes, while her expression became filled with pure joy. It was all she could manage, but it was enough as Hawk wrapped her into his arms and pressed her head against his shoulder, lying a cheek against her hair.

"It's unbelievable, isn't it?" He seemed to mock

himself. "I want to marry you. I want you to be my wife."

She laughed, overflowing with happiness. She lifted her head to look at him, proud and jubilant. "I'll marry you, Hawk. I don't care if we live in a cave or a hogan or—"

"I care," he stated and stopped any further expansive declarations with a hard kiss, then buried his mouth against her throat, muttering against her skin. "You and your damned thinking must have finally reformed me."

His mouth found hers again and Lanna pressed herself close against the male body she had come to know so well. No matter how familiar it was to her, it still had the power to excite her. Lanna knew it always would because of the man he was.

The kiss was long and deep, promising to be the prelude of more until Hawk abruptly ended it, his muscles tensing. He lifted his head in alert pose, and pushed her shoulder away from him.

"We have visitors coming," he announced and glanced at her. "They haven't seen us yet. We can make it to the cave if you want to run."

Lanna saw the cloud of dust and felt the vibration of the ground beneath her feet. "No. I'd rather stay and face Chad," she decided.

Hawk looked pleased, smiling faintly as he let her go, and pivoted to stand beside her. He sent a quick glance behind them in the direction of the cave.

"What is it?" she asked.

"I was just wishing I had my rifle. It might even the odds if they decide to get nasty."

Her confidence was shaken. "Hawk—" she began.

"Don't worry." A reckless gleam danced in his eyes. "We'll handle it."

The wind blew a lock of hair across her eyes, momentarily blinding her before she could brush it behind an ear. There was a pickup truck with the trio of riders approaching the canyon. She could hear its motor, but it was obscured behind the cloud of dust kicked up by the horses. Her heart began to beat faster, pumping adrenaline through her system. Hawk took a half-step, putting himself slightly ahead of her.

He felt a surge of recklessness. All his senses were working at full speed, yet he was totally in control. It was a good feeling. The riders pulled up a good twenty feet away and the truck stopped next to them. Hawk was unaware of the cold smile that curved his mouth. Chad slammed from behind the wheel of the truck and barged forward like an angry bull. Hawk identified Carol and Katheryn as his passengers before centering his attention on Chad, keeping an eye always on Rawlins.

"Hello, Chad. It's so good of you to drop in like this," Hawk taunted. "It looks like the gang's all here, doesn't it?"

"Let her go, Hawk!" Chad ordered.

"I'm not holding her." He lifted one shoulder, then threw a challenge to Rawlins. "What are you accusing me of this time? Kidnapping?" The foreman gave him a cold look but didn't reply.

"You took her from the camp," Chad accused. "I want her back."

"I'm not coming with you, Chad," Lanna answered him. "I'm staying with Hawk because it's what I want. I know what you tried to do to me."

"I don't know what you're talking about," he denied.

"You might as well get back in the truck and leave. It's all over, Chad. You tried, but it didn't work. Lanna is willing to leave it at that," Hawk stated calmly.

"No, it isn't over!" Chad shouted, a wild desperation stringing through him. "You aren't going to screw this up for me! I'm not going to let you! Now, get out of the way! Lanna is coming with us!"

"No." Hawk saw the movement and heard the low order Rawlins gave the two riders. His hand unfastened the strap that held the hunting knife in its sheath. Sliding the blade out, he faced Rawlins. Chad wasn't a threat at the moment. "Don't get out of that saddle, Tom," Hawk warned and flashed the blade toward him. "If you do, I'll have to forget you're an old man."

Help came from an unexpected source. The outside rider, Luther Wilcox, pulled his rifle from its saddle scabbard and swung the muzzle at his two companions. "We ain't gettin' involved in this one, Bill. Tom, you just sit where you are. If there's any fightin' to be done, it's between Hawk and Chad. And I'm goin' to make sure the odds stay even."

"Put the rifle away!" Rawlins ordered. "If you don't want your walking papers, you'd better point that gun in another direction."

"I ride for the brand right or wrong," Luther announced, his rifle never moving from its targets. "But I think you're forgettin' that Hawk owns half the ranch, Tom."

"It's up to you, Chad," Hawk challenged now that the most dangerous threat was under Luther's rifle. "Are you going to pull in your horns?"

He saw the hesitation, the indecision flickering through his half-brother's expression. Then Katheryn murmured to him, "You can't let him get away with it, Chad. You can't trust him."

His blue gaze swept over the older woman, noting the feral gleam of hatred in her eyes. Hawk realized how twisted she had become, willing to pit her own son against him, encouraging the fight. No doubt she had accompanied them for the express satisfaction of seeing him beaten up. Carol's eyes were wide and green as Hawk briefly met her look. He sensed an urgency in them and guessed she was remembering another time when a similar scene had been played out for her benefit.

"I never could stand you, Hawk." Chad's arms were rigid at his side, and his hands were clenched into fists. "Why don't you put that knife down and we'll see how tough you really are?"

Blood sang through his veins. Hawk was vaguely startled to realize a fight was what he wanted, too. Twenty years of backing away was bottled up inside him. Now it was being released. Moving sideways, he stepped away from Lanna to an area where the land was cleared of brush and sage. The blackened ashes of a campfire marked its center, the place where Rawlins and his men had spent the night. Without taking his eyes off Chad, who had begun a wary circle, too, Hawk buried the point of the knife blade in the half-blackened remains of a log.

In those few seconds, he mentally considered his opponent. Chad had the advantage of weight and possibly reach, but he lacked stamina. At the private military academy and later at college, Chad had acquired a reputation as a brawler. His instincts might be rusty, but Hawk didn't regard him lightly.

Their wary circling drew them close as Hawk waited for Chad to make the first move. When it came, it was fast. A cell in Hawk's brain registered the fact that Chad was neither slow nor clumsy, as the point of Chad's shoulder caught him before Hawk could side-step the charge. He grabbed hold of those shoulders to keep from being driven to the ground. They grappled, neither finding the advantage, and Hawk broke away. When Chad turned to follow him, he had his first chance. He beat aside the arm Chad raised and slammed a fist into his mouth, feeling his knuckles rip across the lip. His opponent was stunned and Hawk quickly added more, sending solid blows to the chin and temple. Blood flowed dark red from the cuts and Chad's eyes filled with a murderous rage.

He came at Hawk like a wild animal. He deflected one blow, but the next slashed aside his arm and slammed him squarely on the point of his chin, ringing bells in his head as it hurled him backward. Chad leaped on him, crushing him to the ground and driving his fist into Hawk's neck like a hammer.

Rolling and wrestling savagely on the ground, they struck and missed and hit. The heavy breathing was guttural, heaving with battle and coming in bitter gusts. Hawk couldn't separate the labored sound of his own from Chad's. They struggled and fought, using elbows and knees. Finally, Hawk landed a fist that lifted Chad off him, hurling him backward into the black ashes. He quickly rolled to his feet. There was blood in his eyes, blurring his vision. He blinked and gave a quick shake of his head to clear it, crouching low for Chad's assault.

"Hawk!" Lanna shouted an alarm. "The knife!"

He almost missed the flash of steel in Chad's hand. He jumped backward, eluding the slashing arc of the blade, and grabbed for the arm as it went by. They scuffled, Hawk trying to twist the knife out of Chad's grip. Hooking a heel behind Chad's knee, he forced him off balance. Hawk went down with him. Chad landed heavily, the air whooshing from his lungs, as he fell squarely on his back. His fingers momentarily relaxed their grip on the knife and Hawk tore it out of his hand. A-straddle his enemy, the lust of battle hot in his veins, he stared down at Chad, his features bloodied and bruised, no longer handsome. The man was beaten. Hawk could see the defeat in his eyes.

The hand with the knife raised. There was a faint cry from somewhere as Hawk's arm came down in a driving arc. He plunged the knife all the way to the hilt into the ground near Chad's head. Gasping for breath like a winded animal, Hawk rose and staggered to the side, his body beginning to hurt with the blows that had landed.

"Kill him!" A voice shrieked. "Hawk, kill him!" He turned to the sound, dazed by the screaming rage of it. Carol raced toward him, a frenzied gleam in her eyes. She stopped to grab hold of his torn shirtfront. "You've got to kill him, Hawk!" This time her voice was low, threaded with desperation.

"What the hell are you talking about?" He stared at her.

"Don't you see?" There was something repulsive about the avid look in her eyes. "With Chad dead, I'll inherit his share. We can get married, and between us, we can own everything. It will all be ours—the way it should be!"

"You're not making sense." But he had only to look at her to realize her mind had snapped.

"I am, Hawk. I am," she insisted. "As Johnny's real father, you'll have control of his trust fund—"

"Johnny?" Katheryn's confused voice inserted itself into Carol's explanation. She was kneeling beside Chad, tears streaming down her suddenly aged face. He was trying to sit up, managing to support himself on one elbow.

"Yes, Johnny!" Carol hurled at her with malicious delight. "You didn't think I would have *Chad's* child! I never lost any children of his. I killed them! Every time I found out I was pregnant, I got an abortion! No child was going to have any share of what belonged to Johnny and Hawk!" She turned back to Hawk and he was sickened by the twisted sight. "I made sure it would all come to you."

"Not all of it," Hawk reminded her tiredly. He was slowly beginning to discover that Chad had only been a pawn in Carol's plan. "Chad never got Lanna's signature."

"No, but I did!" Carol declared and released her hold on his shirt to dig into the pocket of her slacks and produce a document. Eagerly, she unfolded it to show him the signature page and handed it to him. "She's signed everything over to you."

He stared in disbelief at Lanna's name written on the bottom. "How did you get it?"

"It was easy," Carol laughed. "I waited until midnight, when she was on a peyote trip. I told her she was signing a letter to Johnny." Then her look became wild again, driven by the maniacal plan she had concocted. "But you have to kill Chad. It was self-defense, don't you see?"

Lowering his head, he closed his eyes for an instant. He reached out and gently took hold of her shoulders. "Chad is my half-brother, Carol."

"But you have to," she argued, then became pleading. "I've made it all up to you, haven't I? You can have all of J. B.'s money—everything. The ranch, the way it should have been. I got it for you so we could be together. We can be married, Hawk. You're rich. No one can dare say anything against you now."

He shook his head. "I'm not going to marry you, Carol. You and I were finished a long time ago."

"No." She didn't believe him. Wildly, she searched his face. "No!" She screamed and twisted out of his arms. "I did it for you!"

Her gaze swept the group, staring at her in frozen silence. With a stifled cry of madness, she whirled and raced for the open country. Rawlins spurred his horse, his face wet with tears as he went after his daughter. Hawk turned sadly away from the sight of the golden-haired girl racing toward the sun. His gaze lighted on Chad.

"Johnny is your son?" Chad's voice was choked.

"Carol is sick, Chad. Don't believe what she said. She might be convinced it's true, but I'm not," Hawk replied in a weary voice.

"What if it is true?" he whispered.

"What if it isn't?" Hawk countered. "Don't let her madness infect you."

He felt the touch of Lanna's hand on his arm and looked down at her pale face. There was relief in her eyes and a silent message meant only for him. The feeling of ugliness that had been around him went away and he smiled. This woman would be the mother of his sons and daughters.

"Let's get our horses and get out of here," he suggested quietly.

Lanna touched a finger to the cut on his face and nodded her agreement. Turning, Hawk curved an arm around her waist while she slid an arm behind his back, linking them together. They started toward the cave.

"Poor Carol," Lanna murmured.

"Yes." Then Hawk realized the document she had given him was still in his hand. He folded it and stuffed it in his shirt pocket.

"Do you think that's legal?" she asked a little absently.

"I don't know. I doubt it, since you were drugged when you signed it."

"I don't care if it is," she said and looked up at him, her eyes tenderly bright. "I never wanted the money. I have what I always wanted."' With a faint and contented sigh, she faced the front and let her head rest lightly against his shoulder.

A surge of warmth seemed to fill his chest. Hawk looked up to the sky, clear and blue, its horizon limitless. His hand tightened on her waist and curved her body a little closer to his.

"In beauty it is finished.
In beauty it is finished.
In beauty it is finished.
In beauty it is finished."